MISSION ACCOMPLISHED:
High praise for
CINDY GERARD
and the scorching hunks of her bestselling
BLACK OPS, INC. series!

"Exciting, taut, sexy, and just plain fun to read."
—Sandra Brown, #1 *New York Times* bestselling author

"Kicks romantic adventure into high gear."
—Allison Brennan, *New York Times* bestselling author

"A great writer . . . head and shoulders above most."
—Robert Browne, author of *The Paradise Prophecy*

"Gerard artfully reveals the secret previously known
only to wives, girlfriends, and lovers of our military
special-operations warriors: These men are as wildly
passionate and loving as they are watchful and stealthy.
Her stories are richly colored and textured, drawing
you in from page one, and not simply behind the
scenes of warrior life, but into its very heart and soul."
—William Dean A. Garner, former
U.S. Army Airborne Ranger

"Gerard just keeps getting better and better."
—*Romance Junkies*

Also by Cindy Gerard

CINDY
GERARD

KILLING
TIME

Pocket Books

New York London Toronto Sydney New Delhi

Pocket Books
A Division of Simon & Schuster, Inc.
1230 Avenue of the Americas
New York, NY 10020

This book is a work of fiction. Names, characters, places, and incidents either are products of the author's imagination or are used fictitiously. Any resemblance to actual events or locales or persons, living or dead, is entirely coincidental.

Copyright © 2013 by Cindy Gerard

First Pocket Books paperback edition February 2013

POCKET and colophon are registered trademarks of Simon & Schuster, Inc.

For information about special discounts for bulk purchases, please contact Simon & Schuster Special Sales at 1-866-506-1949 or business@simonandschuster.com.

The Simon & Schuster Speakers Bureau can bring authors to your live event. For more information or to book an event, contact the Simon & Schuster Speakers Bureau at 1-866-248-3049 or visit our website at www.simonspeakers.com.

Manufactured in the United States of America

10 9 8 7 6 5 4 3 2 1

ISBN 978-1-4516-0683-6
ISBN 978-1-4516-0687-4 (ebook)

There can be no other dedication: To the men and women of the U.S. military, for all the reasons we know and all the reasons we will never know.

And to Kayla, Blake, Lane, and Hailey. You bless my life with untold riches.

Acknowledgments

One of the best parts of writing any book is the research. I love delving into the history, geography, and political climates of my settings. And one of the best parts of the "digging" is the contacts I make with the many individuals who are so willing to provide valuable information that contributes so greatly to the texture and flavor of each book. On that note, I'd like to give a very special thank-you to my Idaho connections, Larry Stone and Emma Scott, for ferreting out such incredible details on the Squaw Valley area of the Idaho panhandle and helping make the portion of the book set there so rich.

One-Eyed Jack: \wən\-\ˈīd\-\ˈjak\
Noun: 1: being, of, pertaining to, a face card or cards on which the figure is shown in profile, such cards being the jack of spades, the jack of hearts. **2:** a loner who has a hard time trusting anyone. **3:** Navy term for a greasy hamburger topped with a fried egg. Often served during midrats—midnight rations.

"Nothing fixes a thing so intensely in the memory as the wish to forget it."
— Michel de Montaigne, February 28, 1533–
September 13, 1592

1

El Tocón Sangriento—the Bloody Stump—was a back-alley, low-rent cantina that hadn't changed in clientele or décor since Mike Brown first set foot in the dump eight years ago. The class of women, however, seemed to have catapulted to new levels.

The sun had been down less than an hour when he turned his back to the cracked, smoky mirror, a shot of pisco in one hand, a timeworn jack of hearts in the other. He slid his aviator shades to the top of his head and propped his elbows behind him on the edge of the scarred bar. Then he watched the dance floor with interest as one particular woman, who had caught his eye when he'd walked in two hours ago, moved sensuously to the rhythm of a slow, Spanish guitar.

Absently flipping the playing card back and forth between his fingers, he squinted through the tobacco and marijuana haze at the dark-haired Latina beauty stirring up trouble and testosterone with the seductive sway of her hips. She was way too hot for this dive. And while he didn't have a clue why she flashed her flirty smile his way, he wasn't going to question his good luck. Just like he wasn't questioning the reason he was tying one on like there was no tomorrow.

He tossed back the shot and exchanged it for a full one from the neat row of soldiers lined up on the bar behind him. Screw the fact that he'd been clean and sober for 364 consecutive days . . . a record he never seemed to beat. Today, like every other July 15 since Operation Slam Dunk had gone south, he was getting flat-ass drunk.

The end of days. That's how he thought of the debacle in Afghanistan eight years ago.

Sobrietus interruptus. That's how he thought of his annual commune with alcohol and self-pity.

He was holding a postmortem. Throwing a pity party. Conducting a wake for the friends who'd lost their lives eight years ago. For the life and career *he'd* lost.

Hell, call it whatever you wanted—a guilt trip, grief, suppressed rage, self-destruction—he didn't give a rip. It was happening. The only new wrinkle in his yearly bender was that it was starting to look like he might also get laid.

Talk about poetic justice. He was already fucked up in the head . . . might as well make it a clean sweep.

Eyes on the prize, he slammed back one more shot, pocketed the bullet-ridden playing card, touched the unlit cigarette tucked above his right ear for luck, and pushed off the bar stool. Then he tried like hell not to stagger as he walked unsteadily across the room toward the spicy little enchilada who seemed to only have eyes for him. Big dark eyes. A little sleepy, a little slutty, a *lot* interested.

Damn, she was something. Centerfold something. A petite, hot mess of raw sexuality. Long, satiny black hair escaped in sleek, bed-mussed strands from the silver clip she'd used to secure it in a loose knot on top of her head. Elegant neck. Smooth, bare shoulders. A lot of soft, caramel skin. And that red bustier—its B cups not having a lot of luck harnessing a generous pair of Cs—worn with black spandex pants that stopped at her ankles where the straps of her four-inch stilettos took over and played hell with the fit of his pants.

"Hey, gorgeous," he said. Because she was. And because he was too wasted to come up with anything original. He moved in close—crowded the hell out of her personal space—and the way she slid up real close and cuddly told him that she was totally fine with the invasion.

"Hola." She smelled sweet and musky and sexually charged as she tipped her head back with a bold, inviting smile and pressed those amazing breasts against his chest. "Nice bling." A long-nailed fingertip—slick, shiny, red—tapped the diamond stud in his left ear, then lingered at the tip of his lobe.

"Nice, um"—he let his gaze slide down to that

magnificent cleavage before easing back to her face—"smile."

She laughed and tilted her head to the side in blatant invitation, giving him an even better view of all that dewy, soft flesh.

"Wanna take this somewhere private?" Might as well cut straight to the chase.

The lady knew what she wanted. "Thought you'd never ask," she said, her English laced with a sultry, lyrical Spanish accent.

Her hand was small and hot—like the rest of her— when she took his and led him toward the back door. He followed like a love-struck puppy, mesmerized by the smell of her hair and the sway of her hips and the way her sparkly purse hung from a silver chain looped over her shoulder and rhythmically bumped her gorgeous ass with every step she took.

Outside, the alley was already shadowy and as dark as the desire that ripped recklessly through his groin. Somewhere in the back of his mind, a warning bled through his lust-induced fog, telling him to slow the hell down, reminding him that if he hadn't been so drunk, he might have asked a few more questions. That maybe, if he added two and two together he might come up with something other than *four*nicate.

Just because he wanted her to be a working girl didn't mean she was one. And just because he was drunk didn't mean he should let his guard down. He started to rethink this entire proposition . . . but then she leaned back against the wall, gripped his T-shirt with both hands, and pulled him flush against her.

Good-bye, presence of mind.

She was all hot, wet, open mouth and ripe breasts rubbing up against him, her left leg wedging super sweet between his thighs and moving up and down over his rapidly expanding package as he pressed her against the wall with his body.

He groaned and scrabbled for a hold on his sanity. "Maybe we should get a room, wild thing."

She laughed, a husky, naughty purr, and bit his lower lip. "That comes later, *gringo* . . . but *you're* gonna come right now."

Holy mother.

When she reached into her purse, another spike of alarm jabbed him out of his stupor.

"Condom." She flashed that dimpled smile and damn if he didn't almost weep with gratitude.

What the hell. It was still early, but it was dark. He was gone. And all this lush woman's heat had him hypnotized by the prospect of her doing him right here, beneath the flashing neon QUILMES sign.

He skimmed his palms down her sides, pressed the heels of his hands against her superior breasts, then slid them lower again, gripping her hips and rubbing her against his raging erection.

All the while, she had one hand on her purse, while rooting around inside with the other.

"Damn, sweetheart. If you don't find that thing soon the party's gonna be over."

Just then he got wind of a scent . . . and got sober real fast.

He grabbed her wrist, pressed her harder against the wall, and pulled her hand out of her bag. A loop of thin, stiff plastic dangled from her red-tipped nails.

"Well, now." He glanced at the flex cuffs. "Speaking of bling. I'm all for kinky sex, but there's no way in hell you're going to slap that bracelet on me."

She wasn't smiling now.

"And nice perfume, by the way. Eau du le gun oil?" He felt the outline of a pistol inside that sparkly purse. "Shoulda gone for Shalimar, *chica* . . . the smell of that stuff makes me stupid."

"That's not all that makes you stupid," she muttered and jammed a knee hard into his gonads.

He doubled over with a gasp of pain, helpless to fight her when she yanked his arms behind his back, expertly looped the strip of plastic around both wrists, and jerked it tight.

"We can do this easy," she whispered close to his ear, all traces of her Spanish accent gone, as he groaned in agony, "or it can go real hard on you."

Well, of course he wasn't going to go easy.

He drove a shoulder toward her midsection. She dodged like a pro and he landed on his face in the alley's pocked, filthy pavement.

By the time he felt the prick of the needle in his neck, it was all over but the headache he knew he was going to have when he woke up. *If* he woke up.

Which, unfortunately, he did.

2

When Mike finally came to and managed to blink through the cobwebs clouding his vision, three things registered in disjointed tandem . . . each one worthy of a nightmare.

One—he was spread-eagle on his back on a mattress in a room he recognized as standard-fare fleabag hotel. Two—flex cuffs bound his wrists above his head to the bars of an iron headboard. And three—the woman staring at him in stony silence from a chair at the foot of the bed looked vaguely familiar.

And even though the only light in the room of mustard yellow walls and cracked plaster came from a low-wattage bulb hanging from a frayed cord in the middle of the ceiling, he could still clearly see the *very* familiar Beretta 92FS she held in a confident grip. The gun was his, which not only made him stupid, it made him officially—if not literally—screwed.

Interesting. Sort of. Because there was some good news here. If she wanted to shoot him, she'd have done it by now.

So if she didn't want him dead, then what *did* she want? And where, exactly, did he know her from?

He breathed deep. Fought to remember. Anything. Then he snapped to with a painful jolt when a memory as blinding as headlights cut through the fog.

Cantina. Pisco. Hot tamale. Leading with his dick.

He clenched his jaw. Dumb ass. He'd let her get the drop on him. She must have juiced him with something. Yeah . . . he remembered now the sting of the needle . . . then stumbling down an alley, his arm slung over her shoulders, her arm around his waist . . . falling into a cab . . . staggering down a narrow hallway, up a flight of stairs.

Collapsing on a lumpy bed that smelled of mildew and cheap disinfectant and where—judging by the fact that he was still zipped and tucked—he was willing to give pretty good odds that he hadn't gotten laid.

He squinted and framed her between his boot tips, trying to get a read on where this was going, who she might be. But she'd stacked her deck rock solid with the three c's—cool, calm, and in control. Her unwavering gaze wasn't giving anything away. He could still smell her above the sour, low-rent hotel room odor, but gone was the sultry temptress with the bed-mussed hair. She'd pulled all that black silk into a sleek, utilitarian ponytail and bound it snug at the nape of her neck. She'd also replaced her "slut suit" with a blinding white T-shirt, tight jeans, and a pair of lace-up leather boots that had seen a fair share of wear. And yet, if you overlooked the gun, she was still damn sexy—in a kick-ass, GI Jane, ball-breaker kind of way.

But sexy didn't hold much sway right now. Too bad he hadn't realized that half a dozen shots of pisco ago.

So . . . was she local *policía*? No. That didn't fit. He'd be locked in a cell by now, most likely beaten, more likely dead. Besides, his nose was clean this trip. And despite the Rambo-ette persona, she didn't have enough sharp edges to be a hard-nosed cop. Not that he hadn't been fooled by dangerous curves before.

Extortion? Good luck, *chica*. His plane was the only thing he owned of any value and that was hocked up to his eyeballs. Woman scorned, then? Did he know her from somewhere? Had he *done her wrong*? That didn't fit, either. He wouldn't have forgotten a face or a body like hers.

So . . . what? What did she want?

Nothing good. The only thing he knew with any degree of certainty was that so far, he didn't much like her agenda.

"Tell me what happened in Afghanistan," she said without so much as a blink and with absolutely zero warning.

His heart stopped.

Afghanistan?

And oh, hell, no, he didn't like her agenda at all.

Eyes narrowed, he searched the face that had turned his mind to mush and landed him in this fix.

Nothing computed. Nothing but the knot tightening in his chest, tripping a defense mechanism that demanded he not let her see him sweat.

"So." He focused through a blinding headache. "You're one of *those*."

A finely arched brow lifted. "One of *those*?"

"One of those women who likes to talk before she does the big nasty."

She gave a small shrug of her shoulders. "I've got more needles. You want another one? Go ahead. Keep giving me crap."

He didn't have much more crap to give. He was running on empty here. His mouth was bone dry. His head spun. And then there was the obvious. He tested the cuffs with a disgustingly weak jerk. The plastic dug painfully into his wrists.

He gave her a squinty-eyed look that was all for show. "You got a name? Or should I call you Mata Hari?" He had a sick feeling he'd want to call her a lot of things before this was over.

She sat back with a sigh and crossed her arms. His Beretta—a little over two pounds of cold steel nestled snug against her left breast—presented an image he would not soon forget. Neither would he forget the scent that stirred in the stagnant air when she moved.

"The only thing you need to know about me, flyboy, is that I'm the person asking the questions. Now tell me what happened in Afghanistan. Tell me about Operation Slam Dunk."

The look on her face and the authority in her voice suggested that she already knew.

That couldn't be. No one knew about OSD. No one was supposed to know. Not his family. Not his friends. And sure as hell not this woman who stared at him like he was week-old roadkill.

He dragged his gaze away from her chest and smiled to hide his panic. "That would be a big go to hell."

She leaned forward and gave him a cold, calculated once-over that made his gut tighten. "Fine. Then I'll tell *you*."

He shot her his best "I could give a rip" grin and kept up the pretense of a man who didn't suspect his past was about to come crashing down around him in an avalanche of shit. "Since I'm what you call a captive audience, go ahead, sweetheart. Knock yourself out."

"*Hola*, señor. I need a room, please. One night only." Jane Smith—per her passport—deliberately spoke in less than perfect Spanish as she set her utilitarian duffel bag on the floor at her feet and her Lonely Planet guidebook on the check-in desk in front of her.

She knew what the bored desk clerk would see if he ever bothered to glance away from his Angry Birds game long enough to look at her: a tired, thirty-something Anglo testing her limited Spanish skills, dishwater-blond hair twisted into a haphazard knot on top of her head, pale blue eyes behind an unfashionable pair of glasses, her unremarkable face flushed from the heat of the city and drawn a little tight with stress—no doubt caused by having to check into this decrepit hotel on *Calle San Ramon*. Her matching TravelSmith vest, khaki pants, and nondescript olive drab camp shirt, with her passport carrier looped around her neck, resting on modest-sized breasts, cemented the image. The weak, carefully staged, "I'm not an ugly American" smile added the perfect camouflage.

Even if he bothered to look at her, the night clerk would never remember her in the morning. She looked like every tourist on a budget who had ever walked through the front door.

"Second floor, please—street side, if you have it," she added almost apologetically. She already knew he did—the key to room 205 hung on an antiquated peg board mounted on the wall behind the desk. That was the room she wanted.

She'd already done a quick recon of the three-story building by sneaking in through a rear service door and catching up with the assignment she'd followed from Langley to Lima. The woman had half-carried, half-walked her drunken mark up the first flight of stairs and into room 203.

The clerk dragged himself away from his laptop, swiveled on his creaking chair, and rolled over to the board. He snagged the key to room 205, rolled back, and slid it across the counter without ever meeting her eyes.

"Up the stairs, third door down the hall," he mumbled in thick Spanish, then asked for cash up front as she signed the register.

She carefully counted out several 10 nuevos soles bills—she was a tourist on a budget, after all—then inspected her change. "Gracious, señor."

He'd already dismissed her from his thoughts, his full interest back on his game. She picked up her duffel, smiled serenely to the two elderly gentlemen bent over a card game in the corner of the timeworn lobby, and headed down the hall.

The soles of her sandals where whisper quiet as she walked over the tile floor and climbed the single flight of stairs. Once on the second floor, she slipped off the glasses, stowed them in her shirt pocket, then paused briefly by room 203. The murmur of voices assured her they were indeed inside, and she moved on to her room.

Once inside, she checked her watch. The night was young. It was barely nine p.m. There was much to look forward to.

She set the duffel on the bed, withdrew the briefcase containing her specially fitted Heckler & Koch MP5KA4 and two boxes of ammo. In her line of work it was the perfect weapon, designed for close quarters battle because it didn't even have a butt stock, just a flat end cap with a sling loop on the outside. Perfect also, because this particular MP5K could be operational, if necessary, with a squeeze of the briefcase handle. Control freak that she was, she'd hand-loaded the 9mm, subsonic-blended, metal-armor-piercing, antipersonnel bullets herself. A quick and devastating kill had to be a certainty. Hands-on loading insured that component.

She set the briefcase on the bed and opened it up. Almost had an orgasm just looking at the gorgeous weapon. With care, she removed and inspected each piece before she assembled it, double-checked the magazine, and screwed the sound suppressor onto the end of the barrel. No, it wouldn't muffle the bulk of the sound but before anyone in this dive decided to investigate, she'd be long gone, the job done.

If an elimination ended up being the job.

Her heart rate picked up just thinking about it. She stroked a finger over the barrel, then laid the gun on the bed and drew a deep, steadying breath. She needed to settle herself down, check the adrenaline spike. Shaking her hands to encourage circulation to her fingertips, she walked into the bathroom and turned on the cold-water faucet.

She bent over the sink, splashed tepid water on her face, then straightened slowly and studied her reflection in the small mirror. Several more deep breaths restored her rock-steady composure. Finally satisfied with what she saw, she touched her fingers to her lips, kissed the tips, and pressed them to the mirror with a grin.

Then she returned to the bedroom, dug her surveillance gear out of her bag, and set up shop.

3

Eva Salinas recrossed her legs and stared at her captive. He looked like hell—drugged, cuffed, and maybe . . . just maybe . . . almost as scared shitless as he needed to be.

But not quite.

Desperate times, desperate measures—and she was damn close to desperate.

Somebody was after her, trying to run her to ground, somebody with a connection to Operation Slam Dunk, and she didn't have a clue who it was— or, for that matter, who had passed her the info that had put her in the crosshairs.

But there it had been one day, the OSD file, landing smack in her lap from out of nowhere. No name, no chain of command, no nothing, just her and the death warrant that had gone into effect the minute she'd started asking questions—and she had plenty of questions. Had OSD been a bait and switch funded by black money? A major screwup that power and corruption had covered up? Or had it come down exactly the way the file said it had and Mike Brown was responsible?

So far, she had damn few answers. She was certain of only two things: One: Whatever had happened that night, security had been breached and a whole lot of people had died—one of whom she still missed with an ache that kept her up at night. Two: Whoever had passed her that file wanted her to ferret out the truth as badly as someone else wanted her stopped.

The sorry piece of work cuffed to the bed had been part of it all. The OSD file had named him as the operator who had screwed the pooch and gotten his teammates killed. She needed him to talk and Mr. "Go to hell" was going to do exactly that before this night ended.

"The *legendary* Mike Brown," she said, watching him carefully, looking for a reaction, any reaction. "Or should I call you Primetime? That's what your team called you, right?"

He worked hard to convince her with a bland look that the use of his nickname and reference to his team hadn't sliced him to the quick. She didn't buy it. The man had once had a conscience. He'd been one of America's best of the best, and he had to be feeling a little raw right now despite the lingering hold of the Ketamine.

She'd dosed him with just enough of the drug to possibly give him a hallucination or two—it wasn't called Special-K for nothing—and make him malleable, to get him where she wanted him. Defense-less. Vulnerable. At her mercy. Nice of him to drown himself in booze to help the process along.

"Primetime and the One-Eyed Jacks." She tossed out the name of his old unit like a gauntlet—or a piece of bait.

He bit, dropping any pretense of indifference. His eyes hardened as he watched her stand and walk closer to the foot of the bed.

And yes, she got it. Got why he had a rep for women falling all over him. She'd had no trouble picking him out in the bar. Despite the fact that he looked a little frayed around the edges with his too-long hair and several days' growth of beard, he was the perfect male package: tall, dark, and broad-shouldered—danger-ous. Add a face with ridiculously intriguing angles and planes, a touch of some ancestral Spanish blood, and thick brown hair, and he definitely lived up to his lady-killer billing.

Even in his current state, Brown was Hollywood gorgeous—primetime TV gorgeous. The quintessen-tial all-American male. Born and raised in Colorado ranching country, star high school and college ath-lete, Naval Academy standout . . . blah, blah, blah. But his wild-card rep—supported by the diamond stud in his left ear—pegged him as a renegade and a troublemaker. So did the flirty smile, laser blue eyes, and an alpha male swagger that was too natural to be staged.

But according to the OSD file, beneath that spectacular exterior beat the heart of a screwup and a coward.

Well, she needed his help, and he was going to give it to her, one way or the other. She had no intention of dying for the justice she would see done—and by God, she *would* see it done. And she *would* get out of this alive.

She pulled her thoughts back together. She was on a mission and determined to make him squirm. "Let's back up a few years. To Annapolis and the Naval Academy. You graduated with honors. Impressive."

"We do aim to please."

"Started out your military career as an E-2 pilot," she continued, impervious to his smart-ass smirk. "Except flying the carrier-based turboprops and conducting electronic surveillance over the Gulf ended up being a little too boring for you, didn't it? A little too routine."

Though his face gave nothing away, he appeared to have stopped breathing. He didn't like it that she knew so much about him. Too bad. Psych ops 101: Make 'em sweat to make 'em talk.

"So you decided to change to the C-12 King Air and then, even though it made no sense to your CO, you asked to switch to helos and ended up transporting covert-ops teams—Task Force Mercy originally— in and out of hot zones because you wanted to get closer to the action."

He jerked hard on the plastic cuffs, then swore

when all he got for his effort was pain. No doubt about it. He'd begun to unravel nicely. And she'd just gotten started.

She *so* had his number. Then as now, Brown was a loose cannon. Only now he was also a struggling, re-covering alcoholic and though her research said he'd quit smoking years ago, when she'd spotted him in the cantina, an unlit cigarette was tucked above his right ear—a crutch for a weak man.

From the moment she'd committed herself to seeing this thing through, she'd made it her business to know everything about him. He was a lean, mean six foot three, one hundred ninety-five pounds, and he was her one and only living, breathing connection to Operation Slam Dunk. The file had detailed his wounds from the disas-trous Afghanistan op. He'd taken some shrapnel in his leg, dislocated his left shoulder, and sustained some nasty third-degree burns on his right thigh. A small price, considering so many others had paid with their lives that night.

He made her sick. He'd once been one of the Na-vy's best and brightest, but for the past eight years, since Afghanistan, he'd been hiding out in South America running a semi-legit, mostly bogus air-cargo business.

Now he was no longer anyone's best and brightest. And like it or not, right now he was hers; he knew it, and he wasn't having a lot of luck hiding his anger over that fact.

"All that action brought you to the invincible unit, right?" she pressed on, letting him know he had no place to hide, not from her. "An elite team, hand-picked by Spec Ops command."

He strained against his cuffs, then swore again when the plastic strip didn't budge from the metal head rail. "Who the hell are you?"

She ignored his question. "The One-Eyed Jacks, a multibranch military task force formed in 2002 and disbanded in 2005," she stated from memory. She'd read his jacket so many times she knew every line of it by heart. The One-Eyed Jacks had been loosely patterned after Task Force Mercy, a highly classified covert unit that had operated all over the Middle East and Africa right before the Bush administration took the reins.

"Got your nickname because of the uniqueness of your experimental unit, your tight camaraderie, and your reckless reputation. Oh, yeah, and you all loved to spend your down time playing cards. Poker. Spades. Blackjack. You name it. You played it."

"Let me guess," he interrupted. "With your winning personality, Old Maid is your game, right?"

A wiseass to the end.

But when she held up the jack of hearts she'd lifted from his pocket, all that bravado folded. The worn playing card was tattered around the edges and faded with age. A 9mm round punctured it dead center.

"You all made a pact. You all carried a one-eyed

jack—either a jack of hearts or a jack of spades. The cards were a sign of unity, and your lucky charms." She paused a beat, then flipped the card toward him. It landed on the chest that heaved rapidly beneath his black T-shirt, making it clear he wasn't nearly as calm as he wanted her to think he was.

"Only your luck ran out eight years ago, didn't it, Brown?" She moved to the side of the bed and leaned in close. "Ran out big-time during Operation Slam Dunk, when *you* screwed up and got most of your unit and dozens of innocent civilians killed." His eyes went hard as stone.

"I need to know why. I need to know who paid you to sell out your team."

Fire burned in Mike's gut like a bonfire. From the cheap booze. From the drug. From the anger at himself for getting caught like a fucking stooge.

But most of all from the mention of Operation Slam Dunk. The memory of that night still ate at him like a cancer.

Sell out his team? He'd rather die a thousand times over than ever sell out the One-Eyed Jacks. But he'd burn in hell before he'd defend himself to her.

She stood over him, cold, hard, demanding, and with the upper hand. He couldn't help but hate her for that—but not nearly as much as he hated himself. Something had gone terribly wrong that night and all he'd gotten was an impossible choice—life imprisonment, or a deal that had ended up costing him his soul.

He'd never gotten answers, not one, and he sure as hell didn't have any to give her.

". . . *you screwed up and got most of your unit and dozens of innocent civilians killed.*"

Even though the accusation sucked what little fight he had left out of him, he had no intention of rising to her bait.

"That's it?" She finally straightened, leaning away from him. "No defense?"

Her goading tone pissed him off even more. "You've already tried and convicted me. What's the point in defending myself? And speaking of points, what's yours? Either shoot me, screw me, or set me the hell loose."

That threw her. She'd expected answers, not demands. And not a crude indictment of her staged seduction. Judging from her sudden stillness and an unmistakable hint of disappointment in her eyes, she might even have wanted him to deny her charges.

Now that was interesting.

Or not. God, he was tired of this crap. He'd drunk himself stupid tonight so he could forget about Afghanistan, only to have this woman throw it in his face like a gallon of acid.

So much for plan A.

"It wasn't me who decided you were guilty," she said, back in attack mode. "It was a military court. Oh, wait." She smiled humorlessly. "There was no actual guilty verdict, was there, or you'd be rotting in prison right now. Instead, you cut a deal. Bought yourself a less than honorable discharge in exchange for your freedom and the promise that the incident got buried."

"Not deep enough, apparently." His gaze narrowed on hers. "How do you know about Operation Slam Dunk anyway?" Even the press hadn't gotten wind of what had happened that night. He had his own theory about the tap dancing that had gone on behind the scenes to accomplish that silence.

"Like I said. I know everything about you."

And then she proved it, nut-shelling the case that the Navy had laid out against him with cold-blooded accuracy.

He tried not to listen as she hammered him with bullet points.

Dereliction of duty . . .

Disobeying direct orders . . .

Reckless endangerment . . .

The list went on and on, and all led to the conclusion that he *had* been responsible for the death of his men and those villagers.

He closed his eyes and breathed deeply, but couldn't stall a cold sweat that compounded his queasiness as vivid memories of that night gnawed at him like rats.

The helo spinning out of control . . . the ground rocketing up to meet them as he fought to right the bird.

The crash . . .

The explosion . . .
The fire . . .
The stench of blood and burned flesh.
The deal that had cost him everything.

Not a day or night went by that he didn't see those images. Didn't hear the screams. Didn't do his best to forget.

And this woman had brought it all back.

Who was she?

And how the fuck had she gotten that information?

He couldn't get past that question. The after-action reports, the court-martial transcripts . . . everything about OSD was supposed to have been deleted from the DOD database. No one was supposed to have access to any of it.

Taggart and Cooper, the two other surviving members of the One-Eyed Jacks, had been brought up on charges with him. He knew they wouldn't talk. He hadn't had contact with either one of them in eight years and yeah, they hated his guts now, but there was no way in hell they were going to talk—they had the same stakes riding on silence as he did.

"Truth hurts, doesn't it, Brown?" she asked into the thickening stillness.

"What do you *want* from me?" he ground out. And then it hit him.

"You lost someone over there." The sudden insight blared through his headache and the nausea. *That's* what this was about. Someone she cared about had died in Operation Slam Dunk. Somehow she'd gotten hold of the file and she held him responsible.

Join the club. *Everyone* held him responsible.

"No, I didn't."

He honed in on her eyes, knowing what he'd see in them even before he called her on it. "You're lying."

"And you're avoiding. Seven men in your unit died that night. Dozens of civilians . . . many of them children. All because you decided to play Captain America."

He clenched his jaw until he thought his molars would crack, hating her for throwing the lies in his face. Hating himself for taking it.

"You led those men to their deaths." She got right in his face again. "You got those people caught in the crossfire. Because you were hotdogging. Because you were playing games with people's lives."

"The hell I was!" he roared so unexpectedly she flinched and stumbled backward. "The hell I did!" He strained violently and futilely against the cuffs, desperate to get at her.

He collapsed back on the bed, defeated. Wrung out.

Silence rang in the wake of his shouted denial. He despised himself for the sudden weakness that washed over him, obliterating his bid for apathy. But, Christ, now that he'd said it out loud, he didn't seem to be able to stop saying it.

"The hell I did." It came out on a whisper this time, his voice broken, his defenses destroyed.

Humiliated that he'd let her crack him, beyond

his limit with her bitch goddess accusations, he turned away, his eyes stinging, his vision blurred — but not before he saw pity momentarily soften her features.

Fuck her. He didn't need her pity.

But goddamn, he could use a drink.

4

Eva steeled herself, watching Brown's façade crumble. It was a painful thing to witness. Stripped down, naked emotion—that's what she'd just seen in his eyes. Anguish. Pain. It was all there. Because he was guilty? Because he *wasn't* guilty? Because he'd sold out rather than fight to prove his innocence?

She pulled it back together and fought the unwanted compassion she had promised herself she would not feel toward this man. No matter how beaten he looked. Guilty or innocent, it didn't really matter. What mattered was finding out who had dropped the OSD file into her life, why they'd done it, and who was after her because of it.

She was a smart girl. She figured she'd been chosen to open this can of worms because she had the means and skills to delve into the underbelly of the defense department's dirtiest secrets—and she had the motivation. Ramon.

"If you were innocent of the charges, why make the deal? Why not defend yourself in court?"

For a long moment, he wouldn't look at her. Finally, he swiped his cheek against his shoulder . . . and she steeled her defenses again. She was actually relieved when he turned his head and Primetime was back—all attitude, arrogance, and defiance.

"You're the one with all the answers, *chica*. You're telling me you haven't figured it out?"

"Enlighten me," she said, her voice firm.

He made a weary sound, then actually answered her question. "You can't fight city hall. Or the combined might of the U.S. military."

She moved back toward the bed. "But if you're innocent, as you claim you are—"

"Oh, please. Prisons are full of innocent men. Just ask 'em. They'll all tell you the same thing. They didn't do it. No one buys that, either."

She breathed deep, fighting the urge to believe him. "So . . . what? Someone set you up as a scapegoat?"

"Scapegoat, slow-moving target. Take your pick."

"Then who *was* responsible for what went wrong that night?"

He pushed out a humorless laugh. "If I knew the answer to that question, do you honestly think we'd be having this conversation?"

"You've got to have some ideas."

He slowly shook his head. "None. And you know what? I don't give a shit anymore. But I do care about how you got your hands on that file."

He held her gaze for a long, challenging moment,

making her uncomfortable for reasons she couldn't explain. Maybe because underneath all that bluster, an unexpected hint of vulnerability bled through.

Or maybe because she really did want Brown to be a good guy after all. Ramon had been a good guy— one of the best.

"It's Jane," she said when Stingray answered his phone. Jane Smith was one of the many aliases that protected not only her identity, but her bank accounts—many of which the man on the other end of the line had filled quite nicely. He wasn't her only source of income but he was one of her most lucrative. He was, however, the only one who shared her bed.

"I'd started to think you'd forgotten who signs your paychecks."

Even though he was thousands of miles away, his voice rang crystal clear through her earbud. Before they'd finally met face-to-face, she'd known him only as Stingray. But after doing a couple of jobs for him, she'd had more than a passing curiosity about what this particular man looked like. She'd been fairly certain he was American. Now she knew everything about him. "Yes, well, I've been a little busy."

The smell of exhaust from the busy street one story below rolled in through the open doors that led to a small, narrow terrace adjacent to the one belonging to room 203, where her assignment plus one were totally unsuspecting. The plus one both intrigued and amused her.

Perspiration trickled between her breasts as she moved away from the doors and lay down on the bed. "Your girl's a mover." She stared at the languid ceiling fan that did little to cut the night's suffocating heat. "Keeping up with her has pretty much taken all of my attention."

"She's not *my* girl. She's your assignment. Please tell me you haven't lost her."

Because she understood he had much on the line, and because the sound of his voice tripped a lot of triggers other than anger, she let the insult slide. And because she was his business associate first, his lover second, she never forgot her professional code. Always keep the customer happy. "I've got her."

"So what's going on?"

"At the moment we appear to have a little hostage situation."

"You're not serious."

She heard the laughter in his voice along with the surprise. She had always liked his laugh. Liked his no-nonsense manner. The first time they'd ever done business, she'd found herself thinking that if she ever met him, she was going to screw him. His smoke-and-whiskey voice—a pleasant departure from the guttural Arabic or Farsi contacts she so often dealt with—had *that* kind of effect on her.

"Have you ever known me to joke?"

"Point taken. So fill me in on what's happened since you landed in Lima."

"She made a beeline to *El Tocón Sangriento*—I

wouldn't recommend the sangria, by the way—where she came on to this guy like a seasoned *pepera* girl."

"*Pepera?*"

"*Pepera. Brichera.* Streets of Lima are full of girls who rob and drug men who can't keep it in their pants."

"Consider me educated," he said with another hint of a smile in his voice.

Yeah. She had definitely fallen in lust with that voice.

"So, she seduces him—he's already drunk so it's no big trick—lures him outside into the alley, drugs him, and hauls him to this dive of a hotel. Last time I checked, she had him cuffed to the bed." Before setting up her audio surveillance, she'd made a foray out onto the terrace with a mirror on an extendable shaft. It hadn't taken much to size up the situation. "She's keeping a bead on him with his own gun. The drunken fool fell for her honeypot trap like an amateur."

"Who's the guy?"

"I'm supposed to know that? You sent me to watch her, not introduce myself to her playthings."

And as with all of her jobs, even for him, she made a point to limit her information to absolute need to know. She didn't want to know motive, she didn't want to know their history; she only needed to know what he wanted done.

"Describe him to me. No. Wait. I have a feeling I can tell you exactly what he looks like. Big guy? Tall? Diamond stud, left ear? Silver screen material?"

He was spot-on right. "So you know him."

A heavy silence passed. "Yes. I know him."

Despite the pulsating heat of the city sifting in through the open doors, the dangerous undercurrents in his voice shot a chill down her spine. The hair on the back of her arm stood at attention as the adrenaline rush she always craved mainlined through her bloodstream.

"Have you been able to eavesdrop on their conversation?"

"If you mean, did I install a bug, the answer is no. They got here before I did, so there was no opportunity to plant one. I did get a room next to theirs, however. Lucky for you I never leave home without my Stealth Gear."

The little black box amplified sound; the supersensitive ceramic contact microphone fed into a pair of earphones for audio monitoring and allowed her to listen through walls several inches thick. The device was reliable to a fault, unless there was an air gap in the wall that could garble the transmission and provided the batteries didn't die. Unfortunately, there was an air gap so her intel gathering was limited.

"I've only been able to pick up bits and pieces of their conversation. One thing keeps coming up. Something about Operation Slam Duck?"

A long silence, then a correction. "Slam Dunk."

"Yes. That could work. Whatever it is, they're pretty angry at each other. She's accused him of getting a bunch of people killed in Afghanistan. For the most part, he's telling her to go take a flying leap."

"Sounds like Brown."

Whether she liked it or not, now she knew the man's name. "Friend of yours?"

"I'd hoped it wouldn't come to this," he said, ignoring her question, which in itself was telling. He definitely knew Brown. Interestingly, the steel in his voice was heavy with regret.

Her pulse rate kicked up again because she knew where this was heading. Most of her contracts started out as surveillance and ended up as something different entirely. Which was why she never traveled without the MP5K.

"Change of plans," he said abruptly. "Take them both out. Tonight."

Anticipation kicked up her heart rate. Now things got dicey. And lucrative. "It's going to cost you."

"Triple the agreed-upon amount." No hesitation. "Deposit to the same account?"

All righty then. "That will work, yes."

"The money will be there within the hour."

She smiled. "And may I say that I not only like the way you do me, I like the way you do business."

"I don't want either one of them leaving Lima alive." The lethal edge in his voice said that friendly conversation was over. "Make it look like a lovers' spat. A drug deal gone sideways. I don't care. Just get it done and get out of there."

Abruptly, the line went dead.

Thoughtful, she tugged off the earbud and tossed it into her duffel. She stared a little longer at the ceiling, thinking about the two occupants of the room next door. She had already been running kill scenarios through her mind in anticipation of these orders.

The only question was, which option sounded the most enticing? Did she go in fast and hard and take them out before they knew what hit them? Or did she play with them for a while? Even a pro needed a little diversion now and then.

She checked her watch—still early—and glanced toward the terrace doors. And decided she had time to think about it.

5

Mike pulled himself together, pissed that he'd let this woman get to him.

She knew about Operation Slam Dunk. He didn't know how, he didn't know why; he only knew she wasn't going to stop badgering him until she got the answers she wanted.

But then, unexpectedly, she did stop. She stopped cold. She got a look on her face that made him think she might be second-guessing herself.

She broke eye contact suddenly and whirled away. Shoulders tense, back rigid, she walked to a pair of multipaned glass doors that he guessed led to a balcony or terrace. The glass was coated with the grime of the city and backlit by a light haze from the cantina and restaurant signs burning up and down the street below.

After a furtive look outside, she undid the latch and shoved both doors open onto the narrow terrace. Car exhaust, overripe fruit, and the tang of unwashed bodies bled into the hotel room, along with traffic sounds from a story below. A distant church bell chimed ten times. Ten p.m. on one of the longest days of his life. Overlaying it all was the faint scent of *El Río Rimac*. She breathed deep, as if preferring the foul city air to a breath tainted with his presence. Then she stared out into the night . . . like she was searching for something or someone, before quickly closing the doors again.

When she finally turned around, he couldn't decide if she looked relieved or wary. She moved away from the doors, head down, clearly uncertain, possibly scared.

It was the first chink he'd seen in her armor, and he pounced on the opportunity like a fat man on a pile of French fries.

"What's your name, *chica*?" He'd grown tired of playing her game. He had to get out of these cuffs, and the best and only option he had now was distraction.

She hesitated, then expelled a deep breath. "Pamela Diaz."

Another lie. Like a bad poker player, she had a tell that gave away her bluff. He'd noticed it when she'd denied she'd lost anyone. A little lift of her chin. An absent tap of her index finger—which happened to be resting against the barrel of his gun and reminded him to proceed with caution.

But at this point he didn't care if she told him she was Margarita Thatcher. She'd answered a question. It was a start.

"Okay, *Pamela Diaz* . . . I'll consider answering your questions if you answer mine." He didn't wait for her to point out the obvious—that she held the gun and the advantage. "What's your stake in Operation Slam Dunk?" When she hesitated again, he pressed his slight opening. "You know you're going to have to tell me sometime."

A humorless smile tipped up one corner of her mouth. "And why is that?"

"Because you haven't killed me for a reason. And I think we can rule out sex." He lifted a brow. "Yes? No?"

She snorted and he saw another sign of hope. She'd wanted to smile.

"So, that's a yes. Which means you want something else from me . . . and that you need me alive to get it."

She considered him with a long look, then finally walked back to the chair and sat down.

Tick. Tick. Tick. He had nowhere to go and no way to get there—yet. He could wait her out.

He knew instinctively that there was nothing he could say that would make her talk. *She* had to decide what happened next.

But he knew he was right. She wanted him for something other than a whipping boy. And to get his help—good luck with that—she was smart enough to know she had to give him something, because they'd reached gridlock. If she wanted information, she needed to lay her cards on the table. Once she did, he'd let her think she'd softened him up enough to get the upper hand. Then she'd find out how tired he was of playing with a stacked deck.

"I'm a journalist," she said after several long moments.

Tip of the chin. Tap of the finger.

Liar, liar, pants on fire.

"A journalist?" He grunted. "Give me a break."

"Freelance," she insisted. "I'm writing a retrospective piece that chronicles Spec Ops military units and their deployments in Afghanistan."

He actually laughed. "Right. And to accomplish that, you make it a practice to seduce, drug, hold at gunpoint, and"—he lifted his arms as far as the restraints would let him—"cuff your potential sources to a bed. Try again, *Pamela.*"

"You have a reputation as a loose cannon."

"Ah . . . so this was all for your protection. What a line of bullshit. You could have walked up and asked me."

"And you would have told me to take a flying leap."

She had a point. "So, rather than risk that happening, drugging me was the next logical alternative."

"I'm on a tight schedule. Expediency is what matters here, not your tender sensibilities."

She was a ball breaker, all right. New tactic. "Do we have a timetable for when these cuffs come off?" he asked point-blank.

No answer.

"Okay, fine. Could I at least have a drink of water while you work it out in your head? I'm bone dry here."

She thought for a moment, then finally stood and

walked hesitantly across the room toward a door he suspected was the bathroom.

The fact that she was willing to show him a little mercy told him reams about her. No self-respecting tango, street thug, or banger would give two rips about his poor parched throat. While it was clear she could handle herself, this particular skill was not her bailiwick—and knowing that only made him more pissed that he'd let her get the drop on him.

As soon as she turned her back to him, he went to work on the flex cuffs, hoping that all the hours of competitions he and the guys used to stage paid off. There had been a lot of down time between missions, a lot of hurry up and wait. You could only play so many games of cards and basketball, so you got creative. Flex cuffs were plentiful and tying each other up and trying to beat each other's escape times provided not only a diversion but a skill set that might come in handy one day.

Looked like today was the day his uncontested speed record was going to be put to the real test. And when she closed the bathroom door behind her—a stroke of luck that the lady needed some privacy—he made full use of the window of opportunity.

Pressing the inside of his wrists together, he wedged his right thumbnail under the edge of the first of a line of tiny teeth that locked into the plastic band on the catch on his left hand. Stretching, he tipped his head back so he could see what he was doing, then glanced toward the bathroom door when he heard a flush and then the sound of water running.

He had to move fast. Straining to get the right angle, he repeatedly worked his nail over the first tooth until it finally gave and slipped under the catch. The left cuff loosened a fraction of an inch. He repeated the process. Another tooth gave. Another breath of room.

He had the feel of it now. Like riding a bicycle. He repeatedly wedged his thumbnail under the next tooth, pressed, felt it give and immediately loosened another tooth, then another, and another . . .

The bathroom door swung open. He let his wrists go limp so she wouldn't suspect what he was up to.

She walked to the bed, a glass of water in one hand, his gun in the other.

Tricky, but doable.

Eyes narrowed and wary, she hesitated.

"Like I can do anything trussed like a chicken on a spit," he grumbled. "Please. Give me a drink."

He put plenty of helplessness in his tone. Added a dose of self-pity in his eyes.

Scowling, she finally leaned over him, extending the glass toward his mouth.

He lifted his head and drank deeply. Because he *was* thirsty. And because he wanted to give her a reason to let down her guard.

"Thanks," he said, appearing to be clearly defenseless and so fucking appreciative he wanted to gag. "More. Please." Oliver Twist at his humble best.

She didn't hesitate this time. She leaned a little closer, extended the glass. And he struck.

He jerked his left hand free of the loosened plastic

loop, knocked the gun across the room, grabbed her hair with his other hand, and jerked her down on the mattress.

Water flew everywhere; glass shattered on the tile floor. She scrambled to get away but before she knew she'd been had, he flipped her onto her back, straddled her hips, and pinned her wrists above her head.

She put up a good fight, and she didn't fight like a girl. She had some serious moves but he had size, physical strength, and a big dose of pissed-off on his side.

She bucked, jabbed with her elbows and attacked with her knees, giving him all he could handle until he finally managed to secure the cuffs around her wrists, loop them over the head rail, and jerk them tight.

Breathing hard, he pushed himself off her and off the bed. Not fast enough to avoid her flying feet, though. She clipped his cheek good with a boot heel and damn near knocked him on his ass.

Swearing, staggering, and gingerly touching his fingers to his cheekbone, he grabbed his gun from the floor, found his one-eyed jack, and tucked it in his pocket.

"So . . ." Sucking wind and grinning in the face of her anger and his pain, he dropped into the chair at the foot of the bed. "Welcome to my world."

6

Of all the stupid moves, Eva couldn't believe she'd let Brown get the drop on her. She knew what kind of an operative he'd been, knew not to let down her guard around him. But because she had, now *her* head was on the chopping block instead of his.

The sense of dread that had dogged her all the way to Peru went off the charts. Anger quickly outdistanced it. The bastard was enjoying this. She felt only a small measure of satisfaction as she watched his cheekbone redden and swell where she'd nailed him with her boot.

A good five minutes had passed since he'd cuffed her to the bed. Once he'd caught his breath, he hadn't wasted time searching the room.

He didn't find much. She'd been careful. If she was right and she'd been followed to Lima, she didn't intend to make it easy for her shadow to find her—which wouldn't make it easy for Brown to find out anything about her, either, and that, too, was by design. She didn't want him knowing her real identity. Not yet. Maybe not ever.

To make certain, she'd rented the room by the hour. Paid cash and used one of her fake IDs. Multiple passports and extra cash were stashed in a locker at the airport, the combination committed to memory. So he wasn't going to find anything to identify her here. But he did find the extra doses of Ketamine she'd brought along for insurance. And he'd found her Glock 19 in her purse, which meant he now had all the firepower.

Both handguns lay on a squat table he'd shoved against the wall near the foot of the bed, where he stood now—out of reach of her feet. He held a full syringe in his hand, playing with it, playing with her head.

"Ve have vays of making you talk," he said with an arched brow and the worst German accent she'd ever heard.

The hard look in his eyes overrode his sick sense of humor. She had to stay strong. "Ooo. That was original."

"I don't have to be original." He considered the needle. Considered her.

Now he was making her nervous. "You're not going to use that on me." She hoped to God she was right.

"Give me one good reason not to."

She tried to get comfortable and felt a brief moment of guilt over how long she'd kept him bound in this very same position. It hurt her shoulders—and she didn't have the added discomfort of once having had hers dislocated. "You won't get any answers if you knock me out."

"Maybe I don't want answers." The German accent and the joking were long gone as he slowly raked his gaze over her body. "Maybe, after all the shit you put me through, I want what you promised to deliver back at the cantina."

A sick feeling slid through her stomach. "You need to drug and rape your bed partners to get a little action these days, do you?"

"Listen to all that judgmental scorn from the woman who didn't hesitate to use a needle on me." His smile was ugly. His voice was so soft and chilling it made her shiver—especially when he moved closer . . . a prowling, pissed-off lion. "Enough playing around. Talk to me, *chica*. I've reached the end of my patience. Who are you, how did you get your hands on that file, and what do you really want from me?"

He looked dangerous now. Unreasonably gorgeous and mean, suddenly, as the anger that flashed in his eyes turned to an arctic cold rage. "Talk or I walk. Right after I tape your mouth shut and give this wad of cash to the desk clerk of this fine establishment and tell him not to disturb you until the money runs out."

He held up the bills he'd dug out of the front pocket of her jeans—another experience that hadn't lacked in humiliation. "This ought to buy a good ten days of uninterrupted solitude, don't ya think?"

She made herself hold his gaze. "You wouldn't do

that. You wouldn't leave me here to die." Or for whoever wanted her silenced to find her defenseless.

He shoved the cash into his hip pocket. "I'm a cold-blooded murderer, remember? Wasn't that the gist of the charges you leveled against me?"

When she didn't say anything, he walked to the door. "Suit yourself."

"All right." She was suddenly afraid he *would* leave her. After what she'd done to him, could she really blame him? "All right," she repeated when he hesitated with his hand on the door knob and waited.

She swallowed. He didn't need to know the whole truth. Not until she knew if there was even a prayer of trusting him. "You were right. I did lose someone that day. A friend."

He got very quiet. Then he leaned heavily against the door and waited for her to tell him.

"Ramon Salinas," she finally confessed, unable to control the tremor in her voice. She hadn't spoken Ramon's name aloud for a very long time, and it hurt every bit as much as she'd thought it would.

For a long moment they were both quiet—both of them assaulted by their own thoughts about Ramon. When she'd recovered enough to look at him, she realized that he hadn't recovered at all. His somber gaze searched her face.

"How did you know Salinas?"

There had been bad blood between the two men. A part of the reason she so despised Brown was because of the stories Ramon had told her about him.

Ramon had told her that Brown had always done everything he could to undermine him—whether it was throwing wrenches in his bids for promotion, questioning his authority, or cutting into his action with women—before Ramon had met her, of course.

She'd had no reason to doubt Ramon. He'd told her that Brown was a hot dog and an egomaniac who took unnecessary risks with other people's lives—risks that, according to the file that had shown up so mysteriously a month ago, had gotten Ramon and all those others killed.

She had to focus. "He didn't like you much."

He grunted. "You're pulling punches now? The man hated my guts."

"He told me you were a hotshot and a wild card. He even told me that you were probably going to get him killed one day."

That had been right before he'd returned to Afghanistan for a second deployment and hooked up with the One-Eyed Jacks again. It was on that deployment that Operation Slam Dunk disintegrated and Ramon had died.

"So you figure that's exactly what I did," he surmised correctly.

Still slumped against the door, he looked exhausted with the weight of Ramon's memory. "How did you know him?" he asked again with a closed expression.

"I did a story on him," she lied. She refused to give Brown the advantage of knowing how she and

Ramon were really connected. "When he was home recovering from—"

"Shrapnel from an IED," he interrupted with a war-worn look in his eyes. "Took a hit in his leg in a skirmish outside Kabul. It sent him back stateside for a couple months."

"That's when I met him. While he was recuperating." That part was true. "He gave me an interview." That part wasn't. What he'd given her was a ring. They'd been married three months when he redeployed to Afghanistan.

She flinched when Brown pushed away from the door and walked back to the chair. Eyes on hers, he stood behind it, gripped the back with both hands, and leaned on it heavily. "Try again. Active duty Spec Ops soldiers don't give interviews."

He was right. She had to pull it together if she wanted to convince him to believe her. "It was strictly anonymous. I never referred to him by name. It was more of an overview . . . the perspective of a soldier on the ground."

"Did you drug him, too, to get him to talk?"

She expelled a deep breath. "I'm sorry about that." It was a lie and she'd do it again in a heartbeat. She didn't have time to be nice. Nor was she particularly inclined.

She seldom was. Nice wasn't her thing.

He considered her with a hard look. "Now you're sorry? I don't think so. You wanted your pound of flesh. You're happy as hell you made me suffer.

That's why you came looking for me, right? To make me pay?"

She wanted him to suffer, all right, the way she'd suffered after losing Ramon eight years ago.

It had taken a long time to work through the grief. But she'd finally moved on. Then a month ago the file on Operation Slam Dunk with all of its conflicting information had dropped into her hands . . . and somebody spooky had landed on her ass. From that moment to this one, her entire world had shifted.

Eight years ago, she'd been told that Ramon had died on a routine training mission. That he'd made a careless mistake that had cost him his life. So all this time, she'd believed a lie that had told her Ramon had not died a hero's death, but one caused by his own carelessness.

The OSD file blew the lie to smithereens. The "official after-action report" on Operation Slam Dunk, signed off on by the Spec Ops commander, said that Ramon had died on a reconnaissance mission in Helmand Province. A mission that had turned into a bloodbath when Mike Brown had defied orders.

And yet, while the official after-action report laid all the blame squarely on Mike Brown's shoulders, he'd vehemently denied any wrongdoing in his pretrial statements. That denial had compelled her to look deeper.

Nothing she'd found out said Brown wasn't guilty. But every new piece of information she'd uncovered raised more questions. Then the shadow had appeared, and her sources had dried up. Someone had been following her ever since, and Eva didn't have a doubt in her mind that her own life was in danger.

Just like she had no doubt that her shadow had followed her to Lima. She'd never seen the spook, but so help her God, she could almost smell the guy.

She jerked her head front and center when Brown snapped his fingers, commanding her attention. "You're drifting, *chica*. We were talking about Ramon."

She cleared her mind, tried to pick up the thread of their conversation. "Ramon talked to me because he was a friend of my brother's." Another lie, but she was determined to stay this course and somehow regain her advantage.

"How were they friends?" he asked, grilling her the way she'd grilled him. "Your brother in the military?"

"What does it matter?" she snapped. She didn't want to go down this path. It left her open to more scrutiny. "He was a friend, okay?"

He spun the chair around and straddled it. "Seems like maybe a lesson in hostage etiquette is in order. You shouldn't get testy with me, *Pamela*. Remember, I'm the one holding the needle this go-round."

7

Eva breathed deep, regained her composure, and stared him down.

He dragged a hand through his too-long hair, brushing it off his face. Between the hair and his much more than a five o'clock shadow, he looked ragged and worn and still ridiculously gorgeous. His eyes were bright and clear now. The Ketamine had worn off.

"Fine," he said when her silence made it obvious she planned to stick with her story. "Ramon was a friend. You hate me because he died. Got it. So, what? You plot for eight years to find me and tell me what a horrible person I am? Sorry. I'm not buying that."

When she said nothing, he studied her face intently, and when he finally spoke he sounded thoughtful, even a little sad. "Did you come here to kill me, *chica*?"

"If I'd wanted you dead, I'd have put something with a little more kick in that syringe. I told you. I'm doing a story. A tribute to Ramon. A retrospective," she said, restating her original lie, then adding a little extra, working him. "And I waited eight years because I've been on assignment in the Middle East. You might have heard? There are wars on terror, uprisings, military coups breaking out everywhere?"

"You know how it is. Us bottom-feeders tend to live under rocks. We miss things." He gave her a considering look as he gingerly touched his fingers to the swelling under his eye. "Okay. Because you're so entertaining, I'll play along. You've been a busy little war correspondent. But now you're back on Ramon's story. Please, do enlighten me more."

"In the process of doing research about Ramon and his deployments, I was given access to several military documents." Another bold-faced lie. She'd never been given access to anything. If it hadn't been for that top-secret file showing up out of the blue on that flash drive—no explanation, no return address, no postmark, because it had been delivered by a courier service that had *conveniently* lost all information about the sender—she would have never opened up this particular can of worms.

His eyes sharpened on hers. He clearly suspected that she was lying about how she'd gotten the files, yet for some reason, he played along. "And they handed over the OSD file. Just like that."

Relieved that his skepticism seemed to have transitioned to interest, she pressed on with her lie. "No. Not just like that. My guess is they intended to supply me with a press-ready overview of the operations run since the war started. Your basic homogenized and carefully culled material. Declassified, redacted, and already made public in some form. They *weren't* supposed to give me the Operation Slam Dunk file."

His face paled again at the mention of the file. "Then how did you get it? That file isn't supposed to exist anymore."

"It exists. I read it."

His expression grew grimmer. She'd already proven how much she knew about him with information that could only have come from the file.

"Okay." He conceded the point. "Let's back up. Who are *they*? *Who* gave you the information?"

"I don't reveal my sources." She couldn't if she wanted to. She didn't know who her benefactor was or what his or her motive was for dropping the bomb in her lap that had led her here to Lima and Brown.

"It's so reassuring to know that you have some professional code of ethics—drugs and flex cuffs notwithstanding." He lifted a shoulder. "But that could just be me, splitting hairs."

"Those were carefully calculated tactics. You're a big boy. I'm sure you've done the same." She wrapped her fingers around the bars on the headboard and pulled herself up to get a little more comfortable. "Anyway, I'd scanned close to thirty generic, sterilized documents when I spotted the last one on the list. Somebody goofed and hadn't erased the data."

He let out a low groan. "No shit. All right. Let's ride this horse and agree that you 'stumbled' onto the 'official' military report of what happened that night. The gospel according to the five-star gods of war. Still doesn't tell me what you need me for."

"In the pretrial transcripts you repeatedly denied any wrongdoing on your part, adamantly maintained that someone had sabotaged the mission then set you up to be the fall guy—"

He cut her off with a lift of his hand. "They *did* set me up."

"Then why the plea bargain?" It was that abrupt about-face that had compelled her to dig deeper. And that digging had ticked someone off enough to have her followed. "Why would an innocent man cop a plea? Why would you sell out your remaining two teammates, Taggart and Cooper, and take them down with you?"

He considered her for a long time. "You ask that as though you think I might have had a reason *other* than being guilty. Having a change of heart, *Pamela*?"

She hadn't realized she was so transparent. "Okay. Here's the truth. When I came here, I wanted you to be guilty. I wanted you to admit it. I wanted it to end there."

He arched a brow. "And yet—now something is making you wonder if maybe I'm not the scourge of the free world. Goodness gracious, my heart's all aflutter."

She squirmed and rolled her burning shoulders, as weary with this game as he was. "Just because I'm starting to believe you got a bum rap doesn't change the fact that I think you're a coward."

"Give it a rest, *chica*. This is not the path to the truth. You ever hear the expression 'You can catch more flies with honey than Ketamine'?"

"Damn it, Brown. Just give it to me straight. What really happened on the mission?"

He slumped back in the chair, slowly shook his head. "Oh, no. I still haven't gotten my answers. You've been lying to me since you opened your mouth. Why is this *really* so important to you? And seriously, if this is about a story, why not put the screws to the powers that be and leave me the hell out of it?"

The intensity in his blue eyes reminded her that while this was about her wanting answers, it was also about his life. His career. Both things he'd walked away from.

"Because the moment I said the words *Operation Slam Dunk* out loud to someone at the Department of Defense, I lost total access. They quit answering my e-mails, refused my phone calls. I get real suspicious — red-flag suspicious — when doors start slamming in my face." Just like she got scared when she started noticing the same black sedan following within a few car lengths on the freeway each night. The same panel van parked a block away from her house.

He made a tired, cynical sound. "There are no stone walls like the U.S. military's walls."

She strained futilely against the cuffs again, then laid back against the pillows. "Listen, I have my own sources, my own methods. I can get to the bottom of this. But I need you to help me flesh things out, sift through the garbage and get to the real leads."

He jerked his chin back. "Leads? Leads on what? An eight-year-old story that—at the risk of total redundancy—the military is going to stonewall like it's Fort Knox?"

"Leads that might go beyond what happened in that valley that night."

There. She'd said it.

"What are you talking about?"

"I wish I knew. But something . . . something's way off."

He looked completely baffled. "Is that not what I've been trying to tell you?"

"I had to find out for myself, okay? That's why I'm here. That's why I used extreme measures."

He had nothing to say to that, but his expression said plenty. Somewhere, mixed in with the staged indifference and very real anger, was relief that she might actually believe him now. Which meant he wasn't as apathetic about the hand he'd been dealt as he let on.

"Isn't it time you found out?" She pressed her point. "Don't you want to know who was responsible for what happened that night?"

Silence. A slow, methodical shake of his head. He crossed his arms over his chest. "Stone walls, remember? That's not happening."

"But what if it could? What if I could make it happen? What if *we* could make it happen?"

He pushed out a laugh. "What? So . . . now you want to help me clear my name?"

"I want to clear Ramon's name," she said honestly. "I couldn't care less about clearing yours."

He laughed again. "You are *such* a charmer."

"Don't you want to read the files?" she hurried on, ignoring his cynicism.

"Sure, fine. So show them to me. Or wait . . . if I frisk you, will I find them myself?"

His eyes were smug and baiting. And he was enjoying himself far too much at her expense.

"You really think I'd compromise my investigation by traveling with the flash drive? It's not on me. It's in a safe place. Back in the States."

When he looked thoughtful, she pressed her advantage.

"Look. I haven't added it all up yet—I can't add it up without hearing your full story. Detail by detail. Call by call. You were there. You know what really happened. Who was there, who called the shots, who had something to gain. But the bits and pieces I *have* uncovered tell me that if you were set up—"

"We're back to *if* again? You should really do something about this little bipolar thing you've got going on."

She couldn't blame him for doubting her. "If someone set up the team and framed you they could still be active duty. They could still be running bogus reports to cover up other operations that are far from being in the interests of national security."

He held up a hand. "Whoa. You a big Vince Flynn fan? Into spies and double-agent stories? Talk about a major leap," he sputtered with a whole lot of cynicism.

Too much cynicism. So much that she knew he was actually thinking the very same thing but didn't want to admit it. He struggled to hide it but he was interested. Real interested.

She decided to take a huge leap of faith. "Doors didn't just slam in my face when I started asking questions. I can't prove it, but I'm fairly certain that I've been followed."

"Bipolar and paranoid. Throw in schizophrenic and you've hit the trifecta. They have padded rooms for people like you. Some of them even come with a view." He touched a finger to his cheek again, winced.

"You think that didn't cross my mind? That I wondered if I saw things where nothing existed? They were there. I've seen one too many cars, one too many times, behind me on the freeway or in my neighborhood. Sensed something out of place in my kitchen or my bedroom once too often."

Just like she'd gotten that prickly sensation along the nape of her neck and that sick feeling in the pit of her stomach that had her sleeping with her gun every single night.

He had that hard look in his eyes again. The one she'd started to recognize as stubborn but intrigued.

"So why not go to the CIA with your speculations? Or the FBI. DHS. Hell, pick the alphabet agency of your choice. Let them investigate."

Of course she couldn't do either, because she worked for one and the other would go straight to the very people who could be involved in the cover-up. *If* there was a cover-up.

"You know that's not how it works. In the first place, it's illegal for the CIA to conduct ops inside U.S. borders without special dispensation from the president. In the second, the Carter administration destroyed the CIA's human-intelligence capabilities and the current administration has continued the war on the CIA. Third, the FBI has bigger fish to fry. Department of Homeland Security? Forget it. Besides, they'd never believe someone was after me."

He lifted his hands as though she'd just made his point. "Well . . . yeah . . . that's because you're nuts."

8

One hundred percent nuts, Mike thought, holding the line against his growing interest. She'd proven that from the get-go, right? She was nuts to take him on. Nuts to drug him.

"So are you going to help me or not?" she asked, more challenge than question.

He laughed. "That would be a not."

"Not even if it means clearing your name? Not even if it means bringing whoever's behind this to justice?"

"Not even." Jaw clenched, he tried to ignore the pounding of his heart and the voice in his head that suggested he was making a mistake.

"Then you're exactly who I thought you were. A cowardly, selfish bastard."

He rose to his feet, tossing the syringe onto the table. "I do love living down to your expectations."

"You know what your problem is?"

"I'm not the one with the problem." He lifted his chin toward her bound hands as he prowled the room.

"You need to stop thinking about yourself," she accused, not letting up. "Quit wallowing in your own self-pity and think about the men who died that night. About the men who took the rap with you. Ramon and the others deserve to have the record set straight. Cooper and Taggart deserve their day in court—deserve the trial they never got because you sold them out when you took a deal that steamrolled them along with you."

"I didn't sell them out. I saved their lives," he countered, unable to stop his anger. Instead of rotting in a jail cell or six feet under, Cooper was living the good life in Australia, making money off his pretty-boy face modeling, screwing women, and not giving a shit. And for the past several years, Taggart had been doing what he wanted: working with a private contractor and mixing it up with the bad guys back in Afghanistan. Mike had saved their asses, but she didn't get that. No one got it.

"Then save their honor," she shouted back, and damn her, he swore she could see straight through him. See that even though he didn't want to he still did care about what happened.

He still cared a lot.

"Help me find out who did this. Help me figure out if there's more going on."

He stalked toward the terrace doors, braced his palms on the frame above his head, and stared outside while she pecked away at him like a vulture on fresh meat.

"If we can get Cooper and Taggart on board, we can find whoever was responsible and expose them."

"Get them on board?" He spun back around. The fire of conviction brightened her eyes; a flush of color stained her cheeks. A slice of smooth caramel skin peeked between the waistband of her jeans and the T-shirt that had ridden up her ribs. The generous swell of her breasts rose and fell with her agitated breaths.

And as angry as he was, as crazy as *she* was, damn if the sight of her didn't turn him on like a flashlight.

Talk about fucked up.

"What alternate universe do you live in?" he snapped. "The boys and I aren't exactly buddies anymore. They hate my guts. They're not going to help me with anything."

"And if they would?" She dangled the possibility like a carrot.

Damn his hide, he was tempted. *So* tempted to do something other than run from his past for a change. But it was pointless. "You're dreaming if you think you can get either one of them to work with me again."

Her coffee-dark eyes snapped with fire. "I don't dream. I plan. I execute. And I make things happen."

"Said the woman cuffed to the bed."

"We can get Taggart and Cooper to help us," she insisted.

He snorted. "When pigs wear tutus."

"Look, Brown, before you tell me if you're in or

out, you think about this. Think about slinking back to your *own* little alternate universe, where you try to convince yourself every single day that what happened to you, what happened to all those people, doesn't matter. You try to convince yourself that you're going to spend the *next* eight years and all the years after that hiding out from your demons, pretending you don't care, pretending you don't have an obligation to Taggart and Cooper. Pretending that you don't have an obligation to yourself, for God's sake! And what about to your country?"

She cut way too close to the quick with that one. "Are you fucking kidding me? You seriously played the patriot card?" He'd been sold down the river by the very people he'd pledged to protect and serve and almost died for. "I've paid that debt. One hundred times over. Try a new tactic, *chica*, 'cause that dog ain't gonna hunt."

"Fine. Then let's try something you can relate to," she said acidly. "I'll pay you to help me."

He considered how badly she hated him in this moment. It was never more evident than now as she lay there, tied up and helpless, yet making her best play to kill him with her disgust.

He thought about all the reasons he should tell her to fuck off, stay out of his life and out of his head. But the words that came out sealed his fate.

"Well, now. You're finally talking my language." She'd barely had a chance to register surprise, when he reached into his boot and retrieved his jackknife.

And he'd barely sliced the blade through the plastic cuffs, freeing her, when he heard a sound outside on the terrace that shot all his defenses to red alert.

Eva heard it, too. Someone was out there.

Her heart went crazy but she held it together and nodded that she understood when Brown pressed his fingers to his lips, signaling her to be quiet. When he pointed to the floor behind the bed, she didn't hesitate. She rolled off the bed and dropped to her knees, using the mattress as the only available shield as Brown rushed back across the room to the table where their guns lay side by side.

He grabbed both and tossed her the Glock. She caught it and checked to make certain there was still a round in the chamber as, two-handing his Beretta, Brown moved like a big cat toward the wall beside the terrace door. He'd no sooner gotten into position, his back flattened against the wall, when the doors flew open and a masked figure burst into the room wielding an MP5K.

Eva scrambled toward the foot of the bed as the gunman fired a three-round burst at the pillow where her head had been.

She slid to her back and started firing at the same time she heard Brown's Beretta pop off several rounds in quick succession.

The barrel of the MP5K jerked toward the ceiling as the gunman stumbled backward out of the room and fell against the iron rail on the terrace. Brown shot outside after him as Eva scrambled to her feet and raced across the room to the terrace.

Brown was leaning over the railing when she reached his side. Her stomach rolled when she saw the scene down on the street. Their would-be assassin had fallen backward onto the roof of a cab. His prostrate body lay motionless in the dim light from the streetlamp as the startled driver scrambled out from behind the wheel.

"You okay?" Brown turned to her.

Her ears rang like church bells. Other than that, she was fine. "Yeah. I think so. You?"

His answer was a grunt, which pretty much told her that other than his attitude, he was fine. "Friend of yours?"

"I told you I was being followed."

He sprinted past her toward the door that led to the hallway. "Shut those balcony doors. Keep your Glock close and don't let anyone in this room but me."

She didn't have to ask where he was going. He was heading down to check the body. As he left, she ran inside and locked the doors to the terrace. Then she wedged herself into the corner facing the hall door, sank down to her butt, and propped the Glock on her updrawn knees. And she waited. Heart going haywire, her breath tight and strained. She'd trained for such a scenario all of her career—but this was the first real encounter she'd had with someone shooting at her. The blowback of the adrenaline rush shot off the charts. It took everything she had to keep her teeth from rattling and the gun from shaking out of her hands.

When a knock finally sounded, she jumped to her feet like she was on springs and pointed the business end of the Glock dead center in the middle of the door.

"It's me. Open up."

Brown.

She hadn't realized until that point how happy she would be to see him.

"Anything?" she asked after she'd let him in and quickly shut the door behind him.

"Nada. Whoever it was, is gone."

"Gone?" Her eyes widened in disbelief. "How can that be? I swear I hit him."

"Well, somebody hit him or he wouldn't have taken a header off the balcony." He shook his head. "The cab's gone, too. I'm thinking wrong place, wrong time, for the cabbie."

Fear obliterated filters. She couldn't stop herself from asking, "Still think I'm crazy?"

He expelled a heavy breath. "What I think is that we've got to get out of here." He glanced around the room. "I don't want to stick around for the second act. If he's got reinforcements waiting in the wings, they might have better aim."

He didn't have to tell her twice. Eva grabbed her bag and followed him.

And she didn't ask a single question until they were in a cab and a good twenty blocks away from the hotel on *Calle San Ramon* where both of them were supposed to have died.

"I don't know where we're going, okay?" Mike said when she finally popped the question he'd expected long before.

Whether it was from shock or disbelief that she'd almost died, relief that she hadn't, or because she had finally realized she was into something beyond her pay grade, he didn't know. But she hadn't asked one question until they were well away from the hotel.

What he *did* know was that Pamela Diaz, or whatever her name was, had landed herself—and now him by proxy—into some very deep doo-doo.

"Are you ready to fly back to the States with me?"

He grunted. "All I'm ready to commit to at the moment is getting out of Dodge."

He looked at her then. At her coffee-brown eyes, showgirl breasts, and anxiety-stricken expression, and man oh man, all he could think about was how gorgeous she was.

Hot, sultry air rushed through the cab's open window, whipping strands of hair that had escaped from her ponytail into her eyes. Her effort to smooth it back was a bust. The wind grabbed it again, plus did a fine job of plastering her damp T-shirt to those amazing breasts.

Seriously, you stupid wing nut? After what she's done to you, you're still wondering what it would be like to get her in bed?

He shook his head to clear it. He could *not* get

sidetracked by her sex appeal. Thinking with his little head had gotten him in this mess to begin with.

Drugged, flex cuffs, shanghaied, crazy. *That's* what he needed to think about.

He drilled her with his best pissed-off glare. "You do realize the significance of what happened back there, don't you?"

"It means I'm probably right about a conspiracy."

He wasn't ready to go quite that far. "For certain, someone wants you silent, *chica*. Someone wants you dead. Someone, apparently, had you followed here from the States, put out a contract on you, and gave the order to pull the trigger."

"Yeah. I got that part." She shuddered, and damn if he didn't have to resist the urge to put his arm around her and pull her against him.

Little head, big trouble.

He ramped up his glare. "So did you also get the part that, thanks to you, they want me dead, too?"

"All the more reason for you to help me figure out who's behind it."

His jaw dropped before he could check it, but she never missed a beat.

"What? You expect me to tell you I'm sorry for dragging you into this? Well, that's not happening. You've been in it from the beginning."

"I've been out of it for eight years, thank you very much."

"No, you've been *hiding* out. Big difference. Grow a pair, Brown. It's past time."

He opened his mouth. Shut it. Whipped his head toward the opposite window and clamped his fingers around his thighs to keep from clamping them around her throat. Talk about tossing a glass of ice water on a lit match. He wasn't thinking about sex anymore. Oh, no. He was thinking about murder. If she'd been a man, he'd have dropped her.

And if she'd been wrong, he admitted as a flood of self-disgust washed over him, he'd have stopped the cab, gotten out, and told her to go preach to another choir.

Can I get a hallelujah?

He stared blindly out at the shadowed urban landscape scrolling by in the dark. *But she wasn't wrong, was she? She was* so *not wrong.*

In fact, she was so flat-out, dead-on right, it shamed him. Kicked him in the head, punched him in the gut, and shamed him into finally admitting the truth.

For eight years he'd been running. For eight years he'd been telling himself it didn't matter, he couldn't change it, couldn't make it right. He'd only been partly right. He couldn't change what had happened, couldn't bring those men back.

But it *did* matter. On that he'd been head-up-his-ass wrong. It had *always* mattered. Every second, every minute, every hour of every freaking day. Mattered to the point where he'd run and denied and become so mired in the game of avoiding the truth, that he'd totally lost sight of it.

Here, now, was the truth. He was an innocent man. Taggart and Cooper were innocent men. And just because his balls had been nailed to the proverbial wall all those years ago didn't mean he had to be held hostage by lies now.

An even sadder truth? Nothing but his own stubborn determination stopped him from breaking free.

He glanced at the woman responsible for upsetting his cart full of rotten apples. Gave her her due. She was wrong about a lot of things, but she was right about the one thing that counted.

He *was* a coward.

Had been for eight long years.

He set his jaw, breathed deep, and made that final leap from resistance to resolution.

That all changed right now.

As of now, he was officially back in the game, because this lying, conniving, sexy-as-ever-loving-sin, wack-job of a woman had dragged him out of his hidey-hole.

So . . . did he thank her or throttle her? And what in holy hell was he supposed to make of her? Though her conspiracy talk was off-the-charts crazy, that gunman had been sent by someone. Someone she'd either pissed off or someone who wanted her silenced—or both.

He scrubbed a hand over his face.

Okay, so if he bought into her conspiracy theory—and that was a big *if*—who was behind it, and what was their endgame? It was bad enough that he'd lost friends that day. Bad enough that he'd taken the fall. But if she was right—if it was far bigger than an operation gone sideways—then it meant that his being framed was only a microscopic blip on the radar of a far bigger plot. Which reduced the importance of what had happened to him to less than nothing.

And that *really* pissed him off. Because he was *more* than nothing. His team had been more than nothing. And suddenly, because of her, if it was the last thing he did, he wanted not only justice for them, but he wanted this bastard taken out. And he wanted to be the one doing it.

"All right, Ms. Hot Tamale Diaz," he said, deciding to give her what she wanted. "We're going to play this out. We are going to proceed as though we have our fingers on the trigger of a gun that's going to go *boom* in the face of the man who killed a lot of good men, a lot of innocent people, and ruined my life.

"But so help me God," he warned her when relief and satisfaction filled her eyes, "if you don't deliver the goods—"

"I'll deliver," she promised. And though he had a shitload of reasons not to trust her, the conviction in her words made him want to believe—at least part of her story. She was still lying her gorgeous ass off about who she was and what she did. Reporter? Not a chance. She was personally vested in this—her heavy-handed tactics at the bar told that story.

"If you sell me out, *chica,* be warned: There's

not a corner of this earth remote enough for you to hide in."

She had nothing to say to that, but her eyes told him he'd made her a believer.

"*Aeropuerto. Rapido,*" he told the taxi driver, hoping to hell he wasn't going to regret his decision.

9

When Brown decided to move, he moved. They hit the Jorge Chavez International Airport running. First stop was at a small hangar far away from the busy international commercial terminals. With an order for the cabdriver to wait that Brown insured by tipping him with some of the money he'd lifted from her pockets, he grabbed her hand and they raced into the building.

"Do you think we're being followed?" she asked breathlessly.

"If there had been more than one shooter, we'd have met up with him before we left the hotel."

That made sense, but didn't stop her from constantly looking over her shoulder.

The hangar housed several small private planes and as Brown jogged briskly across the concrete floor, she'd either have to keep up or fall flat on her face. He dragged her along behind him at a breakneck pace.

"What are we doing here?" They ducked around

and under several wings before stopping beside a vintage twin turboprop Beechcraft King Air.

"Getting my passport."

The Beechcraft was a sweetheart of a plane—her dad had been a Beechcraft buff so she recognized the make and model immediately. PRIMETIME AIR CARGO was sprawled across the gleaming white fuselage in glittering red, white, and blue letters.

For a man who claimed no love of country, they were interesting color choices, she thought as he unlocked the door with a key he fished out of his boot.

And for a man who didn't want anyone to think he gave two rips about anything, the plane was immaculately clean and well cared for.

"If you sell me out, chica, be warned: There's not a corner of this earth remote enough for you to hide in."

Despite the pulsing heat under the tin roof of the hangar, she suppressed a shiver at the memory of the look in his eyes. He'd meant it. Hell hath no fury like a woman scorned—or like a man who'd been played by a woman.

But that sword sliced both ways. If it turned out he'd lied and he was responsible for Ramon's death, she wouldn't hesitate to throw him to the wolves.

"We'd better ditch the guns here. Stash them in the plane." He held out his hand.

He was right. They'd never make it past airport security. Reluctantly, she handed hers over.

"Wait here." He tucked her Glock in his waistband and pulled down the airstairs. "I'll be right back."

He trotted up the five steps and ducked inside. Curious about what she'd find inside, she ignored his order to wait and followed him up the stairs.

He spun around so fast that if he hadn't grabbed her and pulled her against him, she would have tumbled backward down the steps.

For a very long, very intense several seconds, they stood that way. Him gripping her upper arms, her breasts pressed against his chest, their gazes clashing and hot. For a wild and crazy instant, she thought he would kiss her. For an even wilder and crazier instant, she thought she might let him.

"I told you to wait," he growled, breaking the spell.

Stunned by her reaction to him, she lifted her chin and gave him a "you're not the boss of me" look.

He shook his head and with a roll of his eyes, let her go.

And damn if she wasn't shaking. She steadied herself with a deep breath.

What the hell was that?

Adrenaline. Had to be. And sleep deprivation. And the constant, recurring memory of the pillow exploding on the bed from the gunman's MP5K.

While Brown dug around in the cockpit, she grounded herself by looking around the plane. Pretty basic, totally empty. Apparently the cargo business wasn't merely a front. The passenger seats had been removed and the fuselage was rigged with nylon straps fixed to the floor to secure freight.

"Let's go." Suddenly he was right behind her.

She jumped and whirled around. Hyper-awareness. More proof that she was running on empty.

He stuffed his passport and some cash into his hip pocket.

"You travel light."

"I travel fast." Face grim, he headed down the airstairs.

Whatever that moment had been about earlier, he clearly hadn't liked it any better than she had. Which was fine with her.

"Now what?" she asked after he'd locked up and they were hustling back toward the hangar door.

"This is your show, *chica*. You tell me."

After a quick look around outside to insure that they hadn't been followed, he gripped her elbow and sprinted for the waiting cab.

Her Kevlar vest had stopped two rounds from penetrating her chest cavity. Besides saving her life, the vest had saved her from broken ribs when she'd hit the roof of the cab. Pain ripped through her body with every breath she drew, but she'd recover. It was her arm that worried her. She couldn't feel her hand anymore, and blood still trickled sticky and warm down her arm, despite the makeshift tourniquet she'd forced the cabdriver to tie at gunpoint.

Slumped in the backseat of the stinking, hot relic of a taxi, she felt herself slipping. Blood loss. Shock. Disbelief that she'd blown it so badly. That she'd become the prey. That both targets had gotten away.

She was *so* damn pissed.

"H . . . how long?" she asked in Spanish, disgusted by the weakness in her voice.

The adrenaline that had mainlined through her system when she'd tumbled off the roof of the cab and had made it possible for her to crawl into the backseat had let her down. Her MP5K had easily persuaded him to speed away from the hotel, then park in a back alley several blocks away. It seemed like an eternity had passed since she'd made him use his phone to call the number she'd committed to memory before she'd left for Lima. She never commissioned a job without a contingency plan, and was anal-retentive about backup—even though she'd never had to use it until now.

The cabbie quaked behind the wheel. "Twenty-seven minutes," he said, the fear thick in his trembling voice. He'd learned quickly to be precise.

Twenty-seven minutes. Two minutes since she'd asked the last time.

What was taking so damn long? Someone should be here by now.

She felt her eyes roll back in the sockets and her head fall backward, and she snapped to with a start. This was bad. She couldn't win the battle to stay conscious much longer.

But she had to hang on. Had to. She caught herself going under again and forced herself to a more upright position. Knowing she needed the shock of pain to keep her even semi-alert, she jabbed the barrel of the MP5K against her ribs. And bit back a scream as the blinding, white-hot pain exploded through her brain.

A black SUV suddenly pulled up parallel to the taxi. Two doors opened, then closed. The driver's-side door of the cab flew open with a gruffly ordered, "¡Vaya!" Go.

The cabdriver couldn't get out from behind the wheel fast enough. He took off running down the alley, stumbled, righted himself, and disappeared in the dark as the rear door of the cab opened.

"What took you . . . so fucking long?" she gritted out, fighting both unconsciousness and pain as a pair of strong arms reached inside and helped her out.

"GPS isn't all it's cracked up to be. How bad?"

She didn't know this man or his driver. She only knew their service came highly recommended. "Bad enough."

"The doc is waiting," he said, then picked her up when her knees buckled and her world went blacker than black.

It was 11:10 p.m. by the time Eva had retrieved her passport and extra cash from the locker where she'd stashed them at the international terminal. "Two tickets to Washington, D.C.," she told the ticketing agent. "Earliest flight possible."

Mike's eyebrows shot up. The implications of D.C. being her home base clearly weren't lost on him, but he didn't comment. And that was a huge relief because he *had* made a big deal over her passport.

Make that *passports*. She'd stood, jaw tight, arms crossed under her breasts, after he'd snatched the two fake documents out of her hand, scanned them, then handed both back with a knowing smile.

"My, my. Got yourself a good ink man, there. Creative. And smart. He even included an entrance stamp to keep eyebrows from raising when you go through customs. But I'm so confused. Which is it? Pamela Diaz or"—he glanced at the second forged document—"Emily Bradshaw? Or is Mata Hari still going to turn up somewhere on one of these little blue books?"

What she had was access to the CIA's resources, and a trustworthy friend in the documents department who hadn't asked questions. She was glad now that she'd double-covered her bases. Pamela Diaz was on someone's hit list, but Emily Bradshaw was just another American tourist returning home.

And Brown had no room to talk: They'd booked his ticket under the name John Mason. He knew as much or more about forged documents as she did.

She let him wonder about her true identity. She still wasn't ready to tell him the truth about who she was or what she did. They'd taken a chance on standby tickets and gotten lucky with a 12:30 a.m. flight. Even though they barely made the boarding call, Brown insisted they board at the last possible second, which gave him an opportunity to study every passenger as they filed onto the plane. Only after he was satisfied no one on the flight had any interest in them and that no one could board after they committed did they finally walk down the Jetway.

Fatigue hit Eva like a hammer by the time they found their row and she sank wearily into the window seat. They had about fourteen hours of travel ahead of them, with a stop in Bogota, Colombia, before they finally landed at Dulles in D.C. Plenty of time to decide if Brown was a man she could trust with the whole truth, or if she would cut her losses and turn him loose after she'd mined as much information out of him as she could.

She still had a lot of sorting out to do. Even before she'd tracked him down and flown to Peru to talk to him, even before she'd ended up getting shot at, she'd been a bit of an emotional mess, not knowing what to believe. Nearly thirty-six hours with little sleep and Brown's moving proclamation of innocence had combined to skew her ability to critically assess all the information even more. Did she believe him or the OSD report? Did she believe her gut that something wasn't right? She'd spun everything inside out, upside down, and backward until all she felt was frustrated.

Turning her head, she glanced at Brown. He'd already closed his eyes. His lashes were long . . . the very tips rested above the swelling on his cheekbone where blue and purple would join the red skin. The imprint of her boot heel was going to leave a helluva bruise.

The emotional side of her wanted to believe the worst of Brown . . . but there were still so many unanswered questions that her rational side wouldn't let her commit, especially since her profession had taught her that everyone lied. She just hadn't been prepared for those lies to hit her on a personal level.

Too weary to think about it anymore, she followed his lead and closed her eyes. The onboard safety drill droned on in the background. She was vaguely aware of the plane moving down the apron toward the runway, away from Lima and a gunman who had tried to kill her. By the time it registered that they were airborne, exhaustion had taken over and she'd drifted off to sleep.

Eva awoke slowly. Worked the kinks out of her neck and yawned. The cabin was dark. Only a few reading lights and the exit lights diffused the darkness. The engines were a soft, reassuring drone as she shifted and stared down at the vast expanse of the Caribbean through a thin cloud cover. Dawn broke over the horizon, slow and true and absolute. Death, taxes, sunrise, sunset. About the only things she felt she could count on these days.

And then there was Brown.

He was stretched out as far as the seat would allow, his long legs sprawled, his head turned toward her, snoring softly. She felt an odd little clutch in her chest as an unwelcome wave of tenderness washed through her.

He looked exhausted and tortured even as he slept.

And she didn't have a clue why she cared.

She turned back to the window. Guilt, maybe?

Yes, she'd flown to Peru to bring him back to the States. Yes, she'd used extreme measures to coerce him. And no, she hadn't planned on being so . . .

You hadn't planned on being so what, *Eva?* she asked herself.

Affected, she supposed. By his physical presence. By his smart-ass sense of humor. Or by the vulnerability that he tried to hide behind everything from anger to sick humor to a don't-give-a-damn swagger.

"The hell I did."

She still got chills thinking about the conviction and despair in his voice . . . and the tears he'd tried desperately to hide.

She swallowed hard and told herself it was because she was exhausted. Or, *hello*, terrified? When she closed her eyes she could still see the pillow exploding as round after round from the MP5K pumped into it.

Her head had been in that exact same spot seconds before the gunman had opened fire. If Brown hadn't had a change of heart, if he hadn't cut the flex cuffs, hadn't heard a suspicious sound on the terrace outside the room, she'd be dead.

He'd saved her life . . . and she wasn't even sure yet if she trusted that he'd told her the truth about OSD. She didn't have one solid shred of evidence to convince her that he wasn't in league with whoever was behind it and possibly so much more.

Maybe he'd been coerced. Maybe he'd been in

it for the money—he'd sure changed his tune about helping her once she'd mentioned paying him. If he was innocent, then she needed to corroborate his story and enlist his help in figuring this thing out.

If he was guilty, well, she still needed him to help her ferret out the rest of the truth. And when it was over, then she'd level her own kind of justice.

10

Mike woke up with a stiff shoulder and a pain in his neck.

The pain in his ass was awake, too, responding to the flight attendant's request for her to move her seat to the upright position and prepare for landing in Bogota.

He yawned and stretched and shook the cobwebs from his head. "How long is our layover?"

She reached into her bag and checked her ticket. "Couple of hours."

"Good. That'll give us time to grab something to eat. We'll have a nice little chat and chew. It'll be fun. You can fill me in—no excuses, no stalling this time, clear?"

Her glare had plenty of bite to it, but she finally nodded. "Clear."

The El Dorado International Airport in Bogota was a major Central American hub, and the terminal teemed with travelers. Giving a more-than-passing glance at a bar two doors down, Mike stood in line at a fast-food café where he grabbed sandwiches, a couple of apples, and two sodas.

"I took a guess and went for the ham." He tossed the to-go bag on the table she'd found in a relatively quiet corner of the terminal and dropped into a chair across from her. After digging inside for a sandwich, he shoved the bag across the table to her.

"Start from the beginning," he said after taking a huge bite. He was starving.

She gave him a look. "Can I at least eat my sandwich first?"

He popped the top on a soda, wishing it was a beer, and passed it to her before opening his own. "Multitask. I'll even give you a place to start. Who are you really?"

The sandwich stopped halfway to her mouth.

Here it comes. Another lie.

It was time to lay things out for her.

He met her eyes over his sandwich. "You think that I'm not going to figure that out once we land in the States? I've got a few friends in high places."

His buddies at Black Ops, Inc. had recently relocated their organization from Buenos Aires to the States. He didn't know where they were based, because the nature of their covert activities required a high level of anonymity, but he did know how to reach out and touch them. He'd helped them out on their last two missions and knew that all he had to do was ask and they'd get him what he wanted.

"Biometric facial-recognition program. I'm sure you've heard of it." He took another bite, then swiped the corner of his mouth with a paper napkin. "Amazing software. Compares key features of a subject from a photo—nose, eyes, eyebrows, mouth, face shape—to the faces stored in law enforcement and DMV databases. When a requisite number of features match, bingo. It's gonna spit out a name to go with the face so fast you won't have time to say, 'Whoops, I'm so sorry I lied to you, Mike.'"

The software wasn't perfect, but its proponents called it a breakthrough as significant as the introduction of fingerprint technology. And the BOIs had it.

"Too bad you don't have a photo," she said.

"Yeah, about that." He shifted his weight to his left hip, dug into his right pants pocket, and pulled out his phone, which he'd picked up from the Beechcraft. "Smile." He snapped her picture.

"Oh, wait." He made a face. "You won't like that one. Your mouth was open. Not your best look." He snapped another shot, then admired his work. "Much better. That scowl probably matches your driver's license picture."

The noise she made came close to a growl. For the first time since this all started, he actually felt like smiling.

"So . . . do I hit Send or do you talk?"

He had her, and she knew it.

He set the phone down, wiped his hand on his napkin, and extended it across the table. "Name's Brown. Mike Brown. And you would be?"

She looked at a spot on the wall behind him before meeting his eyes again. She did not return the handshake. "Eva." Her eyes were sober and dark. "Eva Salinas."

Mike withdrew his hand on an indrawn breath as the implication hit him. "Salinas?" He had a sick feeling that he knew exactly what she was going to say.

"Ramon was my husband."

He'd been hit with a bar stool once. It hadn't landed as much of a wallop as those two words.

Now it all made sense. No wonder she hated him. No wonder she thought he was lower than dirt on the sole of a terrorist's boot.

He sank back in the chair. "When? When did that happen?"

"When did we get married?"

He nodded.

"Three months before he redeployed." She sat back, too, crossing her arms beneath her breasts.

Three months. Mike remembered when Ramon had come back to the unit after his recovery time in the States. He'd been full of his usual bravado and swagger, talking about the hot babe he'd hooked up with. He'd never said one word about getting married.

And he sure as hell hadn't mentioned a wife to Lieutenant Hot Body from the communications unit. Salinas had resumed their "secret" affair as soon as he'd been boots on the ground back at the FOB.

Mike looked at Ramon's widow. He could have told her that her husband, the man she hated *him* for getting killed, was not only a braggart with an axe to grind, but he was the camp Romeo who considered anything with estrogen fair game and hadn't considered his marriage vows sacred.

But he didn't say one word. He knew all about the sting of salt in a wound.

"Why didn't you tell me that up front?" he asked softly.

"Because it's private." She avoided his eyes, thought better of it, and drew her shoulders back defensively. "Because I didn't want to."

The pain on her face made him feel bad for her, enough to wish Salinas was alive so he could take the jerk down a notch for not keeping it in his pants when he had a woman like this waiting at home.

A woman who would go to the lengths she'd gone to, to find out the truth about his death.

Eva Salinas, aka Pamela Diaz, aka the woman who'd had the *cojones* to brave the hazards of a foreign country, seduce him, drug him, cuff him to a bed, and kick him in the face, hadn't deserved to be played. Strangled, maybe, but not played.

Mike was a lot of things—a coward, yeah, he'd cop to that, a dropout, and a screwup—but he wasn't a cheat. And he had no time for men who were. Which pretty much explained why he and Ramon had never been *besties*.

"And because I didn't know if I could trust you," she added belatedly, the inference being that she'd decided that now she could. "I didn't know who was following me. For all I knew, you could have arranged it."

He couldn't fault her logic. "And the jury was out until we got shot at."

She shook her head. "Maybe before that."

When I'd damn near blubbered like a baby.

"Look," he said, embarrassed and wanting to get some distance from it, "I'm sorry about Ramon. I didn't like him. He didn't like me. But he was a good soldier and he didn't deserve to die the way he did."

He backed off then, giving her a little time to decide how she wanted to proceed from here.

"Eight years ago," she said, "when they notified me of his death, they told me he died on a routine training mission. Not in combat. Not on an operation. They blamed him for making a careless mistake that cost him his life."

Mike frowned. "Ramon was a lot of things, but careless wasn't one of them. Not when it came to his job."

"I didn't know him well enough to know that. But he was Special Forces. I knew he hadn't earned that green beret by being careless."

"Yet you bought the report of his death."

She tipped her soda to her lips. "I had no reason not to. So yes, I believed that's how he died. Until a flash drive with that file on it was delivered to my apartment a month ago."

Even though he'd lost his appetite, he dug back into his sandwich. His body needed fuel whether he was hungry or not. Then the significance of what she'd just said hit him. "Wait. I thought you said it

was given to you by accident when you were researching your story."

She looked a little sheepish. "I made that up to go
with the journalist cover."

"You're starting to be very predictable," he said, in
lieu of a resounding "aha." "So . . . State Department?
DOD?" He'd been speculating about that ever since
he'd seen her fake ID.

"CIA."

He almost fell off his chair. "Oh, this keeps getting
better and better. You're a field agent?" That would
explain the Glock and her tactics.

"Attorney. Office of General Counsel," she clarified, chasing down a bite of her sandwich with another drink of soda.

No wonder she'd known she'd get cut off at the
knees if she contacted the CIA or the FBI with her
theory.

A woman slogged by, wearily pushing a squalling
baby in a stroller. He let the commotion subside before picking up the conversation again. "Back up to
how you got the information." He'd get details on her
CIA gig later.

"It just showed up," she said. "The flash drive was
messengered to my apartment. After I got over the
shock of what was in the file, I tried to find out who
sent it but the messenger service had nothing on record for that customer. No credit card. No address.
Claimed they must have lost it. And no one remembered having seen him—or her."

"How convenient."

"Too convenient," she agreed.

"So tell me about the file." The file that was supposed to have been deleted. The file that branded him the kind of guy whose ego and inability to follow orders got people killed.

"It was a detailed account of the mission that night. The after-action report was signed off on by your base commander. Every word laid the blame squarely on your shoulders."

Which was why she hated him. Territory they'd already covered. "Who would want you to have that file?"

"You want a name? I have no clue. But it had to be someone who knew I had the means and the motivation to start digging."

"Then the next question is why they wanted you to investigate."

"Because they wanted to expose you? Or because they wanted me to find out the truth? Maybe it's someone who believed your pretrial statements. Someone who wanted me to ask the tough questions."

"And that's when doors started slamming."

She nodded. "And when I started to sense I was being watched."

An announcement on the PA system called their flight.

Appetite gone, Mike stuffed the rest of his sandwich back in the bag. She did the same. She hadn't even eaten half of it.

"You have to tell me, you know." She met his eyes with earnest entreaty. "You have to tell me what happened."

Yeah. He tossed the bag in a trash can and started walking toward the gate. He had to tell her.

And thinking about that took him right back to the night he had tried for eight years to forget, but knew he never would.

11

Afghanistan, eight years ago

"The boys are taking their sweet time."

Taggart was right. And Mike was worried. The team should have been back by now.

He squinted into the night. He'd flown the mission totally dark. No locator or position lights, no cabin lights, used only his night-vision technology and his instruments to guide him down to the landing zone. They were still dark, though the bird was powered up and ready to lift off at a moment's notice.

Behind the controls of the Black Hawk that he'd set down on the unforgiving Afghan terrain with only the night and a jagged wall of rock for concealment, Mike glanced over his shoulder past his copilot, Sonny Webber, to his gunner, Bobby "Boom Boom" Taggart. The Special Forces sergeant had drawn bird-protection duty with him, Webber, and Jamie "Hondo" Cooper, while the rest of the team executed their recon mission—and Taggart wasn't happy about it.

Restless behind the Black Hawk's multibarrel M134 machine gun, Taggart wove a jack of spades in and out between his fingers, using the worn playing card as a diversion from the uncertainty and the wait.

Mike understood why the tough-as-nails Bronx native was getting twitchy. Mike and Webber were used to waiting; pilots always stayed with the bird. But regardless of how many missions they had under their belts, Taggart and Cooper would rather be crawling around on their bellies, planted on a ridge with night-vision binoculars, checking for Mr. Taliban, and covering their team's six. Anything beat staying here in the cramped confines of the idling bird, playing sit and wait for the rest of the team to return.

Salinas, Smith, Wojohowitz, Brimmer, Johnson, and Crenshaw had left over twenty minutes ago to hike less than half a kilometer to conduct a quick sneak-and-peek on a small village. They were following up on a report of Taliban fighters taking over the village and forcing the inhabitants to shelter them.

No engagement with the enemy; observation only. In. Out. Twenty minutes on the ground, tops. Report back to Command Central when they returned.

If this had been a Special Forces team, a Night Hawk pilot would have dropped them in. But this wasn't an ordinary team. This was the One-Eyed Jacks—Uncle Sam's grand experiment incorporating special operations personnel from the Navy, Army, and Marines.

It was such a standard-fare mission that Com Cent

had dubbed it Operation Slam Dunk. Recon only. Easy Peasy.

Mike checked his watch—twenty-five minutes and counting—and stalled a trickle of concern. Even with full packs and dogging it, they should have been back by now. It *was* taking too long. But he was used to waiting. Very seldom did he ever leave the bird. His job was to fly the team in, protect the Black Hawk until they returned, then fly them back out. He was damn good at it, regardless of whether they were taking fire on either end of the op. Taggart and Cooper, however, were used to action. Neither liked getting bird protection on the rotation.

"You're going to wear that thing out, Boom Boom," Webber, a quiet staff sergeant from Arizona, said as Taggart continued to work the playing card through his fingers.

The card was barely in one piece. Taggart had used clear tape on it several times, repairing a cut from a KA-Bar that had almost sliced it in half.

"I'm going nuts here." Taggart shifted behind the big gun.

The munitions and explosive expert was an adrenaline junky. And he'd seen too much action. On his last leave home, he'd had a tattoo inked on the inside of his right forearm: a pair of combat boots supporting a rifle on which a combat helmet hung. Beneath the image were the letters RIP, in tribute to his brothers in arms who'd been killed in action.

"You're already nuts."

This from Cooper, whose jack of hearts—every One-Eyed Jacks team member had a card—was worn and burned around the edges.

While Taggart was proud of his mixed German and French heritage, Cooper liked to say that his Caucasian, African-American, and Latino blood beat them all in the mongrel department. The communications expert kept in shape doing push-ups with his toes wedged to a wall and wouldn't think of marring his skin with a tat.

Cooper was a serious Marine but quick with a smile. Unlike Mike, who'd grown up herding cattle on a ranch in Colorado, and Taggart, who'd mixed it up on the streets in the Bronx, or Webber, the son of elementary school teachers, Cooper had grown up in luxury—compliments of his Colombian-born model mother and his father's lucrative export business. Cooper had been a model himself and an actor, but had enlisted in the Marines when a friend had been KIA in Iraq.

Mike had just decided he might have to send Cooper and Taggart to investigate, when his headset crackled.

"Crenshaw to Primetime, do you read me? Over?"

Relieved to finally hear from the big Minnesotan who towered over most of the guys by a good head, Mike answered quickly. "Read you five by five, Crenshaw. Not like you to miss chow. How 'bout a sit rep? Over."

"Ran into a buzz saw." The details Crenshaw

proceeded to give him on what they'd found made Mike's gut tighten.

The team had not only spotted Taliban fighters in the village, they'd witnessed a brutal execution of a young woman. And it wasn't their first kill. Bodies were stacked up like firewood in the town center that was patrolled by Taliban fighters. It appeared the team had stumbled onto a systematic slaughter that was still in progress.

"Seek permission to engage. Over."

Mike totally got it. Crenshaw and the team wanted to take the Taliban fighters out before they killed any more civilians. But permission wasn't his to give— their orders were recon only. He had to contact Command Central at the Forward Operating Base.

"Hold for further. Over."

"What's going on?" Webber asked from the co-pilot seat.

The three men had heard only Mike's side of his conversation with Crenshaw but they all sensed the news wasn't good.

Mike changed radio frequency and immediately tried to raise the FOB. As soon as he made contact he recounted the situation on the ground, then waited for the radio operator to relay the intel to the commander. He didn't have to see the other men's faces in the dark to know they were chomping at the bit to engage. They'd heard his side of the radio commo loud and clear.

Mike listened, his body tense as he received his orders.

"Roger that," he replied. "Over and out."

"We going in?"

Mouth tight, Mike answered Taggart with a single shake of his head. "They're sending air support. We're to call the chicks back to the roost and return to base."

Behind him, Cooper swore. "It'll be sixty minutes before they get gunships up here."

No one knew that better than Mike. He knew how hard he could push the Black Hawk in this climate and terrain. Crews could gear up in a matter of minutes and aircraft was always at the ready. The distance was the problem.

And air support with civilians in the area, being executed? JDAM smart bombs were wickedly accurate, but not accurate enough to take out a bad guy with civilians within ten or twenty yards.

Puzzled by his commander's call, but keeping his opinion to himself, he changed frequency again and tried to raise Crenshaw and call them back to the bird.

"He's not answering," Mike muttered aloud after several attempts to contact the team leader.

Silence was always bad news.

After several more unsuccessful attempts, he ripped off his headset. He and Webber couldn't leave the bird, but Taggart and Cooper could.

"Go," he told them, knowing he couldn't stop them if he wanted to. Both had already locked and loaded their M-4s. "Keep commo open."

He watched from inside the cockpit as the two men in full camo gear sprinted in the direction the team had taken, then disappeared from sight in the inky black night. Webber climbed behind the mini, just in case.

Long minutes passed. Mike repeatedly checked his watch. Swore. Waited. Watched. Then caught his breath when the two men emerged out of the dark fifteen minutes later.

"The sonofabitches have them. All of them." Taggart's voice was thick with anger and alarm.

"What are we up against?" Mike already assumed that since they'd come back alone, they were looking at big numbers of Taliban fighters. Too big for two men to engage.

He swallowed hard when they told him.

"We can't leave them there." Cooper's face was set hard with determination. "They've got them on their knees in the middle of the village square, rifles pointed at their heads."

Mike told himself that American hostages made good bargaining chips; they'd be foolish to shoot them. On the other hand, dead Americans also added fuel to the radical zealots' fires.

There was no telling what they would do to them.

He got on the radio again. "I repeat," he said, attempting to contain his anger after relaying the gravity of the situation and being told to stand down until the base commander could be contacted. "Situation critical. Request permission to engage. Over."

When the orders finally came down, he was sure he'd heard wrong. They were to return to the FOB. "Say again. Over."

The radio operator repeated the base commander's original declaration to return to base, assuring him that gunships were on the way.

Gunships that were still a good thirty minutes from target.

Mike made a decision. "I can't read you. You're breaking up. Over."

Then he cut radio power.

"Shit. You lose them?" Taggart looked anxious.

Mike shook his head. "They called us off."

Cooper's face said it all. "That's bullshit."

Taggart looked ready to spit nails. "We are not leaving them."

"You're right. We aren't." Mike looked at Webber.

When the copilot nodded in agreement with his decision to disobey orders, Mike spun up the main rotor.

"Don't be shy on that mini." He hitched his chin toward Taggart, who'd climbed back into position behind the gun.

The big turbine engine whined as he glanced over his shoulder at Cooper, yelling to be heard above the roar. "Fire at anything with a turban and a rifle." He lifted off, hoping to hell they got there in time.

Mike's stomach dropped as he flew over a final ridge then dove close to the ground, his NVGs casting the confusing and grisly tableau in ghostly green light.

All he saw were bodies. Piles of them. Heartsick, he could make out Crenshaw's big prostrate form lying facedown in the dirt next to the bodies of several villagers.

"Fuckers!" Taggart roared and leaned on the mini, scattering the Taliban fighters. The cartridge belt pumped out two thousand to six thousand rounds per minute as Taggart strafed the ground.

Mike banked the Black Hawk into a tight turn and looped around, zeroing back in on the village center, sickened and riveted by the carnage. So riveted he didn't see the ball of fire heading toward them until a split second before Hondo yelled, "RPG! RPG! Break right!"

"Brace!" he yelled—but it was too late.

The bird jolted, lurched sideways, plummeted twenty feet, then spun a hard three-sixty. Fire surrounded the cockpit, filling it with smoke. Coughing and struggling to see, Mike fought the collective, the cyclic, trying to steady the bird. But when he lost control of the rudder pedals, he knew they were going down.

Not like this. Jesus God, not like this. Not with his team already dead on the ground, and the possibility of innocents in the path of the out-of-control Black Hawk.

Behind him, Taggart roared like a wild dog and clutched his leg; Cooper yelled out a prayer. Mike heard it all on a peripheral level as he fought to right the chopper. The crippled bird spun wildly, dipping and dodging, and finally succumbed to gravity. They dropped like a meteor and the earth roared up to meet them.

The noise was deafening. The stench of hydraulics and burning fuel choked him. And the pain. Holy God, the pain paralyzed him as the rotors sheered through adobe walls and tile roofs, hurling chunks of debris and fog-thick dust while the engine screamed until, with an agonizing jolt, the chopper jerked to a stop.

The impact stole his breath.

And then all was suddenly still.

All but the ping of the hot motor and the groan of the men in the bird with him. Except Webber. Webber was silent. Blood trickled from the corner of his mouth; his head dropped to his chest at an unnatural angle.

Mike reached over, felt for a pulse in his carotid. Nothing.

God, oh, God. Webber was dead. Like they'd all be dead if they didn't get out of the burning bird. Flames licked at his feet, hot and hungry and mean.

Had to get out.

Had to ignore the pain that seared through his shoulder like an axe blade.

He tasted blood. Choked on smoke and fumes and pain but managed to unbuckle his seat belt with his uninjured arm.

Taggart and Cooper were alive. He could hear them moaning. He had to get them out before they went up in the flames that rolled across the windshield.

He stopped thinking and just moved. Somehow, he freed Taggart.

"My leg. I . . . I think it's broken," Taggart gritted through clenched teeth, strangling a scream as Mike dragged him out of the wreckage and away from the fire. Then he went back for Cooper. The Marine was barely conscious when Mike reached him. Blood poured from a gaping wound near his hairline and he was nonresponsive. Gritting through the pain, Mike grabbed Cooper's arm, steered him toward the hole where the cockpit door had been, yelled at him to stay awake, to move. They had to get away from what was left of the Black Hawk before the fire shooting out the leaking fuel tank blew the bird sky high.

Step by agonizing step they reached Taggart, who had managed to stand, balancing unsteadily on his good leg.

"You're burned." Taggart looked at Mike through a smoke-blackened face, his eyes unfocused, like he didn't understand what was happening.

Mike looked down at his own leg. His flight suit had protected him from the worst of the fire, but part of it had melted into his thigh when he'd crawled back inside for Cooper.

"Wait here," he shouted above the roar of the burning Black Hawk, and with Cooper's arm slung over his shoulder, walked him as far away as fast as he could. Then he went back for Taggart.

They had to take cover. Hard to tell how many Taliban were on the ground and had survived the af-

termath of the crash. All they had were their pistols—
not much firepower against AK-47s. Pain screamed
through his shoulder like a vicious bitch as Mike
managed to get the two men to an irrigation ditch
that ran parallel with the village center. He was about
to dump Cooper into the ditch when the Black Hawk
exploded.

The blowback caught them in a blast of blazing
hot air, lifted them off the ground, and dumped them
into the shallow ditch water.

Mike landed coughing, spitting, fighting to right
himself.

Cooper was totally unconscious now. Taggart was
barely with the program. Swearing, sweating, Mike
helped them up toward the lip of the ditch, and par-
tially out of the water.

There he clung, watching as a huge fireball blasted
into the night and everything within a tenth of a mile
of the village center shot up in flames.

What the hell?

The Black Hawk alone couldn't have made that
big of an explosion.

"It's an ammo dump," he muttered and ducked for
cover as the entire village lit up to the sound of screams
and thousands of rounds of ammo cooking off.

The adrenaline that fueled him let up long before
the cache of munitions shot itself out. Pain screamed
through his leg and shoulder as he twisted around
and searched the site of the crash.

Utter devastation. His men were down there. The

sickening smell of burned flesh and gunpowder and an acid smell he didn't recognize mixed with the billowing jet fuel smoke that blackened the already dark night air. The taste of blood and dirt and despair filled his senses.

That's when he heard the distant *whoop, whoop, whoop* of a chopper.

Taggart roused for a moment, swore through his pain. "Flare. Send up a flare."

Mike reached into the pocket of his flight suit for a flare and was about to crawl out of the ditch and light it, when a sixth sense warned him something wasn't right.

He shielded his eyes and squinted up at the night sky. Toward the rapidly approaching chopper, not trusting what his eyes were telling his brain.

The bird wasn't theirs.

How could that be?

The flames from the fire illuminated a chopper covered in camouflage paint as it sat down a safe distance away from the scene of the crash. It was a Russian-made Mi-8 twin-turbine transport that had been converted to double as a gunship.

He stared, still disbelieving even as he knew exactly what he was seeing. What the hell was a Russian transpo chopper doing out here? Tonight?

The Afghan army had a few Mi-8s, but Mike knew every fixed- and rotary-winged aircraft between here and Kandahar, and there weren't supposed to be any in this area of operations. Even if for some unknown reason there were, the Afghan army wouldn't be skulking around in the dark on the wrong side of a mission gone sideways.

Keeping his head low as the sliding door on the starboard side of the fuselage opened, Mike peeked above the rim of the ditch, wishing for the NVGs he'd lost somewhere after the crash. Making do with the light from the fires, he watched the action as four men jumped to the ground.

All four carried Russian assault rifles. Two were bearded and dressed in Shalwar kameez, traditional loose trousers and long tunics typical of the region. Their faces were hidden behind balaclavas. The other two wore western camouflage fatigues. And they weren't Afghani, they were Caucasian. No mistaking that fact. And *they* were clearly in charge.

Hoping like hell they weren't spotted, he listened in troubled silence. He couldn't make out what they were saying above the whine of the chopper's turbine engine, but he could tell they were speaking Pashto to the Afghanis who were shouting toward the village.

A figure emerged from the far side of the village square. One of the Taliban fighters. He sprinted for the chopper and jumped inside. Several more trotted toward the bird, AKs in hand, and at least a dozen men boarded the bird before the original four climbed back inside.

One of the guys in camo stood surveying the scene for several long moments, then crouched below the slowly winding rotor blades, making certain there were no survivors.

Before he turned and stepped up into the chopper, Mike got a good look at his face. It was a face he would not soon forget. He made Mike think of a ferret. Eyes deep-set under bushy black brows. Narrow jaw. Thin, sinister lips. Sunken cheeks below prominent cheekbones.

Apparently satisfied with the slaughter, he finally ducked inside the chopper and it lifted off, heading north.

What the fuck?

Cooper moaned, still unconscious, and Mike turned back to see what he could do for him. He checked Cooper's vitals—not good—and willed a Black Hawk to set down soon. With shaking, smoke-blackened hands, he fished a bag of quick clot from a pocket, dumped it on Cooper's wound, then wrapped a pressure bandage around his head. Then he got to work immobilizing Taggart's leg.

Ten minutes later, he breathed a sigh of relief at the unmistakable sound of a Black Hawk scooting in fast from the south.

This time he set off the flare.

Only then did he let himself close his eyes and knuckle under to his own pain.

12

Eva's heart started racing the moment Mike began to tell his story. It still raced like she'd run a marathon when he stopped. She'd felt his fear. His pain. His despair over his lost team. Eight years after the massacre had taken place, he'd taken her back in time to that tiny village where so many had died.

Including Ramon.

A tear trickled slowly down her cheek. Only when she reached up to brush it away did she realize that she'd covered the hand Brown had fastened in a deathlike grip on the armrest while the words had tumbled out of him, slowly at first, then lightning fast, as though he couldn't stop the runaway train of memories.

And only as she reluctantly pulled her hand away, feeling the absence of his warm palm against hers, did she realize that somewhere during the telling, he'd turned his hand over and linked his fingers with hers.

As if just now realizing the intimacy they'd

shared, he straightened in his aisle seat, rolled his shoulders.

"Well," he said, attempting to inject a lightness she knew he couldn't possibly feel, "I'm thinking that right about now you're sorry you ever asked."

Not sorry. Horrified. But relieved, too. She knew the truth now. She hadn't realized how much it would hurt to hear how her husband had died.

Just as she hadn't realized how badly she'd wanted to believe Mike Brown.

When had a fact-finding mission transitioned into this desperate desire to prove his innocence? Maybe when she'd finally realized that he worked too damn hard to mask his innate decency behind that smart-ass grin. Maybe because he hadn't been able to conceal a primal, masculine rage that she'd sensed from the moment she'd made contact with him in the cantina. A rage that dated back eight years. The rage of an innocent man.

Reading his pretrial statements from the pages of the OSD files hadn't prepared her for the reality. Those pages had only told half the story. They hadn't detailed the fear, the grief, the utter sense of desolation. Those pages hadn't made her believe.

Brown had.

The trouble with believing, however, was that it opened up an entire new line of questions.

"I don't understand why your CO didn't stand up for you. Why he let it get as far as court-martial proceedings."

Brown stared at the seat back in front of him. "You have to look at it from his angle. The Afghani government was all over the U.S. Joint Command demanding explanations—and justice. There was a village full of dead civilians, dead U.S. military personnel, a downed Black Hawk. Added to that, neither the Afghani or U.S. military radar had any record of an unaccounted-for chopper in the area that night—which left my story full of holes."

"But you saw it. Why wouldn't it show up on their tracking system?"

"Because that terrain sucks for radar detection. Even the antimortar radars have a problem with the mountains and valleys. And let's face it—the Taliban have no air game."

"So, they decided you were making it up?"

"That was the consensus, yeah. Webber was dead. Taggart and Cooper had been unconscious or too disoriented to know what had gone down. I was the only one telling the story. And remember, I was already guilty of disobeying a direct order. They pegged it as CYA—cover your ass—all the way."

"Your decision was mission critical. You couldn't leave those men there to die."

He shook his head wearily. "Everyone was covering their asses. The Afghan government was all over Com Cent. They wanted a fall guy—it became real clear real fast that it was going to be me."

"I still don't understand why you let it happen." She couldn't keep the frustration from her voice.

"You weren't there, okay? So don't judge me."

"Then I'm judging your CO. He never should have signed off on that report."

"You think he wanted to? Look, Henry Brewster was a stand-up guy. He ran the FOB, for God's sake, yet he took time to come to see me in the brig. Told me he was sorry I was taking the heat and the rap, and assured me that after some time passed it would blow over and all go away."

"So you agreed to plead no contest?"

"Hell no. I didn't agree to anything. Not then. I waited. I counted on Brewster coming through. Then I got sent back stateside. To Bragg."

"Wait." She held up a hand interrupting him. "Fort Bragg? You were Navy. Why were they holding you at an Army base?"

"The One-Eyed Jacks team fell under Joint Special Operations Command. JSOC is based at Bragg. And JSOC is all about command and structure. I was a fault line in that structure that threatened their very foundation. They wanted me gone, incident forgotten, end of story. The base commander at Bragg— James Slockem—made sure it happened."

"And Brewster didn't stop it."

"He did what he could," he repeated defensively. "He was still in Afghanistan. Dealing with the troop surge, a complete operational reorg, and a bump from one to two stars—so yeah, he was a little busy."

"Too busy to stand up for his own men?"

His jaw clenched. "Let it go." He stared her

straight in the eye. "You're barking at the wrong dog. Brewster was . . . he was the man, you know? The One-Eyed Jacks was his pet project. He fought for the unit, put it together. No one went to bat for us like he did. No one would have let us get by with the shit we pulled but him. He had our backs time and time again."

"Just not when it counted."

He closed his eyes. "Especially when it counted. Who do you think arranged for the plea deal? Brewster set it up. He pulled the strings, pulled in markers. He made the file go away. He made it all go away. He did the best by me that he could. If he hadn't, I'd be rotting in a military prison somewhere."

"He could have exonerated you."

He swore wearily. "Enough. I don't want to hear any more about it. It was all on me, okay? I'm fucking guilty. That kind of weight doesn't transfer. Not to Brewster. Not anyone else. I didn't save them. That's the bottom line."

She got it. He felt tremendous guilt because he hadn't saved his men. For him, there would never be any getting out from under that guilt. She, however, wasn't saddled with that particular problem. And whether he liked it or not, she was looking into Brewster. The man might be a god to Mike, but she wasn't worshiping at his altar.

She understood something else, too. Mike needed to believe in Brewster. If not his CO, then there was no one he could believe in.

And maybe he was right. But she was going to follow up, and then they'd both know.

"The bottom line remains, someone sold you out," she said quietly.

He swiped a hand over his jaw, an action she'd noticed he used when he felt pressured. "Let's say I was a casualty of war. My JAG attorney convinced me that I wasn't going to beat the rap. He said Brewster had moved heaven and earth to get the military to even consider a plea. So I buckled and went for the less than honorable discharge instead of the court-martial."

Her father had been a JAG attorney before he'd retired two years ago. She couldn't help but think that he'd never have let this happen to Brown.

"Taggart and Cooper?"

His eyes looked bleak. "Got caught in the crossfire. The deal was, I took the plea and they walked with me. If I fought it and lost, we all faced a death sentence."

"Do they know that?"

His silence answered that question. No. They didn't know.

I didn't sell them out. I saved their lives.

He'd done what he'd done to protect them—and to this day they hated him because they didn't know the whole story.

Well, that was something she could rectify. And she would, as soon as they got their feet under them in D.C. She figured she owed Brown that much for the Ketamine alone.

Right now, however, there were still more questions than answers.

"We're still at square one. We have to figure out
who sent me that flash drive," she said abruptly. There
were all kinds of implications that came with it.

When the flight attendant walked by, Mike moved
his leg under the seat in front of him and out of the
aisle. If he was aware that, in the tight quarters, his
thigh now pressed against hers, he didn't let on.

But she was aware. During the entire flight, she'd
been too aware of him too many times to count. So
she swiftly moved her leg out of touching distance.

"Gotta be someone who knew about Operation
Slam Dunk," he said, appearing not to notice her
sudden discomfort. "Someone with high-enough security clearance to give them access to the database
containing the file. Someone who knew your connection to Ramon."

"You're right. It has to be someone who was there,"
she speculated, feeling a thread of excitement. He
was on to something. "Someone stationed at the FOB
when this all went down."

"Makes sense. Still doesn't answer why. Specifi-
cally, why now? What's their stake in this? And why
wait eight years to bring it to light?"

"Maybe they've felt guilty for what happened to
the team but couldn't decide what to do about it.
Couldn't do anything about it without implicating
themselves. But then . . . I don't know. Something
changed? Now they suddenly feel free to bring the

events of that night forward? Set the record straight? And because they knew I was Ramon's widow and worked for the CIA, they figured that I'd do something about it?"

"Works for me. It also rules out anyone currently on active duty. You don't shit in your own nest—not if you want to get ahead."

"Someone who retired, then? Or separated from service recently?" She wondered what Brewster was doing now. Wondered if she'd been too quick to judge. Maybe Mike was right. Maybe Brewster had stood for Mike the best he could by arranging the plea deal— even if he knew he should have done better. Had a fit of conscience prompted him to bring the file to her attention? She kept those thoughts to herself while a trickle of excitement eddied through her.

Beside her, Brown rolled his head on his shoulders, clearly weary of the long flight. "Seems like a good bet. It also opens up a lot of possibilities. There were a lot of personnel on the ground at the FOB."

"But how many knew what happened? I'm thinking not that many. I need to get hold of staffing records for that period."

"You can do that?"

She had access to databases that others didn't. Still, it wouldn't be easy. "I can try." Brewster may be ringing her alarm bell right now, but she was going to ferret out every possibility. Including Slockem, the base commander at Bragg who was so quick to hang Brown out to dry.

"There's a flip side to this, you know." He turned his head and looked at her. "Someone else out there doesn't feel an ounce of remorse. What they feel is threatened. So threatened they want you silenced."

She looked away. Not merely silenced. Someone wanted her dead.

Like Brown could have been dead, right alongside her.

The realization that she didn't want him to die hit her like a bullet. A hard punch of guilt delivered a second shot. How could she be thinking about losing Brown, how could she suddenly be so aware of him as a man, when moments ago she'd discovered the truth about her husband's death?

In her mind's eye she saw the grisly scene in the village. Felt the heat of the fire. Ramon's body had been among the charred remains.

She swallowed hard. Had to ask the part he'd left out. "Did they . . . did they ever recover Ramon's body?"

His jaw tightened. He didn't want to tell her.

"Please. I need to know." Heart hammering, she waited.

"No." He shook his head, closed his eyes. "I'm sorry. His dog tags were all that was left to ID him."

Her chest clenched so tight, she couldn't breathe.

Suddenly she had to move. She had to get some distance—from Brown, from the horror of the image of a beautiful, vital man reduced to ashes—before she did or said something really stupid . . . like break down and bawl like a baby.

"Excuse me." She unbuckled her seat belt, scrambled past him, and made a beeline for the lavatory.

Mike let her go. What could he say? What could he do? She might think she'd hidden her tears, but she was dead wrong.

She'd just heard him confirm, in graphic detail, how her husband had died. Didn't matter that it was eight years ago. It hadn't felt like eight years when he'd been telling it. It had felt like it was yesterday.

He breathed deep, tried to force distance between the present and the past. Not that it ever worked.

And yet . . . inexplicably, he felt less burdened than he had in a very long time.

Because he'd spilled his guts? Lightened his load? Because he'd done a good thing and spared her the pain of knowing her husband had been a liar and a cheat?

Because he was finally doing something other than hiding out?

He gripped the armrests hard when the flight attendant strolled by, asking for drink orders. He thought, instead, of the moment he'd become aware that Eva's small hand had covered his. Not to steady herself, but to ground him. To keep him from nose-diving off the deep end.

He'd latched on like a drowning man clutching a life raft. Clung like she was a rock in a sea of sifting sand.

Surprises. The woman was full of them. And she didn't seem quite so crazy anymore.

What she seemed to be — God help him — was the saner of the two of them. And despite the fact that she'd finally shown her vulnerable side, he admired her for her strength and a whole Pandora's box full of traits he really didn't have any business contemplating.

So he wouldn't. He closed his eyes, surprised to find himself beginning to relax and actually drifting off when he sensed her presence beside him in the aisle. He straightened to make room for her to squeeze past him, her flat stomach directly in front of his face.

Of course, it had to happen. She tripped over his foot — with his size twelves, she hadn't stood a chance. He reached out reflexively, circled her ribs with his hands, and steadied her.

And Lord, sweet Lord, his thumbs brushed against the underside of her breasts as she fell forward, catching herself with her hands on his shoulders.

It was all about timing. And reflexes. And damn bad luck as he looked up to see if she was all right, and his mouth came within a breath of touching her left breast.

Mother of God.

Heat. Lush softness. Need.

The sensations all registered at once, shooting electricity straight to his groin.

He set her aside as if she was a hot potato.

"Sorry," he mumbled, not looking at her as she buckled up beside him.

And said nothing.

Holy hell.

He could *not* be attracted to this woman. A hot enchilada in a seedy cantina, yes. That was allowed. Because he'd been drunk. Because she'd been— hell—she'd *really* been something in that red bustier, skin-tight pants, and fuck-me stilettos.

But he could not be attracted to *this* woman. To Ramon Salinas's widow.

13

"It's not like you to be so late calling in."

Eyes closed against the ripping pain in her side and arm, Jane forced herself to concentrate and clear the cobwebs the anesthesia had created in her brain.

She couldn't allow herself to be so vulnerable again. The nurse hadn't been happy when she'd refused pain medication after awakening from surgery, but she'd needed to regain lucidity for this conversation. She'd already lost several hours.

"I ran into a problem," she said, struggling for a breath that didn't make her sound as though she were dying. Weakness was the last thing she wanted to show him. Just like the last thing she wanted to do was disappoint him. "The targets detected me before I could take them out."

The silence on the other end of the line was as loud as a jet engine. "Explain."

As concisely and accurately as she could, she told him what had happened when she'd attempted to eliminate the woman and the man. She was out of breath and weak with pain when she finished.

"Oh, God. You're injured." The concern that suddenly darkened his voice almost made her weep.

"Unfortunately, yes."

"Jane—"

"It's okay. I . . . I'll be okay." The hot tear of frustration that trickled down her cheek felt like a double dose of defeat. "But I'm not going to be able to fulfill the contract."

Another silence. "How bad?"

The surgeon had briefed her moments ago, telling her it would be six to eight weeks before she could consider any physical activity other than therapy on her arm. He'd also pleaded with her to accept pain medication to assist with her healing. "Not fatal. Just feels like it."

"Where are you?"

She told him.

"I'm sending someone for you."

She couldn't stop the tears this time. No one had ever cared about her before. They cared about what she could do for them, but never about her.

"Thank you."

But the line had already gone dead.

She closed her eyes and made herself focus on something other than the pain and this inexplicable flood of gratitude and relief that mixed with a blinding sense of failure.

She had failed him. She had failed herself.

And a man named Brown and a woman whose true name she did not yet know were responsible.

Which meant this was not over.

Halfway across the world the man she knew as Stingray stared morosely at his file on Jane Smith. With a regretful sigh, he closed it, then tossed it aside, rocking back in his desk chair.

He was disappointed in Jane. Very disappointed and, interestingly enough, extremely worried about her.

In the beginning, it was her total lack of conscience that had intrigued him. He'd often wondered what had been done to her as a child that had produced such a twisted, ruthless killer. The term *cold-blooded* was overused and therefore diminished in its significance, but not when it applied to Jane. She had no remorse. Felt no regret—except in failure.

The humiliation in her voice when she'd called and confessed the unthinkable had been heartbreaking. She'd been in agony, but she was a soldier. She had done her duty and made the difficult call.

He had few rules, and high expectations that those rules would be followed to the letter.

Jane had broken the cardinal rule. She'd compromised herself and therefore compromised his enterprises. Had she been any other contract for hire, he would have had her eliminated.

Instead, he'd dispatched a man to Lima to bring her back to him. He'd broken one of his own rules for her. And he wondered what that said about him. What it said about his feelings for her.

That would sort itself out eventually, he supposed. Right now, he had more pressing matters. He still had to deal with Eva Salinas and Mike Brown.

But first he had to find them.

He picked up the phone, hesitated, then made a call. He had contacts in the CIA. People who owed him. Hackers who could follow up on their leads. If Eva Salinas attempted to access any of her files, he'd soon find out which ones and where she was operating from. Soon after that she'd be dead. Her and Brown.

14

Their Avianca flight had left Peru at 12:30 a.m. and right on schedule, almost fourteen hours later, it touched down at Dulles at 3:28 p.m. Mike was happy as hell not to have to deal with jet lag, since the time in D.C. was only an hour later than in Lima. He was equally happy to finally be out of that cramped seat where touching Eva Salinas, either accidentally or on purpose, had been unavoidable—even with Ramon's ghost hovering between them.

"You realize we can't go to your apartment," he said. They'd cleared the customs gate and she was stuffing her Emily Bradshaw passport back in her purse as they headed through the terminal at a brisk walk. "Our friend with the MP5K may or may not be alive, and may or may not have reported in to his handler. Either way, whoever ordered the hit either knows by now that it was a bust or is wondering why his man hasn't surfaced."

"What do you think the chances are they don't know we're back in the States?"

Mike had been doing the math on that one himself. "I think we're good, for a while. I'd make book that there was no one on that flight interested in either one of us. He's not going to fly charter—too many records. And I checked—the next commercial flight out of Lima to D.C. lands at least four hours after ours. So, even if the shooter somehow managed to recover enough to follow us and figures out we headed north, we've at least got that much time."

"And if he contacted whoever sent him?"

He touched a hand to the small of her back and steered her around a gaggle of teens who were walking five abreast through the terminal. "Whoever sent him is going to be looking for travel records for Mike Brown and Eva Salinas—not John Mason and Emily Bradshaw. But they'll find us eventually, so time is also our enemy. We need to get the flash drive and figure this out. Please tell me it's not at your apartment."

She shook her head and kept on walking. "Lockbox."

"Your regular bank?" Whoever was after her had no doubt already tossed her apartment, so they'd be looking for her to have stashed the file someplace safe. A bank made sense.

"No. I opened up an account and a lockbox at Independence Federal on Ninth. Under Emily Bradshaw."

"And the key to the box?"

"Was in the lockbox with my passports. Now it's in my purse."

The longer he was around her, the more she proved how smart she was.

Man. He'd come a long way from thinking of her as a lying, conniving, wack-job.

"I don't know about you," she said as they shouldered through the crowd in the busy airport, "but I could use a change of clothes. And a shower."

Mike looked down at himself. She was right. He didn't exactly blend in with city dwellers. In his combat boots, camo pants, sweat-stained T-shirt, and five-day whisker grow-out, he looked like he'd stepped out of the pages of *Mercenaries R-Us*. He needed to lower his profile. And yeah. He needed to clean up, too.

She stopped short beside a women's restroom, then dug into her purse and came up with a half-full packet of Wet Wipes. "My emergency rations. Never leave home without them." She peeled off half of the stack of moist towelettes and handed them to him. "Meet you back here in five."

"Make it three," he said and headed across the wide walkway to the men's room.

"Much better," she said when they met up again and made a beeline for the rental car desk.

After completing the paperwork for a black SUV, which Eva paid for with a credit card that couldn't be linked back to her real name—the lady had covered her bases—Mike maneuvered the car through the maze of airport parking.

"Next stop—a change of clothes."

"Fine," he agreed, knowing it was necessary but anxious to get to the bank.

They'd only traveled a few miles on the freeway before she had him take an exit, then gave him directions to the great American hunting and gathering spot: the mall.

Less than fifteen minutes later, he stood with his hands on his hips in the middle of a Tommy Bahama store, more than a little intimidated.

"What size shirt?" she asked, quickly rummaging through a spinning rack. "Pants, too."

"Large or maybe extra large for the shirt?" He shot off what he thought was his pants size, trying to remember the American size charts.

It had been a damn long time since he'd bought anything but T-shirts and camo cargo pants, so he was fine deferring to her advice on casual wear for D.C. in July—until she grabbed a shirt and shoved it into his hands. A shirt that felt like silk and looked like a city slicker's version of a rain forest in shades of moss and gray and white.

"No," he said and shoved it back at her.

She gave him a look. "Seriously? You want to waste time arguing about clothes?" She thrust the shirt back at him. "Don't be such a diva. Go try it on. These, too." She handed him a pair of tan chinos that at least had a few pockets, but still made him think of white sand, hammocks, and fruity rum punch.

Jaw tight, he took both pieces and headed for the

dressing room. She added a pair of brown sandals to the stack of clothes as he went by. And a package of boxer shorts.

"What are you, my mother?"

"What are you, five?"

Because she was right—he was acting like a spoiled adolescent—and because they didn't have time to argue, he bit the bullet and tried them all on. Unfortunately, everything fit, so he kept the clothes on, then paid for them and a pair of aviator-style shades he snagged off a rack on the counter. The clerk—a girl who couldn't have been more than sixteen or seventeen—gave him a blatantly flirtatious smile when he asked for a shopping bag and stuffed his old clothes inside. Biting back the urge to ask her if her mother knew she acted like that, he slipped on the dark glasses and walked to the front of the store to wait for Eva.

He'd never admit it to her, but he was surprised how comfortable the clothes were—and how much he liked what he saw when she walked toward him looking fine. Glad he was wearing the shades, he took his time checking her out. Her dress was formfitting, V-necked and sleeveless, and gathered like a fan beneath her left breast. The skirt hit her above the knee. Her bronze sandals had fancy straps covered with beading and bling.

Chic, understated, and so damn sexy he almost swallowed his tongue. Superimposed over all that cosmopolitan cool was the memory of her breasts spilling out of that red bustier and her hips swaying on the dance floor at *El Tocón Sangriento*.

"What color do you call that?" he asked to diffuse the image, the memory of the taste of the pisco, and to keep from thinking about the way her breasts bounced beneath the soft, stretchy fabric.

"Eggplant."

A vegetable—good, he needed to think about vegetables. Not ripe, luscious fruit, which was what she made him think of. *Beans, legumes, squash*. That's what he needed to think about, because she'd also pulled her hair out of the utilitarian ponytail and wound it into a loose, thick braid that looked sophisticated and exotic.

The woman was a chameleon. She was also a woman of extremes. He'd known her for less than twenty-four hours, and during that time she'd effortlessly changed from sex kitten to commando to metropolitan sophisticate.

The only constant was the sexy part and, Lord love a duck, did she ever have that nailed.

"Two bags?" he asked, relieving her of one of the full shopping bags she carried in each hand.

"As long as I was there, I picked up a few extra changes of clothes. For you, too," she added with a small but pleased-with-herself smile.

"Oh, goodie. A man can never have enough flowered shirts."

She actually laughed. A first. And the sound did something to his nerve endings that he didn't want to dissect. *All* of his nerve endings, and holy God, he needed to get a grip.

It had been way too long since he'd gotten laid. And he'd gone far beyond having a need-to-know curiosity about this woman.

"Give me five more minutes," she said. "There's a drugstore two doors down. I need to pick up a few personal things."

Since he needed the space, he didn't argue. Good to her word, five minutes later she was back with another bag full of stuff. A woman who could speed-shop. Impressive.

As they left the mall and hurried across the blistering hot parking lot toward the SUV, he wondered if he would ever know the real Eva Salinas. More disturbing was the realization that he might want to know. Intimately.

Now who's crazy, Brown?

Back in the SUV, he dug his phone out of his pocket, dialed a secure number, let it ring three times, then hung up. He could feel her curious gaze as he pulled out into traffic, and gave her credit for not asking what the call was about. He'd have an answer for both of them soon.

She dug into the bag from the drugstore—lipstick, a compact, lotion, deodorant, and such—and was sorting through them when his phone rang less than a minute later.

He grabbed it on the first ring. "That was quick."

"Figured it was important." The familiar voice of

Joe Green sounded reassuringly close although Mike knew he could be anywhere from here to Singapore. "After all, it's been a year."

Green was a member of Black Ops, Inc. And yes, it had been a little over a year since the team had enlisted Mike's services to help Joe and the woman who was now his wife escape Sierra Leone after Joe had been falsely imprisoned. Of course, nothing was ever that simple, and Mike and his brother Ty had ended up helping Green uncover a corrupt government official, dodge a few bullets, and save a couple of lives along the way.

Mike and the team went way back. He'd been their pilot during their military days, providing air transpo for their Task Force Mercy missions in South Africa and the Middle East. After TFM had been disbanded Mike had redeployed to Afghanistan, was drafted into the One-Eyed Jacks unit, and the rest, as they say, read like a bad B-grade movie.

"I'm in D.C.," he told Green, peripherally aware that Eva had pulled down the passenger-seat visor and was using the mirror to apply makeup. "Need a place to crash. A safe place. There'll be two of us."

Green didn't hesitate. "That all you need?"

He'd just offered his services—most likely the support of the entire BOI team—and for that Mike was grateful.

He also felt a resurgence of guilt. As far as he knew, none of the BOI team knew about what had happened in Afghanistan. The shame and disillusionment he felt over rolling over and playing dead when he'd copped that plea and taken the less than honorable discharge wasn't exactly something he wanted to broadcast to men he respected and admired.

"For the time being," he said, pushing past it, "but how 'bout I give you an IOU for a six-pack and you can consider yourself on retainer?"

"That'll work."

"Appreciate this, man."

"Tit for tat and all that."

It was good to know that a team as skilled and connected as BOI felt they were indebted to him. Joe, after all, was married to the daughter of the new Secretary of State, and Black Ops, Inc. was now a sanctioned entity of the Department of Defense. He didn't intend to call in that marker unless it was absolutely necessary, but he had a feeling that before this was all over, it would come to that. Shooters wielding MP5Ks tended to make him a tad paranoid.

"Hi to Steph, okay? Give her a kiss for me, a big wet one. And just because you need the occasional reminder, that woman is way too good for the likes of you."

Green grunted. "No argument from me on that front. Keep the line clear. I'll be back asap with an address for you."

"Hey, man, there *is* a little something you could do for me. Hold on for a text, okay?"

"You got it."

As soon as Green disconnected, Mike pulled into a liquor store parking lot and fired off the photo he'd snapped of Eva at the Bogota airport. He followed up with a text message asking Green for a detailed search on Pamela Diaz, Emily Bradshaw, and Eva Salinas. Insurance was king in this game.

Mike felt Eva's gaze on him as he eased back into the stream of traffic. For the first time, he noticed the scent of flowers and musk as she lavished lotion on her bare arms. "One of your friends in high places?"

He turned onto Ninth Street, heading for the bank. "Yup."

She toed off a shoe, propped her bare foot on the dash, and started smoothing lotion onto her leg. Her very bare leg, left that way when her skirt slid up her thigh. "You asked him to run a background check on me."

He dragged his gaze back to the street, tightened his grip on the steering wheel. "On all three of you."

"I thought we'd started to trust each other."

He laughed—it was either that or swallow his tongue as she shifted legs and started the lotion motion all over again. "You wouldn't do the same if you were in my shoes?"

She let out a big sigh. "They won't find anything."

He laughed again, this time in relief, when she smoothed her skirt back down her thighs and slipped into her shoes. "Oh, yes. They will. Anything you want to spill before they dig up the dirt?"

She shook her head—more a gesture of disgust than a response.

"There's parking over there." She pointed toward the lot when they reached the bank.

"Wait here." He held his hand out for the lockbox key. "Let's play it safe, on the off chance someone followed you here when you rented the box and still has eyes on the place."

"That's not going to work. The bank will want photo ID."

Right. "Then we go in together. They won't be looking for a couple."

His words stopped him short as it occurred to him for the first time that she may have hooked up with someone in the eight years since Ramon's death. She was an outrageously attractive woman. Intelligent. Driven. Wore the hell out of a red bustier. And right now, she smelled like hot sex on a summer night.

"Or would they?" He looked across the seat at her. "Is there a Mr. Right Now in your life?" If there was, Mike disliked him already. Call him a chauvinist, but in his book a man who would let his woman traipse off by herself to hunt down a no-good like him wasn't a man at all. Unless she hadn't told him where she was going or what she was doing, which was totally her MO.

She hesitated, then shook her head. "No. No one would be looking for a couple."

It was on the tip of his tongue to ask her if Ramon

had spoiled her for any other man, but that would have been just plain tacky and maybe even a little mean.

He'd stopped feeling mean toward Eva Salinas somewhere over a half-eaten sandwich at the Bogota airport, when she'd told him Ramon was her dead husband.

15

Mike had checked the time on his phone when they'd walked through the bank's front doors and he checked it again as they walked back out. In and out in eighteen minutes. No hitches. Not even a close look. In fact, he was fairly certain that if anyone had bothered to look at them, they'd have been as fixated as he tried not to be on the blatant sexuality Eva exuded with every move she made.

Well, *hello*. He grinned when he finally realized what she was doing. Eva Salinas knew exactly what effect she had on people. Knew it and used it. If questioned, no one in that bank would remember a woman doing business and accessing a safety deposit box. They'd remember a pair of amazing breasts, a blatantly suggestive walk, and off-the-charts sexuality. A trophy every man would go home and secretly fantasize about and every woman would want to forget because she felt inferior.

Once again, he appreciated her intelligence as they walked out into the sunlight and got into the

SUV, the flash drive with the data on OSD tucked safely away in her bag.

And he let up on himself a little bit in the hitting-himself-over-the-head department. Sober, he might have had a fighting chance. But stone cold drunk in that cantina? Hell. She'd had him at spandex.

Green called again as Mike settled behind the wheel.

"Are you serious?" he asked after Joe told him where they'd be staying tonight and given him the address. This was the last thing he'd expected.

"As a heart attack." The line went dead.

Mike grinned, picturing the former CIA, former Task Force Mercy, current Black Ops, Inc. operative. Green stood roughly six foot five, was tough as nails, and the word *joke* was not in his vocabulary. The man had seen and done things—for his country, for his team, for his woman—that would spawn nightmares for the rest of his life. But Mike had seen Green with his wife and knew that, like the wives of the other BOI team members, Stephanie would help keep those nightmares at bay. Never thought he'd see the day when those guys would all end up married. Very happily married.

Just like he never thought he would quietly envy them for the lapse in judgment that had prompted them to give up their freedom for the ball and chain of monogamy.

He squashed back an unexpected rush of melancholy. Fought the way he felt like a kid with his nose pressed against a candy-store window when he saw them all together, witnessed the love, the devotion.

Cripes. What was up with that? Domestic bliss was not the path for him.

Then why so blue, buddy boy? Damned if he knew.

File it under fatigue. File it under the anticipation of reading the contents of the OSD file. And yeah, okay, fine. Maybe point a finger at the woman sitting beside him in the SUV.

For whatever reason, she tripped triggers and rang bells he'd never heard before. Sure, he loved women. Lots of them. Just never singularly and never for more than a night or two. And never with any promises. Easy in, easy out, no hard feelings, it's been good to know you. It worked for him. At least it always had.

"So . . . were you planning to sit here all day or do you have an address?"

Eva's slightly bemused question snapped him out of his thoughts, made him realize how far he'd let himself wander down justification lane. He didn't have to justify his relationships—or lack of—with women. Not to himself. Not to anyone.

And he sure as hell didn't need validation for staying away from her. She was Ramon Salinas's widow. Enough said.

He spit out the address Green had given him and shifted into gear. "You know how to get there from here?" he asked gruffly.

The startled and wary look on her face told him how cranky he'd come across. Not fair to take out his bad mood on her. Or hell, maybe it was. Twenty-four hours ago, life had been simple. Fucked up, but simple.

"Not precisely but we'll find it." She entered the address into the onboard GPS.

Feeling guilty but not really knowing why, he tried to make amends with a less abrasive tone. "Used to know my way around. Things have changed since I spent any time here." When he'd been in D.C. a year ago helping Joe and Steph, all he'd seen was the airport and a nearby hotel before they'd gone wheels up again.

Forty-five minutes later, they pulled off the street and into the underground parking garage of a high-security apartment complex. He was about to tell her to wipe the GPS history clean—he didn't want to take any chances on someone finding out where they'd been—when she leaned forward and took care of it. He wasn't finished being silently impressed with her when she grabbed her shopping bags and opened the door. Not long after, Mike punched in a series of security code numbers that Joe had given him to get them into the building, then into the elevator and finally to the tenth floor.

They were walking down the wide, well-appointed hallway, peripherally aware of a zillion security cameras monitoring them, when the door at the end of the corridor opened up.

A big man with an imposing build and eyes that could drill holes through steel limped into the hallway to meet them. "Nice to know you can still follow simple directions."

Mike broke into a broad grin. "Hello, Angel Boy. Long time no see."

"Call me that again, smart-ass, and you won't be seeing anything but stars."

Mike laughed and shook his old friend's hand. "Missed you too, buddy. Eva—meet Gabe Jones. Word to the wise: Don't try to drug him. He's not as forgiving or good-natured as I am."

Mike leaned against the terrace wall, nursing a soda while Gabe stretched out on a chaise longue amid potted plants and a playpen.

Except for their quick sponge baths at the airport and her brief run to the drugstore, it was the first time Mike and Eva hadn't been connected at the hip since she'd seduced him. They'd arrived at Gabe Jones's apartment only a few minutes ago and she'd excused herself to use the restroom. They needed to get to work on the OSD file, but at the moment he couldn't muster the energy. He'd practically been mainlining caffeine in the form of soda since they'd landed and for the moment he simply needed to chill.

This terrace was the spot to do it. His gaze landed on the playpen again. If he hadn't seen it with his own eyes, he never would have believed it. Mike grinned at Gabe. He had to hand it to Gabe's gorgeous red-headed wife, Jenna. She'd tamed the beast.

Gabe "The Archangel" Jones was one of the

toughest, meanest, most reclusive operators he'd
ever worked with. Dedicated, driven, focused. A
warrior to the end.

He'd either led or been part of teams that had
pushed through everything from triple-canopy
jungles, urban ghettos, mountains, and swamps for
months on end, hunting the bad guys. One time
when Mike had picked them up, their clothes were
ragged to the point of falling off their bodies, everyone had lost at least twenty pounds, and they hadn't
had a square meal or decent rest in months. But
Gabe's force of personality and leadership had made
them go way the hell over and beyond to complete
the mission.

He'd even lost a leg a few years ago on an op but it
had barely slowed him down.

Yet, here he was, all cozied up in a high-security
D.C. apartment complex with designer deck furniture, flowering plants, and toddler toys, reeking of
domestic tranquility.

"What?" Gabe narrowed his eyes in response to
Mike's grin.

"Never saw you as a baby daddy."

"Yeah, well, it's called maturity. You ought to try it
sometime."

Mike laughed and glanced down at the street ten
stories below where rush-hour traffic zipped along.
"Sorry I missed Jenna."

He turned back to his friend, propped his elbows
on the terrace wall behind him. Gabe's wife, who

his friend had just informed him was five months pregnant with their second child, was having a girls weekend in West Palm Beach. Jenna had taken their eighteen-month-old daughter, Ali, to visit their friends, Amy and Dallas Garrett, who along with Dallas's brothers and sister ran E.D.E.N., Inc., a high-risk securities firm. Amy and Dallas had a daughter close to Ali's age. Jenna and Amy had been close friends ever since they'd bonded during an investigation that had ultimately brought down a secret third-generation neo-Nazi camp in Argentina that practiced mind-control experimentation on unwilling victims. The two women tried to get together whenever time and schedules allowed.

"Might be a good thing Jenna and Ali aren't here," Mike added soberly. "And seriously, man, this is a safe house?"

He'd never been in one but had assumed it would be sterile—no personal possessions of any sort, not even art on the wall. Reason: If it was compromised, there'd be no clues for the bad guys as to who was there and possibly why.

"It's my home. But no one makes it past the front entry that I don't want inside."

Judging from all the surveillance cameras and combo locks, Mike didn't doubt it.

"Anytime you want to tell me what you've gotten yourself into," Gabe added, "I'm all ears. But that's your call."

"Appreciate it." Mike glanced toward the terrace

doors, wondering what Eva was up to inside. "In the meantime, I'm still sorting things out."

Gabe followed his gaze, then tipped up his beer. "So, what are the chances she's tossing the place?"

Mike grinned and said cheerfully, "I'd say they're pretty good."

He'd seen the indecision in Eva's eyes. She might think she knew everything about him, but she didn't know Gabe Jones from Adam and that made her nervous. With good reason. Gabe Jones was someone to be wary of even though he was one of the good guys.

"She have anything to do with that?" Gabe lifted his beer, indicating the swelling on Mike's cheek.

"Yup," he admitted and carefully pressed the cold soda can against the ripening bruise.

He was going to have to tell him everything— including what he did and didn't know about Eva Salinas. Which meant telling him about Afghanistan.

So he did. Drew a deep breath and purged. It felt like a bloodletting, and he didn't stop until he'd spilled every last drop.

When he finished, along with the relief of unloading, he also felt a landslide of shame.

"About time you got that off your chest."

He blinked at Gabe. "You *knew*? Jesus. The guys? Do they all know?"

Gabe lifted a shoulder. "We knew something had gone sideways for you. You were career Navy all the way, back in the Task Force Mercy days. And then after Afghanistan, suddenly you weren't. The next thing we heard, you were hiding out in South America, playing fast and loose with your little cargo business and supporting the local pisco trade."

Mike stared at the top of his soda can. That pretty much summed up his first couple of years post-Afghanistan. "Couple of years of that hard drinking was all I could take. So I sobered up." Except for one day each year. And except for wanting a drink every single other day of every year.

"We knew that, too, or we'd never have tagged you for the Sierra Leone mission. You should have come to us," Gabe added. "We could have helped."

"No," he said. "You couldn't. I was too . . ." He thought of all the things he was, none of them good.

"Stupid?" Gabe suggested.

In spite of himself, Mike grinned. "Yeah, that, too."

Gabe lifted a dismissive shoulder. "We all have ghosts. Nut up and get over it."

This prompted a laugh. "How touchy-feely of you. I'm tingling all over." He held out an arm. "See? Goose bumps."

Gabe gave him a rare smile. "What can I say? I'm a giver."

Mike looked up at his friend, who clearly didn't think less of him, who absolutely had ghosts of his own.

Gabe hitched his chin toward the apartment again. "Want me to run a check on the mystery woman?"

Mike's phone pinged. He held up a finger and fished it out of his pocket. It was a text from Joe with a document attached. "Funny you should mention her," he said, "because it looks like Joe came through on that front."

"Good to know you're thinking ahead. I'll go check and see if she needs me to move any furniture so she can look behind it."

Mike was barely aware that Gabe walked back inside the apartment. He was already engrossed in the background on his mystery woman.

"And we have a winner," he said under his breath and quickly read the file on Eva Salinas. Good to know she was actually capable of some truth.

Holy crap. Her sheet read like the overachievers handbook. A little reading between the lines and it became clear that little Eva Montoya had been born on a mission. Her parents had set the bar high. From the time she could crawl up on her attorney mother's lap or charm her JAG attorney father, whose service in the Navy had apparently prompted her to pursue her own career in service to her country, she'd been setting wrongs right.

Girl Scout, student council president, captain of the debating team at University of Virginia and graduated summa cum laude, top of her class at U of V law school. Impressive.

And while she did not follow her father's hellishly big footsteps into the military, she'd had instructor-level credentials in Muay Thai—no wonder she'd made such quick work of him in the alley—and was an expert marksman rank in both long gun and pistol. In short—she was kick-ass.

Right out of law school, she'd joined the CIA as an attorney in support services out of Langley, where she'd met Ramon Salinas, fallen in love, and after a whirlwind courtship, married him.

Should have been a happily ever after, Mike thought. A woman like her sure as hell deserved one. Ramon would have ripped her heart out and stomped all over it, but Mike wasn't about to tell her that she wouldn't have gotten that Cinderella ending. He would not talk trash about a dead man to anyone. Sure as hell not to his widow.

He only looked up when he heard the terrace door slide open again and Gabe stepped back outside.

"Everything okay in there?"

Gabe nodded. "I offered her a shower and she jumped at the chance. You look like you could use one, too."

"For a fact. Might wake me up. We've been on the move for longer than I care to remember."

"That would explain the need for the ugly shirt. Sucker's so loud it would keep a narcoleptic awake."

"Listen to you. Another joke from the Archangel. Jenna really has mellowed your ass out."

"I suspect she'd say that she *straightened* my ass out. Come on. You can use the shower in our bedroom. Give you a chance to change into something that doesn't shout South Pacific."

"I'll let that pass."

"As if you could do anything about it."

Gabe headed back inside, his limp reminding

Mike what he'd given up in service to his country and for Jenna. He had saved her from a bomb blast, taking shrapnel in his leg that eventually resulted in amputation below the knee.

"That way." Gabe pointed down the hall.

Mike hesitated and for a second considered hunting up Eva's purse and digging around for the flash drive. He'd been itching to plug it into Gabe's computer and read the information that had driven her to Lima to find him.

But that might break this fragile trust they'd developed and frankly, right now, he wanted a shower more. And he wanted to think about the information Joe had turned up on Eva Salinas, who was not Pamela Diaz or Emily Bradshaw.

The woman was nothing if not inventive.

"Here." He handed Gabe his phone. "For your reading pleasure. It's the lowdown on your other houseguest—aka CIA legal eagle."

16

It wasn't often Eva was given license to snoop. While she wasn't a pro, she'd searched as much of the apartment as she could manage under the ruse of using the restroom before Gabe had stepped back inside and offered her the use of the guest shower.

Not that she'd found anything. Not that she'd expected to, she conceded as she stepped out of the shower and into the bedroom. A good operative—and despite the evidence of a toddler in residence, Jones had *operative* written all over him—would never leave anything in plain sight. What she needed was access to her CIA database so she could find out who, exactly, he was.

What she got, however, was Jones, alone on the terrace, loading salmon steaks on a grill.

"So . . . I figure you have questions," he said, without turning around. "I know I'd have them if I was in your position."

Then he gave her the last thing she'd ever expected: full disclosure. And she immediately felt ridiculous for not recognizing who he was the moment she'd met him.

Jones wasn't merely an operative. He was a member of Black Ops, Inc. Everyone in the intelligence community knew about Nate Black's band of merry men who, until a few months ago, had run covert ops for Uncle off the grid out of Buenos Aires. The team had recently relocated to Virginia, where they were now a sanctioned entity under the direction of the Department of Defense.

Jones was not only a linchpin on the team, he was a legend in the intelligence and black ops community. She should have tuned in when Brown had called him Angel Boy. He was the Archangel.

Holy, holy God.

Jones had gotten his nickname for his deadly skill with an Arc-Angel butterfly knife—solid titanium, razor sharp, ten inches fully open. No one but a master could handle it the way it was reputed that Jones handled it.

The Archangel and his ilk were the ultimate shadow warriors, rogues who played by their own rules and damn the consequences, often skirting around the dark fringes of international law. Until this past year, when the Black Ops, Inc. team was made legitimate.

"Why?" she asked, opting for wine when he offered her a choice.

"Why tell you who I am?" He extended a glass of chardonnay. "Like you weren't going to figure it out?"

She gave him a narrow-eyed look.

"You're CIA. It was just a matter of time."

"It's that obvious?"

He adjusted the fire under the salmon. "Relax. You didn't give anything away. Mike had Joe run your sheet. There are no secrets among spies."

She joined him by the grill. "I'm not a spy. I'm an attorney."

One corner of his mouth drew up in a ghost of a smile. "It's your story. You can tell it any way you want to." He glanced at her then. "From the sound of things, you've been telling a lot of stories."

Because he hadn't said it unkindly, she relaxed a little. Apparently Mike had also told him about Lima, which meant he must also know about Afghanistan.

"Where *is* Brown?"

"Shower."

"Speaking of showers, thanks. And thanks for letting us crash here." She lifted a hand toward the grill. "And feeding us."

"You both look like you need fuel. You'll work better with some food in you. Then you two can have a sit-down and figure out where you go from here."

They lapsed into a silence then that didn't exactly feel comfortable, but was much less tense than before he'd told her who he was.

Eva took the opportunity to size him up. Gabe Jones and Mike Brown could have been cast from the same mold. Jones had a couple inches and maybe twenty pounds on Brown, but both were big men. Both unreasonably attractive. And they both had a look about them. Even though Brown had been out of the game for a few years, his Spec Ops background was evident in the way he walked, the way he constantly scoured the space around them for threats. There was a poised readiness, a situational awareness about him and about this man. When the door opened behind her and Mike stepped out onto the terrace to join them, she had to stop herself from staring.

His hair was still wet. He'd shaved and the effect was stunning. He wore another one of the print shirts she'd bought mostly to tick him off, but partly because he looked so hot in the first one. She could smell him on the light summer breeze wafting across the terrace. Something citrus and spicy and 100 percent male; he must have helped himself to Jones's aftershave.

He looked refreshed and vital and as gorgeous as the Primetime handle billed him to be.

Their eyes met and held for an explicably long moment before she looked away. Tipping up her wine, she attempted to act as though nothing out of the ordinary happened. But the exchange had rattled her.

The little rush, the undeniable shimmer of attraction was so unwise. If she could have ignored it she would have, but Mike Brown was a difficult man to ignore. So were these unexpected reactions she kept having to him.

Jones made a sound that could have been a laugh when he saw Brown. "For the love of God. Who puked a rain forest all over you?"

Brown walked over to inspect the salmon steaks. "You can thank her. Just my luck I finally get a personal shopper, and she misses the memo about cargo pants and black T-shirts."

Jones turned back to his grill. "Well, I think you look real cute."

"See what you've done?" When Mike turned to Eva, there was a smile in his eyes that prompted her to smile back before she could check it. "He's disrespecting me now."

"I never respected you in the first place," Jones said with a grin that indicated he lied. "So you can't hang that on her."

"*Your* fault," Brown insisted with a pointed look at Eva that she made a valiant attempt not to find endearing.

She could *not* go there.

She walked over to the waist-high wall of the terrace, let the coolness of a soft evening breeze wash over her, and listened without comment as the two friends talked, gave each other grief, and laughed softly—their way of keeping the tension of the current situation under control.

They'd been through the fire together. Their bond ran deep. Men like Jones and Brown didn't give that kind of trust recklessly.

Reckless wasn't something she could afford to be, either, but trust was mandatory. Someone wanted her dead and she had no choice but to trust both of these men with her life.

• • •

For her sake, Mike was glad they'd taken a little break. If a quick shower and quicker meal could be considered a break. All in all, it had been less than forty-five minutes since they'd invaded Gabe Jones's very private sanctum. Gabe had gone to clean up, making himself scarce, leaving them alone in the home office with the computer.

Mike had pulled a chair up beside Eva, chomping at the bit as he waited for her to boot up Gabe's PC and open the file on Operation Slam Dunk.

He wasn't sure why he was so anxious. He already knew what was in it. Maybe it was the thought of seeing the lies in black and white all these years later. Or maybe it was that he'd spent the last eight years trying to forget it, and now he was about to lance open a wound that was still painful. Back when it had happened, he'd gone through it in sort of a fog. He'd been in mourning for his lost team, zoned out on the pain meds for his broken collarbone and the debridement of the burns on his leg—and in a state of shock that he had been fingered as the bad guy.

Gabe was right. He'd planned on being career Navy. He'd lived it, breathed it, loved it. And then suddenly the Navy no longer had any love for him. The entire U.S. military had wanted his head on a platter. It had been too much to absorb, to process, and most of all, to deal with.

So he hadn't. He'd skated through the days, lying to himself, blindly reassuring himself that Brewster would come through. That everything would be straightened out. He'd be released back to active duty, exonerated. A wronged man.

His head had been buried so deep in the proverbial sand that the court-martial proceedings had caught him completely off guard. And he'd folded in on himself, defeated, manipulated, too shocked to even be angry.

The anger had come later—self-destructive, angry years that he'd spent seeking restitution at the bottom of a bottle.

"Mike?"

Eva. He'd zoned out on her.

"Yeah. Sorry. What?"

"Where'd you go?"

To a very bad place.

He glanced into her concerned eyes, and it hit him how dark those eyes were. So brown they were almost black. And God, she smelled good. Like that rain forest Gabe had accused him of wearing.

And, whoa. She'd called him Mike.

She'd *never* called him Mike before. Always Brown. He'd understood; it established a line of demarcation. *We are not friends*, it said clearly. *We are merely working together by necessity.*

But she'd just changed the game.

Like when he'd joined her and Gabe on the terrace after his shower. He'd thought then that he'd read more into her expression than was warranted. But no, he'd been right. She'd been glad to see him.

And then she'd looked away. Probably as surprised by her reaction as he'd been.

"Sorry," he said. Not the time. Not the place, and sure as hell not the woman to be bonding with. Sure, he wanted to take her to bed. Any man with a pulse would want her.

But he was smart enough to know that an entanglement with Eva Salinas would come to no good end. So, no. Never. No way. This woman had complication, complication, and had he mentioned *complication*? written all over her.

"Is that it?" he asked with a no-nonsense nod toward the monitor and the document she'd opened up.

"Yeah. That's the first one of several."

She scooted her chair to the side so he could move in close and start reading.

It was all there. Spelled out nice and neat and military sharp. I's dotted. T's double crossed. Just the facts—and they were all wrong. All lies.

He hadn't realized he'd started to sweat until he felt a trickle of perspiration inch down his temple.

"Looks like a cut-and-dried case against me," he said, closing out the first document and opening another. "No wonder you wanted me dead."

She sighed heavily. "I wasn't going to kill you."

"Well, no, not after my boyish charm won you over."

Crap. He could not flirt with her.

"Yeah. The way you stumbled across the dance floor and gagged me with your pisco breath made my heart go pitty pat," she flirted back.

Not good. Not good at all.

He could see in her eyes that she'd realized it a split second after he had. She quickly nipped it in the bud with a sober scowl.

We are totally on the same page here, chica.

He cleared his throat, all business again, and leaned closer to the screen to put a little distance between them and that floral scent that made him crazy. Or maybe he was making himself crazy. He'd had plenty of practice in that area the past several years.

"I figured at the very least you were guilty of collusion with whoever had called the shots," she said. "But I decided that until I could confront you face-to-face, I wasn't taking any chances. That's when I started digging past the file."

He listened as he scrolled. Closed one document, opened another, not seeing anything he hadn't known before.

"So who all did you bump about this?" he asked absently.

"It's more like who *didn't* I talk to." She stared morosely at the screen over his shoulder. "So when doors started slamming shut in my face and I began to get the sense that I was being followed, I turned my focus in another direction. It didn't make sense at that point that you were behind whoever was stonewalling or following me. You couldn't have connections that reached that far.

"So the question was," she continued, "who

did that leave? That's when I started giving serious thought to a cover-up."

"Maybe that's what your mysterious benefactor wanted when he gave you the flash drive," he speculated, opening the next file. "For you to investigate the possibility."

"I wondered the same thing. But no matter how I spun it, I hated the idea. I've spent my entire career in service. To believe that you were innocent was to believe that my own government had conspired against you. But to what end? Why throw a decorated Navy pilot under the bus?"

"Lots of questions," he agreed absently and clicked on another file. The first thing to open was a photograph.

His heart stopped dead before his mind fully engaged. Then he leaned in close, taking a really long look, making sure his eyes weren't deceiving him.

17

"I have no idea why his photo was included along with the OSD files," Eva said over Mike's shoulder. "But in case it wasn't by accident, I checked him out anyway. His name is Joseph Lawson." She hit the print button and waited for the printer to spit out the photograph. "I didn't find any connection to him and Afghanistan or you or Ramon."

Only when she turned back to him did it register how deadly quiet he'd become. So quiet, she knew something big was going on.

She watched his face as she handed him Lawson's photograph. "You know him, don't you?"

Several seconds ticked by while he read all the information she'd compiled on Joseph Lawson.

He stood abruptly. "We need to share this with Gabe." Shouldering around her, he headed out of the office.

They found Gabe on the terrace talking on his cell. The minute he saw the look on Mike's face, he said,

"I've got to go, babe. Call you back later. Love you, too. Kiss Ali for me." He ended the call. "What?"

Mike handed him Lawson's picture without a word. Just as he hadn't spoken another word to Eva after announcing that they needed to talk to Gabe.

Eva watched the exchange and shivered, sensing they were on the brink of a major breakthrough.

She breathed deep as Gabe studied the photograph. The July evening had cooled a little; that daylight was now a memory. Light from strategically placed sconces bathed the terrace in a soft glow. The fragrance of flowers spilling from a dozen planters scattered around the tile floor drifted on a soft breeze. But the soothing summer scents and colors did nothing to cut the tension that emanated from Mike in troubling waves.

She was worried about him. Which was crazy; he was a big boy. And while he wasn't exactly her enemy, he wasn't exactly her friend, either. Still, ever since he'd seen Lawson's photograph, something had changed inside him. Something profound. Until that moment, she'd sensed he was only here because he'd felt he had no choice, not because he wanted answers.

There was no question that he was fully invested now.

Gabe's expression was thoughtful as he squinted from the photo to Eva. "And?" Eva looked toward Mike for a clue.

"Tell him what you've got," he said.

Eva turned back to Gabe. "That photo was included along with the OSD files. I didn't understand why—still don't understand why—since it didn't seem to have any connection, but I ran it through the CIA database anyway."

Gabe smiled. "See, you are a spy."

"Because I'm an attorney," she reminded him, "it's in my nature to investigate all angles of any situation. Anyway, I got a hit. His name is Joseph Lawson."

Gabe glanced at Mike. "Should the name sound familiar?"

Mike looked grim. "It's going to."

"I pulled as much intel on Lawson as I could find," Eva continued. "And when I butted up against security clearance restrictions, I leaned on some of my friends in-house."

"Let me guess—it was about that time your sources dried up and you started to sense you were being followed," Gabe said.

"Now that I think about it, you're right. That's exactly when the stonewalling started. But not before I found out about the organization Joseph Lawson founded."

"UWD. United We Denounce," Mike filled in the blank when Gabe's brows furrowed. "A radical militia survivalist group that denounces all allegiance to the U.S. government."

Mike drew a deep breath and dropped down on a chair, his hands clasped together between his knees like he was physically attempting to get a grip, Eva thought, watching him.

Gabe held up a finger. "I remember now. Saw Lawson's name on a government watch list several years ago. Has a big compound full of followers living somewhere in the mountains out west, right?"

Eva nodded. "UWD headquarters are in Idaho, at a commune on land Lawson's parents left him when they died."

"Perfect place to build a communal colony, isolate his followers from the outside world, and brainwash them," Gabe said grimly and lifted a hand for Eva to continue.

"It's estimated that between one hundred and one twenty-five UWD members and their families are in Idaho, but Lawson's recently branched out. He's started up smaller settlements in five or six states and over the past year the membership has multiplied like rabbits. UWD is now the fastest growing antigovernment group of the decade."

"So what's the background story on Lawson?" Gabe turned directly to Eva since Mike had grown quiet.

"Former Spec Ops. Gulf War veteran. Reports indicate he suffers from untreated PTSD with violent tendencies. Took to using his wife as a punching bag. Several years ago, when she finally filed a restraining order against him and left him, taking their only child with her, he turned radical zealot and started gathering disciples. His numbers are estimated to be pushing three hundred now."

Gabe scratched his jaw. "So how much trouble have they stirred up?"

Eva shrugged. "They've actually been pretty quiet,

so the FBI has been content to list them on their watch list as a cult and monitor their activities."

When she fell silent, Gabe looked at Mike, then back to Eva. "I'm guessing that silence I hear precedes the sound of a shoe about to fall?"

She drew a deep breath. "Because of the escalating extremist rhetoric on his underground website, it's now suspected that UWD is a front for a paramilitary operation. Recently, he was spotted in a surveillance photo meeting with a known member of the Juarez drug cartel's La Linea."

The Juarez organization had far-reaching tentacles, with contacts and suppliers all over the world. They were also ruthless. Too many headline stories showed crime scenes with the decapitated bodies of their victims. Recently, Acosta Hernandez had been sentenced to ten consecutive life sentences after pleading guilty to charges of racketeering, drug conspiracy, money laundering, firearms violations, murder, and conspiracy to kill in a foreign country. Hernandez had been linked to over 1,500 homicides in Mexico alone.

Gabe's expression hardened. "So we've got a wacko running a cult tied to the Juarez cartel. Talk about a goatfuck." He turned to Mike. "I still don't get the connection to you."

When Mike's eyes met his friend's, he looked haunted and hunted.

"He was in Afghanistan," Mike finally said, his voice gruff with emotion. "The night OSD went

down. I saw him. I saw Lawson. The sonofabitch was
in the Mi-8 when it landed."

Mike was low on sleep and high on fatigue. Yet as he
stood alone on the terrace, he was as revved up as an
Indy race car. Adrenaline, hate, and the need for re-
venge fueled him. His fingers were clamped so tightly
around the terrace rail they ached, yet he couldn't let
go. Consumed by rage, he was afraid he might grab
the first thing he could put his hands on and heave it
over the side. Potted plants, furniture, he didn't care.
He wanted to throw something. He wanted to hit
something. He wanted to destroy something.

His entire life had been kicked to the curb because
of Lawson. For eight years, he'd told himself to forget
what happened. Tried to "nut up" and carry on.

But he finally wanted his life back. He wanted pay-
back. First, though, he needed answers.

They had to find out what Lawson had been doing
in Afghanistan. Had he been gunrunning even then?
The village had lit up like a bomb site when that
ammo had started cooking off. Had the One-Eyed
Jacks team stumbled onto one of Lawson's weapons
caches? Had he needed them all dead to keep from
being discovered? Was that why he'd needed a fall
guy when he'd found out there'd been witnesses—
Mike, Taggart, and Cooper?

If that was the case, then Lawson had to have a
pipeline directly to someone in the military to pull it
off. Someone with clout. Someone who had been on

board and on his payroll, who had driven the locomotive that ran Mike out of the service.

His mind spun in circles trying to figure it out. Maybe it had been something even bigger than an ammo dump or weapons cache. Their FOB in the Pashtun Helmand Province had been within a hundred kilometers of the epicenter of Afghanistan's poppy and opium pipeline. Had Lawson been cashing in on the rampant opium trade? Had he been supplying the Taliban with weapons in exchange for the opium? Was he still supplying them, in addition to dealing with the Mexican drug cartel?

They'd get their answers eventually—including answers about who Lawson was in league with and had helped him with the cover-up.

Yeah. Now that they knew where to start, they *would* find out. Gabe had headed inside to his office over an hour ago and alerted the BOI team. All their resources were now invested in digging up every piece of intel that existed on Joseph Lawson and his known associates, and in finding out who leaked the OSD information to Eva, and why someone wanted her dead because of it.

He breathed deep. Willed his fingers to unclamp from the rail. He needed to chill. Needed to level himself out. This was far from over. It was just beginning, and this was about more than his own personal vendetta. Another deep breath.

Boom Boom Taggart and Hondo Cooper hadn't merely been his OEJ teammates. They'd been his friends. His brothers. Like the Black Ops team were brothers.

He hadn't allowed himself to miss them.

But he missed them tonight. Missed their trash talk. Missed them having his back, and him having theirs. He wanted desperately for them to know he hadn't sold them out to save his own neck. Wanted things back to the way they had been between them.

Right. He might as well wish for world peace. Neither was going to happen.

"You okay?"

He hadn't heard Eva step out onto the terrace. So he guessed that would be a no. No, he was not okay.

"I'm fine," he lied. "You should turn in. Tomorrow's bound to be a long day."

Tomorrow they'd have enough intel to decide how to proceed. Mike already knew the basic game plan: Get Lawson. The man's thin, ferret face and beady eyes had haunted him for too damn long. When he found him, Mike intended to make him squeal like a stuck pig, bleed him for information, then tear him limb from limb.

Eva joined him at the terrace rail. He should warn her away. Right here, right now, was not a good place for her to be. Not when he felt this raw and achy, in need of something to release the emotions that had built up inside him like white-hot steam.

But one look at her face and he knew he couldn't send her away. He'd known her for . . . what? A little over twenty-four hours? And yet he could tell she was troubled.

She had something she wanted to say.

Exercising more patience than he thought he had left in him, he waited. Let her take her time.

"Lawson . . . knowing who he is, knowing he was in Afghanistan." She glanced at him, then looked away again. "It's a game changer for you."

He pushed out a breath that sounded a little like a laugh, a lot like a groan. As understatements went, that was Guinness World Record–worthy. "Little bit, yeah."

"I can't . . ." She stopped and the emotion that clogged her voice made him turn toward her again. "I can't imagine what you must be feeling."

Her dark eyes glittered with tears that made it clear she *could* imagine the tumult of emotions inside him. This changed things for her, too. She now had a name and a face of the man who'd had a hand in her husband's death.

Don't do it, he warned himself. *Do not touch her. Do not comfort her. Not unless you're prepared to start something that she's not going to want to finish.*

He was so close to the edge right now, it was all he could do to keep himself together, to keep from howling at the moon, beating his chest and demanding the entire world look at him, listen to him, believe him. *I did nothing wrong.*

"I'm so, so sorry for what this has cost you." The compassion in her voice rattled him.

She rattled him. He'd seen the way she'd been watching him since they'd connected Lawson to Afghanistan. She was worried about him. When had she started caring? And man, she shouldn't. She had her own adjustments to make. Thinking her husband died on a mission was one thing. Knowing her husband had been betrayed by another American . . . that was no easy weight to bear. Not to mention, someone wanted her dead.

Do not touch her.

But he couldn't stop himself. He lifted a hand, made the slightest contact with her shoulder. "Eva—"

And she moved into him.

18

Mike held his breath, finally giving in and drawing her against him. To comfort her. That's all.

The breath left her in a sigh as her arms wrapped around his waist. She pressed her cheek against his chest and nestled against him, and God, oh, God, she felt small and fragile and so uncharacteristically vulnerable, it made his chest hurt.

"For years, I thought Ramon died because of his own careless mistake. He was a warrior. You're a warrior. You understand. It wasn't how he would have wanted to go out. And then I find out I was lied to. And lied to again."

She stopped, worked at composing herself, and Mike wished he could feel something other than contempt for Ramon Salinas. She didn't deserve what he'd done to her, and Salinas did not deserve Eva's grief.

"But none of that is going to bring him back." She lifted her head, tipped her face to his. "For you, though . . . *everything* changes for you. I lured you back here on the promise of a chance to clear your name, but I never really believed it was going to happen. I used you to get to the truth."

He knew too much about feeling guilty. About how it made you feel about yourself, about how demoralizing it was. "Everybody uses, Eva. It's the way of the world."

A sad smile lifted one corner of her mouth. "Spoken like a man jaded by life."

"Jaded? Resigned? Fine line. And it doesn't matter how you got me here. I don't care. The end result is that because of you I might get my life back. Whatever that might look like."

He'd seen his brother, Ty, last year when he'd tagged him to help with Joe's problem. He hadn't seen his mom and dad in years, though. Talked to them, yes; he kept in touch and kept tabs on them, made sure they were all right. But he'd been too ashamed to face them.

"You didn't deserve what happened to you." The regret and compassion in her voice joined forces with the look in her eyes and completely undid him.

He'd done a lot of stupid things in his life. Some he'd thought about. Some he hadn't. But as they stood there with Jenna's flowers all around them and the sky doing its moonlight and madness thing above them, he quit thinking about the fact that the woman watching him with soul-deep eyes was Ramon Salinas's widow. He quit thinking about the fact that she'd drugged and shanghaied him.

He only thought about how much he wanted to kiss her. How much he needed a connection to someone. No, a connection to *her*. Someone who had lost as much as he had.

Screw smart. He'd wanted to do this from the first time he'd seen her, drunk on his ass and looking to get laid. He'd wanted it sober, cuffed to a bed and determined to wring her neck. He'd wanted it at a noisy table at the Bogota airport, when she'd finally dropped her act and confessed who she really was.

But most of all, he wanted to kiss her because she looked like she needed to be kissed. Because she looked both tentative and on the brink of something she didn't understand, but in this moment didn't want to fight.

Eight years away from a loss they'd both suffered, miles from where they'd started, they'd reached a moment where they were kindred souls. Souls in need of solace, and a respite only they could give each other because of their common bond.

He cupped her cheek in his palm and, holding on to what he chose to read as an invitation in her eyes, he lowered his mouth to hers.

Insane, but perfectly, unerringly right. God, she tasted sweet and sad, and like someone who didn't want to be sad anymore.

Her lips were lush and soft and open as they met his, accepting and yielding and needy. It completely unhinged him.

It had been a long time since a woman had needed

him. A long time since he'd wanted one to. But he wanted to be important to her, strong for her, and even weak for her so she would understand how much she was giving him in return.

With a low groan, he deepened the kiss, drew her tighter against him, and took things to a different level. Tentative and sweet shifted to demanding and dark as desire outdistanced tenderness. They both fed from it, built on it, until his leg was wedged between her thighs, her hands tunneled under his shirt, and their mouths devoured each other's.

The wet heat of her tongue sent shockwaves of longing straight to his groin. He pressed his hips against her, letting her feel what she was doing to him, and got so lost in the heat firing between them that it took a while to tune in to the sudden tension in her body.

She'd stiffened against him. The hands that had threaded through his hair now pressed flat against his chest, resisting.

He lifted his head, relaxed his hold, and gave her the distance she suddenly needed.

Long, long moments passed with nothing but heavy breathing and wildly beating hearts separating them. Below, the traffic continued to rumble. A soft light glowed from inside the apartment. A dewy dampness had fallen on the night. And where there had been heat, he now felt a clammy cold.

"Well." He forced a deep, steadying breath. He'd started this; he needed to be the one to restore the status quo. "I guess that was probably inevitable."

She tucked her chin to her chest, slowly removed her hands. "Yeah," she agreed, sounding breathless. "I guess it was."

She backed away then, crossed her arms beneath her breasts, and shook her head. "Doesn't mean—"

"Anything," he cut in, so she'd think he was on the same page. "I know."

She smiled ruefully. "I was going to say, it doesn't mean it was smart."

"Oh. Right." So it had meant something to her, too?

"But you're right about the other, too. It didn't mean anything. We . . . we're both processing a lot of information right now. We're both running on empty."

He should have felt relieved. Instead, he felt unreasonably deflated.

"And you're right on another count," she said on a bracing breath. "I need sleep. I'm going to turn in."

"Good night," he said and waited for her to leave him so he could figure out what had just happened, and why it took everything in him to let her walk away.

When she stopped and turned back, his heart slammed into his ribs. And when she slowly walked back to him, and reached for his hand, his mouth went bone dry.

"I came out here to give you this." She pressed a folded paper into his hand. "Call him."

This time she left him there, closing the terrace door behind her.

For someone who prided himself on his reaction time, he stood like a freaking lump, in a lust-induced stupor, staring at the space she'd just occupied. And yeah, it *was* lust. No way in hell could he have feelings for that woman. Not this fast. Not . . . not Ramon's widow.

He shook his head. Shook it off. And finally looked down and unfolded the paper.

It was a phone number he recognized. He'd committed it to memory long ago, but had never dialed.

"Call him."

He stood there for a long time, staring blankly at the night.

Finally he walked over to a deck chair and sat down heavily. His heart beat like crazy. He could feel it in his throat . . . right there with the knot that damn near choked him.

His hand wasn't exactly steady when he reached into his pocket and pulled out his phone. It took a full minute to work up the nerve to dial. Took more nerve to keep from hanging up as he waited for the connection to Sydney, Australia.

Finally it started ringing.

He propped an elbow on his thigh, dropped his head into his hand, and pinched the bridge of his nose. And waited, a split second away from hanging on or hanging up.

Hanging up had about won out when he heard a pick-up on the other end of the line.

"Cooper. Leave a message."

• • •

Jamie Cooper lay utterly still in bed, fingers clutched around his phone. The message light had been blinking when he woke up. He'd listened to it four times now. And he still felt dead inside.

Finally, he rolled to a sitting position; his feet hit the cold wood floor beside the bed and he shivered. It felt like a ghost had just drifted over his shadow.

Brown. Eight years ago, all he'd thought about was what he wanted to do to the man he had once called friend. Then he hadn't thought of him at all—except when he thought of home and all the reasons he couldn't go back there.

"Come back to bed, babe."

Lonnie. He'd forgotten she was here. Why *was* she here? He dragged a weary hand through his hair. Oh, yeah. The party had run late, he'd drunk too much, and she'd convinced him it was a good night for a sleepover. Since it was pushing four in the morning by the time they hit the sheets, he'd been too wasted to argue. But he didn't do sleepovers. Not with women who would read way too much into a "good night" followed directly by a "good morning."

He squinted at the bedside clock. Two p.m. Okay. Not morning.

"Babe?" she repeated, raising up on an elbow behind him and touching a warm hand to his bare back.

"You probably need to get going," he said, to keep from telling her to mind her own business. He was not her "babe" and this entire setup reeked of manipulation and expectation on her part. "Help yourself to a shower before you go," he said, standing. "I'm going for a run. You want me to call you a cab before I head out?"

Yeah, it was cold but he'd been straight with her from day one. He had nothing to give a woman beyond a good time and a fast good-bye.

"No. I'm fine," she said in a small voice and he knew he had hurt her.

He should be more sorry about that. His mother would not be proud. "Take care, then." He pulled on a pair of running shorts and jerked a sweatshirt over his head. He grabbed a pair of socks and his running shoes before he left the room, closing the door behind him.

Then he headed out into the cold damp afternoon and ran as if he could outdistance his past.

A past that Primetime Brown had dusted off, shaken out, and aired like a bag full of dirty laundry and bad memories. Hard feelings. Big regrets.

None of which he was able to outrun in nine miles, so he pushed it to twelve. When he returned to his cottage he was soaked with sweat, breathing hard, muscles quivering. And Brown's call was still on his mind.

"*Please call,*" he'd said just before ringing off and leaving two different numbers for him to call.

Fat fucking chance.

Thankfully, Lonnie was gone. All he felt was relief as he put on a pot of coffee, stripped, then hit the shower. Where he stood beneath the steaming spray and told himself to forget about the call. Forget about the lump that had lodged in his throat the moment he'd recognized Brown's voice. Forget that they'd once been as close as brothers.

He wasn't the one who had betrayed that bond. Brown was.

"Urgent, my ass," he muttered under his breath.

Fuck him and his eight-years-too-late explanation and appeal for help in setting the record straight. What was the point?

There wasn't any.

In a foul, crappy mood, he finally got dressed and poured himself some coffee. For a long time he stared broodingly out his kitchen window at the thick clouds rolling in from the west. Finally, he booted up his laptop and checked his e-mail. A note from his agent. A message from Lonnie—already? He didn't bother to open either.

Instead, he clicked on Create Mail. Let his fingers hover over the keys for a long moment before finally typing Bobby Taggart's address. He debated even longer over the subject line, almost hit Delete a dozen times. In the end, he finally hammered it all out—everything Brown had said, what had supposedly happened, what he was planning, the name and phone number of some Jones person if he couldn't reach Brown—and hit Send. It wasn't as if he and Taggart were pen pals—he had Brown to thank for that split, too. He kept track of him was all. Last he knew—over nine months ago—Bobby was back in Afghanistan. Still in the thick of it, working for a private contractor, still taking fire. Still as pissed as Jamie was that Mike Brown had sold them down the river.

Only now he claimed he hadn't.

He should go hit the weights. He had a big shoot scheduled in two weeks at Bondi Beach. Swimwear. Hot models. Big money.

Instead, he walked back to the bedroom, opened his bureau drawer, and dug until he found it. His one-eyed jack. The card—a jack of hearts—was timeworn, yellowed, and burned around the edges. He rubbed his thumb over the faded surface, thinking of what it had once meant to him. What it still meant to him.

Several long moments later, he tucked it back in the drawer where it belonged, packed a bag, and headed for the gym.

Bobby Taggart lay on his narrow cot, trying not to think about how fucking hot he was as the Afghan sun baked down on his tent like a blowtorch.

Outside, engines gunned and revved; the scent of diesel and gunpowder drifted inside on the ever-present dust that seeped into every nook, cranny, and crevice known to man and machine.

He'd returned to base after a sixteen-hour patrol. Exhausted, bone dry, and so hot he thought his head would explode, he'd stripped down to the bare essentials—boxers, T-shirt, and his AR-15—and collapsed.

He was about to let sleep take him when Arnold poked his head inside.

"There's a computer open," his battle buddy said, standing in the open tent flap.

That snapped his eyes open. "Appreciate it."

"No prob." Then Arnold was gone.

Their civilian commo setup was primitive at best. Five computers shared by upwards of two hundred men did not make for easy access.

He forced himself up off the cot and walked barefoot across the thirty yards of dirt to the commo tent at the center of the base. The free computer had already been taken, but since there was only one other guy ahead of him in one of the lines, he decided he'd stick it out. Such was life on this all-expenses-paid getaway to beautiful bombed-out Afghanistan.

Twenty minutes later, he sat down in front of a screen and keyed in his ID and password. It had been two weeks since he'd checked his mail, and while the sad lack of people reaching out to touch him was no surprise, the fact that there was a message from Hondo Cooper was.

The subject line read: Primetime.

Bobby's knee-jerk reaction was rage. A thick, bone-deep rage that he'd buried deep and only let out when he was drunk or certain he was going to die.

Why the hell was Cooper e-mailing him about that bastard? Maybe Brown was dead? Cause for celebration.

Or not.

Maybe he didn't want to know.

He almost deleted the message unread, but curiosity got the best of him.

And by the time he finished reading, he didn't know whether to laugh, cry, get drunk, or wish to hell he'd never opened the damn e-mail.

Eva headed straight for the guest bedroom after leaving Brown on the terrace. She needed some real distance from him, real fast. Unfortunately Gabe glanced up when she walked past his office door and swiveled around in his desk chair.

"I put a T-shirt and a pair of boxers—Jenna's go-to sleepwear—on the bed. Help yourself to anything else you need."

"Thanks." She hung uneasily in the doorway, not wanting to appear unappreciative but hoping he'd realize she wanted to move on. "That was very thoughtful."

He watched her with eyes that were far too perceptive. "Everything okay?"

"Yeah," she said, but everything was not okay. She'd let Mike Brown kiss her. And she'd liked it. There were more things wrong with that picture than she could begin to sort through. She forced a smile. "I'm just tired."

"He's a good guy, you know." Jones was still watching her. "A smart-ass, but a good guy."

She didn't have a response for that. It rattled her that he was sensitive to the fact that Brown was on her mind. Was she that transparent?

She met Gabe's eyes, hesitated, then walked into the office. She found a piece of paper and pen, wrote down a name, and handed it to him.

"A project for your spare time."

"Brewster?" Gabe looked from the name to her. "Something you want to share with me?"

"It's the name of Mike's CO in Afghanistan." She lifted a shoulder. "Might be worth checking out."

"Checking out for what, exactly?"

She'd been thinking about this a lot, was now willing to give Mike's CO the benefit of the doubt. "I have a feeling he might be my Deep Throat."

"Seriously?"

"I don't know. Word to the wise? Don't mention this to Mike unless you're up for a lecture."

After shutting herself in the guest bedroom she stripped, pulled on the borrowed sleepwear, and crawled into bed. Exhaustion hit her like an anchor. She was dead on her feet. She should probably feel guilty that Mike was left with the sofa, but she couldn't go there. Just like she couldn't let herself think about that kiss.

As tired as she was, though, she did think about it. Couldn't stop thinking about it. She closed her eyes and smelled him, felt the solid heat of him, the softness of his lips, the rapid beat of his heart pounding against her breasts.

This was not good.

Restless, she rolled to her back. Hot and achy, desperate to get the taste of him out of her head, she stared into the dark, a thousand other thoughts keeping her from sleep. Thoughts that started with Ramon and ended with how good it had felt to be kissed by Mike. She'd married the last man who had stirred her that way.

It was irrational, but even the thought of getting involved with Brown seemed like a betrayal. Ramon had hated him. Based on what Ramon had told her, she'd believed that Brown was a misogynistic, arrogant prick. A user, a grandstander, a bad human being, and a worse teammate.

Because of that, she'd flown to Lima and laid her trap without any guilt. All that had changed, however, once he'd dropped the smart-ass act and she'd seen the anguish Mike lived with.

"You led those men to their deaths." She got right in his face again. *"You got those people caught in the crossfire. Because you were hotdogging. Because you were playing games with people's lives."*

"The hell I was! The hell I did!"

That kind of passion and conviction couldn't be faked. She'd realized right then that he was innocent. At least, intellectually, she'd realized it. Her emotions, however, were dragging their feet. She'd wanted to believe he was guilty. Because believing in Brown meant no longer believing in Ramon.

Her dead husband.

Brown was very much alive. And because of that kiss, *she* felt alive in a way she hadn't felt in a very long time.

Groaning, she rolled to her stomach and pulled the covers over her head. She'd become a cliché. A sex-deprived widow, looking for a little strange to get her through a rough spot.

Sad as that thought was, she almost wished she could chalk it up to that. It had been a long time since she'd been with a man, and she had a healthy libido. But she had never been ruled by her hormones. There had to be more than animal attraction for her to consider a physical relationship. There had to be respect. Affection. Trust. None of which she felt for Mike Brown.

As Gabe had glibly put it: That was her story and she was sticking to it.

What happened between them had been about fatigue. About their startling discovery that Joseph Lawson had been in Afghanistan on the night that had changed her and Brown's lives forever. It was about what they'd both been through to get to this point. It was about raw emotions and anticipation. Her goal couldn't change. Ramon deserved vindication and she was getting close to making it happen.

And Brown—well, he had to be as exhausted as she was. His emotions frayed beyond reweaving. Everything had changed for him tonight. His past. His future. It stood to reason he'd be responsive to and even intuitive about what she'd been feeling when she'd stepped out onto the terrace.

So that kiss, the lingering pangs of longing . . . it was simply about action and reaction, nothing more. This she could comprehend. It made sense.

If only it was even remotely true, because, damn it, she was thinking about him again.

Was he lying awake, too, thinking of her?

Or was he thinking about Cooper? Had he made the call?

It couldn't have been easy for him.

The thought sobered her.

"Oh, for God's sake," she sputtered and threw back the covers. She wasn't going to get any sleep. Not until she knew.

On a deep sigh, she sat up, finger-combed her hair away from her face, and got out of bed. Because he probably could use someone to talk to, she told herself. He wouldn't talk to Gabe because guys didn't spill those kind of personal pains with each other. They trash-talked, joked, and skirted the tough issues. A slap on the back, a quick silent glance. Problem solved.

Not so much. She opened the bedroom door. She knew what it was like to be alone. To cope. To deal. To try to make sense of something that was senseless. Why she felt that it was up to her to make certain Brown was okay, she didn't know.

Or maybe, she thought with disgust, she did.

19

Gabe's office was dark, but there was a light on in the kitchen. She followed the smell of brewing coffee — and found Brown. Alone. Standing with his back to her at the counter, shirtless, barefoot, wearing the pants she'd bought him.

Tan chinos hung low on his hips, emphasizing taut, hard buttocks and a narrow waist, the whipcord leanness of his ribs. There wasn't an ounce of fat on him. He was all defined muscle and ropy sinew. Canned ceiling lights in front of the cabinets cast soft light and shadows on his broad shoulders, showcased a scar beneath his left shoulder blade. It was about three inches long, the skin puckered and raised.

She stared at it, wondering how he'd gotten it, suddenly knowing she'd made a major mistake. She needed to go back to the bedroom.

Then he turned around.

For a long moment neither of them said a word. The soft gurgle of the coffeepot, the ticking of the clock above the sink, and her uneven breathing were the only sounds.

She needed words to break the quiet. "Couldn't sleep?"

He nodded. "Apparently you have the same problem."

Oh, she had lots of problems. Most of them were wrapped up in six-plus feet of this ridiculously gorgeous, shirtless male.

She cleared her throat. "Did you call Cooper?"

Raw emotion put gravel in his voice and so much vulnerability in his eyes that it made her heart hurt. "Yeah. I called."

She didn't know why she was so sensitive to him, and yet she was. "Is he . . . is he coming?"

He leaned back against the counter, crossed his arms over his chest, and propped one bare foot on top of the other. One broad, bare shoulder lifted in a shrug. "I don't know. Doubt it. I got his machine. Left a message."

Her heart dropped. "I'm so sorry you didn't make a connection."

He compressed his lips, gave another shrug, but he wasn't fooling her. He was hurting.

"Look, Eva. I'm a little raw around the edges. Lack of sleep. Ketamine. It's probably not a good idea for you to be here right now."

She agreed, this was not a good idea at all. And yet she stood there.

"Probably not," she said finally, her gaze locked on his.

His eyes were so dark and so tortured as he watched her, trying to get a read on why she was still standing there.

God, why was she? She should definitely go.

But she didn't want to leave him. She wanted to wrap him in her arms and hold him. To feel the press of his lips and be more to him than a warm body who understood this kind of pain.

She stood there. Heart racing. Breath caught.

While he watched her, eyes piercing, eyes searching. Finally understanding what she was offering.

He slowly unfolded his arms, stood up straight and pushed away from the counter, never taking his eyes off her face.

Her heart nearly exploded when he started walking toward her. She held his gaze, smothering a cry of relief when he finally stood in front of her, their bare toes touching, his strong arms drawing her hard against him.

She tipped her head up to his. It was all the invitation he needed. His mouth slammed down on hers and she stopped thinking, stopped doubting, and reacted. She opened her mouth under his, met his tongue with wild, hungry strokes, and wound her arms around his neck when he picked her up and carried her back to the bedroom.

There was no talking. No reasoning. What happened now was all about feeling, all about loss, all about giving as his rough hands tunneled under her shirt and slid against her bare back, then reached for the hem and dragged it over her head.

She gasped as he bent her backward onto the bed and followed her down, his mouth hot and wet and ravenous on her breast. Electric shocks fired to her core as he suckled and licked and fed like a man whose appetite had not been satisfied for a long, long time. Like a man whose desire was in frantic need of slaking. Like a man whose heart was in desperate need of healing.

She arched against him, reached between them, and slipped her hands inside his pants to cup the hard, pulsing length of him. He groaned and gently nipped her, hard enough to sting, soft enough to excite, and rocked his hips into her clasping hand.

Out of body. Out of mind. Her responses were primal, raw and consuming. When he reached down and undid his pants, shoving them away, she was right there with him, wriggling out of her borrowed boxers and parting her thighs, making room for him there, where she was wet and achy and . . . *Oh, God* . . . so much in need.

She bit his shoulder when he touched her, rubbing her all the right ways until she rocked against him, digging her nails into his back and begging him to come inside her.

She didn't know where he got the condom. Only cared that he got it on. Then he was holding himself above her, his biceps bunching, his hands braced on the bed on either side of her waist, nudging her center with the tip of his erection, asking her with his eyes to guide him home. She raised her knees to her chest, open, vulnerable, and did exactly what he wanted. She surrounded him with her hands, tilted her hips toward him, and centered him over her core.

"Hurry," she begged. "Deep," she demanded, gripping his hips and offering everything she had as he slowly entered her. "Hard," she all but whimpered as he stretched her with the thick hot breadth of him and drove to her very center.

Sweet, hot, rough friction, unbelievably perfect. She didn't question how she could barely know him yet *know* him. Instinctively. Know his rhythm as well as she knew her own heartbeat. Know what pleased him. Know what moved him. It wasn't possible to feel this level of intimacy and trust, to feel his need and know exactly how to fulfill it—and yet she did.

He thrust; she met him stroke for stroke. He plunged, she tightened and flexed; losing herself in the union, the incredible sensations, and the welcome weight of him pressing into her.

And then the rush consumed her, transported her to that place where body met mind and pleasure courted pain and nothing, *nothing* mattered but the wild, reckless release that shot her into a pulsating orgasm that had her gasping and grasping him closer and deeper, marrying body and soul.

Mike sat on the bed in the dark with his back to Eva. His feet were on the floor, elbows propped on his thighs, head in his hands. Utterly, totally spent. Lightheaded and sweaty.

She'd fallen asleep behind him.

He was still reeling.

He wasn't a man to rhapsodize about sex. It was a basic human function. Sometimes necessary. Primarily physical, and if done right, purely pleasurable. No hearts, no minds, no souls involved.

But what he'd shared with Eva went beyond anything he'd ever experienced. And he was an experienced man.

"How will I know she's the one, master? The final one? The only one I'll ever want to be with?"

"Well, Grasshopper, when the top of your head blows off and your heart explodes along with it, you can pretty much bet your sorry ass that you've entered dangerous new territory."

He dragged a hand through his hair and fought a flat-out panic that told him he was in some deep, serious shit here.

The woman had played him, for God's sake. She'd drugged him. Cuffed him to a frickin' bed. Held his own gun on him and accused him of every crime known to man short of killing puppies.

Not much more than a day later, he wanted to crawl back under the covers with her, saturate his senses with her scent, the touch of her skin, the taste of her breast, and stay there for the next millennium.

What a putz.

Gabe had known he was in trouble even before he had. Just before he'd turned in, he'd pressed a couple packets of condoms into Mike's hand. "Jenna and I don't need these at the moment."

Mike had glanced at the foil packets with a snort. "And what makes you think I do?"

"Because the chemistry between you two could blow up a science lab."

Had he been that transparent with her, too? Had he let her see how damn needy he was? Is that why she'd come to him? Because she'd known how important—yeah, important—what they'd shared would be to him?

God, he hoped not. Because this couldn't go any-where.

And he didn't want to be *that* man. The man he'd never understood, who needed a woman in his life.

Carefully, so as not to wake her, he made himself leave her bed. Made himself, because he sure as hell didn't want to go. Another first.

He groped around in the dark and finally found his pants, dragged them on, then walked quietly out of the room. Once outside, he leaned back against the door, made a gun out of his index finger and thumb, pointed it at his temple, and pulled the trigger.

20

Thin wisps of daylight peeked beneath a closed blind when Eva woke up after not nearly enough sleep. She hadn't expected to find Mike in her bed come morning and wasn't surprised that he was gone. She *had* expected to feel exactly the way she did: weighed down by a mix of satiation, stupidity, and second thoughts.

Brown knew his way around a woman's body; she'd have been shocked if he didn't. What *had* shocked her was his attention to her needs. Men who looked like him leaned more toward selfish than selfless, in her experience.

Guilt stopped her cold when she realized she'd been comparing him to Ramon. *Don't go there*, she warned herself as she rose and got dressed. Thoughts of Ramon did not belong in a bed she'd shared with a man he had despised. And second thoughts about last night were pointless. There was no taking it back, and she wouldn't if she could. But a replay wasn't going to happen for too many reasons to count, starting and ending with the fact that they both had too much baggage to make any kind of a relationship work.

Relationship? Okay. That soaked it. They'd had great sex, and yes, maybe they'd even tapped into something deeper. They'd both needed an emotional outlet, had given and taken mutual comfort, but that's where it ended.

Her head back on straight, she stepped out of the bedroom. When she saw that the light was on in Gabe's windowless office, she stopped in the open doorway. Both men were already hard at it. Neither saw her there, and she took advantage of the moment to look, really look, at the stunningly beautiful man who was so much more than she'd expected him to be. If he'd lived down to her expectations, this would be much easier.

She could tell by the fatigue etched on Mike's face that he hadn't slept much. Still, he was clearly revved and chomping at the bit to get things moving. Just like it was clear that he was as determined as she was to avoid revisiting last night. Because when he sensed her standing there, he looked up, then directly away.

A classic case of buyer's remorse. *Well, take it times two, buddy.*

She moved on to the kitchen in search of coffee, glad they were on the same wavelength. They had bigger fish to fry. Armed with caffeine and her own determination to let that sleeping dog lie, she walked back to the office and joined them at the small conference table.

"What's happening?"

Without looking up, Mike handed her several sheets of paper.

"And this would be?"

"A roster of known members of United We Denounce."

She scanned the pages of names, then glanced at Mike, who was still practicing zero eye contact. "Who's Barry Hill?" His name was highlighted in yellow on page three.

"Big dog in UWD. And it so happens that I know him—sort of. He was in the Navy around the time I was in boot camp in San Diego. I didn't cross paths with him all that much but I knew who he was. Everyone did. He was a radical even back then. Made a habit of pissing off the wrong people. Wasn't much on respect for authority. *Was* already spouting an antigovernment doctrine."

"While in uniform? Interesting."

"He pulled a lot of other stunts, too. Ended up with a big chicken dinner."

Big chicken dinner, military slang for a bad-conduct discharge, was a step above a less than honorable discharge and generally didn't result in a court-martial.

"Until three months ago," Mike went on, "Hill was Lawson's second in command at UWD. Ran the Idaho operation when Lawson wasn't around."

"So what happened three months ago?" She handed him back the list of names.

"Hill got busted on a weapons charge," Gabe said. "Rather than have his trial draw unwanted attention to UWD, he took one for the team. Pled guilty, did not pass go, did not collect two hundred dollars, and went directly to jail. He's currently doing eight to ten in California State Prison."

"Okay. I get the connection and the story. But how's any of it going to get us what we need from Lawson?"

"Maybe Lawson's still looking to replace Hill," Mike said. "Maybe with a rec from Hill, I could be that man—going in under the name of Dan Walker."

A rush of apprehension hit her broadside. She glanced from Mike to Gabe then back to Mike again. "You're going to try to infiltrate the Idaho compound?"

"Unless you can think of a better way to access Lawson. If I can get close to him, I might find out what he was up to in Afghanistan."

She had to talk him out of this. He could get killed if he went in there. She didn't know which terrified her more: the fact that he could die or the fact that she cared so much about what happened to him.

"Okay, wait. This is a horrible idea. If Lawson and UWD are on the FBI or ATF watch list, how do you know the feds haven't got a team inside already? You could muck up their operation."

"They're not inside. Not yet," Gabe assured her. "But my contacts tell me that's about to change, possibly within a few weeks. As soon as they can assemble a team, they're planting some agents and setting a sting in place. They want to nip in the bud any possibility of Lawson brokering a weapons deal with La Linea."

"That's why I need to do this now," Mike added. "If they get in before I do, it's bad news."

"How could that be bad news? They'd be doing our work for us."

"Get real. They either arrest Lawson and he lawyers up and makes like a clam, or they spook him and he flushes like a quail and goes to ground."

"Either way, there's wildlife involved," Gabe deadpanned, making her grin in spite of everything.

"Either way," Mike restated with a glare, "we'll never get to him if they get in before I do. Nothing changes for either of us."

"You seriously want to interfere with a government operation?" She was determined to find a way to keep him from this crazy scheme.

"You weren't listening. So far there *is* no government operation. I'm not interfering with a damn thing. If anything, I'm helping them out . . . launching a preemptive strike. They'll probably want to give me a medal," he added, unable to keep the bitterness out of his voice.

"Look." He finally met her eyes, and the emotions she saw there made her heart weak. "If going in gives me an opportunity to clear my name, I'm going to do it. That's what this is about, right? Wasn't that your selling point when you goaded me into coming back?"

Yeah. And right now she'd give anything to not have been so convincing. "There's got to be another way. This is too risky."

"What's risky is doing nothing when there's someone out there wanting both of us dead. Or were you planning on hiding out the rest of your life?"

She didn't have an argument for that.

"It's the only way, Eva. UWD is Larson's home base. Everything he is, everything he has, will be in that compound. Personal papers. Photos. Mementos. Spoils of war. Hell, one photo of him on the ground in Afghanistan, shoulder to shoulder with a Taliban operative or in that Mi-8, and I've got proof he was there. Best case scenario, he spills the beans. Worst case, I find enough evidence to get the Joint Spec Ops Command at Bragg to reopen the Operation Slam Dunk file and investigate, and we flush out the top dog."

She still didn't like it. "But if Lawson knows you—"

"He only knows my name. I never saw him face-to-face. And even if he saw photos of me, it was eight years ago. I'm betting he won't remember."

"I'd take that bet." She couldn't believe he'd bank on a memory lapse.

"I've changed since then. I've ma—"

"Do not say *matured*," Gabe put in without looking up from a report, breaking another small chip off the iceberg of tension.

"*Physically* I've matured," Mike clarified without missing a beat. "Probably put on a few pounds. No military buzz cut. No uniform. So I look different. And I'll be going in as Dan Walker, so he won't have any reason to connect the dots."

"The team's already reaching out to Hill." Gabe glanced up and the look on his face told Eva that he understood her concern. "We figure he's going to like the promise of a few perks, possibly a good word at his next parole hearing, in exchange for vouching for 'Dan' if someone from UWD makes the call to verify his story."

Eva knew all about the maneuvering that sometimes took place behind the scenes to get someone to step up and tell the truth—or in this case a bald-faced lie. No harm no foul, as long as no case was affected. No doubt they'd offer Hill better conditions—a single cell, some extra rec time, conjugal visits, help with his family—to get him to play ball.

She still wasn't ready to jump on board. "Even if Hill vouches for you, an organization as secretive and paranoid as UWD won't accept just anyone into their ranks. Lawson will run his own check."

"And he'll find exactly what we want him to. By the time we get done with him, not only will Dan here be besties with Hill, he'll have a documented vendetta against Uncle for all the reasons UWD loves. He'll be a poster child for the cause."

"I still don't like it."

Mike lifted a hand in frustration. "You don't have to like it. I just have to do it."

That pissed her off. "You're right. I don't have to

like it." She looked at Mike, who was busy avoiding eye contact again. "But I can do something about it. I'm going in with you."

That got his full attention. "The hell you are."

"Seriously?" His Lord of the Manor look was *so* not going to work on her. "You're going to dictate what I do? I don't think so. I've got as much at stake in this as you do. Someone's trying to kill me, remember?"

He lifted his chin and shifted gears. "Exactly. And it could be Lawson."

"I've thought about that. It doesn't make any sense that he'd be after me. I wasn't in Afghanistan. My *husband* was, and he's dead."

A shadow darkened Mike's eyes, but she pressed on. "But you're alive, so if Lawson was behind this he should have come after you first. You, Taggart, and Cooper. You're the loose ends."

"You made yourself one when you started digging in the OSD file, Eva."

"Agreed, but I'm not Lawson's loose end. I'm a problem to whoever's calling the shots, and they're above him on the food chain. Possibly on the top. Lawson's tied to him in some way, no doubt about that, but the only reason that shooter aimed at you is because you were with me."

"We've come to the same conclusion." Gabe's admission earned a scowl from Mike. "Haven't pinned down the specifics yet but we agree. The intel we've turned up says Lawson's not top dog in this pack. The money, the calls . . . it's all coming from higher up. Lawson is definitely high on the pecking order, maybe even an equal partner, but he's not making the calls by himself."

"So . . . what are you thinking? An Al Qaeda splinter group? Russian mafia? Chinese Triad?"

"Could be," Mike put in grudgingly, "but our money's on a smaller-scale 'for-profit' organization or someone cutting a deal with one. These guys are in it for the money. That's their bottom line. And while we figure they have business ties to any number of international organized crime syndicates, we see this threat as much smaller potatoes—or it would have been on everyone's radar from Interpol to Langley long before now."

"Agreed," Gabe said. "They're suppliers and their puppet master has hidden himself behind layers of front men and smoke screens. Lawson's still our best lead to get to him. We figured he's had his fingers in illegal weapons and international drug trade for years. Most likely he was into both in Afghanistan, and hasn't changed his MO since. This tie with Lawson and the Juarez cartel? It's just another link in the chain. We're thinking that they might have been locked out of the cartel until Hernandez was caught and convicted. New leadership equals new openings, and they didn't waste any time getting their foot in the door."

"Do you think that whoever leaked the OSD file to me is tied up with them?" She and Mike had talked about this on the flight and they had agreed that it was most likely someone on the ground in Afghanistan at the time OSD had gone down.

"Like someone in the organization with a vendetta?" Gabe shook his head. "That doesn't wash for me. In the first place, disgruntled lieutenants generally turn up dead. End of problem. In the second, even if there was some infighting going on, why would someone in the organization give it to you? Yeah, you're CIA, but there are other channels they could have taken with much more impact if they want to bring someone down.

"I agree with Mike. Your Deep Throat has a personal connection to either you or Ramon. Possibly to the One-Eyed Jacks. We think we're looking at a bid for restitution here, setting wrongs right. Something this person couldn't do before."

"So he waited for the right time to give me the file," she concluded.

"Or waited for the courage," Gabe agreed.

She and Gabe exchanged a look that told her he was with her in thinking Brewster might be their man.

Mike grunted. "Takes a real hero to feed info anonymously, then lay low while someone else takes the flack."

Gabe stood and stretched. "We're running records on any name that turns up that's even remotely connected to Lawson, United We Denounce, and Operation Slam Dunk. That's a lot of names. So far, nothing, but we'll get there." He headed for the office door with his coffee mug. "Anyone need a refill?"

Mike held out his mug.

Gabe took it and headed for the kitchen but stopped at the door. "Eva, Mike said you mentioned having access to staffing records for DOD. We can backdoor access them eventually, but if you have more direct access, we might be able to find your mystery source a lot faster."

"Absolutely. How secure is your computer?"

He grinned.

"Got it. I'll write it all out. Once your people get in, they won't have any trouble running a search."

Gabe left for the kitchen, and suddenly she and Mike were alone in the office with a silence as big as the bed they'd made love in.

He leaned back in his chair and clasped his hands behind his head. "Let's get this settled right now. You're not coming with me."

"Look. If it's about what happened last night—"

"It's not," he said quickly. Too quickly. "It's about you slowing me down."

She laughed. "Try again. Or have you already forgotten who got the drop on whom in Lima?"

"I was drunk."

"You were stupid. And you weren't drunk when I clipped your cheek." Though the swelling had gone down a little, he had the beginnings of a shiner this morning.

And oh, he was looking at her now. He suddenly stood, did the old rooster strut, puffed out his chest, and stuck his face right in hers. "You're not going, Eva. End of discussion."

"Said the king of the world." She decided she didn't feel bad about the bruise on his cheek after all. "You are such a piece of work."

"Children," Gabe cut in as he stepped back into the office. "Do I need to put you both on time-out?"

They stood for several long moments, noses almost touching, gazes locked and blazing . . . until something other than irritation fired through Eva's blood and warned her to stand down. A vivid, visceral image of last night, two bodies moving together in the dark, so close no air moved between them, so hot the touch of skin on skin set them on fire.

She backed away, crossed her arms over her chest, and settled herself down. Judging by the sudden weight of his breaths, Mike had experienced a little midnight flashback, too.

"She could be an asset, Mike." Gabe broke the uncomfortable silence.

Mike whipped his gaze to Gabe.

"It's true." Gabe held the line in the face of Mike's glare. "Lawson knows he needs to keep the ranks content. Content men equals malleable disciples. Going in as a couple enhances your cover," he added, building on his point. "Not to mention it gives you twice the eyes, twice the ears. And it's pretty clear to me that Eva can handle herself."

Mike clenched his jaw. "Traitor."

Gabe arched a brow. "Sticks and stones, bro? That's all you've got?"

The look on Mike's face said, yeah, it was. He

knew as well as Eva did, as well as Gabe did, that there wasn't one good reason she shouldn't go with him and a dozen reasons why she should.

"Fine." His tone said it was not fine. "But let it be known I'm agreeing under protest."

"I'll make sure to write that down," Gabe said with an eye roll. "Now quit pouting and let's hammer out a plan of action."

21

When you worked for a bureaucracy as large as the U.S. government, even an agency as clandestine as the CIA, you got used to wheels turning slowly. But slow apparently wasn't in the Black Ops, Inc. agency's wheelhouse, because by one p.m., the team pretty much had Mike and Eva's backgrounds in place.

"Study everything in each folder inside out and backward, so by the time you touch down tomorrow, the stories will be as natural as breathing." Gabe handed them both thick files that had arrived by courier a few minutes ago.

They'd moved out to the terrace after being cooped up in the small office most of the morning. Birds sang, flowers bobbed, traffic rolled by in a muted rumble ten stories below. Eva found some shade from the hot July sun, sat down on a chaise, and paged slowly through her folder. In addition to a detailed background sheet, there were various forms of ID and credit cards.

"So where's mine?" Mike asked, looking over her

shoulder and noticing that he hadn't gotten a credit
card.

"Dan's credit rating sucks, I'm afraid," Gabe said
with a smile as he spread duplicate information on
a patio table and got comfortable. "Okay," he continued, "let's go over this. Eva—as you can see, we
kept it fairly simple. You're going in as Maria Walker,
Dan's wife. Maiden name: Gomez. We want both
Dan and you to offer something of value to UWD.
Your cover is an attorney."

"If I can't be convincing at that, we're in big trouble," she said, scanning the detailed background information as Gabe thumbnailed it for her.

"You're the only child of a single mother, an illegal alien, which makes your history and family ties
harder to trace. You grew up in Miami, got into a
little trouble as a juvenile—shoplifting, some petty
larceny—and ended up before a judge who gave you
the option of doing time or enlisting in the Army. You
wisely chose the Army."

Eva was impressed by the depth of the background
they'd created for her.

"During basics, your story goes that you were assaulted by a senior enlisted soldier," Gabe went on,
"but the Army swept it under the rug and told you to
soldier up and keep your mouth shut. It pissed you off."

"And between the inequitable treatment and the
fact that my male attacker got off scot-free, I made a
decision that I'd never be that helpless again. Good
thinking."

Gabe nodded. "So you took advantage of all the educational opportunities the service provided, including the GI bill, after you separated. You were a staff sergeant by that time, by the way."

It was all in there. Dates of service, what college she'd attended, where she'd gone to law school.

"When you passed the bar—first attempt, by the way—you ended up a public defender in Sacramento, which is where you eventually met handsome Dan here."

"Apparently I was even irresistible in my prison orange," Mike said absently as he pulled out a chair and sat down at the table opposite Gabe.

"Mr. Irresistible," Gabe said dryly, "is a little more hard-core. Grew up in the mountain west, which is true, so that helps. He was the child of a far, far right-wing father who was also a strict disciplinarian. Read: He did not believe in sparing the rod to spoil the child. Dan hightailed it off the farm as soon as he graduated high school but with no skills, no college degree, and no money, he couldn't find work. He eventually enlisted in the Navy—where he encountered Hill, someone his own age, who spouted the same doctrine as his old man. And suddenly the whole "less government, more people" message began to resonate."

"I was very impressionable," Mike said.

Eva had his number by now. His sense of humor was his coping mechanism. Tension, anger, guilt . . . he hid it all behind a wisecrack. He couldn't help himself.

"So you did your four-year hitch in the Navy, got out, couldn't find steady work, and drifted from odd job to odd job for several years. Began to resent the establishment that you felt repressed your earning ability. Got mixed up with a bad crowd in Sacramento. Got nabbed on a couple B&Es and got off on technicalities, but not learning the error of your ways, you got busted knocking off a liquor store where a clerk was shot. Not killed, and you weren't responsible, but you were an accomplice in an armed robbery so you were pretty much screwed."

"Enter Maria Gomez, my court-appointed attorney?" Mike speculated.

"The same. She repped you, got your sentence reduced from ten to eight, of which you served six— early out for good behavior—in California State Prison. You kept to yourself while you were there, kept your nose clean, no gang affiliations, but—"

"But I ran into Barry Hill again in prison. Seemed like kismet, right? And Hill became my new best friend."

"Exactly. Now back to Dan and Maria. Romance blossomed while Dan did his time. Maria resigned from her PD position and moved to Soledad to be closer to the facility and you. While there, Maria did pro bono work for a local woman's shelter and paid her rent working part-time for a small law firm.

"Dan, on the other hand, had become a student of Lawson's teachings and a devotee of him and UWD.

When you got out last month, you and Maria got married and you convinced her you wanted to join the movement."

He stopped and looked from her to Mike. "Any questions? Issues?"

"Yeah. Maria will be of value to UWD because she's an attorney. What do I bring to the table— besides my good looks and malleable mind?"

"There are so many places I could go with that, but I'll restrain myself." Gabe actually grinned. "You're offering up a strong back, a military background, proof that you aren't afraid to mix it up—your recent record supports that—and the possibility of bringing in more recruits. Numbers are king when you're trying to sustain a movement. Mob mentality and strength in numbers aren't just clichés. They're the foundation for these radical organizations.

"So once you've earned Lawson's trust, you convince him you have a couple buddies who believe in the cause and want to recruit them."

Disappointment flashed in Mike's eyes for an instant. She knew he was thinking of Taggart and Cooper. He was thinking that they should be the ones going in with him.

"Most likely it'll be me and Joe," Gabe said, breaking a silence suddenly rife with regret. "The more boots on the ground, the more we find out about Lawson and his extracurricular activities."

"This is really good work," Eva said, "but you know they'll run a records check—you have to figure they've got someone in the ranks that can hack into IAFIS."

The Integrated Automated Fingerprint Identification System was a national fingerprint and criminal history system available to local, state, and federal partner agencies to assist in solving and preventing crime and catching criminals and terrorists. She had no doubt that UWD had someone in law enforcement they could tap to run both Maria's and Dan's backgrounds.

"And Dan Walker's history will all be there by the time you two make contact with UWD. It'll also be supported by strategically planted federal reports that, prior to his conviction, mark Dan as a low-level activist with a pattern of sporadic radical rhetoric against the government—a few arrests involving protest rallies, maybe a concealed-weapons charge or two prior to his big downward slide."

Mike scratched his jaw. "I've been a busy boy."

"The perfect candidate for anarchy, madness, and mayhem. Maria's military background, education history, employment, everything will be on file where it needs to be. Same for Dan's criminal record. All you have to do is sell it."

Very clearly implied was that they also had to sell the married-and-in-love act.

Gabe glanced at the diamond stud in Mike's ear.

"I know. I need to lose the rock."

"A long time ago." The look on Gabe's face told a bigger tale of what he thought of the earring.

Mike laughed. "What? You don't like my bling?"

"You're lucky someone hasn't ripped your ear off, going after it in a bar fight."

"Lucky's my middle name."

"Well, leave the hair, Lucky. If Lawson saw photos of you it would have been with a military haircut. Plus that scruffy I'm-pretty-but-I'm-not-anyone's-bitch look has *badass* written all over it."

"So glad we're not talking skinhead." Mike ran a hand through his hair. "I can fake the low IQ but I don't have the tats to pull that off."

"UWD has been very careful to disassociate themselves from the white-supremacist movement," Eva said. "The Randy Weaver case was the first nail in their coffin, but the Aryan Nation still held a strong presence in Idaho until about a decade ago. You remember the Victoria Keenan incident, where guards at the AN compound were found responsible for the assault on her and her son?"

Both men nodded.

"That pretty well sank them. The Aryan Nation has effectively become history in Idaho. A multimillion-dollar civil suit followed and basically bankrupted the organization. Everything I've read says Lawson has been smart and sensitive to the bad feelings the local residents have about the white-supremacist group. He doesn't want the bad press, so he's limited his rhetoric to his anarchy platform. It's just as wrong but not as distasteful to the public."

"Show's how savvy he is," Mike agreed.

"We should probably do a little something about your look, Eva," Gabe said, turning to her. "You good with that?"

"Whatever it takes."

"I need to take shots of both of you and e-mail the pictures to B.J. and Stephanie so they can pull together your photo IDs."

B.J. and Stephanie, Eva had learned, provided much of the intelligence gathering and dissemination, and coordinated ID documentation for the team. B.J.'s background included the military and the Defense Intelligence Agency—DIA. Stephanie came directly from the National Security Agency—NSA. Both had joined the BOI organization after marrying operatives Rafe Mendoza and Joe Green respectively. Both, Gabe had assured her earlier, were digging into Brewster. So far he was whistle clean.

"Almost forgot." Gabe opened another envelope. Two wedding rings fell out into his palm.

As he handed one to each of them, Eva and Mike both glanced up and locked gazes. The heat that flashed in Mike's eyes told Eva he was thinking exactly what she was: They were going to be spending several days and nights in close quarters as a married couple.

She knew all about close quarters with Mike Brown. Close quarters in the dark, naked and begging him to come inside her.

Gabe cleared his throat, and she snapped her gaze to his like a kid caught cheating on a spelling test. He didn't mention the very obvious exchange between her and Mike but he couldn't have missed the sexual tension. The small office felt like it had heated by fifty degrees.

"Might as well start getting used to wearing them." She'd slipped hers on, not surprised they knew her ring size, when a phone rang from inside the apartment.

"That would be the bat phone." Gabe pushed away from the table and stood. "HQ," he clarified. "Be right back. In the meantime, everything we've got on the UWD compound grounds and surrounding area is in there." He handed them each another envelope. "Have fun."

Eva was glad for the diversion. Apparently Mike was, too. He dug into the packet like it was the Holy Grail.

As she sifted through photographs, aerial maps, and detailed diagrams of the topography, waterways, and roads, she couldn't help but glance surreptitiously at his long, strong hand and the plain gold band circling his ring finger.

When Gabe joined them outside again a few minutes later, the look on his face had the hair on Eva's nape standing on end. "What? What's happened?"

"I asked Joe to go check out your apartment this morning to see if there were any signs anyone had been there. The fire department had already arrived in force when he got there."

"Oh, God." The blood drained from her head and a rush of dizziness filled the vacuum.

"I'm sorry, Eva. Your apartment and the two adjacent ones were destroyed in a fire that broke out right before dawn."

She felt Mike's hand on her shoulder.

"Was anyone hurt?" Please, God. Don't let sweet Mrs. Bolger be hurt . . . or worse, dead. If anyone was harmed because someone was after her—

"No," Gabe broke in before she could finish the horrible thought. "Everyone got out okay." He gave her a kind smile. "Even your neighbor's cat. I'm sorry. Of course it was deliberate, but the arson report will no doubt come back that it was faulty wiring, a gas leak . . . whatever. These guys after you are pros. They'll make certain there won't be an investigation."

She breathed deep, working to regain her composure. She willed herself not to think about everything she'd lost. The artwork, her favorite chair—those were just things. She could replace them. But the photographs of family, friends. Ramon. Those were gone forever.

The sense of loss and violation she felt could be crippling if she let it. She was determined not to.

"The police are going to be looking for Eva." Mike glanced up at Gabe, his brows drawn. "When she doesn't show up, they'll start a search for anyone not accounted for in the fire."

"It's okay." She breathed deep, marshalling her

composure. "My parents and my boss all think I'm on vacation in Italy. But they'll try to reach me to tell me about the fire. If they can't get in touch, they'll panic. I need to tell them."

Mike looked at Gabe. "Can we make that happen?"

Gabe looked grim. "I think we have to."

22

He stood in front of floor-to-ceiling windows of bulletproof glass, in a lushly appointed apartment overlooking the sprawling, bustling city. And felt like a fucking prisoner. While five thousand square feet of luxury did not equate to a prison, the fact that he was basically captive here did. He was a captive of circumstance until this Eva Salinas/Mike Brown mess was sorted out and it was safe to resume normal operations. Anyone who might be suspicious of his absence assumed he was on a much overdue vacation in the French countryside.

Twenty stories below, sun baked a pavement lined with compact cars maneuvering the Quebec rush hour like a string of worker ants, all hot-wired to serve their queen. The queen in his world was the mighty dollar. Always had been. Always would be. He was only paid, however, if he kept his suppliers happy. And he could only keep them happy if he didn't blow his carefully nurtured cover. That cover was his first line of defense.

Because of Eva Salinas, that line was threatening to crumble. Because of Eva Salinas, he was hiding like a common criminal. The rage that indignity dealt him was eclipsed only by his determination to repair the damage before it got out of control.

Crossing his arms over his chest, he brooded about his dilemma. She had to die, of course. Both her and Brown. If Jane had fulfilled her obligation, all of this would be behind him. But she hadn't, and they'd both paid the price. He'd been relieved when his man had delivered her, weak and in pain, but stoically bearing up, a few hours ago. She rested comfortably now. A doctor had seen her. And he had insisted she take the pain medication, unable to bear seeing her in such agony.

He was not accustomed to feeling tenderness for a woman—for another human being, for that matter. That Jane provoked not only tenderness but an unfamiliar fear of loss was not something he chose to analyze. She mattered in a way that his well-bred wife and pampered children had never mattered.

On an equally disturbing front, neither Brown nor Eva had turned up yet. Which royally pissed him off.

Jaw clenched, he walked to the bar and poured two fingers of whiskey from a $2,500 bottle of Bruichladdich Forty. He savored the first sip, then walked across the Italian marble floor and sank down onto one of a trio of white leather sofas flanking a spectacular saltwater reef aquarium that spanned the width of the room.

A spotted ray—his favorite, next to the stingray from which he'd taken his code name—floated across the panorama, blissfully unmindful of a reef shark skimming along the white sand below him. Flashes of purple, red, and yellow darted by, all fish of various sizes and shapes. The variety of colorful sea life, live rock, and luminous, undulating corals was designed to soothe and mesmerize, but the brilliant spectacle barely registered. He was looking inward. And all he saw was red.

He'd made a huge mistake. He'd attempted to handle Eva's inquisitiveness by monitoring her activities, waiting for her to back off on her impromptu investigation. He still didn't know what had set her off in that direction. He just knew it couldn't be good. And that he'd let sentiment blind him to grim necessity. He'd also underestimated her determination. He would never make either mistake again.

Where the hell had she gone? Where was Brown?

Deductive reasoning pointed to one or both of them returning to the States. Probably D.C. It only made sense. And it only made sense that they were working together—whether as adversaries or allies, time would tell. Either way, they were more dangerous together. Like dynamite was dangerous.

He had to get to them, silence them, before they found out the truth. If that happened, his current problems would look about as lethal as an overdue book fine.

All of his resources were focused on finding them. While he had hoped the team he'd sent to toss her apartment would lead him to her or Brown, or at the very least turn up some clue to what had triggered her investigation into OSD and Afghanistan, they'd found nothing.

Her apartment had been clean, but in case she'd hidden something damaging there, he'd made certain it was destroyed. Because his team was competent, any possibility of determining the fire was due to arson was a solid 95 percent in his favor. An empty apartment, with a coffeepot negligently left turned on or a faulty TV or other small appliance, would be the first place an investigator would look for cause. And the only place when they had evidence that an electrical fire had, indeed, been the culprit.

Regardless, they were still at square one. The only positive note was that if Salinas and Brown had what they needed to expose him, it would have hit the papers by now. He'd have been notified that charges had been filed and an international manhunt would be underway. None of that was in the wind.

Which meant the clock ticked for all of them. If he found them first, they died and he won. He had every intention of winning.

His secure phone rang. When he saw the return number, his pulse spiked. The call was from Mark Barnes, his cyber-surveillance guru. "Tell me you have news."

"Someone hacked into the CIA database using the Salinas woman's user ID and passcode."

That someone had to be Eva or someone acting on her behalf. For the first time since Jane had called to inform him of her failure, he felt some relief.

23

Mike and Eva left Dulles at 8:30 the next morning and after an eight-hour flight with a connection in Denver, landed in Spokane, Washington, around 2:30 p.m. mountain time. The black Jeep Cherokee that was waiting for them was well used and rode like a lumber wagon as Mike drove down Highway 2, heading for Squaw Valley, Idaho, and the UWD compound. If Mapquest and their calculations were correct, they were looking at another hour or so tops.

Beside him in the passenger seat, Eva consulted an area road map. He still couldn't get used to the way she looked as Maria. They'd done their best to drab her down. Her face was free of makeup. A quick dye job had turned her hair a muddy brown that she'd pulled back into a no-nonsense ponytail. And just in case her washed-out jeans, loose blue tank top, and worn tennis shoes didn't finish the look, they'd given her a pair of wire-rimmed glasses.

In theory, everything combined should have transformed her into the equivalent of a brown paper bag.

Fat chance.

They could shave her head and dress her in a gun-nysack and she'd still take his breath away. She was that stunning. Add in the vulnerability factor that the loss of her apartment had triggered, and piggy-back that onto a rock-solid—some might call it pig-headed—resolve to see this through to the end . . . and hell, he was flat-out, un-freaking-believably cap-tivated by everything about her.

Yeah, *captivated.* Who was he, Lord-freaking-Byron, all of a sudden? He didn't think in those terms. Hot. Smokin'. Sexilicious. Those were his kind of words. What the hell was wrong with him?

Concentrate, sucker. And cut yourself some slack. Spending hours on end on a plane and now in this ve-hicle with her didn't help. Thinking about last night, when he'd wanted to haul his sorry self up off the sofa where he hadn't been getting any sleep, knock on her bedroom door, and invite himself back into her bed, didn't help.

Dipstick—party of one. Your table is ready.

He did *not* get why this woman messed up his head so badly. He hadn't met a bottle of pisco that screwed him up this much.

But right now, *right now,* he had to get his head out of his ass, get it firmly in the game, and keep both of them alive.

A deer shot up from a ditch and he had to break hard and swerve to miss it, forcing his attention back to his driving.

"That was close."

He glanced at Eva, then back at the four-lane highway, glad he was wearing shades so she couldn't read his thoughts through his eyes. Close? She didn't know the half of it.

"Been a long time since I've used anything but a GPS for directions." Her businesslike tone grounded him to the task at hand.

In keeping with her living-on-a-shoestring budget and with his just-out-of-prison-with-no-work cover, they were running strictly low-tech. They had one buy-minutes-as-you-go cell phone between them, and the paper map since they had no GPS capability.

They also had two handguns tucked in the glove box—a Makarov, the commie version of a Walther PPK that Dan, recently released from the pen, would have bought on the sly and on the cheap, and hers was a Taurus PT92, a reasonably decent version of the handgun that Maria had carried in the Army before she'd separated from military service over a decade ago. They had no doubt that the cell and both guns would have to be surrendered before they stepped one foot into the compound. All fringe groups had a tendency to be a tad bit paranoid, but to come in carrying showed allegiance to the cause. *Can we say trigger-happy, ladies and gents?*

But without weapons they were toast if things got dicey, because once they hit that compound, they were on their own. The Squaw Valley compound was 540 acres surrounded by mountains and tall timbered forest. The moon wasn't this remote. There would be no backup team lurking within earshot and no way to get a team anywhere close. Planning was their backup. Luck was their backup. Good acting was their backup. Stupid? Probably. Other options? None.

They did, however, have a contingency plan that had been put into play before they'd lifted off from Dulles, and could potentially even up the odds a bit if push came to shove. They'd flown to Spokane under yet different aliases, then ditched those IDs and became Dan and Maria Walker once they'd landed. As promised, Gabe had everything set up. BOI contacts on the ground had left the Jeep in airport short-term parking, the keys wired under the license plate.

Carrying a small amount of cash and two duffel bags with lightweight black night gear for recon hidden in the lining, a few regular clothes and basic necessities, they'd gotten in their ride and headed toward the Idaho panhandle.

"We stay on Highway 2—we'll be down to two lanes soon, by the way—and take it all the way to Priest River. Shouldn't be much more than a half hour. Then it's only twenty miles, give or take, to the UWD compound."

Before they went any farther, Mike wanted to check out the gear Gabe had set up for them.

The forest had been cut way back from the highway to make room for power lines and waterways, but when he turned off onto a gravel road less than a half

mile later, they were suddenly up close and personal
with towering pines, dense forest, and total isolation.
A harbinger of things to come.

To make certain no one would see them, he
turned onto what looked like a park access road and
drove about a tenth of a mile until they were swallowed by trees.

"Let's see what we've got."

He tossed his shades on the dash, then got out,
rounded the vehicle, and opened the passenger-side
door. Reaching into the glove box, he dug around
under the pistols until he got his hands on the screwdriver he knew he would find there. With Eva keeping watch, he started loosening the screws securing
the interior door panel. When he carefully removed
the panel and got a look inside, he let out a low, appreciative whistle. "Lord love a duck. Would you look
at that."

Along with an emergency phone they were to use
daily to check in with Gabe and a pair of mini night-
vision binoculars, both affixed to the metal door with
Velcro straps, was a short-barreled M-4 rifle with a
seven-inch stock. Two full magazines and several
boxes of ammo were also strapped into the door.

"Nice." He ran his fingers over the stock. "Not for
dinking people in the head at five hundred yards, but
one of these babies can hit a golf ball at one hundred
yards. And up close, the muzzle flash would probably
blind God." He glanced at Eva. "Ever shot one of
these?"

She nodded. "Firing range only. But I can handle it."

He replaced the panel, then quickly checked the driver's-side door. Two pistols identical to the ones in the glove compartment, plus ammo for both, were fastened inside.

"I think you could call that a very special delivery," Eva said.

Mike grunted in agreement. "Let's hope we don't need to use them."

After putting the door panel back in place, they headed back to the highway.

Neither of them had had more than snacks on the go since they'd gone wheels up that morning, and since this might be their last chance to grab a square meal for a while, Mike stopped in the little town of Priest River long enough for them to eat. The Feed Store was a combo restaurant and yes, livestock feed store, and sat right next to the railroad tracks and the Pend Oreille River.

It was a good time to sit down on something that wasn't moving, take a deep breath, and reassess. A little over a half an hour later, they walked back outside. It was almost four thirty, but he wasn't worried about losing daylight. In July the days were long, even in the mountain west. But he had done a lot of reassessing over his burger and fries.

He took a good look around him as they walked down Main Street toward the Jeep. They were in a valley surrounded by mountains on every side. *In the middle of nowhere. With nothing but our wits and our purpose to get us through what happens next.*

This was it, he realized, as he settled in behind the wheel and slipped his dark glasses back over his eyes. The point of no return. He knew that he might not walk out of the UWD compound alive, and he was willing to take that chance—with *his* life.

But not with hers.

They were 100 percent on their own. The guns had made it real. The isolation as they'd driven deeper and deeper into the panhandle made it clear. No cavalry would ride in at the eleventh hour to save them if things went sideways. Help would be hours away. He was squared away with that. But Eva—God, he never should have let her come along.

Feeling the weight of her safety like an elephant on his shoulders, he made one last-ditch effort.

"It's not too late." He looked across the seat at her, wishing that just once, when he looked at her, his heart didn't jump like a frog on speed. "I can put this off until tomorrow. Drive you back to Spokane tonight, get you on a flight back to D.C. It's not a problem."

She already had that closed look on her face.

"Damn it, Eva, listen to me. You don't have to do this."

She stopped in the process of buckling her seat belt, lowered her chin to her chest, and let out a heavy breath. After a long moment, she met his eyes. "Take off those glasses so I can see your eyes and know you're listening."

He did as he was told, then waited. But not for long.

"I'm only going to say this one more time," she said with crisp efficiency. "Whatever happens out here, it's not on you, okay? It's on me. Going in is *my* choice. So stop feeling responsible for me. Stop trying to protect me. I can handle myself, but if you don't start treating me as an equal, this is never going to work."

Her brown eyes were almost black with conviction, and damn if he didn't fall a little deeper into whatever mess he was falling into that he refused to give a name.

"And stop calling me Eva," she added with a glare. "It's Maria. I may be your loving wife, but you're indebted to me for getting you an early out and for sticking with you until you got released. And you are definitely not the boss of me. Get used to it."

The last thing he'd expected to punctuate the end of this conversation was a grin. But damn, if she didn't worm one out of him.

"Okay, *wife*." He shifted into gear, checked in his rearview, and pulled out onto the street. "If it's not too much to ask, please navigate us the hell out of here, would you? It's time to get this show back on the road."

And it was time for him to accept that she was in to stay. She was also right. If they were going to pull this off, he had to stop worrying about her and start working with her.

• • •

"Aside from the fact that this land already belonged to Lawson, it's pretty clear why he picked this valley as UWD's base of operations," Eva said as they drove deeper and deeper into endless stands of tall pine and cedar.

They'd turned off the highway onto gravel several miles ago. Spindly birch and maple trees sprouted up here and there but the ponderosa was king, so towering and dense that in most places sunlight never hit the forest floor.

"You want seclusion and privacy, it doesn't get any better than this," Mike agreed.

The five hundred–plus acres that made up Squaw Valley was private land surrounded by the Idaho Panhandle National Forest—unless you were a long time local who still called it by its original name, Kaniksu. This road was the only way in or out, if horsepower under a hood was involved.

"In addition to the Priest River, two creeks run through the UWD property," Eva added, studying her map. "The Upper West Branch and Good Creek. So there's their water supply. Where do you suppose they get their power? Generators?"

"Could be. More likely, they've tapped into the electrical lines that run along the road. The power company probably wouldn't even know if they did it."

"Do you think we can get cell service up here?"

He'd been wondering the same thing. "Guess we'll find out." With the size of the mountains they'd been driving through, there were bound to be dead zones.

"I'm thinking it's a good thing we're here in July," Mike said. At Eva's instruction, he turned off the gravel and onto a dirt road. The power lines that had run parallel to the main road disappeared from view. "Bet this sandy dirt turns into mucky ruts once it starts raining."

"Slow down a little." Eva looked from her map and concentrated on the road ahead of them. "We should be getting close to the next turnoff."

"Within a couple of miles, if those 'Keep Out' and 'No Trespassing' signs are any indication. Can't say they don't give fair warning."

"There's supposed to be an old forest-fire lookout tower around here. Wait. There it is. Turn left there. The entrance should be at the end of this road—less than a quarter of a mile."

He braked suddenly. Jammed the Jeep into park, turned off the ignition, and stared at the dark glasses he'd whipped off and held in his hand.

"What?" she asked after several seconds ticked by.

He turned his head slowly. "I need a moment."

She looked puzzled, then amused. "A *moment*? You need a . . . *moment*?"

"Okay, fine. I *want* a moment."

Then he reached for her.

She had to know what he was going to do. The question was, would she let him? He didn't give her time to decide. He dragged her against him and kissed her. Kissed her as if yesterday was nonexistent, tomorrow would never come, and *this* moment was all that mattered.

Because it was. All of his fear for her, all of his second-guessing, his bafflement over this crazy hold she had over him—*all of it*—dissolved into feelings that only made sense when he had her in his arms and his mouth was pressed over hers.

Her taste alone was insane, intoxicating. Yet unbelievably grounding. The feel of her in his arms was, hell, it was perfect. And if he'd learned anything that one single night, those few amazing hours in her bed, it was that what he felt for Eva Salinas didn't have to make sense. Not when he was kissing her. Not when he was inside her. Not when she was gasping his name and moving against him with an abandon that she could never have given in to if there wasn't something important happening between them.

But that wasn't happening now. He pulled away, pressed his forehead to hers, and dug for control. There were other important issues they still had to deal with. Ramon was one. History was another. The snake pit they were about to set foot in was yet another.

"We will finish this," he whispered, then dove back for one final taste. "When this is over, we will figure this out and we will finish it."

As abruptly as he'd grabbed her, he let her go. Sliding back behind the wheel, he cranked the ignition and glanced at her. Her lips still parted, her nipples erect against her thin knit top, her expression was slumberous and sexy—and damn if it didn't make him smile.

"Ready?" he asked as if he hadn't just kissed her into next week. He was pretty pleased with himself for not only catching her off guard but for bringing her on board. If they weren't where they were, he'd have dragged her out of the Jeep, flattened her up against the door, and taken her right there. And she would have let him.

"Ready?" he asked again, his voice low this time, intimate, and she finally snapped to.

"Um . . . yeah."

Oh, yeah. She definitely would have let him.

He felt smug as hell. So sue him.

To be continued. "Then let's do this."

Her hand on his arm stopped him. The dreamy look in her eyes had been replaced by something that sobered him.

"This isn't going to be easy for you, Mike. Coming face-to-face with Lawson. Buddying up to him. Pretending to drink the Kool-Aid. You sure you can handle it? Because you really need to be sure."

She wanted guarantees that he could keep his cool, contain his anger, and play nice with the man who had ruined his life and was responsible for ending the lives of some of the best men he'd ever known.

"I can handle it." He *had* to handle it.

She searched his eyes, then squeezed his arm. "Then let's do this."

He put on his sunglasses and shifted into gear.

They were as prepared as they could get. They both knew their own and each other's cover as well as they knew "Twinkle, Twinkle Little Star." They'd studied the intel on the Squaw Valley area and the encampment. They knew the United We Denounce doctrine as well as they knew their own faces. All they needed was to get into the compound.

Which would be no easy feat, if the size of the guns held by the men in the camouflage pickup that suddenly roared up to meet them was any indication.

24

"You can't read the signs?" The guy riding shotgun—literally—stepped out of the pickup, a big-ass, 16-gauge double-barrel propped against his shoulder. Dust rolled up from under the truck where its oversized tires had skidded to a stop on the dirt road.

Mike squinted through his shades and sized up Mr. Personality with the 16-gauge. He put him at around forty. He was broad-shouldered, beefy, bald, and judging by the swagger and the scowl, saw himself as bad to the bone. Two guys, a few years younger with more wiry builds, sported short dark hair and beards. Both stood in the truck bed, elbows propped on the roof; each had one foot hiked up on the rim of the box in a combative stance. One carried an AR-15 assault rifle. The other held a shotgun that would have been a twin to Mr. Personality's if the barrel hadn't been sawed off to next to nothing. All three wore camo T-shirts, cargo pants, combat boots, and varying degrees of a Hitler complex. Mike guessed that the guy behind the wheel was decked out and armed pretty much the same, but couldn't see him clearly behind the dust on the windshield.

Mike glanced at Eva. "Showtime." Then he opened the door and stepped out of the Jeep.

"That's far enough."

He lifted his arms away from his sides to show he'd come in peace. "I'm looking for Joseph Lawson. Maybe you boys can help me."

Dead silence. Stone-cold glares.

"This is the UWD compound, right?"

"Don't matter what this is," Sawed-off said, all slow and hostile. "'Cause it's no business of yours. You're on private property, *boy*. Best you turn around and head back the way you came."

Mike stood his ground. "Came a long way, fellas. All I want to do is see Lawson." Not deal with jerk-offs like you, his tone made clear. "I was told I could find him here."

Personality glanced over his shoulder at Sawed-off, then back at Mike. He was close enough by now that Mike could see SIMMONS stenciled on the pocket of his T-shirt. "Is that a fact? Told by who?"

Mike returned his glare for a tense moment, then finally gave it up with a hint of exasperation. "Barry Hill."

Hill's name got exactly the reaction he'd been shooting for. Simmons wasn't the brightest bulb in the fixture, and the look on his face gave away his surprise. "Hill? What have you got to do with Hill?"

"That's between me and Lawson," Mike said, making his impatience clear. "Look. I'm not here to cause trouble. I'm just here to talk to your boss. Now is he here or not?"

Simmons got a real mean smile on his face. "I asked you to tell me how you know Hill." It was no longer a question but a demand.

"I don't have to tell you anything." Another show of irritation that Simmons found amusing.

"Now, see, you're wrong about that. You don't get to Lawson unless you get through me."

Mike pretended to consider, then surrender. "Yes. I know Hill. He said he and Lawson were tight. Brothers in the movement."

Simmons still wasn't buying it. "I got a little problem with your story. No way you coulda talked to Hill."

"Because he's in stir?" When hostility turned to surprise then to interest, Mike put a cap on it. "He joined the club a couple months before I got out."

That had them all looking at him in a new light.

"Look, I'm not on the run. I did my time. Now I'm square. Don't owe anybody anything. I'm not looking for trouble and I didn't bring any trouble with me."

"*She* looks like trouble." Sawed-off glanced at Eva.

Mike ignored the reference to Eva. Just like he ignored Eva, something he knew instinctively that these Neanderthals would respect the same way they grudgingly respected his show of arrogance. This was men's business. A woman had no part in it.

"So is Lawson here or not?" he asked Simmons point-blank.

"You still haven't told us who wants to know."

"Jesus," he swore, a man beyond tolerance and weary of their games, then he met Simmons's combative expression with his own and stepped out on a limb. "The name's Walker. Dan Walker. But you know what? Forget it. You're not looking for recruits? Fine. I'm outta here."

He jerked open the door and moved to get back behind the wheel.

"Hold on there." Simmons made it clear that he made the decisions around here and he would decide if and when Mike went anywhere. He scowled a while longer, then turned to the driver with a clipped nod. "Call him."

Inside the shadowed interior of the truck, the driver punched some keys, then held a phone to his ear.

Mike glanced at Eva. She sat stone still, eyes down, hands clasped in her lap. Like a good little subservient of an alpha male would do. It was a nice touch.

A raven flew overhead as they stood there, playing the waiting game. A fly buzzed his ear. The July heat, cut only by the pines that blocked direct sunlight, bore down in evergreen-scented waves.

And time turned agonizingly slowly as they all waited on a conversation that could seal or stall the deal.

Everything hinged on Lawson's response.

Finally, the driver gave Simmons an almost indiscernible nod and Mike knew they were getting in. It was all he could do not to exhale in relief.

"You carrying?" Sawed-off asked, still perched in the truck box.

"Couple handguns. A Makarov and a Taurus."

"Turn 'em over."

Mike made a weak show of looking reluctant, then leaned down to window level and told Eva, "Get the guns out of the glove box."

"Keep 'em where we can see 'em." Rifleman felt the need to exert his show of power.

With slow, deliberate moves, Eva handed the handguns to Mike, who handed them to Simmons butt end first, to make sure no one got too excited.

"Now your phones."

Schooling his expression to reluctant resignation, Mike turned over the burn phone.

"That's it?"

"That's it."

"How about I check for myself?" Simmons laid his 16-gauge on the hood and walked over to Mike. "You don't want to know how sorry you'll be if you're lying to me."

Mike assumed the position and gritted it out while Simmons did a rough and thorough pat-down.

He straightened with a grunt. "Now her."

Mike had a feeling this would be the first of many moments he was going to regret. He lifted his chin toward Eva, motioning her to get out of the car.

In the end, he couldn't help himself. "Touch her the wrong way and you're the one who's going to be sorry," he warned Simmons when Eva got out and stood by the Jeep. "You can see she's not carrying."

It was true. It would have been difficult to conceal much of anything beneath the tank top and jeans.

Simmons searched her anyway and all Mike could do was stand there, fists clenched at his side, and wait for the bastard to make the wrong move. Apparently Simmons was smarter than he looked. He kept it businesslike, short and impersonal.

"Make sure they stay right where they are," he told Sawed-off when he was finished, then started searching the Jeep.

He popped the hood, checked the trunk, inside the wheel wells, under the seats, then rifled through their duffel bags. All the while, Mike acted bored and irritated. If Simmons found their cache of weapons inside the doors, there wasn't enough BS in the world to talk his way past it.

"Get back in the Jeep," Simmons said, satisfied with his search. "Stay right on our bumper. Keep both hands on the wheel—*both* of 'em. And tell her to put her hands on the dash where we can see 'em. You only stop if we stop. Got it?"

Mike nodded.

"And stay in the vehicle until you're told to get out."

He climbed back into the truck. After a lot of en-

gine gunning and tire spinning, the driver maneuvered the pickup around on the narrow road.

Mike glanced across the front seat to Eva.

She told him, "You've got to get used to things
happening to me that make you uncomfortable, or
you're going to blow it."

He would never get used to some knuckle dragger
touching her. "Yeah. I know."

He shifted into gear, face grim, and tailgated the
hell out of the truck's rear bumper. "In the meantime, looks like we're in."

So why didn't he feel like celebrating?

Up close, Mike could read the name on Rifleman's
shirt—WAGONER. With Simmons behind him and
Wagoner ahead of him, he walked up seven wooden
steps into a log building that looked to be a command
center or meeting place.

Double crossbuck doors opened into a wide
foyer. The floor was made of rough pine planks. The
walls were more of the same, and bare except for
two pine picture frames hanging on either side of
an interior door that Mike suspected led to Lawson's
inner sanctum.

Both frames were three foot by three foot square.
One was a copy of the UWD charter. The other was a
photograph of Lawson decked out in standard UWD
uniform, posed with an AK-47. *The general in charge
of his army.*

"Sit," Simmons ordered, then knocked on the

door, waited for admittance, and disappeared inside.

Mike sat, slipped off his shades, and hooked a bow into the neck of his T-shirt.

Wagoner took a position with his back to the door, the AR-15 cradled in his arms, the barrel pointed in Mike's general direction.

It was a nice touch if intimidation was the game, and from what he'd seen of these yahoos, their game was all about intimidation.

He hadn't liked leaving Eva alone in the Jeep with Sawed-off—Bryant—leering at her, but he had no choice. Counting on her ability to handle herself, he steeled himself for the confrontation to come.

He owed it to himself, to his lost team, and to her to keep it together. Yet when the door opened and Lawson appeared in the doorway it took every shred of his self-control not to launch himself across the room and wrap his hands around the ferret-faced bastard's neck.

On a deep breath, he rose in a show of respect and swallowed back his disgust.

For a long moment Lawson said nothing, only looked him over as if deciding if he was worth the time it would take to draw another breath.

"It would seem you've gone to great lengths to find me," Lawson said finally.

"Yes, sir. I have." He infused his few words with just enough humility and respect to show he was aware that he was in the presence of greatness.

Apparently it worked.

"Bring him in," Lawson told Simmons, then told Wagoner to stay outside and guard the door.

"You heard him." The barrel of the AR-15 lifted, a signal for Mike to move.

So he did, with Simmons's shotgun pointing dead center in the middle of his back.

25

Eva drew a deep breath to steady herself. They'd done it. They'd gotten inside the belly of the beast.

She'd watched Mike, surrounded by thugs with guns, disappear into a heavily guarded building an hour ago. She didn't try to hide the fact that she was worried. She was playing the role of Dan Walker's wife. And what woman wouldn't worry if the man she loved had walked into unknown territory so long ago and hadn't been heard from since?

And it wasn't entirely role-playing. She wasn't Mike Brown's woman, but something was happening between them. Something unexpected and extremely unwise.

"We will finish this . . . When this is over, we will figure this out and we will finish it."

She had no idea what that "finish" was going to look like, or even what she *wanted* it to look like. She knew how he made her feel. Very much like a woman again, alive and vital.

But they were a long way from getting out of here

alive. The full-body pat-down Simmons had given her had almost prompted Mike to hurl himself at the guard. Now Bryant, who'd been stationed in front of the Jeep to guard her with his sawed-off shotgun, had more than guarding her on his mind, judging by the look in his eye.

And Mike was inside the big building in the center of the "city" square, meeting Lawson.

The heat didn't help her sense of apprehension. Here in the middle of the open meadow, the sun beat down on the Jeep's black roof like a blowtorch.

Sweat trickled down her back and between her breasts. She'd been ordered not to move, and other than opening the door to let some air in, she hadn't.

"Roll down the window," Bryant had told her when she'd asked if she could open the door.

"It's broken."

That was a lie, but with the weapons and ammo hidden in the door, she didn't dare roll the window down. Since the Jeep had seen better days and looked the part, he'd finally conceded—thank God, or she'd have had a heat stroke by now. So here she sat, one foot propped on the open door's armrest, arms crossed over her breasts, helpless to do a damn thing but commit the layout of the compound to memory.

The aerial photos, while accurate, told only part of the story. She felt like she was looking at a time-confused scene from *Little House on the Prairie*. She hadn't expected the compound to be so breathtakingly beautiful. Just a few minutes in, the narrow dirt road had opened up to a stunning valley. Tall green grass, bobbing white daisies, and soft yellow and pink flowers peppered an expansive, idyllic meadow that cradled the epicenter of the UWD compound.

Half-plank logs had been used for siding on the buildings, which had all the earmarks of a small, crudely constructed village in the middle of nowhere. She kept expecting to see teams of horses pulling lumbering wooden wagons. Instead, ATVs, pickups, and Jeeps lined what passed for streets, parked in front of a motor pool and maintenance shed, a first-aid station, food and supply storage, a guard post, and several residence buildings.

Wooden shakes covered the roofs; piles of split wood were stacked under exterior windows and close to entry doors, which were open like the windows to take advantage of the slight breeze.

At the far end of the town's center was a huge communal garden plot. Chickens wandered around free, pecking between the rows and at the garden's edge while women and young girls wearing long dark skirts, blouses, and what looked like prairie bonnets bent over hoes or knelt between rows tending spinach, radishes, onions, and lettuce, along with immature tomato, corn, and squash plants. One girl, so young she could barely be in her teens, carried a toddler on her hip. The sight gave Eva a sinking sensation in her stomach. *Please let that be her little sister.*

The sick feeling increased as she watched the women and girls, all moving with purpose, eyes down, faces somber, always working, rarely resting or even taking time out to take a drink of water under the hot sun. It was as if they were afraid to be idle. Their heads down, subservient, they appeared to be little more than slaves.

Everything she'd read on the UWD movement downplayed that aspect of the culture. But these were the kind of women that men in these movements preyed on. Low self-esteem. Gargantuan need to please and be accepted. Most likely abused, either as children or by a boyfriend or a spouse. It made them weak, yes, but mostly it made them victims. And it made her physically ill.

The boys were an entirely different story. Even though they were also dressed uniformly—jeans, solid-colored T-shirts, and ball caps—the boys were clearly encouraged to be boys. They wandered around kicking rocks down the dirt street, carrying BB guns or fishing poles, or fooling around in a playground that consisted of rope swings, a rope-webbed climbing wall, targets stuck to straw bales, and a wooden teeter-totter.

Holy God. It was Opie Taylor meets the frontier Stepford wives.

Shoulders back, head high, Mike followed the men into what was clearly Lawson's office. From the bank of computers, the camera monitors, and the whiteboard outlining the duty roster and work schedule, this was also UWD command central. Taking it all in, he stood at attention as Lawson rounded a military surplus gray metal desk and sat down, a man confident of his power. The desk was a behemoth: utilitarian, expansive, rusted in spots, dented in others. Not one item on its surface was out of place. It was as clean and organized as the room, as orderly as Lawson himself, who carried himself like a little general lording it over his troops. A pennant that Mike recognized as the UWD banner—a solid red background showcasing a closed white fist—hung on the wall behind the desk.

A straight-backed wooden chair faced the desk but Mike didn't take it. Simmons and Wagoner flanked him on either side, cradling their weapons. He stood military straight, hands at his side, legs planted wide, eyes fixed on the banner, not Lawson . . . the posture of a man who respected his superiors.

He could not wait to bring this bastard down.

"Walker, right?"

"Yes, sir."

"And why are you here, Mr. Walker?"

"Only one reason. To join the movement and help the cause."

Lawson leaned back, clasped his hands over his lean midsection, and regarded Mike with a somber expression. "You'll understand if I'm skeptical."

Now it got dicey. "Yes, sir. I do. You don't know me. You have no reason to trust me or my motives."

Lawson continued to watch him with interest. "So what am I supposed to think? That you're brave, or stupid—or a little bit of both?"

"I'm a devotee, sir. I only want to join the movement."

Lawson lifted a hand. "And yet you show up here, no advance word, no letter of recommendation."

"Barry Hill's my recommendation."

"Says he knew him in stir." Simmons was clearly not a believer.

Mike turned to Simmons. "I don't need you to do any talking for me."

As he'd hoped, this amused Lawson. Not so much Simmons; the big man's face turned blood red. Mike figured that was a good thing. Let Lawson know he had Simmons's number—big, dumb muscle—and Dan Walker was a little higher on the evolution ladder.

He turned back to Lawson.

"I was in the pen in California with Hill. But we go back further than that. We were both in the Navy at the same time. San Diego. We were of like minds even back then."

"Like minds? What the fuck does that mean?" Simmons growled.

Knowing he was making an enemy, but calculating that it might play well for him to stand up to the big man in the long run, he ignored Simmons again. "When our hitches were up, Hill ended up going one way, I went another. My way didn't work out. Did six of an eight-year stretch. I was three months from release when Hill showed up. I saw it as a sign, that we crossed paths again, you know? And I still liked what he had to say. He told me to come find you. That you'd have a place for me."

"Convenient that there's no way to verify it." Simmons again.

"Would you shut the fuck up?" Mike said very quietly but with deadly intent, then turned back to Lawson, who lifted a hand motioning Simmons to settle himself down.

Like a good little toy soldier, Simmons backed off.

"With due respect, sir," Mike went on, "knowing what I do about the sophistication of your organization, I would be very surprised if that was the case." He nodded toward Simmons.

The subtext in that statement could fill a football field. One, he'd thrown a gauntlet and basically invited Lawson to check out his story. It showed that he had nothing to hide. Two, he'd let Lawson know he was privy to some inside information—which invited the assumption that Hill had confided in him. And three, it cemented the notion in Simmons's and Lawson's minds that he was not intimidated by loudmouths like Simmons.

If the slight glimmer of interest in Lawson's beady eyes was any indication, he'd scored major points on all counts. He hoped to hell that Gabe and the BOIs had gotten Hill to play along. The chances of Lawson not following up and checking with Hill were slim.

Mike forced himself to hold Lawson's measuring gaze. He was so thin he looked emaciated. His features were so sharp edged and severe they were almost cartoonish. Only there was nothing remotely laughable about this man.

Mike schooled his expression to remain impassive while he played out a mental fantasy of launching himself over the desk and choking the life out of the bastard.

"Explain the woman." Lawson jarred Mike back to the room.

"Maria Gomez. Sorry. Maria Walker. We got married a month ago . . . right after I was released. Maria was my attorney. She can be an asset to the movement."

Lawson tilted his head, interested. "An attorney. One would also assume, then, that she is a strong-willed woman."

"An *intelligent* woman. Who bows to my will." His slight smile was genuine; he was thinking of Eva's reaction if she heard this exchange.

"And what if she is asked to bow to my will? To the will of the movement?"

Mike knew where this was going. "Maria has no allegiance to the current government. She has her reasons. She's prepared to contribute what is asked of her."

Apparently Lawson liked his response. "And you. What do you bring to the table?"

Mike could bullshit with the best of them, and it was time to put the spin on the plate. "I grew up in Colorado, so the mountains here feel like home. My old man believed in less government—he'd have been a follower if he was alive today. Not that I gave a shit what he thought back then." His smile was jaded.

"But then I found out what life in the real world was about . . . and I finally understood how badly the government screws its people."

He had Lawson's full interest now. The UWD leader had started to think he might have a true believer on his hands.

"I tried the Navy when I couldn't get work. Like I said, that's where I ran into Hill the first time. Liked what he had to say even then."

Then he turned the hatred he felt for Lawson and everything he stood for into a passionate line of party rhetoric that would have made a Quaker want to pick up a gun and declare war against Uncle Sam.

Lawson was too proud of what he had created not to feel triumphant over Dan Walker's impassioned and fanatical declaration. And when Mike put the spit on the polish by reciting the closing lines of the UWD doctrine—

"United we stand against corrupt politicians. United we face an enemy from within. United we prevail over a failed ideology. United we denounce allegiance to a government that has forgotten the people."

Mike stopped abruptly, and made a show of reining in his enthusiasm.

"You've read the manifesto." The fire in Lawson's eyes made it clear that he'd begun to see the possibility of promise.

"Anybody can read the manifesto," Simmons grumbled. "It's on the website."

"I've read it many times," Mike said, again ignoring Simmons who seethed beside him. It might not be wise to make an enemy before he'd made a friend, but he needed everyone in the room to know that he understood Simmons's position in the pecking order. Simmons was an enforcer. A bootlicker. He was not a thinking man.

Dan Walker was.

Lawson was smiling now, but the reservation in his eyes told Mike he wasn't home free yet.

"Simmons," Lawson barked.

"Yes, sir."

"You may speak now. What do you think we should do with our uninvited guests?"

Simmons got a mean, real smug look on his face— and Mike got a sick feeling that things were about to take a turn for the worse.

Eva checked her watch again, avoiding eye contact with her guard, knowing that what she'd see in his eyes would compound her case of the creeps.

Another five minutes had passed. She breathed deep. Realized how thirsty she'd become sitting here. Since she'd rather swallow her tongue than ask him for a drink, she continued her study of the compound.

At the very far end of the meadow, it appeared that most of the men had congregated. They were playing war games, running drills, participating in target practice. The constant, steady barrage of automatic weapons fire from the training site was a muffled *thwup*, *thwup*, *thwup* in the distance.

Back toward the heart of the compound, rows of single-story residence buildings flanked the meadow to the north. At least a dozen individual cabins backed right up to the forest on the south and again to the east. The residences made a U that faced the military hub of the compound and the main building Mike had been led to.

What was taking so long? And what were they doing in there?

A door slammed like a shot and she jumped, making her guard laugh. Ignoring him, she turned toward the sound . . . and briefly closed her eyes in relief when she saw Mike walking toward her, flanked by the two enforcers who had led him into the building.

None of them looked happy.

26

"And here I was expecting ankle chains and whipping posts. Hell, these are five-star digs."

Behind him, Eva grunted. "If you're into *Little House on the Prairie*."

Mike peered out the front window of a small, rustic cabin, watching the activities outside that mostly consisted of women working and men playing war. Wagoner sat in a pickup about twenty yards away, AR-15 still in hand, picking his teeth and playing jailer.

The fun never ended.

It had been touch and go for a while, but despite Simmons's suggestion to "run the cocky bastard's ass all the way to the Idaho border," Lawson had decided to take a chance.

"You will remain here tonight as my guests," he'd decreed like the petty dictator he was.

Translation: Lawson was going to tap his resources and find out the full skinny on one Dan Walker and Maria Gomez, and neither of them were going anywhere until it was decided if they were legit or candidates for target practice.

"That's very generous," Mike had told him, then showed Lawson that he knew the score. "I want only to be a part of this, sir. But I understand, you need to run a check. I have nothing to hide. Neither does Maria."

Lawson's expression had been unreadable as he'd ordered Simmons to get them settled. The irate flunky had snapped to like a dog used to having his chain jerked when he got out of line.

"Provide our *guests* with everything they need. And Simmons," Lawson had added with an arch look at Mike, "they've had a long trip and are no doubt weary. Make certain they don't want for anything that would require them to leave the cabin tonight."

It hadn't taken a degree in language arts to understand the subtext of Lawson's order. The cabin door would be locked behind them to make certain they didn't get out.

Wagoner, the watchdog, would make doubly sure of that.

Feeling confined, fighting off memories of the time he'd spent in the brig, Mike moved away from the window, and to make certain he hadn't missed anything, did a second sweep for bugs.

Not that he expected to find anything this time, either. The camp's living conditions were pretty primitive. The computers and surveillance equipment in Lawson's office were cutting edge but Mike strongly suspected resources were focused on the camp's perimeter areas. Still, Lawson's dossier said he was paranoid. So, just in case, as soon as they were alone, he'd dug the ink pen that was actually a bug detector out of his duffel bag. One of Gabe's toys. The sweep hadn't taken long, and it didn't take long the second time, either.

The cabin wasn't much more than fifteen by twenty feet. One door in, same door out, only with Wagoner there, out wasn't an option. There were only three windows, one on each wall except the one with the door. A bare lightbulb hung in the middle of the ceiling. The living room/bedroom were one single, open area. A double bed, a small, square table with two wooden chairs, and a single chest of drawers were the extent of the furniture. A kerosene lamp sat on top of the dresser, along with a thick bound volume: the UWD manifesto. Eva had picked it up and sat at the table thumbing through it.

A row of ten wooden pegs had been fixed to the wall beside the door. A small closet—barely large enough to hold a jacket—had been built into a corner. Roller shades covered the windows. There was no bathroom. Communal showers and toilets—one for the men, one for the women—were located at the north edge of the village, about one hundred yards from the cabin. He knew where the toilets were because prior to being delivered to their "guest house" he and Eva had been given an opportunity to use the facilities.

That had been over an hour ago, and they

hadn't seen anyone other than the guard since. They had, however, been informed by Wagoner that someone would bring their dinner and that sometime before sunset they would be escorted to the showers, should they wish to take advantage of them. Sunset apparently was the bewitching hour, because that's when electricity and the camp as a whole shut down.

"This is such a load of crap," Eva sputtered under her breath. She tossed the manifesto aside in disgust. "I'll never understand why so many people buy into cults."

Mike matched her hushed tone. He may not have found any bugs, but Lawson might decide to post someone right outside a window and listen the old-fashioned way: by eavesdropping.

"It's the same mentality that almost allowed Hitler to take over the world, and made it possible for Bin Laden to launch his war on democracy and free will. Ten parts bullying, ten parts fear, fill in the blanks with disenfranchised, desperate zealots who are look- ing for a cause and a place to fit in, and bingo—you've got yourself a world war, or a 9/11, or something as small but significant as a Waco."

She rose, walked to a window, and looked outside. "I hate this waiting around. What happens next?"

"Nothing. Not until we find out if Gabe and the BOIs convinced Hill to play ball. When Lawson con- tacts Hill, we're up crap creek if he rats us out."

"What a lovely visual." The rough pine floor

creaked under her slight weight as she turned and walked back to the table.

"Hey. I've got a big mouth. Sorry. And don't worry. They'll make it happen."

She'd folded her arms beneath her breasts, a gesture he recognized. When she felt vulnerable, she tightened in on herself.

"So," he said, wanting to move her out of that place, "want to talk about the elephant in the room?" He glanced at the bed, then at her, then wiggled his eyebrows.

She actually laughed. "And here I thought maybe you'd want to talk strategy."

He smiled. "Saving that for when Wagoner falls asleep."

The click of a key turning in a lock had them both turning toward the door, effectively tabling any further conversation—strategic or otherwise.

Wagoner swung the door open and a young woman walked inside carrying a covered tray and what looked like a folded charcoal blanket under her arm. She was dressed in the standard uniform—long dark skirt, dark button-down blouse, and prairie bonnet. Without a word, she walked over to the table and set down the tray.

"General Lawson wishes for you to enjoy your dinner," she said without raising her head.

"For you." She shoved the blanket in Eva's hands.

Before Eva could thank her, she quickly crossed

the room and hurried back out the door, which Wagoner locked again.

"Complimentary bedding?" Mike asked.

Eva unfolded the blanket . . . which turned out *not*
to be a blanket. "I should be so lucky."

"Do not say a word," Eva muttered as the cabin door
was locked behind them yet again, shutting out a twi-
light sky that fast faded to dark.

An armed escort had just walked them back from
the showers. She wore the getup that had been delivered with their dinner. And since her voice was filled
with a healthy dose of pissed, Mike thought it best
that he not laugh.

He'd been wrong about something, though. The
long, dowdy skirt and matching navy blue blouse *did*
manage to drab her down. But then, *drab* was a relative term when it came to Eva.

He tucked the bug detector back into his duffel
after doing another sweep in case Lawson had gotten
crafty and installed something while they used the
showers. He hadn't.

"You saying you don't want to know how you look?"

"There's a reason there aren't any mirrors in here."
Her mouth pulled tight when she saw his grin. "Okay
fine. Get it over with."

"You look, darling wife, like a subservient, Kool-
Aid–drinking disciple of the UWD doctrine. And better you than me, by the way. I don't think I could run
in that thing."

"But oh, wouldn't I love to see you try." She gave him a tight smile. "I itch all over. How do those poor women wear this stuff in this heat?"

"Guess you're going to find out," he said with a sympathetic smile. She was, unfortunately, going to find out a lot of things before this was over. He thought of Simmons touching her today when he'd searched her. How Bryant had watched her every move. How the women of the camp worked like dogs while the men played soldier.

"For the record, you've been a rock through all this."

She scowled. "What did you expect? That'd I'd fall apart and start crying for my mommy?"

"Actually I thought I might do that. I still might. Hold me?"

He couldn't quite pull off the hat trick; this time she didn't smile. She made a twirling motion with her index finger instead. "I'm getting out of this itch fest."

She wanted him to turn around? Seriously? Seemed a little like closing the barn door after the horse got out, but his momma hadn't raised no dummy, so he did what he was told. She had good reason to be on edge. He wasn't going to add to her tension.

Back turned, he thought about strategy instead of the sound of her rummaging around in her duffel for the T-shirt and boxers that she'd brought along to sleep in.

He thought about slipping outside when the camp

was asleep for a little look-see. He thought about the meal that had been limited but surprisingly good: honey-cured ham on fresh-baked bread and fresh spinach salad. He thought about the communal shower and how the last time he'd used one, he'd been in the military. Which made him think about the One-Eyed Jacks. And Taggart. And Cooper.

And he thought about how badly he wanted to nail Lawson.

But when he heard the sound of a heavy wool skirt hit the floor, all of his carefully schooled good intentions and diversion tactics dropped with it.

Suddenly everything he thought about was totally hot and totally wrong. Like the fact that she might now be standing naked behind him, in transition between itchy wool and soft, worn cotton. All he could picture was that double bed with the plain white spread and creaky springs, which he'd discovered earlier when he'd tested it for firmness. And he thought about how small that bed was for a man his size, when that man was expected to keep his distance from a woman who looked like her. From a woman whose skin was as supple and soft as satin, whose body was responsive and giving and . . .

"You can turn around now."

There was nothing else in the cabin to look at. No TV. No computer. No distractions. There was only her. And she was magnificent.

"Lord, you're beautiful."

She was wearing the same T-shirt and boxers he'd

taken off her two nights ago. The marriage of the memory and the reality combined to give him some serious issues in a certain area of his body that had a tendency to swell in her presence.

Once more with feeling: Little head, big trouble.

It didn't help that the glasses were gone. She'd shaken her hair out of that confining elastic; it curled softly over her shoulders and down her back. And speaking of unconfined—she'd ditched her bra. And her feet were bare. And he was suddenly sinking fast.

He could blame it on the adrenaline. On the very dicey situation they were in. All of his senses were overloaded and ready to stage a riot. It stood to reason he'd be revved in the testosterone area.

Or, he could own up to the truth. This wasn't all about raging hormones and randy sex. This was way bigger. And damn scary. He'd fallen in love with this woman.

And he still didn't know how it had happened. It sure as hell didn't make sense. Especially in just three days, give or take a period of unconsciousness or two.

"You don't pick the time, Grasshopper. The time picks you."

Again with the Confucius voice invading his head?

He needed to snap out of this, fast. Despite her studied reserve, he caught definite vibes that she had a few issues with this captive-in-a-box intimacy, too.

He needed to fix that. And he only knew one way to go about it.

"Any chance you'd do a guy a solid favor and put those woolies back on?"

Another attempt to make her laugh. But clearly, she did not find him amusing. "Seriously? We're being held hostage while an anarchist decides whether he's going to kill us or recruit us, and you're thinking about sex?"

If it was easier for her to pretend this was just about sex, then hey, he'd give her that to hold on to. "I'm a guy. I always think about sex."

She gave him a look, turned back the covers, and climbed into bed. End of discussion.

"Just make sure you stay on your side and keep your hands to yourself, or I'm going to cry foul," he grumbled—and right then the lights went out.

27

Deep breaths. Forced yawns. Meditation. None of it worked. Eva couldn't get to sleep. It didn't help that Brown lay awake beside her. On top of the covers. Fully clothed. On his side, facing away from her. They'd played this "pretend to sleep" game for over an hour now and it wasn't working for either of them.

She knew he'd been kidding about the sex issue — sort of.

But she wasn't laughing, because he wasn't the only one having trouble. That metaphorical elephant was way bigger than this damn bed. And as wired as she was on a combination of adrenaline, anticipation, and a healthy dose of apprehension, she didn't see sleep coming anytime soon.

It didn't help to know that one word, one touch, was all it would take to put them both out of their misery.

Would that be such a bad thing?

Yeah. It would. The fact that she even entertained thoughts about going there showed how wrong her thinking was.

"We will finish this . . . When this is over, we will figure this out and we will finish it."

Threat? Promise? His words had hovered at the fringe of her conscious thoughts since he'd had his *moment* and kissed her.

Frustrated, she sat up and propped the pillow behind her head. She stared into the dark, stared down at his utterly still form, and gave it up.

"What do you think the chances are of Lawson finding us out?"

For a moment she thought he would keep up the pretense of sleep, but then he let out a perturbed sigh and rolled to his back. "About the same as me getting any sleep, if this is the start of a game of twenty questions."

Well, good. That made it the both of them who were cranky. "I thought you were going to sneak out and do some recon."

"And I will," he gritted out, stacking his hands behind his head. "Once they lift the twenty-four-hour guard. All I want to do right now is sleep."

She snorted. "Liar."

"It doesn't count as a lie if you're trying to do the right thing."

Oh, God. Why did she always want to laugh at his stupid comments?

"Why aren't you asleep?" he asked into the dark.

"Like you don't know."

Silence. Then, "Do you want me to sleep on the floor?"

That might be a good idea. "No."

More silence. Then in a very soft voice, "Do you want me to sleep on *you*?"

She would not laugh. She pulled her knees to her chest and wrapped her arms around them. "What is wrong with us? I mean, it's not like we're sixteen and shacked up at the local Holiday Inn on prom night. There are high stakes here. If these people find out who we are, they're going to kill us."

"So," he said after the quiet had settled again, "what do you know about shacking up on prom night?"

"Damn it, Brown. Stop with the jokes."

"I wasn't joking. Well, not about sleeping on top of you."

She expelled a deep breath. "All right. You know what? Let's just *do* this. How's that for an engraved invitation? Maybe it'll relieve the tension and we can finally get some sleep."

"You want a tension reliever, take a Valium."

"Seriously? You're turning me down?"

She blinked down at him in the dark.

"You haven't asked me nice yet."

She growled in frustration. "Everything's a game to you, isn't it?"

He moved so fast, she flinched as he rolled over, hiked up on an elbow, and looked up at her. "You think this is a game?" His somber tone sent her heart pounding. "You think I make it a habit of getting stupid over a woman? That I turn myself inside out drumming up reasons not to have sex?"

She didn't even know what to say. She could only stare at his moonlit face. His beautiful, tortured face.

"Well, how's this for *not* playing games? You scare me to death, Eva. You . . . make me feel things . . . and want things . . . and realize that I need things I've never let myself need before."

He sat up, then pressed his forehead against hers and let out a breath that spoke of longing and frustration. His voice held a sincerity she had never expected. "Look. I know this is sudden. I know you might not be totally over Ramon. I know that I'm a constant reminder of that part of your life. It sucks. For both of us.

"I also know," he went on, pressing the softest kiss on her temple and making her melt a little at his tenderness, "that a thousand obstacles stand between us and the finish line with Lawson. But I'm going to get you out of here. We're both going to get out of here and accomplish Mission One, which is to expose Lawson for what he did in Afghanistan. I don't want to muck that up by adding sex to the mix."

He'd managed to silence her again. And make her feel bereft when he rolled to his side with his back to her again.

"Oh. And for future reference, 'let's just do this' is an ultimatum, not an invitation. I don't do real well with ultimatums these days."

For several long moments, she sat there. Processing what he'd said, mulling over how she felt about it. He was right. There were a thousand obstacles standing between them and their goal.

But there was nothing lying between them in this bed, and the one thing she *was* sure about was that she wanted him. Wanted this devastatingly gorgeous man who was funny and sincere and conflicted, and so, so much more than she had thought he was.

She wasn't going to think about this any longer. It was a no-brainer. She peeled her T-shirt over her head, shimmied out of her boxers, and pressed herself full-length against his back.

His skin was fire hot when she tunneled her hand up under his shirt and spread her fingers over his flat abdomen.

"Eva," he warned on a low growl and covered her hand with his, stilling it as she slid it toward the snap on his jeans.

"Shh," she whispered, pressing her lips against his nape. "This is me, asking nice."

He turned toward her then, his big hand finding her bare hip and squeezing. "You sure about this?"

"Um . . . I'm naked. So yeah, I'm pretty sure."

To erase any doubt on his part, she wedged her hand inside his pants and, with a thrill that shot through her like electricity, found him, hard and hot and pulsing.

"Well," he said on a groan as she squeezed her fingers around him, "since you asked so nice."

She laughed, then gasped when he flipped her to her back and found her breast with his mouth.

She held him there, knotted her hands in the coarse silk of his hair and showed him with a whimper how much she loved what he was doing to her. His mouth . . . she hitched in a breath and arched into him . . . his mouth was ravenous. His tongue masterful as he flicked it over her nipple, never letting up on the suction, finessing her to an edge that was sharp and thrilling.

"You drive me crazy," he murmured, trailing kisses between her breasts to her other nipple, which he sucked and lightly bit and tugged into his mouth with equal measures of greed and gratification.

When he pulled away to shed his clothes she helped him, frantically working the snap on his pants and lowering the zipper. He left the bed long enough to strip to the skin, dig around inside his duffel—thank God he'd brought condoms—and lay back down beside her.

"I know we talked about *me* sleeping on *you*," he said, handing her the packet.

God love him, he was irrepressible. And she loved it. She pushed to her knees, then threw a leg over his hips and straddled him.

"Don't. Move," he ground out as she settled herself over him.

"Yeah . . . like that's a possibility."

He laughed and groaned and circled her waist with his hands and held her down on him—open and vulnerable and weak with desire for him.

Holding the packet between her teeth, she ground herself against him, loving the feel of him hot and damp and thick against her. Loving the ache that built in her belly, making her wet and wanting to forget the condom and feel him move inside her, skin on skin.

He reached between them, caressed her clitoris with his thumb, and she almost came in his hand.

"Mike . . ." She whispered his name on a sigh. She lifted her hips and reached for him. She wanted him inside. She wanted him there now.

"Oh, no." He gripped her waist and lifted her, then pressed a kiss against her pubic mound.

"I can't . . ." She couldn't catch her breath, couldn't stop him, didn't want to, as he lifted her higher, guided her knees above his shoulders, then buried his mouth in her heat.

It was like riding out an electrical storm, all fire flashes and lightning bolts and turbulence. She groped for the headboard, desperate to ground herself. She clamped her fingers around it and hung on as he took her through a vortex of sensation she wasn't sure she would survive.

His tongue was relentless as he probed and plied and sucked, until she pressed her mouth against her arm to keep from screaming.

And still he licked and suckled, until the insane pleasure burst in an explosion too perfect to comprehend.

She was crying softly by the time he drew her down his body and wrapped himself around her, while she trembled and fought for a breath that wasn't a sob.

"I'm going to go out on a limb here," he whispered

against her hair, "and guess that that was good for you."

She weakly pounded once on his chest. "Shut up. You know you destroyed me."

He cupped her head in his big hands and kissed her hair. "In a good way, right?"

She found the strength to push up to an elbow. "You can't help yourself. You have to gloat, don't you?"

He skimmed his fingertips along her shoulder. "I didn't think you could possibly look more beautiful." Trailed his fingers through hair that had been tangled by his hands. "Look at you."

"And look at you," she whispered, and dropped her gaze to the gorgeous, jutting length of his erection. Pushing to her hands and knees, she moved deliberately down the bed. "We need to do something about that."

She knelt over him, shoved a handful of hair over her shoulder, and met his eyes. Then she took him in her mouth and showed him a few relentless tactics of her own. Tactics that had him clenching his teeth, and breaking a sweat and arching off the bed as though what she was doing to him was the beginning and the end of everything that mattered in his life.

28

Feeling humiliated and mean with it, Lawson slapped the girl across the face, then shoved her off him.

"Get out. And stop whimpering."

She was sixteen. Skin like ivory. High, firm breasts. The brightest flower in his harem, and she had come with her mother's blessings. Not that blessings mattered; everyone knew the rules here. He maintained absolute power. He took what he wanted. And he'd wanted her tonight. That mouth had finished him off like melting ice cream more times than he could count.

But not tonight. Tonight he lay here, flaccid and impotent and glaring at her naked ass as she gathered her clothes and scrambled for his bedroom door.

Fucking prostate.

He hated getting old. He shouldn't feel this old; he was only sixty, for chrissake. Prime of his life. A warrior. He'd done things, seen things, made things happen. Hell, he commanded his own army—ragtag bunch of misfits that they were.

He propped the pillows behind his head, then reached for the glass of scotch sitting on his bedside table. Took a slow sip. Stupid fucks, all of them. Not a day went by that he didn't want to clock Simmons for saying or doing something so stupid he shouldn't be allowed to live. To a man, they actually believed the bullshit he fed them about overthrowing the government. And the women were nothing but sheep. Stupid, mindless sheep. It made him sick to be around them.

He needed Hill back to rule the camp and free him up to do what he did best: making deals and money.

He craned his neck, found the open bottle of scotch and refilled the glass, then sipped some more. They didn't get that UWD was all a front. A way to keep Uncle focused on a backwoods anarchist group so he could continue to run his main operation without interference.

He'd picked the right horse to run with fifteen years ago. Stingray was smart. Arrogant bastard, but smart. He'd kept their dealings out of the U.S. for the most part. The Juarez deal . . . that was a little different. And possibly the reason he was stressed to the point of impotence.

He contemplated the amber liquid in the glass he'd rested on his chest. He didn't like bringing their business here. Made him nervous. But this deal . . . this deal was big. His cut alone would net him a cool half mil. His "army" would actually come in handy—provided they could get their heads out of their asses long enough to protect the camp and the shipments.

He lifted the glass off his chest and sat up abruptly.

What this camp needed was new blood. Dan Walker struck him as a man who could provide it. Walker had an axe to grind—unlike most of the men here who simply had no place else to go.

And Walker's wife? The photos his source had pulled off the Internet for him were impressive. A woman, not a girl. His cock stirred when he thought about her . . . which made him smile. Maybe if he'd called on the lovely Mrs. Walker to keep him company tonight, the outcome would have been entirely different.

What better test for them? The ultimate bow to his will? He didn't imagine Dan would like it much. But it was early. He'd give it time. And in the meantime, he'd savor the possibility.

New blood. That's what the Walkers brought to the table. He'd already placed a call to Hill, who had backed up Walker's story. Barry had surprised him by going as far as suggesting he consider placing Walker in an officer's position. His former second in command's opinion held a lot of sway. He had a good feeling about Walker, but it was way too soon to think along those lines. So far, everything Walker had told him checked out. So it looked promising . . . but it was far too early to decide if he was trustworthy. He'd see how it went.

At the moment, he had bigger irons in the fire than

vetting new recruits. He expected a call any day now. And he was ready. If he pulled this off, he might actually pack it in and buy that place in Fiji. Or maybe he'd go back to Thailand. The women there knew how to take care of a man.

Even an old one, he thought again with disgust when he realized he had to take a piss. Again.

Fucking prostate.

First light had broken through the thin curtains on the windows a little over an hour ago. Mike had been awake for most of that hour. Awake and watching Eva. She was still asleep beside him, her hair fanned around her head on the pillow that was bathed in a soft morning glow. Awake and thinking.

About a lot of things. Like how she was so stunningly gorgeous, sometimes he had to remind himself to breathe when he looked at her. Like how athletic she was in bed, and how she totally abandoned herself to a dedicated and enthusiastic giving and receiving of pleasure.

About life's little habit of lobbing wrenches into plans and laying waste to the best of intentions. God's truth, he had *not* intended to make love to her—which didn't explain why he'd tossed the condoms into his duffel at the last minute, but that was beside the point. He'd been a Boy Scout. Still swore by the *Be Prepared* motto. So sue him. He was damn glad he'd raided Gabe's supply.

As for his plans . . . he didn't have any. Zip. Nada.

Not one single solitary idea of what happened next in his life other than putting his pants on in the morning and flying his Beechcraft wherever the wind blew him. Until she'd come along, he'd been fine with that. No plan, no pressure. No problem. And no way to live a life.

Eva had clarified that for him. Not only with her very vocal—and spot-on—assessment of all his failings, but with her fire and determination. Her fearlessness. Her honor. She'd been right to look for answers. And she'd been right about him. He'd checked out. For eight years he'd been killing time. Taking up space. And it was wrong.

He owed her for that awakening. Regardless of how this turned out, because of her he wasn't ever going to be content to drift again. Or to settle again. He needed to be the man he'd once planned on being. He needed to be a man worthy of a woman like her.

If she'd have him.

When this was over, he was sure as hell going to find out.

So yeah, he thought, smiling when she stirred and wrinkled her nose and curled onto her side, tucking her hands, prayerlike, beneath her cheek. Maybe giving in to her had been a good thing.

Well, duh. Yeah. She'd blown his mind. All that passion. All that fire. All that vulnerability that she opened herself up to.

Yeah. A very good thing.

But more than that, he'd needed a catalyst to help

him focus on the task at hand. She'd provided it last night. There was no conceivable way he wasn't going to get her out of here alive. Just like there was no way he was leaving without getting the goods on Lawson to expose the sadistic bastard for what he was.

But even more than he needed vindication, she needed closure about what happened to Ramon. As much as she'd given him last night, as much as she'd opened herself up to him physically, he didn't have a chance under the sun of an emotional commitment from her until she got what she'd come for. The chance to clear her dead husband's name.

He wondered what it said about him that he was jealous of a dead man. Wondered what it said that despite his best effort, he still had the urge to wake her slowly and make love to her one more time. He rose instead, careful not to disturb her, and stepped into his pants. He couldn't fault her for wanting to know about Ramon. He thought it was admirable. Heroic. And bullheaded stubborn, which was another trait about her that he respected and yes, damn it, loved.

The idea still made him a little light-headed.

Which was why he decided to table any discussion about love and future for the duration. Grabbing his shirt from the floor, he dragged it over his head and walked over to the door.

The first thing he noticed when he looked through the multipaned window was their Jeep parked in front of the cabin. The second thing that registered was that Wagoner's truck was gone. After checking out as much of the perimeter as he could, he was pretty much convinced that no one had taken Wagoner's place on guard duty.

Interesting. He tried the door—and got another surprise when it creaked open with only a gentle nudge.

"What do you suppose that means?"

He turned around at the sound of Eva's voice. She propped herself up on an elbow; her hair tumbled over the left side of her face in a tangle of silk and trailed down her shoulder, the ends kissing the tip of her left breast that the slipping sheet revealed.

"The unlocked door?" He crossed to the bed and planted a hip beside hers. "I'd say it means that Lawson liked what Gabe and the guys planted about us when he did his cyber-snoop and put out feelers to Hill. The Jeep's parked out front and Wagoner's gone."

She lifted her hand to scoop all that glorious hair away from her face and it was all he could do not to lean into her . . . maybe start nibbling on that pale, delicate flesh on the inside of her upper arm . . . or maybe lower his head and take a pouting, pretty nipple in his mouth, then lay her back, spread her thighs, and find the heart of her again with his tongue and suck until she screamed his name.

"Seriously?"

His eyes must have glazed over because it took a moment to focus. When he did, it was clear he'd been caught.

"Sorry."

She pulled the sheet up over her breasts and glanced pointedly at his lap. "No, you're not."

He laughed. "Okay, I'm not. But if you have any compassion at all, you'll slip into a little something less provocative. "

"Lucky for you, that can be arranged. Hand me my gunnysack."

He was about to double back on his promise to leave her alone when a knock sounded at the door.

Eva slid back down into the bed and pulled the covers up to her chin.

He stood and walked to the door. The same young woman who had brought their dinner waited on the other side, her head lowered, eyes downcast.

Like a good little UWD devotee, Mike played superior male and didn't address her. He waited in silence for her to speak.

"You are to join the general in the communal dining hall for breakfast. Your wife is invited, too," she added with a quick peek into the cabin before lowering her head again. "It's the large building three down from the meeting hall. He's expecting you by seven."

"What time is it now?" Mike demanded briskly.

"Six fifteen, sir."

"Thank General Lawson for the invitation and tell him we'll be there." He shut the door in her face.

"I'm guessing your mom would be ashamed of the

way you treated her," Eva said, hiking herself up in the bed.

"*I'm* ashamed." Mike lifted a shoulder. "When in Rome is great in theory but in practice, it sucks."

"Yeah," she said with a grim nod. "It does. I hate the way they treat women."

"Then let's do something about it. Nothing says we can't do double duty."

She looked skeptical.

"We bring Lawson down. We destroy the movement. These women can get on with their lives again. You'll never convince me they knew what they were getting into, and now they're trapped."

"I hope you're right . . . about changing their lives when this is over."

"It all starts today. Come on." He grabbed her skirt and blouse from the hook where she'd hung them last night. "Get dressed and let's head for the showers. Nothing like ice-cold water to clear the mind for battle."

She put on her bra, shrugged into the blouse, and started working the buttons. "You think there's going to be a battle?"

"Just with myself. It took everything I had in me yesterday to keep from ripping into Lawson."

"The first shock of seeing him face-to-face is behind you now. You should be able to rein it in better today."

"And what about you?" He watched her shimmy into the long skirt. "You haven't met him yet. You going to be able to handle it?"

She kept her head down, messing with buttons and the zipper. "I'll handle it."

Yeah, he thought as she grabbed her tennis shoes and, barefoot, headed for the door. He had no doubt that she would handle it just fine.

Even before Eva stepped into the dining hall—a respectable distance behind Mike for show—she'd suspected her patience would be tested to the limit. One look at the layout and activity in the room the size of a basketball court, however, and she knew she'd underestimated the magnitude of her irritation.

The women who weren't cooking or serving or clearing dishes sat with the children at long rows of tables on the left side of the room, eating breakfast. The men sat in clusters around large round tables at the other side. All of the conversation—save for the little boys mixing it up and laughing—came from the men. The women and girls were silent. As soon as a woman finished eating, she immediately rose and started helping the others. Except for the toddlers, even the little girls rose from the table like robots and started helping with the chores.

She followed Mike, who had apparently spotted Lawson at the table at the head of the room. She felt her stomach tighten as they neared the head table and knew she had to get a grip, to school her expression into one of blind acceptance and bear it.

Lawson stood as they approached and extended his hand to Mike. "Welcome to my table."

"It's a pleasure, sir. Thanks for the invitation."

Eva was grateful that she was expected to stand in silence, her head lowered, so Lawson couldn't see the hatred in her eyes.

This man was responsible for Ramon's death.

She made herself pull back from the thought. She didn't have the luxury of indulging her hatred. That could come later.

Lawson introduced Dan to the men sharing his table, tossing around their titles. Executive officer, intelligence, supply, operations, security officers. Lawson had structured his army after the U.S. military model. He'd even anointed himself with the title of general though he had barely enough men to form a company.

"My wife, Maria," Mike said as if he were presenting a piece of meat for inspection.

She had to look at Lawson now or he'd consider it disrespectful. The predatory look in his eyes made her want to recoil with revulsion, but she kept it together.

"Dan tells me you're an attorney."

She swallowed. "Yes, sir."

"Licensed in Idaho?"

"Yes," she answered again. "I made certain of that before we left California."

"That's very good to know. Should we have need for legal counsel, we may call upon your expertise."

"I would be honored."

He motioned to one of the serving women. "See to it that Mrs. Walker has something to eat, then give her a tour of the compound and assign her to a unit and a work detail."

Like a dutiful wife, she thanked Lawson, cast Mike a subservient glance, and followed the woman who had gotten the task of breaking her in.

And so her UWD indoctrination began.

29

It was after seven p.m. when the door to the cabin opened and Eva walked in. It was on the tip of Mike's tongue to ask, "And how was your day, dear?" but one look at her flushed face and angry eyes told him she wouldn't appreciate the joke. He knew they'd worked her like a mule.

"You would be wise not to talk to me right now." She tugged off the bonnet and hung it on a peg by the door.

"Way ahead of you on that one."

Poor baby. Even though the uniform made it difficult to distinguish one woman from another—part of Lawson's plan to break them down and strip them of their individuality—Mike had managed to catch glimpses of her on and off throughout the day. Once he'd seen her lugging a basket of wet laundry to a clothesline. A couple hours later, he'd spotted her in the garden, weeding. That was around two p.m. The sun had been brutal. The last time he'd seen her was in the communal dining hall. She'd been clearing tables after dinner, which explained why she was a full hour behind him getting back to the cabin.

Her hair was plastered to her head, damp with sweat. Her clothes were dusty and spotted with what he suspected was food from her work in the dining room.

She looked exhausted and irritated and beautiful, and he couldn't stop himself from walking across the room, taking her in his arms, and hugging her close.

"All in all, you look pretty good for a beast of burden." He dropped a kiss on the top of her head.

"I need a shower," she said on a weary breath and leaned back against him. "Then I'll be ready to talk."

"I'll walk you there," he offered even though he'd already had his shower.

She shook her head. "I need a little alone time, okay? I've got a lot to process."

He got it. "Sure. Take all the time you need. Here." He squeezed her shoulders, then reached for a stack of clean clothes. "Someone dropped by with these. I even got my uniform." He spread his arms wide to show his camo pants and T-shirt, WALKER stenciled on the breast pocket.

She stared at his bare feet. "No soldier boots?"

He grinned. "They're under the bed."

"And did you have fun playing war games all day?"

"Thought you didn't want to talk yet."

"You're right. I don't." She snagged the clean clothes and a towel from the chest and headed out the door.

It was almost dark by the time she got back. Not quite as pissed, but still exhausted. Still quiet. But looking a little more in control.

As soon as she closed the door behind her, she stripped out of the confining blouse and skirt and into the T-shirt and boxers she'd washed out during her morning shower.

"Much better," she said on a sigh and crawled onto the bed. She plumped a pillow behind her back, crossed her legs, and breathed deep. "So . . . how was your day, dear?"

He grinned at their like minds.

"Interesting. I got access to some of the workings of the camp. Because I'm good with engines and electrical—"

"You are?"

"I might have fudged a bit, but I'm hoping we won't be around long enough for them to find out. I'm also a crack shot—that, at least, I can back up. Anyway, they showed me their mini power plant. Besides a few gasoline-powered generators for emergencies, the camp gets its electricity from the local electrical cooperative—as I suspected, stolen by splicing into rural power lines. Since the electric company doesn't have a chance of patrolling more than every other year or so, they're pretty much home free. It's located at the south end of the compound. It's also stocked with some large propane tanks."

"All critical information."

He sat down beside her, propped his own pillow

behind his back against the headboard, and stretched his legs out in front of him, wanting to touch her but knowing she needed her space. "Yep. If we have to make a break for it, we can knock out their power source, blow the propane tanks, and at least make it confusing for them to search for us."

"Got it. What else?"

"Lawson's office is the camp's command center. Doubles as the surveillance and communication room. That's where I first met him yesterday. He took me back today, had me sit in on his weekly podcast so he could impress me while he preached to the faithful and spread the word. The sonofabitch clearly sees himself as the zealot enforcer god they all worship."

"Sounds like you're in like Flynn."

Because he couldn't help himself, he lifted a lock of hair away from her face, played absently with the ends. "Not exactly. He hasn't turned over our handguns or the phone, so apparently he sees me as enough of a question mark that he's not yet ready to hand me keys to the kingdom. He's short a training specialist, too. I'm going to convince him I'm the man for that position but that'll take a little more time. Just like it will take a little more time to finagle a tour of the armory. I might have to resort to a sneak-and-peek to see what they've got tucked away in that building."

"You're going out tonight?"

Mike bent a knee and rested his forearm on top of it. "Lots of cloud cover. A little wind. Sounds like good conditions."

"You want company?"

She was so tired, she could barely keep her eyes open. Yet she was ready to go if he asked her. "I think this is a solo gig. Just to get the feel of the place.

"Hey," he said before she could lodge a protest. "I made a friend today." His grin told her he was pretty pleased with himself.

"You and Simmons bond over bullets, did you?"

His grin widened. "Nah, I think I burned that bridge. Guy by the name of Beaver. Even has the buck teeth to go with it. He's not much more than a kid—physically or mentally. Exactly the type Lawson likes to mold. Only Bucky has a little weakness. He's pretty much in awe of me for doing time for that B&E. Sees me as a real badass."

"I'm sure the black eye helps cement the image. How does that feel, by the way?"

"It's fine. As for Bucky, yeah, just about everything about me impressed him. It didn't take long to figure out that all I had to do to prime his pump was tell him a few stories about life in stir while we were on the shooting range."

"That must have been good."

"Oh, it was. Plus he hates Simmons. The big dog has lifted his leg on the little dog one too many times, so we have something in common. Anyway, now he wants to show me he's important and a badass, too. He wants to share secrets."

"What kind of secrets?"

"I don't know yet. But he's busting to let me know

he's got inside info. Important enough to make him feel superior and show me he's got status around here."

"And nothing makes a little man feel bigger than sharing what he knows, to prove his importance."

"Exactly. I'm hoping he can clue me in on where Lawson spends his time. I haven't figured out where the general lays his head yet. That seems to be top secret . . . so maybe when I find his bed, I find where he stashes his important papers." Which was the purpose of their visit.

"Anything else?"

"Yeah. I let Lawson know I had a couple friends wanting to join the movement." Gabe and Green, who were waiting in the wings for the call.

"How'd he react to that?"

"He didn't have much to say. But I know he's think-ing about it—especially after I told him they were disenfranchised former Special Forces. He could use some thinkers with military backgrounds. It's pretty clear his recruits are mostly rejects and derelicts who don't lend much more than muscle to the cause."

"Maybe that's the way he likes it. Men like that are easily led."

"True, but Lawson can't do all the leading—not and keep his fingers in his other pies."

"Like fraternizing with the Juarez cartel."

"Exactly. His executive officer was Army for four years but that's it. No one else has any special skills. Not too many sharp tacks in that drawer, either. I can tell that Lawson knows his top tier is lacking. He tries not to show that he's frustrated by it. He has to delegate at some point and it's apparent he's starting to realize he doesn't have a lot of go-to guys to carry the load."

He grinned again. "That's where I come in. And Gabe and Joe. Military background, school of experience and hard knocks. At least that's the plan."

"So fingers crossed."

"And soon, I hope. We could use more eyes. It's a big compound. And Lawson is as paranoid as we figured he'd be. He's stationed guards everywhere. It's going to be hard—even pulling night recon—so I'm hoping he falls for the bait and lets me contact them."

She yawned then, and he realized how tired she really was.

"So what about you?"

"Oh, you know how it goes. A captive woman's work is never done. Didn't offer much opportunity for recon. But I did figure out their work patterns. They divide the women up into units, then rotate duties every two hours. That way everyone hits the laundry, or garden, or kitchen, or child care duties at some point every day. Makes us well-rounded little robots. When the women change work shifts, I noticed the men changed guard duties as well. So it looks like they run two-hour shifts all the way through."

"Any dissension in the ranks?"

She compressed her lips, shook her head. "If there

is, they didn't share with me—not this quickly. It's going to take a while to gain any trust. I think they're so browbeaten and brainwashed, they simply move with the herd." She fisted her hands, then winced.

"What?" he asked.

"Just a blister. It's really pretty disgusting, how soft I am. I don't know whether to admire these women for how tough they are, or slap them silly for letting these men use and manipulate them this way."

He lifted her hand, inspected it in the fading light, then brought it to his lips and kissed her boo-boo, which made her smile in a way that told him he'd surprised her and pleased her.

"It's the kids that tear me up," he said. "The girls, especially."

She nodded, then yawned again and dragged her hair away from her face. "I don't know what's going to give me more pleasure: exposing Lawson or giving these people a chance to go back to a normal life."

"How about you forget about Lawson until morning, because I think I know exactly what kind of pleasure you need tonight." He got up and flipped off the overhead light, then rejoined her on the bed.

"Oh, Mike—I don't—"

"Shh." He pushed himself to his hands and knees and straddled her. "All you have to do is lie there."

As tired as she was, she gave a pure female shiver when he gripped her hips and pulled her down the bed until she was reclined.

"I've been thinking about this all day," he murmured, pressing a kiss to her flat abdomen after peeling the cotton boxers down her hips.

"And this," he whispered, lightly nipping the point of her hip, then slowly working his way down to the apex of her thighs. "All. Day. Long."

Her low groan of pleasure made him smile as she opened her legs wide for him and let him have his way. Let him open her feminine folds with his fingers. Let him nuzzle and kiss and lick and suck, until her hips were lifting to his mouth and her hands were clutching the sheets and she was coming apart for him, overwhelmed by passion, victorious in her surrender.

30

It was close to midnight before Mike slipped out of the cabin, dressed in his night gear: black pants, black long-sleeved shirt, black gloves, and boots. He'd pulled a black mask over his face to minimize any possible glare from a flashlight beam, in the event he alerted a guard.

He hid in the shadows of the cabin, letting his eyes adjust, listening to the rhythm of the camp, familiarizing himself with the sounds, checking his watch as a two-man guard detail walked by, getting a feel for their level of awareness. It was clear they were pretty relaxed, their threat level low. They'd done this drill many times before and were comfortable with the routine. They weren't anticipating trouble, and he wasn't going to give them any. Not tonight.

He waited five minutes, then sprinted for the Jeep. Before they'd left Spokane, he'd unscrewed the overhead lightbulb. Opening the passenger-side door only wide enough to give him room to work, he took a knee, leaned back into the door frame, and went to work on the door with a screwdriver he'd tucked in the glove box.

He had the interior frame off within a few minutes, laid it on the passenger seat, and unstrapped the phone, NV binoculars, and short-barreled M-4 rifle, which he quickly assembled. The magazines and extra ammo came next. He shoved everything across to the driver's seat.

When a quick glance confirmed that he hadn't roused any guards, he replaced the inside of the door and shut it quietly. Then crouching low, he rounded the front of the Jeep and went to work on the driver's-side door. When he'd repeated the process, he gathered up the two handguns along with the rifle and ammo, and crouching low again, sprinted to the cabin and silently let himself back inside.

He'd searched the cabin for hiding spots while he waited for Eva to return after dinner, but hadn't come up with much. He'd finally pried loose a couple pieces of the pine paneling inside the closet, stuffed the poured insulation down as far as he could, and made a space for the guns and binoculars. It wouldn't take much digging for someone to find them, but it was the best he could do with what he had.

Before stowing the phone, he turned it on and fired off a quick text to Gabe, letting him know they were in. Then, after pulling the battery and hiding the phone and all the guns but the Makarov, he quietly tapped the boards back in place and closed the closet doors. Checking to make sure Eva was still asleep, he tucked the Makarov into his waistband and headed back outside.

Sixteen minutes had passed since he'd let himself outside the first time. If duties and details changed every two hours, that meant the next patrol duty wouldn't be by for over an hour. Plenty of time to do some recon.

His new friend Beaver had pointed out the night watch positions today. "You'll have to pull your fair share of shifts, so you'd just as well know." Consequently, Mike knew which areas of the perimeter to avoid.

Using buildings, vehicles, trees, anything he could duck behind as cover, he divided the encampment into five-block grids and started systematically exploring.

First stop, the armory. He wanted to know what kind of munitions and numbers they had stockpiled inside.

The one-story building was approximately fifteen-by-fifteen square. Mike cut between the motor pool and the power plant and approached it from the rear. As he'd suspected, there were no windows on the entire building—the only way in was the front door. His back pressed to the side of the building, he snuck around toward the front, stopped at the corner, and listened.

He could hear the two guards talking; caught the scent of cigarette smoke as it drifted his way on a south breeze.

Obviously he wasn't going in the front door. He slipped around back again, looked up the building to the peaked roof. Bingo. There was a triangular ventilation grate right where the outside wall met the apex of the roof. Looked about big enough for a man his size to slip through.

He hot-footed it back to the power plant—he'd spotted a ladder on the ground behind it on his way by—and less than five minutes later, he had very carefully propped the ladder against the armory's back wall and scaled it. But even standing on the top rung, he could barely reach the bottom of the grate. He wasn't going to be able to remove it and get inside without creating a shitload of commotion.

New plan. He dug a high-power Maglite out of his pocket, flicked it on and, careful to keep the face of the light flattened against the wall to concentrate the beam there, he stuck the end of the light in his mouth. Then, gripping the bottom of the grate, he pulled himself up so he was eye level with the slates in the grate.

With the flashlight still in his mouth, he hiked himself up a little higher, using his boot tips for leverage against the outer wall, and shined the light inside and down, working the beam across as much of the inside of the building as he could see. And holy shit, did he see a lot.

Enough to know there might be trouble afoot.

Careful to keep the beam of light concealed, he tucked his chin to his chest and, feeling the burn in his biceps, lowered himself back down until his feet touched the top rung of the ladder. Then he switched off the light and shimmied down as fast as he could go.

He'd just hit the ground when he heard voices— close and getting closer. And fuck . . . there was no place to hide. Deer. Headlight. That was him.

He quickly lifted the ladder away from the wall and laid it on the ground. Then he scrambled to lie down full-length behind it. Pressing his back as close to the foundation of the building as he could get, he pulled the ladder snug against him. They would definitely notice a man out of place in the night, but hopefully a ladder leaning against a foundation wouldn't draw much more than a glance. Even a ladder that wasn't supposed to be there. It was dark. They were tired, maybe they wouldn't notice.

Maybe was a piss-poor plan, but it was all he had.

Willing his beating heart to slow, his breath to even out, he lay still as dirt, flattened against the foundation—*be the foundation*—counting on the ladder to provide camouflage. It would be laughable if it wasn't so dangerous.

Holding the ladder steady with one hand placed inconspicuously along the bottom edge, he pulled the Makarov out of his waistband but kept it under his shirt.

No sooner had he locked himself in freeze position than the guards rounded the corner, one with an AR-15 slung over his shoulder, one smoking a ciga-

rette and toting a shotgun. Both seemed bored out
of their minds and he'd bet the last thing they were
looking for was a problem.

God willing, they wouldn't find one.

They were even with his feet now, then his hips,
and he prayed they'd keep moving . . . but the smoker
decided to stop and stub out his cigarette butt, inches
from Mike's face.

He held his breath as a leather boot heel bumped
against the ladder as the guard ground the butt into
the grass.

Shouldn't have been a problem. But the back of
Mike's hand, which held the ladder steady, was flat
on the ground, his fingertips extending beyond the
aluminum slats, and directly under both the cigarette
butt and the boot.

He gritted his teeth to keep from sucking in a
breath as white-hot pain seared into his fingertip.
Then the boot heel ground that ember deeper into
his finger, burning through his thin glove and em-
bedding deep into the fleshy part of his fingertip.

Sweat trickled in his eyes as he lay there, fighting
the pain and the involuntary urge to jerk his hand
away. Jaw clenched, eyes bulging, he willed himself
not to move. Swore a litany of curses in his mind to
keep focused and stone still. He thought of ice, of No-
vocain—anything to get him through this. Just when
he thought he might pass out or roar and hurl the
ladder at the guard's head, they moved on.

Still holding his breath, Mike slid his hand out

from under the ladder, tugged the glove off with his teeth, and lightly fanned his burned finger in the cool night air.

The guards had moved out of sight, no doubt back to their positions at the front of the building. He waited for several more minutes, then decided it was safe to get up. Carrying the ladder with him, he returned it to where he'd found it.

After checking out the motor pool and the storage building, he ended his recon for the night. He stripped off his mask and the other glove and tucked them in his pants pockets. Then he shucked the shirt, tossed it onto his shoulder, and headed straight for the communal restroom — nothing suspicious about a man making a nighttime run to the head.

Feeling like a weenie — his damn finger still burned like it had been stuck in acid — he ran cold water over his stinging digit until the fire had cooled a little, then headed back to the cabin.

"Where were you?" Eva whispered, half-asleep as he skinned down to his boxers and climbed in bed beside her.

"Working on a Purple Heart."

"You're hurt?" Alarmed, she started to sit up. He stopped her by banding an arm around her waist.

"Only my pride." The damn finger still hurt like hell. *Mikey has a boo-boo* . . . God, he'd gotten soft. "Go back to sleep," he whispered, making a place for her against his shoulder. "We'll talk in the morning."

He loved the way she snuggled trustingly against

him. Within seconds, her breath had slowed again and she was sound asleep.

It didn't quite work that way for him. He couldn't stop thinking about what he'd seen in the armory. And what the hell it meant. Plus his finger throbbed like a bitch.

Weenie times ten.

The next morning before breakfast, Eva listened as Mike gave her a rundown on his recon of the armory. His near miss scared her half to death, but that's why they were here—so she kept her concern to herself.

"A freaking ton of AK-47s, AR-15s, a wall of shotguns and pistols, and a shitload of ammo to go with it. I even spotted some frag grenades and Claymores," Mike told her.

He reached for his boots and tugged them on. "He's got his little army; he needs to arm them. The kicker, though, was the explosives. There're enough spools of det cord and boxes of plastic explosives to blow up a small city."

She watched him lace up his boots, noticed he favored the middle finger on his left hand. "Maybe he has plans to target a government building. That would make a statement."

"It would fit the profile, yeah." He tied the final lace and stood. "Guess time will tell if they decide to read me in on their long-range plans. Not that I care. We're going to stop Lawson before he ever gets one of his plans off the ground."

"What did you do to your hand?"

He grunted and, sounding embarrassed, told her. "I'm a candy ass. You'd better hope I don't get shot. I'll probably bawl like a baby."

Grinning, she grabbed her duffel and rifled through her "necessity" kit. "Come here. This will help."

"Ouch."

She laughed. "I haven't touched you yet."

"I can tell by looking that it's going to hurt. Maybe you'd better kiss it first. Better idea. Kiss this."

He lowered his mouth and touched his lips to hers. "Much better."

"You're still getting the ointment. Hold still. It should take the sting out of it and keep it from getting infected."

"I'm starting to dig this. Can we play naughty nurse later tonight?"

"As long as I don't have to patch up anything more than a burned finger." She got serious suddenly. "So *don't* get shot. I . . ." She felt overwhelmed with dread suddenly, felt the sting of tears before she could stop them.

"Hey. Hey. I'm not getting shot, okay?" He tried to pull her into his arms.

She wasn't having any of it. Her display of weakness embarrassed her and she pushed away. "Like you can guarantee that."

"I can. I will. Nothing's going to happen to me. Nothing's going to happen to either of us. Now, let's go see what kind of slave labor Lawson's got lined up for you today, while I go play fun and games with my new pals."

Because he wanted her to—because she needed to—she smiled and pulled herself together. "Fine. But next gig? You get the beast of burden role."

He dropped a kiss on top of her head. "I'll flip you for it."

Smiling, she headed out the door.

And wondered when things had become so easy between them.

And when she'd started thinking of a future with him in it.

31

During the next few days, they fell into a routine. Up at dawn, off to what Eva had started to think of as the coal mines, back to the cabin by seven p.m., quick text to Gabe, then midnight recon missions that had so far turned up nothing of value.

Tonight, however, the routine was off-kilter—and it worried her. It was almost ten p.m. and Mike wasn't back yet. There wasn't a lot of time for socializing or fraternizing and when there was, it consisted of a command performance by Lawson, where the entire camp was expected to show up and listen to one of his speeches that denigrated the government and sang the praises of the UWD movement. Last night was one of those nights.

"Soon, brothers and sisters. Soon we will be in power. Until then, patience and diligence and devotion are required of every man, woman, and child."

Eva couldn't believe that people bought this crap. But the mob mentality kicked in, and that's all she wrote.

She willed herself not to look out the window again, and thought instead of what they'd accomplished. She'd started to gain a measure of trust from a few of the women, but for the most part they remained guarded, more out of subservience than from a sense of self-preservation. It was sad.

Mike had more freedom around the camp and had been assigned as a team leader to a small group of men. A test, they suspected, to see how he handled a leadership role.

Their guns and phones hadn't yet been returned and Mike hadn't been assigned a weapon like the rest of the troops but, again, that was to be expected during what Lawson now referred to as a probationary period.

The daily texts to Gabe let him know they were fine and to stand by. Mike hoped to be inviting Gabe and Joe to the fold soon. Maybe with four pairs of eyes, they could hunt down Lawson's secrets.

Her thoughts returned to Mike. Where was he? He should have been here hours ago.

"I liked what I saw on the shooting range today."

Mike acknowledged Lawson's compliment with a nod, and smiled across the desk, not surprised the lights-out-at-sunset rule didn't apply to the big dog. The office was well lit. Too well lit. He'd seen too much of Lawson's ugly face today. "The AR-15's a sweet weapon, sir."

He was dead beat, hot, and two hours late getting back to Eva. He'd rather dive into a snake pit—and he fucking hated snakes—than spend one more second

in Lawson's company, or call the bastard "sir," but the
UWD leader had extended a special invitation. No
way could Mike pass up the chance to suck up and
get his foot a little further in the door.

So here he was. In Lawson's office, buddying up
across the ancient gray desk, an uncapped bottle of
scotch calling to him like original sin.

"Sure you don't want one?" Lawson lifted his shot
glass.

Hell yes, he wanted one. "Thanks, but no. Never
acquired a taste for it." As long as he was lying, go big.

"If it's not too presumptuous, sir, I have some ideas
that might improve the men's overall shooting accuracy."

Lawson leaned back in his chair. "By all means."

Because the range and the equipment disburse-
ment was so slipshod, it didn't take much for Mike to
lay out a good case for making changes. Since Lawson didn't know that he was aware of the contents of
the armory, Mike ran a laundry list of all the things he
thought it would make sense to stock—all of which
Lawson already had on hand, of course.

"Impressive."

Mike said nothing. A humble man, wanting to
help the cause.

"You ever see any action?" Lawson asked after re-
filling his glass.

"Some."

"Where?"

Mike took a chance. "Afghanistan."

Lawson nodded. "Navy played a bigger part over there than most civilians realize. When?"

Mike shot out a date a couple years after he'd left Operation Slam Dunk, hoping it would trigger some conversation. It did.

"I spent some time in that rat hole. Whole fucking country should be blown to hell." Lawson shotgunned the scotch, slammed the empty glass on the desk. "Lot of money to be made there, though, if a man knows how to get it." He smiled, showing disgusting, pointy little yellow teeth. "I could tell you stories."

Mike got a sick feeling in the pit of his stomach that he was about to do just that as he poured another two fingers. He was getting sloppy. The sonofabitch couldn't hold his liquor. Must be the total lack of body fat. Or his ice-cold snake blood.

Lawson was quiet for a while, lost in the good old days, Mike thought sourly. Then he started telling war stories, bragging about his kills. He was slurring his words now.

Mike fought the urge to vomit and forced himself to bait him. "Country's crawling with opium, right? Lot of profit there for a tight operation."

"Hell. There was money to be made everywhere in that part of the world. I ran guns to Chechnya rebels, then turned around and supplied the Taliban. It was all a big fucking game."

He leaned in, grinning confidentially. "There was this sting I ran once . . . a favor, let's call it, for someone high up on the food chain. Someone who had a vested interest in the U.S. not getting a toehold in Helmand Province."

This was it. OSD had gone down in Helmand Province. The "someone high up on the food chain" had to be Lawson's big boss.

"Because of the opium trade?" Mike asked, hoping to lead him into more details.

"No shit. This certain Spec Ops unit was mucking things up for my—let's call him a business partner."

Business partner? Oh hell, let's call a spade a spade. He was a ruthless motherfucking murderer.

"How so?" Mike asked in a strangled voice. Lawson was too wasted to notice Mike's tension.

"They were putting the screws to the local warlords who were the main supply source for our lucrative little opium trade. We needed them gone—but it had to look like someone screwed up."

Mike swallowed back bile. "That had to be a neat trick."

"Just called for a little creativity. Ended up a real bloodbath. Wasted a bunch of locals to lure the team in, then took most of them out. Made it look like a goatfuck."

When Lawson chuckled, it was all Mike could do to keep from killing him with his bare hands.

"See, I worked it so the whole deal got pinned on some schmuck—a hotshot chopper pilot."

"Nice." Mike felt his eyes glazing over.

"Killed two birds with one big stone. Got the unit

out of the area by killing most of them off, and put a lid on anyone who lived to talk about it."

"So you actually took out a Spec Ops unit?" Apparently he sounded impressed because Lawson puffed out his chest.

"Damn straight. Showed that bunch of gung-ho, rah-rah, take-one-for-the-team patriots. Jerk-offs called themselves the One-Eyed Jacks."

Mike saw red, then black, and literally had to force himself to breathe.

"And you know the really funny part? One of their own was on my payroll."

The blind rage consuming him took a backseat to shock.

"Latino guy. Arrogant prick. Fancied himself a real lady-killer."

Ramon had been working with Lawson?

"Joke was on him, though," Lawson went on, seeming so lost in his fond memories, he'd forgotten Mike was even there. "Greased him on the spot. He burned up with the rest of his asshole buddies. Fitting end for a sellout, don't you think?"

"Yeah. A fitting end," Mike said grimly.

Eva was beside herself. It was almost midnight, and Mike still wasn't back. To pass the time, she'd showered, braided her hair, and rebraided it. Paced. Paced some more. There was nothing else to do, and she was way too upset to sleep.

Had something happened to him? Had they

found him out? Was he being held captive? Was he hurt?

Footsteps out front had her rushing to the door. Finally! Light-headed with relief, she swung the door open wide.

Mike barreled inside, almost knocking her over in the dark.

"Where have you been?"

He scowled down at her. "Shrew much?"

Worry shifted to anger in a heartbeat. "Uncalled for. I was worried. I thought something happened to you."

He let out a long breath. "You're right. I'm an ass. I'm sorry."

She followed his lead and settled herself down. "I'm sorry, too. I didn't mean to pounce on you."

He hugged her against him, then let her go and walked over to the bed. He sank down on the edge and began unlacing his boots, his movements sharp and jerky. "It's just . . . hell. I couldn't get away. When the general decides he wants your company, you don't decline because the little woman's waiting."

The hard edge in his voice undercut his attempted joke. A hard, dangerous edge. She took a good look at him, and saw more than fatigue and tension lining his face. He was beyond angry and trying to hold it in.

She sat down beside him. "Tell me what's going on."

For a long time he didn't say anything, just kept working the laces. When he finally got them loose, he toed off the boots, picked them up as though to put them away, then slammed them back down.

Then he sat forward, shoulders hunched, elbows on his thighs, and stared at a spot on the floor.

Eva waited, understanding that whatever was working on him was taking much bigger bites out of his peace of mind than the issue that had been eating at her all day.

"Mike? Talk to me."

Stocking feet still flat on the floor, he lay back on the bed and stacked his hands behind his head. "The asshole bragged about it, Eva," he said finally. "He bragged about slaughtering my team."

A sick feeling rolled through her stomach as he started talking and didn't stop until he'd purged himself.

"He was so fucking proud of himself. It wasn't about human lives. It was about the game. And the money. 'Lot of money to be made over there back then,' he said with this good-old-days look in his eyes. Opium trade. Gunrunning. Always someone on the take, right? Always someone who needed someone to do the dirty work for them. He was glad to be that man. Loves the irony of sticking it to Uncle."

He stopped again, a sick look on his face. "He's one brutal, sadistic bastard. Completely without a conscience. And I had to sit there and look awestruck, and encourage him to tell me more."

His voice broke then and he dragged a hand over his face. And grew deadly silent. Silent and brooding, his big body literally vibrating with a rage that was tearing him apart.

"Arrogant, immoral, egotistical, murdering bastard," he swore in a voice that was so softly menacing, it would have frightened her if she hadn't known him so well.

And she did know him, she realized as she encouraged him to lie lengthwise on the bed, then wrapped herself around his big, tense body. What she knew was that he had wanted to kill Lawson tonight. But he hadn't. He'd sat there and taken it. Sat and listened as Lawson bragged to him about how he'd annihilated women and children as though they were lab rats, killed honorable men who had been as close to Mike as brothers.

One of those men had been her husband.

"His only regret," Mike's voice was weary as he lifted his arm and made a place for her next to him, "is that it's harder to keep in the game these days.

"'A smart man like you,' I told him, pimping for more information, 'I figure you can still find a way to keep on sticking it to 'em.'"

He was so smart, she thought. "I don't imagine he was able to resist the opportunity to impress you even more."

"Yeah—that would have been my bet, but he got quiet then. Maybe I pushed a little too hard, because all he said was, 'You're right. I am smarter than them. They'll find out soon enough, too.' Then his phone rang. Whatever it was, he stood abruptly and told me he was calling it a day. That was my cue to leave.

"I came this close to killing him," he said after a long, heavy moment. "I've never felt that way in my life. I signed up for the service to protect and defend. But tonight I wanted blood. Wanted it as much as I've ever wanted a drink. It would have been easy. I outweigh him by fifty, sixty pounds. A blow to the head. A kick to the throat. He'd be gone."

"I want him dead, too," she said. "Ramon is dead because of him. Your life was ruined because of him. But you were right to hold off."

"There's only one reason he's not dead right now."

"Lawson's partner?"

He nodded. "When we find out who he was or is working with, we find out who put the hit out on you."

"And we clear your name," she pointed out, not wanting him to lose sight of that goal. "We have to get him. He can't get by with what he did. What he's still doing."

"I've got to get into his office again. There's got to be something there. Mr. Big's name on a computer file, a scrap of paper. His picture. Lawson has to have an insurance file—something he can hold over this guy in case they ever have a falling-out. And if it's not there, it'll be where Lawson sleeps. I just know he'll keep it close.

"And it's going to get easier starting tomorrow," he added, drawing her nearer. "He asked me to call my friends."

She lifted her head. "Seriously? That was fast."

"They'll be here tomorrow."

"You talked to Gabe?"

He nodded. "On Lawson's private line."

She hadn't realized how much relief that news would give her. It would still be four against over one hundred if things took a bad turn, but knowing that their numbers were increasing with two of the most revered operatives in the black ops community made her breathe easier. For all of two seconds.

"Lawson's put a lot of trust in you. Seems a little too easy, doesn't it?"

"I told you I could bullshit with the best of 'em. Earlier in the day when Lawson admitted that most of the yahoos he calls soldiers are weak-minded, undisciplined, all-talk-and-no-action losers, I told him I could help him with that and do it in triple time if I could call in my buddies. He liked the idea of new blood. So he gave me the green light. Not only that, he said he'd cut me in on a little action if I could cut that time down to less than a week."

She lifted up on an elbow. "What's his hurry?"

"I don't know. Maybe it had something to do with that phone call. But I get the sense that something important is about to happen. Bucky's been making noises about a big deal going down soon. A really big deal. I'll get it out of him tomorrow. In the meantime, I got a bead on Lawson's private quarters."

"You saw them?"

"No. But I hung back in the shadows after I left his office and spotted him heading south."

"I didn't see any buildings on the aerial maps in that area."

"Maybe it doesn't show on the map. Maybe the blood-sucking vampire lives in a cave like a bat."

"I don't remember anything about caves on the topography map, either."

"We've got to figure it out fast. I've got a bad feeling we're running out of time."

He tensed suddenly. "You hear that?"

Yeah. She heard it. The distant, then not so distant grinding gears, air brakes, and roaring diesel engines.

They jumped out of bed and raced to the window.

Then they stared in stunned silence as a line of vehicles slowly rolled by.

A pickup led the way for three semi tractors, each one pulling a long box trailer. Another pickup flanked the procession.

Dumbfounded, Eva turned to Mike. "What's a convoy of semis doing in the middle of nowhere?"

"Only one way to find out. Get your sleuthing shoes on, *chica*."

32

They waited five minutes, then, dressed in black, headed out into the dark and cut around to the back of the cabin. Eva had the Taurus tucked in her waistband and a Maglite in the pocket of her cargo pants. Mike opted for the M-4 in case they ran into a shitstorm. The mini NV binoculars were tucked in a pocket on the leg of his cargo pants. They hadn't gotten two steps when he grabbed Eva's wrist and dragged her back into the shadows.

"Patrol," he whispered, pressing his lips to her ear.

She froze, and like him, measured her breath, barely blinked, and hugged the cabin until the guards passed not ten yards away from them.

"I don't like this," he whispered.

"What you don't like is me going with you. I'll be fine."

She was right. He didn't like it that she was out here. What he liked even less was the surprise Lawson had dumped on him tonight, about Ramon being on Lawson's payroll. A major detail that Mike had left out when he'd filled Eva in. If she ever found out, it would kill her.

"It's clear." Her voice snapped him back. "Let's go."

With him in the lead, they headed out at a crouching run, ducking behind buildings, fences, trucks, whatever they could find for cover. While they couldn't track the semis' route, they'd figured out the path they had to take, based on the layout of the camp, and the direction the trucks were going when they rolled by. They were headed for the northern border of the meadow.

It was slow, treacherous going. They had to stop several times again and wait for patrols—which were double what he'd run into last night—to pass. Finally they reached the shooting range, cleared the earth berms built up behind the targets to stop the bullets, and headed out into the woods.

Using the edge of the tree line for cover, they worked their way slowly toward the northernmost quadrant . . . and stopped abruptly when they heard an idling motor and the murmur of voices in the distance.

Mike glanced at Eva. She nodded. She'd heard it, too. Slowing the pace and making sure they stayed concealed in the trees, they moved as quietly as possible toward the sound. A light materialized out of the dark. Then two. Headlights. Then several more lights. Flashlights. A diesel engine revved. Gears ground. Men shouted.

When they were within thirty yards of the activity,

Mike dropped to his belly and dug out the binoculars. Eva was right beside him—a good soldier, alert, light on her feet, sensing instinctively what he wanted her to do.

"I count five . . . make that six men on the ground," he whispered, adjusting the focus on the binocs.

"What are they doing?"

"Best guess? They're directing the semi drivers to back up the trailers. Let's get a little closer."

Under the cover of the gunning engines as the powerful diesels' gears engaged, they belly crawled, digging with their elbows and knees until they cut the distance in half.

Mike refocused the binoculars and scanned the area of activity. "What the hell?"

"What?" Beside him, Eva sounded anxious.

"They're gone. The semis. They've fucking disappeared."

He raised the glasses again, scanned slowly this time. All he saw were men milling around the pickups, talking, slamming tailgates, stowing gear. He couldn't see behind the smaller trucks but there was a flurry of activity, then everyone piled in and they took off.

After the taillights disappeared back toward the encampment, Mike checked things out one more time. Satisfied that there was no one left behind, he pushed to his feet.

"Let's go check it out."

• • •

"I thought I was kidding about the vampire cave." When he was satisfied that no one had been left behind on guard duty, Mike shined the Maglite through inch-thick iron bars that had been welded in six-inch squares to form two huge gates, padlocked together. Tire tracks in the dirt disappeared under the locked gate. "Wait. It's not a cave after all. See those old timbers? This is a mine shaft. We need to get inside."

He handed her the light and had her shine it on the padlock so he could check it out. "I don't remember anything about picking locks on your bio," he said, after inspecting it. "Don't suppose that's a hidden talent."

"Sorry. Way above my pay grade. Can we break it?"

"Not without letting them know someone was here."

He held out his hand and she handed back the light. He shined the beam around the perimeter of the opening, which was approximately twelve feet wide and fifteen feet high.

"Our lucky day." Because the opening of the shaft was slightly rounded and the top of the iron gates were level, there was a gap about three feet wide and eighteen inches high at the apex. "It'll be tight but I think I can get through it. You first."

He watched as she easily scaled the grillwork, holding the light so she could see where she was going. Once she made it to the top, she kept low, swung one leg over, then the other, and a few seconds later, hit the ground on the inside of the mine shaft.

He passed the Maglite through the bars and she returned the favor as he climbed to the top of the gate.

"Can you make it through?"

He grunted as he worked his body through the narrow opening. "Kind of like trying to squeeze a watermelon through a keyhole, but yeah. I'm good."

"Let's see what we've got." She handed back the light when his feet hit the dirt beside hers.

He shined the flashlight over the shored-up beams of the long horizontal shaft, then down to the very clear tire tracks that led to the three semis. The trucks were parked end to end down the length of the long, narrow tunnel that Mike guessed stretched a good one hundred feet. "So . . . the trucks arrive after dark and get tucked out of sight. Somebody doesn't want anybody seeing these bad boys."

"'Anybody' as in satellite surveillance?"

"That, too," he agreed and shined the light along the first trailer. "This is a refrigerated box. They all are," he added after trotting back and checking the other trailers.

"So why aren't there any generators running?"

"Good question."

They climbed up into the cab of the first semi, and Mike dug through the glove box until he found the manifest. "Check this out." He handed her the papers. "This truck's out of Canada and is supposedly carrying meat. I'm betting they all have the same papers."

"Let's go look in the back."

They found keys for the trailer with the manifest. After making quick work of the lock, he swung open one of the rear doors.

"I'll give you a boot up."

Eva placed her foot in his cupped hands, grabbed onto the other door, and he lifted her up and inside. Seconds later he was right beside her, shining the flashlight into the dark.

Hundreds of boxes, about three feet by two feet, were stacked on pallets to the ceiling. All of them had PORK and an expiration date stamped on the outside.

"In a pig's eye," Mike said.

"Seriously?"

"Sorry. I never back away from a pun."

He pulled out his Leatherman, flipped open the blade, and very carefully cut the tape on one of the boxes.

"Holy shit."

"AK-74s?" Eva peeled back the plastic that was covering the rifles to get a better look.

"Yeah. About the same caliber as the M-16, but more controllable at full automatic than its older brother, the AK-47. Someone plans to start a war." He shined the light up and down the inside of the trailer. "Let's say this trailer's around fifty feet long."

"Sounds right."

"Okay. Figure twenty-five pallets per trailer. But let's say at one point there was some legal cargo to make this work—just in case they got stopped at the border."

Eva saw where he was going. "So they place some pork loins here in the rear, making it look like the whole cargo was meat. Those boxes that actually contained the pork are probably in the back of the pickups that headed back to camp."

Mike nodded slowly. "That would work. A constant stream of trucks drive back and forth between the States and Canada. There wouldn't be a reason in the world to single one out and question if it was legit. Walks like, talks like, looks like refrigerated cargo, so anyone searching the trailer would hurry because the driver would be on their case about all that expensive meat spoiling.

"So," Mike continued, frowning, "let's say six decoy pallets—a couple on the back, the others on top, surrounding the boxes of guns."

Eva started calculating. "One gun per box times twenty boxes per pallet times twenty pallets. That's four hundred rifles per trailer."

"I'm betting there's ammo and mags tucked in here somewhere, too," Mike added and worked the rest of the math. "So each trailer's carrying around two hundred thousand dollars wholesale. Easily a half a mil per truck on the open market if they plan to sell them."

"Wait." Eva looked at him sharply. "Sell them?"

"Think about it. Lawson's armory is already overstocked. I saw that firsthand. Even if he planned a siege on a major city, no way would he need this much firepower for an operation. So this isn't about waging war. This is about supplying someone who plans to wage a war."

He saw in her eyes the moment she reached the same conclusion that he had. "Oh, God. The Juarez cartel. La Linea is his buyer."

"The 'big deal' that Lawson was hinting about going down."

She lifted a hand toward the gun shipment. "So they're storing them here until they decide it's safe to truck them south?"

Mike shook his head. "Maybe. But try this out. Million and a half in weapons, right? If you were Lawson, would you risk delivering the goods before you got payment in your hot little fist? No, you wouldn't. And if you were the badasses on the receiving end, would you fork over the cash before you received the shipment?"

"Whoa. You think the exchange is going to take place here?"

"If it was my deal, that's what I'd do. It just makes sense. Just like it makes sense that if this is their first business transaction, all the key players are going to show up for the dance. Have a little face-to-face, you know? Cement the new relationship."

Her eyes had grown wide. "Holy God."

"And all his angels," Mike added on a deep breath. "I'm not thinking just cartel members, either. Another big gun might be heading this way, too."

"Lawson's partner."

Mike nodded. The man who had called the shots on OSD. The man who had put a hit out on Eva.

For a moment they both stood there, working through all the revelations. Finally, she looked at him. "We can't let this exchange happen. We've got to call Gabe."

Shit. She was right. Gabe and Green needed to be stopped so they could regroup.

"They need to contact ATF. Hell, contact DEA, Homeland Security, and the FBI. Get them all down here. We can't let the cartel get their hands on these guns."

She was right again. But if they called in the big guns, Mike's chances of taking out Lawson himself shrank from slim to nonexistent.

His face must have shown his thoughts, because she put her hand on his arm. "Mike. This isn't just about us anymore. It's way bigger than that. It's about national security."

Life was so un-fucking-fair. "It's ironic, right? I come back to the States to clear my name, and I end up fighting for the team that benched me."

"It's that patriot gene of yours. You can't help but do the right thing."

She had a lot more faith in him than he had in himself. And something about that faith made him feel like a better man.

But yeah, this was a game changer. Lawson could no longer be the primary target. Clearing his name, setting things straight for Ramon's legacy . . . they had to let all that go, and stop the cartel from getting their hands on these guns. With Gabe's help they just might be able to do it. But they had to reach him first.

Face grim, he shut the gun box, then maneuvered it in behind several others so no one would notice the shipment had been tampered with. "Let's get out of here. That ticking clock we were working against just turned into a time bomb."

"Phone."

Jane's groggy whisper penetrated his sleep from a distance.

"Your phone is ringing."

Her hand touching his arm finally roused him.

Shaking himself awake, he groped for the switch on the bedside lamp and flicked it on. Squinting against the sudden glare, he reached past the clock that told him it was three a.m., and fumbled for his phone. The screen showed Barnes's number.

"What?" he said.

"You said to call, no matter the time, if I had actionable information," his cyber-security man said.

"Tell me you found them."

"This is what I can tell you. Whoever is using the Salinas woman's CIA access codes is not a traceable entity. I've tried everything. The system using her codes is hardened against external attacks—firewalls, RSA encryption . . . you name it, they've got a safeguard."

"And this helps me how?"

"This helps because it tells me that whoever it is has major resources if they can protect themselves with this level of sophistication. We're talking NSA kind of security here."

He sat up, thought about what Barnes was saying. "So you think we're dealing with a branch of the government?"

"Or a black ops unit."

This was not good news.

"While I can't pinpoint who's using it or where the activity is based, I was able to capture and trace some of their search threads using a zero-day exploit in their browser."

"Save the tech talk for someone who appreciates it and cut to the chase."

"Lawson's name came up a lot on those search threads. So did Afghanistan and UWD."

Fuck.

"On a hunch," Barnes went on, "I started monitoring cell phone transmissions out of the UWD camp."

"And?"

"There's been one text per day for the past several days, each time to a new phone number that was disconnected after it was used. Each number appears to have been forwarded to another phone or a series of phones. But the original numbers were all in D.C., and the phone exchange for each call was the Department of Agriculture's."

The bastards were real comedians. The Department of Agriculture was a standby beard. But they weren't as smart as they thought they were.

"Call Lawson. Find out—"

"I just got off the phone with him. He hasn't contacted anyone in D.C. And control freak that he is, he's the only one on base with a cell phone."

"Then who made the call?"

"This is where it gets interesting. Seems Lawson got a couple new recruits this past week. A man and a woman. What do you want to bet the texts were sent by them?"

His heart rate picked up. "Did you get their physical descriptions from Lawson?"

"I did. It's them."

33

"These beefed-up forces make me nervous," Mike whispered as they hid from yet another traveling patrol. They'd left the mine nearly two hours ago, tripling their return time because they'd run into double the usual number of security details. In another hour and a half it would be daylight.

"The increased patrols have got to be because of the guns," she whispered as they crouched low behind the food storage building and waited for the four-man patrol to pass. "I'd be nervous, too, if I was sitting on that many dollars' worth of weapons."

Mike placed a finger to his lips as the men grew closer, then faded away into the night. Several seconds passed before he tapped her shoulder—time to take off again.

They darted between the shadows and finally reached the rear of the cabin. With Mike taking the lead, they circled around to the front and crept up onto the porch. Eva kept seeing those semis loaded with weapons. She'd never seen so many fricking guns in her life.

The cabin was dark. Eva silently slipped inside and sprinted across the room. She only had one goal—get to the hidden cell phone—but she'd no sooner opened the closet door than a burst of light flooded the room.

She spun around, ready to rail at Mike, but the words died on her tongue.

They weren't alone—and neither was the man who held the monster flashlight that lit up the room and half blinded her.

Three other men stood just inside the doorway, all of them with rifles shouldered and pointed at them.

Mike looked from Simmons to the other three and slowly lifted his hands in the air. "Look who's here. The Welcome Wagon committee. Nice to see you again, fellas."

Simmons ignored him. "Looking for this?" He held up their cell phone, then dropped it to the floor and stomped it with his boot heel. "Whoops. Guess it's broken."

Eva glanced at Mike, who gave an almost imperceptible shake of his head. *Say nothing*, his eyes said.

"I always knew there was something off about you, Walker. Oh, wait. Make that Brown." Simmons walked up to Mike, a self-important sneer on his face. "Not as smart as you thought you were, huh, asshole?"

Mike gave the big man a huge, fake smile and Eva knew he was about to say something that was really going to piss Simmons off.

No, she mouthed.

"And yet, you're the dumb fuck letting a loser like Lawson run your life. What's that say about you . . . *asshole?*"

Red-hot rage spread up Simmons's neck, over his face, and mottled the top of his bald head.

"If he fights back"—Simmons handed Bryant his rifle and the flashlight—"shoot her."

Then he slammed a closed fist into Mike's gut with a force that doubled him over.

Mike landed on the floor, folded in on himself, gasping for breath. "That . . . the best you got . . . pussy?"

Eva screamed when Simmons hauled back and kicked him in the ribs. "Mike, shut up! For God's sake, shut up!"

But it was too late. Simmons unloaded on him like a bull, blinded by rage and seeing red. By the time Wagoner pulled Simmons off, Eva wasn't even sure if Mike was breathing.

When Mike came to, it was to screaming pain, a hard floor, a hot, dark room, and a soft woman cradling his head in her lap. "What'd I . . . miss?"

"Oh, God. Thank God. You're conscious."

Even though she kept her voice low to keep from being overheard, Mike heard the fear and the tears. And he hated that he'd put her through it.

"Unfortunately. Yeah. I am." Everything hurt. Breathing. Talking. Blinking. But most of all, it hurt to know he'd scared her.

"How long?" he whispered, lifted his hand to her face and discovered his wrists were flex-cuffed together in front of him. Bastards had tied her up, too.

"How long have you been out? Hours. Many, many *fucking* hours. It must be close to noon."

Okay. Pissed off had officially muscled out worried and scared.

"So what was the plan, Brown? Was there a reason you invited Simmons to beat the snot out of you?"

How one small woman could pack so much venom into a whisper was beyond him.

"Yeah . . . sure." He struggled to sit up, sucked in a breath when fire shot through his ribs. "Damned if I can remember why, but I must have thought it was a good idea at the time."

Actually, he'd wanted Simmons's focus on him. The big man had been working his way into a mean, dark snit, and rather than take a chance of him going off on Eva, he made sure Simmons unleashed on him.

"He could have killed you."

Because he heard more regret in her voice than anger now, he figured she'd forgiven him. "But he didn't. At least not yet."

"Because Lawson wants you alive."

He grunted, then regretted it. "For the time being. No doubt he's got big plans for us. We've got to get out of here before that happens. More to the point . . . we need to head off Gabe and Green."

The two men would be arriving anytime, unaware

that they'd been found out. He couldn't let them walk
into an ambush.

With Eva's help, he staggered to his feet. Through
swollen eyes and a blinding headache, he checked
out their prison. Slivers of daylight filtered in through
windows that were boarded shut. July heat seeped
through the walls, searing and suffocating in the stagnant air. The main light source was from a triangular
ventilation grate like the one in the armory, where
the back wall met the peaked ceiling. The room was
approximately twelve by twelve. Bare-bones construc-
tion. Plywood floor, open rafters, and wall studs.

"Do you know where we are?" he asked.

She wiped sweat from her forehead with the back
of her bound hands. "It's the overflow food storage
shed—empty now, but I'm guessing it's where they
keep their winter supplies. Why wouldn't they have
a jail or a brig like any other military operation, since
Lawson fancies himself a general?"

He hadn't wanted to tell her this before, but there
didn't seem to be much point withholding it now. He
shuffled over to a wall, leaned against it to keep from
keeling over. "Remember my buddy, Bucky? He
made it pretty clear one day that I needed to keep my
nose clean. You break a rule around here? You cross
the boss? One shot. Back of the head. The coyotes eat
well that night. There is no discipline. Just death."

"Well. It's efficient, I'll give him that."

No whimpering. No hand wringing. *Way to take it
on the chin, Eva.* God, he loved this woman.

"How many guards?" he asked.

"I counted six—three at the door and three more stationed around the perimeter of the building. Inside? It's just you and me and the mice."

"So . . . thoughts?" God, his head hurt.

"None that I see working. Even if I could climb up to that ventilation grate and get outside without making enough noise to raise the dead, I'll never get past the guards. And you? Right now, you're pretty much worthless thanks to your smart mouth."

Okay. So she wasn't totally over being pissed at him.

"But you've got a plan, right?" He knew she had one. Eva wasn't a reactor. She made things happen.

"Yeah. I've got a plan. But you're not going to like it."

"Try me."

"We wait for Gabe and Green."

He carefully let his head fall back against the wall. Closed his eyes on a fractured breath as sweat trickled down his spine. "You're right. I don't like it."

"You don't have to like it. We just have to do it."

Now she was throwing his own words back at him. Guess he had that coming.

"At least with them inside, we've got enough numbers to make something work. And unless you sprout wings and a machine gun, we aren't going anywhere anyway."

Very slowly he sank back down to the floor. Breathed through the pain. "Fine. We wait."

He closed his eyes and dozed on and off, so he wasn't sure how much time passed when a key rattled in the lock and the door swung open. He squinted up to see Simmons standing in the threshold, carrying his shotgun. Then he flipped on the light switch and an overhead bulb blinked on. "Special delivery, asshole."

Simmons stepped aside and Wagoner and Bryant shoved two men into the room, their wrists bound with flex cuffs, their heads covered with hoods.

Even though he'd been expecting it, it ripped a hole in Mike's chest to know that he was responsible for putting Gabe and Joe in this position.

He propped himself up on an elbow. "Four people? This small room? Gotta be breaking some fire code for maximum capacity. Who do I see about lodging a complaint?"

Simmons backed toward the door. "You're a real funny guy. What do you wanna bet you aren't laughing tomorrow at this time? Oh, wait. Tomorrow at this time you're gonna be dead. You and your bitch and your buddies. If it was up to me, the deed would already be done. Make a joke about that."

He stomped across the room, flipped off the light, slammed the door, and locked it behind him.

Mike swallowed back the lump in his throat, feeling a despair unlike anything he'd felt since Afghanistan. He thought of Gabe's little girl. Of the baby on the way. Of Jenna and Stephanie—the wives and lovers these men might never see again.

"Sorry, guys." His voice broke. "Didn't exactly see it going down like this."

Both men reached up and wrestled off their hoods.

And for the first time that he could remember, Mike couldn't have uttered a sound if his bare feet had been held to a fire.

He squinted his eyes into focus, certain he was hallucinating, but there was no getting around it. It wasn't Gabe Jones staring back at him. It wasn't Joe Green.

"Long time no see, Primetime." Bobby Taggart stood there grinning at him as if he'd just checked into a resort and eight years of hating Mike's guts had never happened.

What the hell?

"You just can't help yourself, can you?" Jamie Cooper's Hollywood smile was as blinding as it had ever been. "Always landing your sorry ass in a sling."

What the holy hell?

"And dragging us along for the ride," Taggart added, then directed his attention to Eva. "Ma'am. It's a pleasure to meet you—present circumstances notwithstanding."

All Mike could do was stare. At those far-too-familiar faces that looked so much like he remembered, yet had changed in ways he understood too well. He still couldn't believe what he was seeing. After he'd left a message on Jamie's machine and never heard back, he'd figured that the bridge was well and truly burned.

"Wh . . ." He stopped, shook his head, unable to form the words. *What are you doing here? Why did you come?* "What happened to Gabe and Joe?"

Even before Cooper spoke, he knew. Cooper hadn't just gotten his message—he'd believed him. Then he'd convinced Taggart and, knowing Taggart, he'd needed a helluva lot of convincing.

"Your buddy Jones says 'hey,'" Cooper said.

"And to not fuck this up," Taggart added.

Since they both had candy-eating grins on their faces, Mike knew Gabe had probably had a lot more to say.

The fact that the two of them were here, though, said everything he needed to know. When they couldn't reach him, they'd called the number he'd given Cooper to reach Gabe, who had read them in on the mission, and they'd asked to take his and Joe's place.

Pig simple. And not simple at all. They were here because they needed to be. They were here because they had to be.

Because they were his brothers.

His vision misted over as a relief so huge and so consuming threatened to drop him to his knees.

"Not that we don't appreciate the stellar digs"— making a point of giving Mike a chance to pull himself together, Cooper craned his head around, checking out the possibilities—"but it's a little stuffy in here. I'm all for going for an upgrade to oh, say . . . anywhere but fucking here."

"I'm down with that."

Mike recognized the gravel in Taggart's voice, since the same rock of emotion had lodged in his.

Sonofabitch. They'd come.

• • •

Eva sized up Taggart and Cooper, deciding the two men were as different as tequila and scotch. Taggart was tall, fair, wore his light brown hair in a military buzz cut, and was built like a tank. Cooper clearly had Latino blood running through his veins. The man gave Mike a run for his money in the drop-dead gorgeous department. He was also muscular, but more like a runner or a swimmer.

And regardless of the trash talk that passed between the three of them, that indefinable bond that united them still held strong. Not that they weren't feeling their way carefully around each other. Eight years of distance and resentment, no matter that it was founded on lies and misunderstanding, rode heavy on the air between them. But the team mentality had fallen back into place like well-oiled gears.

The looks that passed between them made Eva's heart break. Typical men, they couldn't come out and say what was really on their minds. Years of regret. Years of pain. Years of loss. And all they exchanged were looks and trash talk. No handshakes. No hugs, because, God forbid, contact might trigger an emotion they'd have to actually deal with.

Okay. She got it, she thought, as Mike filled them in on the semis full of guns and their speculation that a deal with key members of the Juarez cartel was about to go down. Now wasn't the time for a sentimental reunion. Now wasn't the time to voice forgiveness and repent. Neither was it the time to sort out her link to

Lawson, although she suspected that Gabe had connected the dots between her and Ramon when he'd
read them in on the operation.

But so help her God, if they got out of here alive,
she was going to make sure that the three of them
confronted the ghosts that haunted them. They were
going to have a touchy-feely moment if she had to
knock them all in the head with a hammer.

But first they had to get out of here. Cooper and
Taggart were already making a visual sweep of the
room for possible escape scenarios when a commotion outside had them all turning in that direction.

Mike gave her a *What now?* look.

"Open it." Lawson's voice was unmistakable on
the other side of the door.

Eva's heart sank. This couldn't be good.

Was this it, then? The end? Why else would Lawson be here?

Mike moved close against her side just as the door
swung open and the overhead light flipped on.

Lawson walked in, flanked by Simmons and Wagoner, both of them armed to the teeth. Lawson glared
at Taggart, then Cooper, let his ferret gaze drift over
Eva and finally land on Mike. The smile that tilted
his lips was ugly. "You've got yourself a little problem,
Walker. Excuse me. Brown."

"I'm guessing this means I'm not going to get that
promotion?"

Anger flashed in Lawson's eyes, but his smile never
wavered. "What it means is that you're a dead man.

You and your friends. But not just yet. I'm not without compassion. So as long as we've got this reunion theme going, I want to give you an opportunity to say hello to an old friend."

Lawson stepped aside. First into the room was a woman Eva didn't recognize. She was blond and totally unremarkable except for her eyes. And the coldness Eva saw there chilled her blood to ice. She was dressed all in black. In one hand she held a wicked Heckler & Koch MP5K. Her other arm was immobilized in a sling. And though she'd never seen her before in her life, Eva got the distinct impression the woman's ice-queen exterior was a wall holding back a red-hot hatred.

A man stepped in behind her. Big man. Tall. Late fifties, maybe early sixties. Like Lawson, he was dressed in camo pants and a neatly pressed broadcloth shirt. An officer's shirt, complete with a shiny nameplate pinned to his breast pocket.

She squinted to make out the letters . . . then sucked in her breath on a gasp.

BREWSTER.

34

"Well." Brewster looked from one shocked face to another. "I guess we can safely say you hadn't figured it out."

He'd been close to these men once. They'd believed in him. Trusted him. Whatever regrets he harbored, however, held little sway when stacked up against the money he'd made over the years.

"I could have had you taken out eight years ago, you know. The three of you are only alive now because I arranged it."

"Gosh." Cooper was the first to break the silence. "Does that call for a thank you very much or a fuck you very much?"

Brewster grinned. "I always liked you, Jamie. Hell. All of you were damned entertaining."

Brown glared at him. "So glad we could be of service."

"And that," he said, lifting a chiding finger, "was the crux of your problem. Your dedication to service."

"You sonofabitch," Taggart swore under his breath.

Again Brewster smiled.

"You sold us out." The calm edge in Taggart's voice did little to hide his outrage and hatred. "You murdered our brothers. And for what? Money? Power? The fucking fun of it? *Sir*," he added mockingly.

Brewster shook his head and let out a sigh. "I misjudged you. That was my mistake. I hadn't expected a bunch of flash-and-dazzle party boys to pull together and turn into a cohesive and, frankly, exemplary unit. Figured it would be all about the hotdogging, right? That's what you all did best. Thought I could keep you contained. But I didn't take into account the Boy Scout factor. You really did believe in the greater good. Well, all except Salinas."

Oh, that got a reaction. Pretty little Eva went ghostly pale. And Brown's eyes flared with hatred.

"Shut up," Brown warned. "Just shut the fuck up. She doesn't need to hear this."

"Interesting. You never liked Salinas, Michael, yet you don't want to sully his name in front of his widow?"

"Leave her the hell alone." Brown couldn't keep his emotions in check.

"No." Eva took a step forward. "I want to know. Tell me."

His gaze swung to the lush and lovely widow Salinas. Under other circumstances he might have looked for a reason to save her, but this was a done deal and he was finished with leaving any loose ends.

"Your husband wasn't the man you thought he

was, dear." A hard truth, but few men were the heroes their women thought them to be. God knows he'd never been, but he'd sure convinced a helluva lot of women that he was Superman, and they'd all seemed happy to believe him. "Ramon was easy to corrupt, a greedy bastard who couldn't keep his dick in his pants, or his hand out of my till."

Her face paled, and he could see her struggling to find some way to push her long-dead husband closer to the purer end. A lonely guy too far from home and his beautiful wife, just needing a little solace in another woman's arms, a hardworking man who realized his boss was on the wrong side, and tried to right some wrongs.

Wasn't going to happen. Not with Ramon Salinas.

From the tight, sad expression on her face, he figured she knew. Smart girl.

"So if he was working for you, why did you kill him?" she asked.

"Because every time I turned around, he was standing there with his hand out. When he started bitching about either getting a bigger cut or else running his mouth to the wrong people, he left me no choice. I buried the bastard. Frankly, my dear, you're better off without him. Well, relatively speaking." They'd all be dead by morning, and not one of them was naïve enough to doubt it.

Not even the lovely Eva.

He let his gaze run over her from top to bottom and back up again, not missing a curve. The lady was built. He had a soft spot for smart, gorgeous women, and this one was starting to look like a lost opportunity. He should have done the right thing eight years ago and been there to console the grieving widow.

Oh, well. Jane was a safer bet—and she had the same mean streak he did, which made them a good team.

"You weren't supposed to make it out of Lima," he said, holding her gaze. "Jane was contracted for the hit." He gestured to the kick-ass blonde at his side, and saw dawning recognition in Eva's and Mike's faces. "She still wants to finish the job, professional pride and all that. She wants her pound of flesh." And he was inclined to let her have it. His boys deserved the best, and Jane was the best.

He slid his gaze over the three of them, all that was left of the One-Eyed Jacks. That's what they'd been— his boys, and he couldn't help but feel a small twinge of regret. They'd been the best team he'd ever had, and they'd been their own worst enemies.

"You were too good," he told them. "You couldn't keep your heads down and ignore what needed to be ignored. It was a simple deal: drugs and guns. Lawson and I delivered the guns, and the Afghani warlords delivered the opium. But you guys"—he shook his head, and a small grin curved his mouth—"you guys just kept screwing their pooch. I don't want you to think I gave you up. There wasn't a choice to be made. It was purely a question of logistics. You had to go."

"OSD was a setup from the get-go," Mike concluded.

"And your own Salinas lead you into the trap."

"Why not just kill all of us that night?" Cooper looked genuinely puzzled. "You knew we were out there hiding."

"Ah, that was the genius of the plan. We could have killed you, yes, but then how did we explain what happened? Nothing like a whodunit to bring on a major investigation."

"So you deflected the attention to us. Put the blame on us for killing those civilians."

Brown always had been intelligent.

Brewster nodded. "Which got Karzai good and riled. He put pressure on the White House. Told the President that if he wanted to maintain any kind of presence in the region, he needed to pull all Spec Ops teams out or he'd blow this incident up in the international press to the point where it looked like Abu Ghraib all over again."

"How'd you get it buried from the media?" Taggart wanted to know.

"Same way every potential political bombshell gets buried. Money. Karzai made out like a bandit. Plus he got his warlords off his back when the Spec Ops teams were booted—which was exactly what Lawson and I wanted. It got you out of our hair so we could continue to run our opium pipeline without interference."

None of them had anything to say to that.

"If you had just left it alone"—he turned back to Eva—"everything would have stayed status quo. You'd all still be alive tomorrow."

"Then why did you leak the OSD file to me?"

He frowned, puzzled, then let out a soft chuckle. "Someone leaked the OSD file? To you? God, that's what set this whole thing off? Well, that explains a lot. Leak the file? No, that wasn't me. Though now that I know someone's playing fast and loose with information I had made certain was buried . . . well, when I find out who did it, they'll be as dead as you're about to be. And that's the irony, isn't it? Apparently they thought they were doing you a favor. Instead, they signed your death warrant along with their own."

"So why are we still alive? Why not get it over with?"

Taggart. Always impatient, to his own detriment.

Brewster looked at the men who had once been under his command and actually felt regret. "Don't worry. We will. But right now we have pressing business that can't wait."

Lawson's walkie-talkie squawked, then a disembodied voice crackled over the radio. "ETA on the chopper, five minutes."

"Stand by," Lawson said into the radio, then looked at Brewster and nodded. "We need to cut this little reunion short. Our guests are about to arrive."

"Your pressing business?" Cooper was insolent as ever.

"'Fraid so. Duty calls," Brewster told them, then

regarded them with a regretful look. "I know you don't believe this, but I am sincerely sorry about the way this turned out."

Cooper, Taggart, and Brown all looked at him, looked at each other, then as one, lifted their bound hands and flipped him twin birds.

Arrogant bastards. "And that attitude, gentlemen, is exactly why you're going to die."

35

The silence that fell over their prison after Brewster and his entourage left could have filled a football stadium. It lasted all of five seconds before Taggart cut it off at the knees.

"Let's get the fuck out of here. Steak dinner to the first one out of the cuffs."

"You are *so* buying." Cooper flashed a grin full of arrogance and attitude. "Sixteen ounces minimum. Not one of those baby cuts."

Like old times, Mike thought, going to work on the plastic straps binding his wrists. They'd felt invincible once, and found out the hard way that they were far from it. But their lives weren't going to end here. Not like this. No way. Not like rats in a cage.

Jesus. Brewster. He still couldn't believe it. The man had been a verifiable hero in the Spec Ops community. He'd had the chops, done the deeds, and he'd made good, all the way to a three star—and then he'd gone bad. So fucking bad.

But there was no time for that now. He had to

get Eva out of this rat hole, and to do that *he* had to get out.

Thwup, thwup, thwup. They all heard it at the same time and everybody looked toward the vaulted ceiling. Chopper. A big one.

"The nice men from Mexico must have arrived." Cooper looked grim. "Sounds like a Shithook."

Eva scowled. "A what?"

"A civilian version of the CH-47 Chinook," Mike explained. "Big bird. Can carry a lot of cargo." Like guns, they all thought, but didn't voice.

"We've gotta boogie."

It had to be over a hundred degrees in the small, airless room. Sweat ran down Mike's forehead, burning like fire when it trickled into the cuts on his face, as he went back to work on the flex cuffs.

"Winner and new champeen," Cooper crowed in a whisper as he lifted his hands, free of the restraints.

"I'll make sure you get a medal," Mike grumbled. "If my friend Simmons hadn't tried to beat my face into hamburger, you'd still be second best."

"Nice try, but your face has nothing to do with ditching the cuffs." Cooper went to work on Mike's cuffs. "Did sort of improve the way you look, though. Too bad you've lost your edge."

As soon as Mike was free, Cooper helped Taggart finish up. Mike helped Eva.

"You up for this?" she asked as she worked the circulation back into her hands.

He got why she was concerned about him. One

eye was swollen shut, he could barely see out of the other, his lips were busted up, and he couldn't draw a deep breath without gasping. Probably had a couple of bruised ribs, maybe broken.

"*Chica.*" His tone was tender yet chiding as he touched a hand to her cheek. "You have to ask?"

"Macho to the end," she whispered.

"Anyone have any brilliant ideas?" Cooper glanced around the room, brows raised hopefully.

Taggart grunted. "Asked the man with the highest IQ. We rely on *you* for brilliance."

"Ambush?" Mike suggested, staring up at the rafters.

Taggart looked up, too; checked out the electrical wire running from the switch by the door to the overhead light tacked to the center rafter. "I like it."

"What do you want to bet there's a big pomp and circumstance meet and greet going on right now?" Taggart wandered around the room looking for anything they might be able to use as a screwdriver.

"First deal with the cartel?" Mike grunted. "Hell, yeah. Brewster's going to want to show them all around the facility, show 'em the guns, let them test them out. Make sure they know this is an operation that delivers. That there will be more deals in the future."

"The kitchen staff has been working on something for days," Eva said. "I didn't put it together at the time, but they must have been getting a feast ready for this meeting."

"So we probably have until after the shindig before Brewster sends the ice bitch for us," Cooper speculated.

"That woman was flat-out spooky."

Mike agreed with Taggart. "Wiki wiki, people. No time to waste."

They spent the next few hours working out the details of their escape plan, gathering weapons, and waiting for dark, when they would have their greatest advantage.

Eva had found a rusty nail in the corner on the floor, and as night began to fall they got to work, with Taggart using the nail to quietly unscrew the switch plate from the light switch.

On Taggart's nod, Mike let out a bellow— "Simmons! I need to *pee*, man"—to cover the sound of Taggart ripping the wires loose from the box.

"Go piss up a rope," Simmons shouted back.

"If you really cared about me, you'd bring me a beer," Mike wheedled, which netted him a "fuck you."

"He loves me," Mike mouthed around a grin that made him wince in pain.

With the electrical wire loose from the switch plate and the room effectively without a light source, Taggart gave Cooper a boost up. He grabbed onto the rafters, pulled himself up, then, agile as a monkey and quiet as a shadow, swung up until he was straddling the middle rafter. He scooted toward the center and unscrewed the lightbulb from the porcelain base. Then he tossed the bulb down to Taggart, who whipped off his T-shirt and wrapped it around the bulb to muffle the sound of the glass he was about to break. After another nod to Mike, who started badgering Simmons again, he cracked the bulb against the floor.

They now had a knife. The jagged glass was thin and could never land a killing blow, but it could still cause a lot of pain if twisted directly into an eye socket, an ear, or a hand.

Using the same rusty nail Taggart had used on the light switch, Cooper went to work loosening the individual staples that secured the electrical wire to the rafters.

"Taking too long," he whispered. "Give me a distraction."

Taggart walked over to the door and started pounding and swearing a blue streak. Cooper gave the wire several hard, swift tugs. Staples popped like popcorn as the wire broke free all along the rafter and down the wall studs.

"My friend has a temper," Mike pointed out when Taggart wound down. "You really don't want to see him mad."

"You don't zip it," Simmons growled back, "I'm coming in there and shutting you up."

Cooper still straddled the rafter, working the nail into the screws holding the porcelain light fixture. He finally got it loose and tossed it down to Eva. The fixture was heavy and round, and since it was still attached to one end of the twelve-plus feet of electrical cord, it would make a helluva projectile missile if swung with enough velocity.

"Okay," Mike said, barely able to make out their silhouettes in the dark, hot room. "Let's do this. No shots fired, if at all possible, or we'll have the entire camp on our asses."

"Places, everyone." Cooper softly clapped his hands together.

Taggart gave him a look. "Who are you, Cecil B. DeMille?"

Grinning, Cooper shimmied forward so he was hanging directly over the door.

Eva and Taggart, each gripping one end of the electrical wire that they'd strung low just inside the threshold, squatted on either side of the door.

They all glanced at each other in the thickening dark, just barely able to see as four thumbs went up in the air.

This was it.

"Oh, Simmmooonnns," Mike sing-songed, doing his damnedest to irritate the hotheaded guard. He'd planted himself on the floor, legs stretched out in front of him at the far wall, dead center with the door so he'd be the first thing Simmons saw when he burst inside. If he played this hand right, the knuckle-dragger would be blinded by rage. "I know you're out there, big guy. Got a question for you."

"Shut the fuck up," Simmons grated through the door.

Mike grinned, regretted it when his split lip let him know it wasn't happy.

"Oh, come on. Don't be a Mr. Cranky Pants. Just

got a couple questions. Lawson ever share any of his high-priced scotch with you? Man of your stature, seems he'd pony up some of that private stock. He shared with me, after all."

Silence. Oh, yeah. Simmons was simmering in the stew Mike was dishing up. Mike loved baiting this guy.

"But, hell, there're probably other perks. Gotta be to make up for tonight, right? I mean . . . important man like you, pulling a shit job like babysitting duty? Shame you're missing the big shindig and all. Doesn't that bug you? Seems like you should be out there rubbing elbows with the cartel. They should know what a key player you are."

"If you don't shut the fuck up, I'm coming in there. I've had it with your smart-ass digs."

"Never have figured out your official title," Mike went on, ignoring him. "Bootlicker in chief? Supreme bootlicker? What's he pay you to do that, anyway? And do you get bonuses for all that ass kissing?"

A chair scraped against raw wood.

A key rattled in the lock.

The door swung open, and there stood Simmons in all his pissed-off glory. "I told you to shut up," he said, planted like a tree in the doorway.

"Ask me nice." Mike made a kissing sound.

Predictable to the end, Simmons roared, storming into the room, and Taggart and Eva snapped the electrical wire tight.

Simmons tripped midstride, landing flat on his face.

Taggart was on him like sweat on a hog. He jammed his knee between Simmons's shoulder blades with all of his weight, grabbed his jaw in one hand, the back of his head in his other, and jerked hard right. Simmons was dead before Taggart jumped off of him and dragged his carcass to the side of the room.

It was over in less than seven seconds.

And they now had a pistol and a shotgun.

"One down," Mike mouthed and Taggart and Eva assumed their positions on either side of the door again.

For several seconds, nothing happened. But when the silence stretched, it didn't take long for Bryant and Wagoner to check on their comrade.

"Simmons? What the fuck you doing, man?"

"I think he might have hurt himself, guys," Mike said cheerfully. "But that could just be wishful thinking on my part."

Bryant appeared at the door in a shot. When he couldn't see into the dark, he peeked inside, then tentatively walked in. Eva jammed the broken lightbulb into his hand. He dropped his gun and opened his mouth to howl like a coyote — but Taggart was right behind him. He looped the electrical cord over his head from behind, jerked it tight and down. Bryant fell to his knees clawing at the cord. Taggart slammed his knee between his shoulder blades with the force of a Mack truck and drove him face-first into the floor.

Wagoner charged in the door right behind Bryant. "What the —"

Cooper dropped out of the rafters, landed on his shoulders, and rode him all the way to the ground. Wagoner's head hit the floor with a loud thud, and it was lights out.

"I've got to say, I'm impressed as hell." Mike struggled to his feet. "But I probably could have done it better if I wasn't on the DL."

"Still got some work to do on that humility issue, I see." Taggart made sure both Bryant and Wagoner were well out of commission, then tossed Wagoner's AR-15 to Mike. He kept Simmons's shotgun for himself while Cooper confiscated Bryant's sawed-off.

Taggart tossed Eva a pistol that he lifted from Bryant's hip holster. "Figure a woman who can handle a lightbulb like that can sure as hell handle a pistol."

"I'd rather it was a Glock," she said, chambering a round, "but this'll do."

"And so will you," Taggart said with a grin. "You'll do just fine. Shall we boogie, boys and girl?"

"Remember," Mike said. "No shots unless you absolutely have to."

Cooper took the lead, with Mike and Eva sandwiched between him and Taggart, who was pulling up the rear. When Cooper reached the corner of the building he held up a hand, two fingers extended.

Two guards.

Taggart skirted Mike—who really was in no condition to be contemplating any full-body contact—and snuck a peek around the corner.

"They're taking a smoke break," he whispered. "One on the left is mine."

Cooper nodded and grabbed one end of the electrical cord. Taggart started swinging the other end with the porcelain fixture attached. When he had a good head of steam worked up, he gave Cooper a nod. "Stand by."

He swung the cord several more times, building up speed, then let it fly. The fixture connected with a thud just behind the guard's left ear. He dropped like a rock.

Before the second guard could react, Cooper shot out of the shadows and used his end of the cord as a garrote. The man fought, twitched, then finally went still.

Cooper was letting him slide to the ground when the third guard rounded the corner, checking up on his two buddies.

"Hi." Eva stepped out of the shadows, a big, flirty smile on her face. "I don't suppose you could give a girl a light."

In the split second it took him to get past flummoxed to "holy shit," Mike rammed the butt end of the AR-15 into his stomach. The guy doubled over and got a second hit on the back of his head.

"Well, hell," Cooper whispered with an approving grin. "Guess we'll take you out of the dead weight column."

"Damn straight." Mike winced at the pain that grabbed him in his ribs. "The motor pool's this way."

"Wait." Eva's hand on his arm stopped him. "The motor pool?"

He laced his fingers through hers and took off running. "Unless you've got a better idea, but I have serious doubts about them giving us the keys to that chopper."

"Stop." She planted her feet, dragged him to a halt. "We're leaving?"

"Yes. We're leaving."

"But I thought we'd decided . . ."

"I'm making an executive decision. Change of plans. I'm not sticking around to give them the chance to plan our execution. Did you see that woman's eyes? She's insane. Now come on. We've got to go."

"But what about the guns?" She forced him to look at her. "I thought the plan was to stop the cartel from getting the guns."

He looked poleaxed. "That *was* the plan . . . when we thought Gabe and the BOIs, and ATF and DEA, *and* the FBI would be charging in with enough firepower to blow this place to kingdom come. But they don't have a clue what's going down out here. And in case you've forgotten, there are over one hundred of them." He jabbed a thumb over his shoulder, where special lights had apparently been rigged for tonight's festivities and glowed from the big outdoor rally that appeared to be staged somewhere in the vicinity of the shooting range. "I'm getting you out of here. We'll get word to Gabe as soon as we can. He can figure out a way to deal with it later."

"Later will be too late."

He stared at her, flabbergasted. "No. I let you do this to me before. I let you shame me into going for the guns. Well, we tried that. And we ended up locked up and almost dead. I'm not falling for it again."

When she stood her ground, he appealed to Cooper and Taggart. "Help me out here, damn it. Tell her there's nothing we can do."

Cooper glanced uncomfortably at Taggart. "He's probably right."

"Probably?" Mike swore under his breath. "What is *wrong* with you? If we don't get her out of here right now, *right this very now*, we may not get her out of here alive."

Taggart compressed his mouth, shrugged. "I don't think Eva is as concerned about getting herself out as you are."

Mike glared at him. "Seriously? You're going to take her side in this?"

"This isn't about sides," Eva insisted. "It's about doing the right thing. If La Linea gets those guns, a lot of innocent people are going to die."

"For the love of—" Mike dragged a hand through his hair. She was making him crazy. He was not going to lose her. He was *not* going to—

"Mike . . . this is bigger than us," she appealed softly. "Way bigger."

"I told you *not* to play the duty and honor card again. All it got me was a less than honorable discharge, my career down the tubes, my life stolen. My friends dead or gone." He glanced at Taggart and Cooper.

He finally had them back. He couldn't lose them again. And for the first time in his life, he had a woman worth holding on to. He would not lose her.

Yet if he didn't stand and fight, he would lose her anyway. As he stood there in the dark, with the PA system ramping up and Lawson's zealot voice booming across the meadow, he knew he would lose them *all* again if he insisted on saving them.

Just like he would lose what he'd recovered of himself, if he walked away from this challenge.

"Fuck," he muttered. "Fine. But if she loses one freaking hair, I'm going to make you all wish you were never born. Especially you," he told Eva, just before he dragged her against him and kissed her.

"Aw." Taggart's teeth glowed white in the dark. "Group hug?"

"I'm in." Cooper opened his arms.

"Fuck you both," Mike grumbled. "Let's just get this done."

36

"You sure you can make this happen?" Cooper huffed under the weight of almost eighty pounds of coiled det cord as the four of them snuck around the back perimeter of the camp and headed for the mine in the dark.

"Am I sure the sun's gonna shine tomorrow?" Taggart humped a large canvas bag filled with blocks of C-4 on his back.

"Not sure that's the best comparison," Cooper muttered, "considering we might all blow like a JDAM if you screw things up."

"I won't screw it up. Why do you think they call me Boom Boom?"

"Because you douse all your food with chili sauce?"

"TMI, boys." Eva kept pace behind them with the detonators.

Mike led the way carrying the blasting caps, reaching deep to outdistance the pain. They stayed as far away from each other as possible, because one tiny zap of static electricity could cause the detonators or blasting caps to blow like an action scene in a Rambo movie.

"And I'm still gonna have all my fingers and toes when we're through?" Mike gritted out, struggling to keep a steady pace as the sharp pain in his ribs nearly brought him to his knees.

"Save your breath and lead the way, flyboy. I'll get you in, we'll set the charges, get out, and this place will blow sky high."

But Mike knew that even if Boom Boom was right and this worked, there was no guarantee they were getting out of here alive.

Breaking into the armory had been a piece of cake. All the other men in the camp were attending the rally. The women and kids would not have been allowed to attend the rally, which meant they were all tucked in their cabins and would be well away from the fireworks when the C-4 detonated.

Still, Mike wasn't going to breathe easy until they set the charges and beat feet away from the blast site.

"How much farther?" Cooper carried the heaviest load.

"Just a hundred yards or so. Now quiet down. There are bound to be guards."

"Fuck," Cooper sounded exhausted. "Can nothing be easy?"

Mike stumbled and almost went down, but dug deep and kept on going.

"Hold," he whispered when they were within twenty yards of the mine shaft.

Everyone dropped to their bellies.

Taggart lifted the NV binoculars he'd tagged from the armory. "I count four."

"I don't have another hand-to-hand in me. Shoot 'em." Cooper had rolled to his back. He was sucking wind, recovering from the hard pull with his heavy load. "Damn, I'm out of shape."

"Taggart?" Mike glanced at his friend.

"I just happened to snag a sound suppressor. Lawson knows how to stock an armory."

"Clock's tickin'." Mike hardened his mind against the ugly part of war. Simmons and the others deserved what they got. These guys might, too. But cold-blooded killing was one of the worst parts of combat.

Taggart handed Mike the NV binoculars, dug the suppressor out of his pocket, and threaded it onto the end of the AR-15. Balancing the rifle barrel on a fallen log, he got a bead on his targets through the NV scope and on a long exhale, popped off four rounds in rapid succession.

Through the binoculars, Mike watched each man go down.

"Let's go," he said, and the four of them rose to their feet and sprinted toward the entrance to the mine shaft.

"Problem," Mike said once they'd broken the lock with bolt cutters and scrambled into the mine. "One of the semis is gone. What do you want to bet it's sitting on the chopper pad, ready to offload onto that bad boy?"

"So they . . . what? Just fly across U.S. airspace uncontested?" Eva asked.

Mike answered, "If they fly at night, under radar, they're not going to be detected. Sounds crazy but it works."

"Let's worry about one problem at a time." Cooper started uncoiling the det cord, which looked like brightly colored clothesline rope—only much more lethal. "Where do you want this?"

Taggart dug into the pack and hauled out several blocks of C-4, then paused to admire it. "Beautiful. Like Play-Doh that goes boom."

"Where do you want it?" Cooper repeated, edgy and impatient.

"Chill, bro. You can't rush with this stuff—not unless you want to be reduced to particles that someone cleans up with a dustpan. If I do this wrong and one charge blows prematurely, another could go off due to sympathetic detonation.

"So deep breaths, all right?" He looked from one to the other, and when he was satisfied they were calm, got down to business. "For starters, we're going to wrap each block with a loop or two of det cord, then string it around the mine shaft. Start with the timbers that brace the ceiling and walls—put extra charges near the entrance. If for some reason the trucks don't blow, we'll make damn sure no one gets in here to retrieve these guns."

With Cooper and Mike busy rigging the mine, Taggart turned to Eva. "I need you to wrap these blocks of C-4 with det cord, okay? I'll crawl under the trucks and stick 'em under the trailers. Once everything's in place, you all clear out, I'll crimp on the blasting caps, and hook everything up to the remote detonator."

"There's a remote detonator?" Cooper looked relieved as he returned to Taggart's side.

"Well, I thought about having you light a fuse, but what would the world do without your pretty face?"

"Mourn," Cooper said, deadpan, and set about his deadly work.

When Taggart was satisfied everything was ready, he handed Mike a black box with an antenna to which he'd attached wires to two terminals. "Head outside with this."

"Detonator?"

"You're not as dumb as you look."

Mike grunted. "I'm *here*, aren't I?"

"Relax. I've got around three thousand feet of wire. We'll be well out of the blast zone when this baby blows.

"Come on," Taggart added after double-checking all of his connections and the work the other three had done. "Let's beat feet."

On Mike's order they grabbed the rifles from the dead guards, then they all took off, running like hell, back toward the camp.

"I'm out of wire." Mike's ribs screamed at him as he tried to suck wind. They'd run for a little more than a quarter of a mile through dense forest, careful not to break the connection between detonator and cord.

"Must be stuck." Taggart blew out a breath. "Fuck it. Find a tree of your choice, people. We don't have time to go back and check it."

Mike grabbed Eva and they dropped to the ground behind a huge deadfall tree.

Taggart checked to make certain everyone was as concealed from the blast as possible. Then he called, "Fire in the hole!"

He flipped the detonator switch, then ducked and covered.

The C-4 detonated with a roar so loud, Mike swore it broke his eardrums. The earth rumbled, fire spewed into the air a quarter mile high, and a pressure wave hit him so hard it knocked the wind out of him, leaving him deaf and speechless and in excruciating pain for several vibrating seconds.

By the time he gathered his senses around him again, shrapnel, dirt, and dust laced with embers rained from the shaft, whizzing projectiles that had him covering Eva's head. When he felt he could chance it, he looked up. A small mushroom cloud rose and boiled against the night sky.

From Brewster and Lawson's perspective, it must have looked like Armageddon.

Taggart's head popped up. "Lord, that was pretty."

"What?" Cooper poked a finger in his ear, shook his head.

"I said you were pretty," Taggart said with a smart-ass grin and sprang to his feet, holding out a hand to help Cooper up.

"Ya think you used enough C-4?" Cooper stared at the cloud in awe.

Taggart looked smug. "Go big or go home, I always say."

The two men high-fived.

"Can we hold off on the gloating until we actually get out of here?" Mike pushed slowly upright. His ears were ringing. His balance was off. He'd intended to help Eva up, but the pain in his ribs stabbed like a knife and he dropped back to his knees with a groan.

She ended up helping him. "Can you make it?"

"We're going to get run over with UWD troops in less than five, so that pretty much says I'd *better* make it. And I am *not* over being mad at you, by the way."

When Taggart moved in with a he's-not-heavy-he's-my-brother look on his face, Mike held up a hand. "I'm good."

"Like hell."

"I'm good," he insisted and forced himself to stand up straight to prove it.

"Mike." Eva's eyes implored him to let them help.

"Mollycoddle me later," he grumbled. "If we don't get to the chopper pad and figure out how to stop it from taking off, we're screwed."

Then he headed out, ignoring the pain and their worried looks.

• • •

"So . . . not all of the soldiers headed for the mine."
Cooper passed the binoculars to Mike.

They were on their bellies, using a berm on the target range for concealment as they checked out the he-
licopter pad. Their sense of urgency magnified when
they saw the big Chinook and the third semi parked
beside it. Heavily tattooed, machine gun–toting men
guarded it while UWD members offloaded guns from
the semi to the chopper.

"I make six La Linea total—three at the front,
three at the rear." Cooper scanned the area. "As many
UWDs doing the grunt work. And, lookie who just
showed up to protect their investment."

"Brewster and Lawson," Mike speculated correctly. "Psycho babe there, too?"

"Yup. And their new business associates don't look
any too happy."

Mike lifted his rifle, sighted through the scope,
and found the men involved in the big powwow in
his sites. He didn't have to hear the conversation to
know there were a lot of threats being made on the La
Linea side, and a lot of cajoling coming from Brewster and Lawson. If they couldn't control and contain
their own compound, how could the cartel count on
them to deliver on future shipments?

"Can we say, 'ass in a sling'?" Beside him, Taggart
also sighted through his rifle scope.

"Wonder how they're explaining how they couldn't
contain four hostages—one of them a woman." Eva
sounded a lot more calm than Mike felt, since it was

a pretty safe bet that they'd undoubtedly launched a full-out manhunt. They were still a long ways from being out of the woods.

"So," Mike moved wrong, then silently cursed the pain in his ribs that was steadily getting worse. "What's the plan?"

"You're the chopper pilot. How do we keep it grounded—no, wait." Taggart refocused the binoculars. "How do we drop it out of the sky? The semi's pulling out and the main rotor blade is starting to spin up."

"Forget about the rotors. Those suckers are strong enough to chop down trees."

He thought about the bird's vulnerabilities. "Chinooks are very slow on takeoff, so we might have a chance to keep her grounded. Eva—hammer the hell out of the engine. I'll be right there with you. You two aim for the fuel tanks," he said decisively. "They're located right by the side wheels. I'm guessing the civilian models don't have self-sealing fuel tanks, so they should be susceptible to small-arms fire. If we can get the engines burning, that fire will race right back to the leaking tanks and we might get lucky. And now, by the way, would be good."

Mike had confiscated an AK-47 from one of the guards at the mine site. He took aim and popped off several three-round bursts—and got immediate results.

The men on the ground by the chopper scattered and ducked for cover. Then, spotting their muzzle flashes, they fired back.

Mike ignored them, pecking away like a rooster after grit. Beside him, bellied down in the dirt, Taggart, Cooper, and Eva followed his example.

"Holy shit," Cooper sputtered when several rounds zipped past his head. "Bastard's either a deadeye or damn lucky."

Luck was something they needed a lot of, if they were going to keep that bird grounded and keep from getting killed in the process.

Mike kept firing; burning sweat poured into the cuts on his face, fire seared through his side. It was dark, the nightscopes were difficult to focus, the distance was not desirable—the chances of them taking down the bird were growing slimmer with every minute, which meant Brewster and his boys would be on them as soon as the threat was over.

They were sitting ducks out here. UWD soldiers behind them, Satan's spawn in front of them, wilderness in either direction. And him with a broken rib and, *fuck*, an empty magazine, he realized when he squeezed the trigger.

He quickly ejected the mag and rapid-loaded a second thirty-round clip. His last one.

"She's about to lift off," Taggart yelled, his focus and his shots steady on the Chinook.

"Keep firing!" Mike yelled.

"I'm out of ammo." Cooper lowered his gun.

Pick a doomsday cliché, they were living it.

Eva, rock-solid steady, kept her eye glued to the scope and methodically fired again and again.

But it was too late. The bird hovered, then lifted, and spun slowly skyward.

"Fuck." Taggart watched the flight lights as the chopper gained elevation.

Mike roared in frustration and emptied his magazine, knowing it was hopeless—until the engine cowling blasted off the bird in an explosion of sound and a huge, raging fireball. Smoke roared out of the damaged fuselage, billowing in a black, spiraling plume. The chopper listed sideways, spun, dropped, and corkscrewed down fast.

"No way." Mesmerized, Cooper stood, shielding his eyes from the white-hot blaze of fire as the chopper fuel combusted, and twenty tons of electronics and metal slammed to the ground and blew anything within thirty yards into fireballs, dust, and rubble.

"No freaking way did we drop that chopper," Cooper uttered again.

Stunned, Mike stared at what was left of the Chinook. No one on the ground nearby could have survived that explosion.

The La Linea lieutenants were dead. The woman with the empty eyes was dead. Lawson and Brewster—dead.

His satisfaction was undercut by disappointment. The sonofabitches had gotten off way too easy.

"Listen." Eva touched a hand to his arm. "Hear that?"

Above the roar of the blaze, the ammo in the bird exploding, and the blood pounding in his ears, Mike finally heard what she had. The sound of choppers. A bunch of them.

Mike looked up and finally spotted the flight lights of four Black Hawks zooming in. Their searchlights flashed on, the wide beams sweeping the crash site like a scene out of a SWAT movie. The remaining UWD members had to be running for the hills.

"You're right, Cooper," he said, grinning because he knew who had to be in one of those birds. "We didn't take it out. Gabe did."

37

"Do you know how much freaking paperwork I'm going to have to fill out to explain how a 'borrowed' freaking Black Hawk and a 'borrowed' freaking flight crew somehow managed to fire off its mini and shoot a freaking Chinook out of the *freaking* sky? You said this was a training mission. You didn't say a word about live fire!"

Mike sat on the bumper of one of several ambulances that had arrived at the UWD site on the tail of the Black Hawks, watching and grinning as Gabe patiently waited for the red-faced DEA officer to finish spitting out his tirade. All around them, ATF, DEA, DHS, and FBI agents worked the scene, some of them arranging a makeshift holding area for the UWD members who had been rounded up in the woods surrounding the camp.

Gabe had covered all the bases. There were even female agents on the ground, dealing with the shell-shocked wives, daughters, and sons of the compound.

Mike didn't know yet how Gabe had managed to charge in and save the day, but he had no doubt the Archangel would be able to appease the infuriated agent.

"You should be lying down."

Eva. Beside him. Safe and sound. That was all that mattered now.

"I should be right here." He looped his arm over her shoulder and kissed her beautiful dirt-and-smoke-streaked face. "Besides, you heard Collins. He's the paramedic. That makes him the expert, and he says my ribs are just bruised."

"I don't care what he says. I can see the pain on your face. You need to be horizontal. You need to rest."

"*Chica.*" He nuzzled his nose around the shell of her ear. "If I get horizontal, it will be with you. And trust me. We won't be resting."

"This dipstick giving you a hard time, Eva?"

Mike groaned when Taggart and Cooper ambled over to the ambulance. "And to think I missed them."

Cooper hiked a booted foot up on the ambulance bumper. "Just goes to show. Be careful what you wish for. You just might get it."

Mike looked into the faces of the two men he had thought he would never see again. They were covered in grime and the satisfaction of a job well done. The same faces that had been full of accusation and hatred the last time he'd seen them eight years ago.

He felt a wave of emotion so strong, so massive, he

didn't know if he could contain it. Then he looked at
Eva and *knew* he couldn't. She wasn't going to let him.

"Yeah. About that." He lowered his head, groped
for the words he needed to say. "Thanks." He met
Cooper's eyes, then Taggart's, and saw the same emotions welling up there. "Thanks for showing. Means
a lot."

Hell. It meant everything.

Taggart looked at his boot tips.

Cooper found a spot in the distance that suddenly
demanded all of his attention before getting himself
back together. "Yeah, well . . . Someone's going to
pay us, right? . . . Because we didn't do this for old
time's sake."

Mike burst out laughing, then regretted it when
fire bit into his ribs. "There was some mention of
money, now that I think about it. Right, Eva?"

She shook her head, disbelieving. "You three are
the most stubborn individuals I've ever met when it
comes to expressing your feelings."

Then Gabe walked over and joined them.

"How you doing?" He studied Mike critically.

"Fit and fine." Mike hitched his chin toward the
DEA agent. "You settle him down?"

Gabe lifted a shoulder. "Once he found out his name
would be leaked to the media in conjunction with taking down six of La Linea's top-tier management, and in
shutting down a major illegal gunrunning op, he decided the paperwork wasn't such a hardship after all."

"Something I don't get." Taggart crossed his arms

over his chest. "I figure when we didn't check in, you put it together that things had gone south. But how'd you know to bring the birds and the mini and all the alphabet guys?"

"We've got a connection at NSA. A friend picked up some cyber-chatter about a gun shipment out of Canada. On a hunch we relayed the info to border control, of which there are two in Idaho. Since Porthill carries the most passenger traffic and Eastport carries the most trucks, it wasn't difficult to pin down which route they were going to take."

A line formed between Eva's brows. "You mean there were more trucks on the way?"

Gabe nodded. "One truck, and the driver couldn't talk fast enough—despite the fact that La Linea threatened to kill him. La Linea, guns, UWD? It only made sense there was a big deal going down, and that you were caught here in the middle of it."

"The guns were in a refrigerated meat trailer, weren't they?" Cooper looked smug.

Gabe regarded him with new interest. "And you know this how?"

Taggart glanced at Mike, who nodded. "You might want to look about half a mile north of the shooting range. They hid them in an abandoned mine shaft. Well, it used to be a shaft. Good luck finding a piece of anything bigger than a cinder."

A slow smile built on Gabe's face. "Nice work."

"It was," Taggart agreed wholeheartedly. "It really, really was."

"So where'd you come up with the Black Hawks?" Mike asked. "There aren't any military bases within five, six hundred miles of here."

Gabe said nothing.

And just that quick, Mike knew.

"Sonofabitch," he said with a grin. "Uncle's got a little top-secret Spec Ops training facility out here in the mountains, huh?"

"I don't know what you're talking about." Gabe had his poker face on, a sure sign that Mike had hit the nail dead center. "I don't mean to change the subject, but—"

"The hell you don't," Mike said on a laugh.

"But," Gabe pressed on and shifted his attention to Eva, "I haven't had a chance to tell you before now. We found your Deep Throat."

The D.C. lunch crowd was long gone at two in the afternoon, when Eva and Mike stepped inside the little corner café. They'd returned from Idaho and what the press referred to as "the assault on Squaw Valley" two days ago. CNN had run an hour-long special on the operation last night, and the Alcohol, Tobacco, and Firearms, the Defense Intelligence Agency, and the FBI had received all the credit for the takedown. That was fine with Eva. Let them rack up the win in their column. She wanted her name kept out of it—so did Mike, Taggart, and Cooper. The fact that Gabe had managed to make that happen and keep the Black Ops, Inc. team off the radar as well, told her just how covert he and his teammates ran.

It was also Gabe who had set up the meeting with Deep Throat. She touched a hand to her hair, nervous, as she scanned the few occupied tables. A young couple, clearly in love and oblivious to anything but each other, laughed and made moon eyes over a shared chocolate sundae. A middle-aged man sat in a wheelchair sipping coffee as a younger woman with a kind face spoke softly to him. A pretty blond mommy fed her young son ice cream and laughed when he smeared it in his hair.

All of them were oblivious to everyone around them and the drama that was about to unfold. Eva was hyperaware of the wild beat of her heart and peripherally aware of Gabe, who occupied the only other spot in the restaurant. He'd insisted on being here, just in case. He didn't acknowledge them, just sat at the coffee bar, his back to the room, his focus alternating between a cup of black coffee and the wall mirror that gave him visual access to the dining area and everyone in it.

An older gentleman with a round belly, wild bushy brows, and a twinkling smile approached them, menus in his hand. "Miss Salinas? Mr. Brown?"

Eva nodded and gave him credit for not staring at Mike—beat up and bruised, his eye still swollen shut.

"Your table is ready. Follow me, please."

Mike's strong presence beside her was both unsettling and reassuring—as was his hand on the small of her back as they crossed the room and settled in at a secluded corner table.

"We'll just have coffee," Mike said, and their host smiled amiably and left them alone.

"You good with this?" he asked, scowling as only he could scowl when he was worried for her.

"I'm fine. I'm eager to talk with him."

"I'd like to do more than talk to him," Mike grumbled.

He didn't exactly feel gratitude toward the man they were about to meet. Mike considered him a coward who had placed her life in danger. Nothing settled the score in his book, not even her reminders that if not for the mystery man, Mike would still be estranged from Taggart and Cooper, and Lawson and Brewster would still be running their nasty business.

"I wouldn't be surprised if he didn't show. That's his MO, right? He's a coward who hides in the background."

"I'm sure he had his reasons."

She'd been so intent on keeping Mike calm, she hadn't realized the man in the wheelchair had rolled up to the table.

When he stopped and met her eyes, she smiled automatically. He wasn't as old as she'd thought he was. Instead, it was apparent that whatever accident or illness had put him in the chair had aged him. "Can I help you?"

"You can if you're Eva Salinas."

Eva glanced at Mike, then back to—"Who are you? How do you know my name?"

"I'm Peter Davis."

She searched her memory banks. Nothing. Other

than the wheelchair, there was little that was remarkable about him. His close-cropped hair was peppered with gray. His eyes were brown. Nothing about him was familiar.

"You don't know me," Davis said, reading her thoughts. "But I know your father."

Her heart picked up several beats.

And then she read something in his eyes. And she understood why he'd come to the table. "Oh, my God. It was you? You gave me the OSD file?"

His expression was grim. "I did. And believe me, I had no idea that my actions would place you in so much jeopardy."

Too stunned to speak, she simply stared. Her brain clicked into stall mode as she attempted to process his words.

"You sonofabitch." Mike glared at him. "You almost got her killed."

Davis shifted his attention to Mike, repentant but not cowed. "I know. Mr. Jones told me everything." He wiped a hand over his jaw. "I didn't see that coming. Believe me. I'm sorry."

"What did you *think* was going to happen when you gave her that file? And why her?" Mike rushed on, not giving Davis a chance to respond. "Why not come to me or Taggart or Cooper?"

"Mike." Eva placed a hand on Mike's arm to settle him. "Let him talk. He didn't have to agree to meet with us."

"It's all right. In his shoes, I'd be angry, too." Davis

faced Mike again, looked him in the eye. "If I could have found you, I might have contacted you. And what would you have done with the information?"

For a long moment, the two men locked eyes. They both knew exactly what Mike would have done. Nothing.

"How do you know my father?" Eva asked, effectively defusing the anger simmering between them. Davis gave Mike a final glare, then turned back to her. "I was active duty until five years ago. Several years before that, one of the enlisted men in my unit had need of a JAG attorney. Your father was assigned to his case. Since I was the aide to the base commander, much of the communication went through me. Your father and I became casual friends. He's a good man."

He smiled tightly, then went on. "A little over a month ago, we had a chance encounter at the funeral of a mutual friend. We caught up. He told me about you. He was very proud that you became an attorney. And he told me you'd lost your husband eight years ago in Afghanistan."

Again he stopped, then drew a bracing breath. "I was in Afghanistan eight years ago. I was General Brewster's aide."

Mike went stone-cold still beside her, then erupted with anger. "You *knew*? All these years, you knew he sabotaged Operation Slam Dunk?"

Davis squared his shoulders. "Not at first, no. But I suspected something was off. Again, I'm sorry."

"In the interest of time and my patience, leave out the 'sorrys,' okay? Just cut to the chase."

Davis cut Mike a hard look, then addressed Eva again. "Brewster ran a tight ship. He was making end rows against the resistance. The One-Eyed Jacks were kicking some serious Taliban ass. Then this guy started showing up."

"Lawson," Mike speculated.

Davis nodded. "Didn't know who he was—not right away. I just knew there was something off about him."

"Other than the fact that he was an asshole?"

A small smile lifted one corner of Davis's mouth. "Yeah. Other than that. The day he showed up, Brewster started making decisions that didn't make sense."

"What kind of decisions?" Eva wanted to know.

"Deployment of resources, mission strategies, calls that undermined the progress his Spec Ops teams had made. Then Operation Slam Dunk went down."

He whipped a hand over his face again. "I knew some of those guys. They were straight shooters. Good men."

He paused again, then met Mike's glare. "I was there the night Brewster made the call to stand down. I'll never forget it. I'd heard your radio transmissions. I knew what was going down out there. And I didn't understand Brewster's orders until several days later, when he gave me a stack of files and told me to shred them immediately. Before I could get to it, we got hit by an artillery strike. I ducked and covered, and when the smoke cleared, the files were scattered all over the floor."

"Let me guess. One of those files was Brewster's after-action report on OSD." Mike leaned forward, elbows on the table, hands clasped together in front of him.

"Yeah. He'd filed that report himself—hadn't dictated it to me, so I didn't know what was in it until I started reading. From the first word, I knew it was all bogus. I knew the op hadn't gone down the way he'd recorded it."

"Back up," Eva said. "Was it protocol to shred official reports?"

"After they'd been transferred to electronic documents and encrypted, yes."

A waitress stopped by the table then with their coffee, and everyone stopped talking until she was out of earshot again.

"And as his aide, you had access to the encrypted files," Eva concluded.

"Limited access. Brewster changed his access code weekly. As soon as I read the paper copy, I knew I was sitting on a potential land mine—so I accessed his computer files and copied the report onto a flash drive before he could change his code and lock me out."

"Why didn't you do something with it?" Mike cut him no slack.

"What *could* I do? I was an aide. Who was going to believe me over a two star? And I'd basically stolen the file. It scared the shit out of me. So I sat on it until I could figure out what to do. In the meantime, I filed the paperwork to get transferred out of Brewster's unit."

He looked down at his legs, at the chair, breathed deep, and faced Eva again. "Soon after, I caught some action and ended up in this chair. And for too many years to count, I wallowed around in a big pile of self-pity."

For the first time, Eva saw a softening in Mike's eyes. He couldn't relate to Davis's lie of omission, but he could relate to what the man had been through. He knew all about how easy it was to get caught in a self-destructive cycle. And about sacrificing for your country.

"But I finally got myself together." Davis glanced toward the table where the woman with the kind eyes waited. She smiled at him and he nodded, then turned back to Eva. "And I knew I had to bring this to someone's attention. So I started researching Brewster. Did you know he was in the Office of the Under Secretary at DOD?"

Mike swore.

"And while I wasn't sure where I was going with the file, I did some research on Lawson. I couldn't get that guy out of my head, you know? Ran across a story about him and this extremist survivalist group, and a lightbulb went on. There was no question in my mind that Brewster and Lawson had been in some unholy alliance in Afghanistan. And no question that someone needed to find out what really happened that night."

"So you picked Eva."

"And I stand by my decision. She was the right choice. She had a vested interest. And a reputation for having a cool head. I knew that if she was anything like her father, she'd work through it the right way."

"So you gave it to her anonymously and your conscience was cleared. Nice, neat, and tidy for you. Deadly for her."

"Do you think I saw things coming down this way?"

"I think you should have."

Davis nodded slowly. "Probably. Wasn't the first mistake I've made. And next to sitting on the file for eight years, it's the one I regret the most."

38

"This is legit?" Mike frowned at Gabe, then darted a quick glance at Taggart and Cooper to check their reactions to the offer Gabe had just laid on the table.

He saw surprise, followed by keen interest, followed by skepticism. The same things he felt.

Gabe tipped up his beer, then, squinting against the charcoal smoke, went to work flipping the steaks. "It's legit." He glanced over his shoulder and chuckled at their slack-jawed expressions. "You guys need some privacy to talk it over?"

"What I need is another beer." Looking like he'd been hit with a stun gun, Taggart walked over to the cooler.

"Based out of Langley?" Cooper considered Gabe through deeply veed brows.

"Yup."

"Complete autonomy?" Mike wanted to make certain he'd heard him right.

"*Autonomy* is a relative term," Gabe said. "So, officially? No. Unofficially? Damn straight. Same ground rules as the BOIs play by. Which means you'll call your own shots."

Mike looked at Taggart's beer with envy. He missed the taste of it sometimes. Not as much as he missed the benefits of a clear head, though. He needed all of his brain cells functioning right now. One of the reasons why was inside the Joneses' apartment with Gabe's wife, Jenna, who'd returned from Florida yesterday.

Eva had been too quiet since their meeting with Peter Davis yesterday afternoon. He didn't know what was going on in her head. Didn't know where they went from here. It was driving him a little crazy.

Then there'd been the conference call from the Secretary of Defense himself in Gabe's office yesterday afternoon. A formal apology to all three of them. Notification that the paperwork was already in the tube for revocation of their less than honorable discharges, and full reinstatement of their honorable service status. Recommendations for Purple Hearts and silver stars for gallantry in action.

He was still processing his reaction to the accolades and the call. Still deciding if he was pissed or proud. If he felt redeemed or played. Eight years. A big chunk of his life, gone. It was also a long time to be angry. On that, all three agreed. Just as they agreed it would take more than a day to shed the resentment and get on with their lives.

They'd talked way into the night, just he and Taggart and Cooper. Talked about the call. Talked about what they'd pulled off at Squaw Valley. Straight-up honest talk about time they'd lost. About the lives they'd been living. About the would have beens and should have beens, and finally about the futility of looking back.

And now . . . this very *now*, Gabe was offering them a future.

"Just for clarity, shoot it by me one more time," Mike said. "I want to make certain I didn't doze off there for a minute and dream half of what you said. And don't burn that steak. That one's mine."

"You let me worry about the meat. You just think about this. Short and sweet, DOD is looking to beef up their nontraditional covert-ops units. BOI was the first one brought on board. Sec Def likes our results. Now he wants the three of you to join the mix—a companion unit. Get away from me with that garlic salt," he warned when Cooper moved in with the shaker.

"Bottom line," Gabe continued, "you'd be signing on to fight the bad guys. Sanctioned by DOD, but you'll run your ops on your terms. Not by committee."

Mike scratched his jaw. "All because we got screwed over eight years ago?"

"No. Because of what the One-Eyed Jacks accomplished. Because you were damn good at what you did. Because you still are. And because we need more good men like you."

• • •

"What do you think they're talking about out there?" Jenna asked.

Eva glanced at the woman she'd decided was not only the queen of the multitaskers, but someone she wanted to get to know better. Just back from West Palm Beach and wearing a body-hugging, neon pink tank top and black biker shorts, Jenna balanced little Ali on her hip and stirred a gorgonzola sauce that would garnish the steaks Gabe was grilling outside on the terrace. "Best guess? Boobs, beer, and bullshit."

Jenna laughed. "I can see why Gabe likes you."

"I like him, too," Eva conceded. Gabe was one of the good ones.

"How did the apartment hunting go today?"

"Not great," Eva admitted as she sliced Roma tomatoes and tossed them into a mixed-green salad. She'd loved her old apartment, but it would be weeks, possibly months before the fire damage would be repaired, and she didn't think she wanted to return there anyway. She would think about Brewster every time she let herself inside. "But I'm sure I'll find something."

Eva had liked Jenna the moment she'd met her yesterday, after the sit-down she and Mike had with Peter Davis. The pretty redhead was a straight shooter, warm and friendly, and held her own in the company of tough men who had a tendency to want to protect their women.

"So—how big does this apartment need to be?"

Eva glanced at Jenna sideways. Okay. Maybe she

wasn't such a straight shooter after all. "Did you mean to ask me if Mike's moving in?"

Jenna got a guilty look on her face. "Well, I was trying not to, but obviously I should stick to what I know since I bungled that big-time."

Eva smiled. "It's okay. And honestly, I don't know how big it needs to be."

"Because you don't know if you want him to move in? Or because you don't know if he wants to?"

She glanced toward the terrace where the men were all standing around the grill, most likely offering Gabe unwanted advice on the best way to charcoal a steak. "A little of both, I guess."

Jenna kissed Ali on the cheek, then set her down on the floor with two wooden spoons and a pie tin. Grinning widely at her mother, the toddler started beating on the tin with gusto.

"Since I've pretty much walked in those same shoes," Jenna said, smiling down at her little daughter, "the best advice I can give you is go with your heart. Advice you can feel free to ignore, by the way. I'm not usually this interfering. Can we blame it on hormones?"

Again Eva smiled. "It's okay. Frankly, it's nice to be able to talk to someone about it." Someone other than Mike . . . who hadn't been doing a lot of talking since they'd gotten back to D.C.

"I like Mike," Jenna said decisively, as if she were talking about fruit or a soft drink. "Do you like Mike?"

That one threw her. "Is that a trick question?"

Jenna laughed. "No . . . it's just . . . these guys are so intense, you know? And so *present*. They're gorgeous, tough, intelligent, a lot driven, a little broken. Sometimes it's difficult to see past the sensory overload and cut to the heart of the matter. And the heart of the matter is: Do you *like* him?"

Eva glanced out the terrace door again and stared at Mike—at that stunning cosmic union of muscle and bone and brain and brawn. At that beautiful man who had been so broken, who would always be a little broken, and was all the more beautiful because of it—even covered in bruises.

Love him? Yes. And that had been a tough admission to make. Adore him? Absolutely. Want to heal him? More than she'd ever wanted anything in her life.

But did she *like* him?

A very astute question.

Jenna was right. She needed to figure this out. Could she step back, divorce who he was from how he looked and what he did, and like him?

How could she answer that? She'd known him all of seven days. Seven intense, wild, dangerous days that were hardly a traditional getting-to-know-you experience.

And she'd loved another man once. A gorgeous, driven and, she'd recently discovered, broken man. A man she'd never known well enough to like, but had married anyway.

Look how that had played out.

Then there was the other side to that question: Did *he* like *her*?

God, what was she, thirteen? This was so junior high school.

But she'd sensed a change in him. Now that the danger and adrenaline rush was behind them, maybe he was having second thoughts. Maybe he was running back-out scenarios in his mind. They'd been back in D.C. two days and he'd spent most of that time with the guys—time he'd needed to spend. Time she was glad he had with them, and she'd been busy, too. But at night, when they were finally alone, they still didn't talk. They made love. Hot, intense, needy love, like each time was the last time.

"When this is over, we will figure this out and we will finish it."

Was that what he'd meant on that gravel road, just before they'd driven into the UWD compound? When it was over, they'd be finished?

"You okay over there?" Jenna asked.

"Yeah," she said, smiling to minimize the concern in Jenna's eyes. "Yeah, I'm fine."

I just don't know what the hell I'm doing.

39

Mike reached around Eva and flashed the key card over the lock on their hotel room door. She'd been quiet on the ride back from Gabe and Jenna's. She was still quiet. And it scared the ever-loving crap out of him.

He shoved open the door and let her walk in ahead of him.

"I'm going to take a shower."

That's all she said as she walked into the bathroom and closed the door behind her. Not, *Plenty of room in the shower for two*. Not, *I'll wash your back if you'll wash mine. Wink wink.*

"Sure. Go ahead," he said to the empty room. "I'll just be out here beating my head against the wall, wondering if 'I'm going to take a shower' is some kind of code for 'It's been fun and it's been real, but now it's time to move on.'"

Then he tried to convince himself that the click of the lock on that bathroom door wasn't symbolic.

Rousing himself from his stupor, he walked across

the room and tossed the room key on the bedside table, along with the keys to the rented SUV. Then he toed off the sandals she'd bought him, stripped off the rain-forest shirt, and flopped down on his back on the bed.

And stared at the ceiling. Feeling gutless and panicked and scared.

Yeah. Scared. He'd never been so fucking scared.

There were times in a man's life when he had to admit he was in over his head. Afghanistan had been one of those times. When he'd laid in that trench with Cooper and Taggart, with the heat from his burning Black Hawk turning the night into an inferno and his buddies lying dead all around him, he'd known that life as he'd known it was over. But he'd survived.

He'd survived a military tribunal that had twisted lies around the truth and destroyed his career before his very eyes. He'd survived assholes like Lawson and Brewster who wanted him dead.

But that kind of fear he knew how to handle. *Don't let 'em see you sweat. Don't let 'em know they've got you by the short hairs.*

That kind of fear he knew he could survive.

But this . . . whatever he was facing with Eva . . . he didn't have a clue. Not one freaking clue how to come out of it in one solid piece.

Not if he lost her. Hell, he'd just found her.

Now she was pulling away.

He couldn't let that happen. But his old standby

bag of tricks wasn't going to help him. He couldn't laugh. Couldn't crack jokes. Couldn't swear or shoot his way out of this one. He simply had to face the fire.

He needed a cigarette.

He needed a drink.

Hell—he needed a game plan.

Lucky for him, one popped into his head.

He bolted up off the bed before he could think about the wisdom or lack of it, stomped over to the locked bathroom door, gave it a hard glare, then hauled back and kicked it off its hinges.

Eva screamed and peered around the white shower curtain.

Eyes wide, she blinked at him, then at the door, then back to him as clouds of steam billowed out from the curtain. "Why did you do that?"

He jammed his hands on his hips, jutted his chin. "Because I wanted in."

She swiped a fall of heavy, wet hair away from her face. "You couldn't have asked?"

"And where's the fun in that?"

Her mouth dropped open. "What is *wrong* with you?"

What wasn't wrong?

He swallowed hard. Looked at the ceiling. Looked at the floor. Finally, looked at her. "You. You're what's wrong with me." He lifted a hand. Dropped it, feeling helpless and stupid and scared. So scared his next words were barely a whisper. "You're shutting me out, *chica*. I'm scared to death that I'm losing you."

His heart beat so hard he could hear it swooshing

in his ears. He hadn't even realized he'd clenched his hands into fists until his knuckles started aching.

She became very quiet. Hung her head. Then, her shoulders started shaking.

Oh, God. He'd fucking made her cry.

But then she looked at him, and she wasn't crying. She was laughing.

Scared and sorry instantly transitioned to pissed. "You think that's *funny*?"

"No." She held out a hand to him. "I think it's hysterical. I think *we're* hysterical."

If he lived to be one hundred, he would never understand this woman. He took a halting step toward her. "If there was a joke, I missed it."

"No joke. Just two very stupid people, thinking very stupid things."

"For the record," he said, feeling hope growing, "what stupid things was *I* thinking?"

"That I was leaving you?"

She nailed that in one. And the look in her eyes, oh, God, the sweet, loving look in her eyes did things to his heart he wasn't sure he could survive. Probably wouldn't survive if relief hadn't revived him. "And what stupid things were you thinking, *chica*?"

"That you were leaving me. No more questions. Come here." She shoved the shower curtain aside, reached for the waistband of his pants, and yanked. "Just come here to me."

Never let it be said that he didn't know how to take an order. He scrambled into the tub and under the shower spray—to hell with his clothes—and pulled that wet, lush, and laughing woman against him.

"Wait!" she covered his mouth with her hand when he would have kissed her.

He groaned. Okay, he whimpered. "You want me on my knees here?"

"Do you like me, Mike?"

"*What?* What kind of question is that?"

"A legitimate one. Please. Answer me. Do you like me?"

He closed his eyes, felt the water wash over his face. What was she *doing* to him? "I like you. I really, really like you."

"In bed."

"Yes, in bed. Also out of bed. In a car. On a boat. In a plane. Eva. What do you want from me?"

"I just got what I wanted." She threaded her fingers through his wet hair, pulled it back from his face. "And for the record I really, really like you, too."

"Wonderful. Can I freaking kiss you now?"

"Yeah. You freaking can."

So he did. He kissed her. And kissed her and kissed her until there was nothing but tongue and teeth and heartbeats and hungry hands and hope. Kissed her until the water ran cold and he picked her up and carried her out to that king-sized bed. Kissed her until he'd stripped off his soggy pants, covered her wet, warm body with his, and buried himself deep inside her heat, where he stayed. Deep and snug and not even a little bit scared.

40

"So," Mike whispered from the pillow beside Eva, "are we gonna do this or what?" He loved that soft spot behind her ear. Nuzzled it until she stirred, then stretched, then made that amazing sound that was somewhere between a sigh and a purr and turned into his arms.

Eva by morning. Somebody ought to write a sonnet. Sunlight filtered in through the slit in the drapes, kissed her skin, shined through her hair.

He sighed in contentment. Nothing in this world compared to the feel of her warm skin, soft breasts, and insanely sexy legs wrapped around him, lying in the middle of sheets that smelled of sex and her.

Last night around midnight, he'd texted Gabe that they were fine but were not to be bothered for at least twenty-four hours—please spread the word to Taggart and Cooper. Then he'd turned off the phone, ordered room service, and gone back to bed.

Where they'd talked. And eaten. And made love. And finally slept.

Lather, rinse, repeat. All night long.

Most of all, they'd talked. About Ramon. About Mike's drinking. About their families. About their dreams.

About the burn scars on his leg. About the scars Ramon had carved on her heart, but that Mike had every intention of healing.

"Gabe made me and the guys an interesting proposition," he'd said finally.

She'd listened intently as he'd given her the details. "And what are you thinking?"

"I'm thinking I need to find a hangar close to Langley for the Beechcraft." Taking Gabe up on his offer wasn't a decision he'd come to lightly. But now that he'd made it, it felt good. It felt right.

She'd kissed him. "The One-Eyed Jacks, back in the game. It's a good plan."

Something else had been weighing on him. He was getting a second chance, and maybe he wasn't the only one who deserved it. "We're going to need an operations manager. What would you think about recruiting Peter Davis for that position?"

The approval in her eyes had made his heart swell.

The touch of her hands had made something else swell.

They'd made love again; gotten hungry again.

Somewhere between the cheesecake, Greek yogurt, franks and beans, spinach crepes, and sparkling cider, he'd proposed.

The first two times he'd asked, she'd been asleep—

make that comatose, after he'd plied her with multiple orgasms—so he figured the stand-up thing to do was ask her again, this morning.

So he repeated the questions. "Are we going to do this or what?"

"Do . . . *this*?" She yawned, let a hand, heavy with exhaustion, rest on his cheek. "Are you taking those little blue pills or something?"

He hugged her. "You're my 'or something.' But that's not the 'this' I was talking about. I was talking about that other 'this.'"

She smiled against his chest. "Is this one of those 'Who's on first' shticks?"

He raised up on an elbow so he could see her face, watch her eyes when he asked her. "Will you marry me, *chica*? Will you be my wife?"

She smiled. "You know I will."

He swallowed back emotions so huge that, if he let them out, he might bawl like a baby. "Wait, there's more. Will you cook for me? Clean for me? Kiss my boo-boos? Wear that sexy little red bustier and pretend you're a *pepera* girl who plans to roll me for my money?"

Her eyes sparkled with laughter and tears, and a whole lot of love. "Since you make it sound so appealing, how could I possibly say no?"

"So . . . that's a yes?"

She pressed her forehead to his. "That is a definite yes."

"Wow," he said and kissed her.

"You want to talk about wow? Wait until I introduce you to my parents."

"Daddy's little girl?"

"For a fact."

"So I should probably do some heavy editing on the details of the night we met."

She smiled into his eyes. "I love you. Promise you'll always make me laugh."

"With me, not *at* me, right?"

"Yeah. Like that." She kissed him.

"Say it again." He wasn't laughing now. He needed to hear it. Lived to hear it.

"I love you. But more important, I really, really like you, Mike Brown."

"I really, really like you, too."

They made love slowly this time, like they were going to take all the time in the world. And they might have, if some knucklehead hadn't picked that moment to pound on the door.

Mike groaned and buried his face in her neck. "Don't make a sound. They'll go away."

The pounding got louder.

He growled and shouted at the door, "Unless this room is on fire, go the hell away!"

"Primetime. Yo. Open up."

Taggart.

He swore into her neck. "And to think, three days ago I was happy to see him."

Eva grinned and gave him a gentle shove. "Go on. Let him in."

"Do I *have* to?" He stopped, looking horrified. "Did I just whine?"

She laughed and gave him another little shove. "Go."

His heavy sigh had her giggling, but he got up, found his pants, and had the pleasure of watching her sweet naked ass disappear behind the bathroom door.

He opened the door. "What the hell do you want?"

"Not a morning person. I just remembered that about you." Cooper grinned and shouldered past him into the room.

Taggart, also grinning because he knew damn well Mike was irritated, pushed in after him. "Whoa. Dude. Looks like you ate the whole menu up here last night."

"Hi, guys."

All eyes turned when Eva walked out of the bathroom, wrapped from neck to ankle in a white terry robe—and still sexier than any woman had a right to be.

"Eva." Cooper sauntered across the room and hugged her. "How's my favorite kick-ass road warrior?"

Mike muscled in between them. "She's not your anything. Now what are you doing here?"

"We thought you might miss us," Taggart said, deadpan.

"Did you get hit on the head with something? You do see her, right? Do you honestly think that I would give you knuckleheads even a passing thought when I'm alone with her?"

Cooper winked at Eva. "Well, when you frame it like *that,* I guess it makes us look kind of silly." He added a Jethro laugh that broke Taggart up.

Mike shook his head. Then smiled. Then gave it up.

He *had* missed them. For too damn long.

These were his friends. These were his brothers.

He looked at Eva. This was the woman he loved.

He was never going to risk losing any of them ever again.

"What the hell. Let's go get breakfast." He pointed a finger at Taggart. "You're buying."

"Oh, no. We settle this like we always did."

He reached into his hip pocket, pulled out his wallet, and produced his one-eyed jack.

"I'll be damned." Mike couldn't believe he still had it.

Then Cooper whipped out his card, too.

Without a word, Mike walked over to the closet. When he came back, he was carrying his own one-eyed jack.

"To tradition." Taggart's sober tone spoke of all that had passed between them.

"To tradition," Mike and Cooper echoed.

"You do the honors, *chica.*" Mike gathered the three battered cards together, and with great care for all they represented, all they'd been through, he shuffled them.

"Close your eyes and hold out your hand. Now pick one."

"Whoot!" Cooper crowed when Eva held up Mike's card. "Breakfast's on Primetime."

Eva gave him a grin and mouthed, "Sorry."

Taggart pecked her on the cheek. "I think I love this woman."

"Yeah," Mike said taking her into his arms, "but I really, really like her."

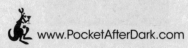

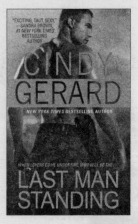